DRAGONS AT THAT AWKWARD AGE

BILL MCCURRY

BOOKS BY BILL MCCURRY

DEATH'S COLLECTOR SERIES

Novels

Death's Collector

Death's Baby Sister

Death's Collector: Sorcerers Dark and Light

Death's Collector: Void Walker

Death's Collector: Sword Hand

Death's Collector: Dark Lands

Novellas

Wee Piggies of Radiant Might

SORCERER OF BAD EXAMPLES COLLECTION

Novels

The Dragon's Manservant

Dragons at That Awkward Age

Men at forty
Learn to close softly
The doors to rooms they will not be
Coming back to.

—Donald Justice

For Arta

ACKNOWLEDGMENTS

My most profound acknowledgment goes to my wife, Kathleen, who patiently listened to my first draft as I finished each chapter. When I read her something I had written and said, "That makes no sense," and she said, "I didn't want to be the one to tell you," I knew our partnership was strong. She has never complained that I've chosen to do such a crazy thing as write books.

The beta readers who devoted their time and energy helped me make this a much better book. They caught simple errors I missed, suggested opportunities I overlooked, and pointed out choices that might make them hate me a little if included in the final draft. They are J. Russell Bailey, Jean Berard, Diane Catanzaro, Stephen Clingman, Steve Krum, Brett LeClair, Michelle McLaren, Reed Richmond, Tom Tolliver, and Lee Vick. They have my deepest thanks.

I also thank the men and women who taught me improv and who performed with me over the years. You know who you are. Thank you for making all my characters have a running improv game in my head.

ONE

I almost died because I was carrying a magic lizard in my hand. I had never needed a magic lizard, nor any kind of lizard. I sure as sheep shanks didn't need this one and could have dropped it, I guess. But striving to be a good lizard custodian was how I gave my wife hope.

Pil, who was my wife, held her own lizard trapped in her hand. We had accepted the little creatures from a surly old crone who claimed to have second sight. Now we had to rush to visit five sacred spots in the city by midday. At each spot, we would hold our lizards' noses near the wall so they could lick it at the same time.

That was supposed to make her love me again.

Old crones who handed out lizards might make that happen, but it seemed unlikely to me. Pil had thanked the woman though, given her too much money, and rushed out of the tidy dwelling with such urgency she might have needed to pee. I followed and didn't complain.

At the next intersection, Pil turned left and gave no sign that this was the stupidest thing we had done since we hit the mainland. Arguing wouldn't turn her aside. She was a barrel of anguish hurtling down a steep hill, and I knew better than to get in front of that. I followed and kept quiet.

Pil said, "Doing these awful things will have been worth it when I get the rest of my memories back—and don't think I don't know what you're saying in your head." She glared at me alongside her and never missed a step.

"Oh, it's nothing bad," I said. "I mean, it's good!" I tried to smile and almost made it.

Pil mimicked me, and she was damn good at it. "Oh, 'This is the stupidest thing I've ever heard of.' . . . 'If they're going to build roads for people to do pointless tasks, at least they could build a couple of alehouses along the way.' . . . 'It's a good thing I love you. That's the only thing keeping me from going back and stuffing these lizards up that old woman's nose.' Am I close?"

I coughed. "That's remarkable. It's as if I was over there talking."

Pil stopped, reached out her empty left hand, and grabbed the wrist of my lizard-toting hand. "I heard something," she whispered. She turned her head and shook her thick mostly black hair away from her ear.

During our many years of wandering in dangerous places, I had come to respect Pil's ability to hear things that I couldn't hear if they were pressed against my head. We backed up to a weathered blue building, which was a leather worker's shop. The smell of salt flowed through almost every part of the city, but the stench of curing leather overwhelmed all the other scents here.

I tried to shift the lizard to my left hand so I wouldn't lose the damn thing, but a scream from across the street and above us stopped me. The scream was packed with fury and contempt. I pulled my knife left-handed and glanced up just as a tall fair woman plummeted three stories to land in front of me.

She would have split my head with her four-foot-long black sword, but I pulled away from Pil's hand and rolled left, keeping the lizard safe in my right hand for no good reason at all.

The woman cut at me from the side without pausing. The black sword was singing. If I heard correctly, it was singing in four-part harmony. With no blade in my main hand, I backed away fast. Her weapon missed my belly by a finger's length. I scrambled aside to assess things while she pivoted to try slaughtering me again.

The creature looked like a divine being to me, or at least semi-divine. By any objective standard, she was one of the most beautiful women I had seen in years. She was tall and straight, with honey-colored hair and slanting blue eyes in a perfect oval face. Her face did seem a bit contrived, though, as if she'd been carved from a block of fine, murderous marble. She wore a long burgundy coat over a shirt of golden chainmail, a fine plum-colored waistcoat, short white trousers, and tall silver boots. Her leather bracers and belt were dyed yellow. A spreading diamond-covered headpiece shaped like a swan held back her hair.

I was wearing yesterday's shirt, which wasn't too clean. It hadn't been all that clean when I put it on yesterday.

The woman stepped back to laugh at me again, I supposed to disconcert me. I glanced to my right and saw another demigod thrusting a pure white spear at Pil. His face and body were so pretty they might make both women and men weep. Pil wasn't weeping. She dodged to the middle of the street and began backpedaling fast to draw him away from me. She picked through a pouch with her left hand and probably didn't want to obliterate me with whatever magic she was planning.

I had learned the trick of doing magic without hand gestures, and I used that trick now. I spun three red bands of power, visible only to me. Their value couldn't be calculated by any normal means because I had purchased that power from the gods with my suffering.

I flung one band to each of the demigod's bracers and the third to her leather belt. Then I squeezed all three so that they'd cinch down to half their normal size.

Well, I wasted that power. The belt and bracers must have been enchanted, which made them immune to piddly sorcerer magic like mine. The demigod thrust at my chest and would have gone through me by a foot if I hadn't blocked it with my long knife. The last two inches of my knife broke off, and I leaped aside.

"Wait!" I shouted.

The demigod hesitated, grinning.

"This will be a profound victory for you!" I said, gasping a little for effect. "Do you know how many of your kind I have killed? At least you can behave like a cultured being and explain who is having me murdered here in the middle of the damn street!"

Every citizen around had fled from the fight, babbling and slamming doors.

The demigod laughed. "You'd like to know that, wouldn't you?"

"Yes, I would. That's why I asked. After guarding the future of your realm and mine for so many years, I deserve that much, don't I?" I edged a foot closer to her. "It's a tiny favor, and the last one I'll ever ask of you."

"Very well. I do respect you, maybe a bit." She stepped forward until she pressed the tip of her sword against my chest. "The Goddess of Life has ordered you killed."

"Trutch? What the hell did I do to her?"

I could see Pil and the other demigod fighting a hundred feet down the street. Something flared in Pil's hand, but the demigod swept his arm in front of his eyes and didn't seem bothered.

"You dare ask what you did?" The demigod facing me sneered. "That which was horrific! Bilious! Nauseating!" She paused. "All right, I don't know what you did. It is not within my purview to understand. I am curious, however. You really don't have any idea what it was?"

I chewed my lip. "Are you sure you used that word correctly?"

"Bilious?"

"Purview."

"Yes, I'm pretty sure I did."

I saw death flare in her eyes as her muscles twitched to thrust the blade through me. I rushed to ask, "What's your name? I want to honor you in my thoughts as I die."

Divine beings loved that kind of crap.

"I am Undinaer, the daughter of Trutch and Bazingall, ruler of the Five—"

Down the street, the other demigod screamed. Undinaer didn't turn to look, but her eyes flicked that direction.

Bixell, my teacher in the Dark Lands and the great pain in my ass, warned me that I would never be as fast as any divine being. I might be as fast as a semi-divine being, but I'd be better off moving first. Sometimes I could move second but arrive first if I was clever. He advised me not to try that for the first twenty years.

I rolled left off the point of Undinaer's sword. It left a shallow cut across my chest. Little flames flared out of the cut, which certainly surprised me, but I didn't hesitate. With her sword on my right, I rushed toward her and hooked my right arm in hers. When she turned toward me, I leaped, and the demigod spun me as if we were dancing on the village green. She paused, probably wondering what to do with an awful little grasper like me, and I used the momentum to thrust my not-so-sharp knife into the side of her neck.

That was the end of Undinaer. She came to destroy us, and I didn't mourn her a bit.

I ran down the street to Pil. Her enemy's body lay smoking on the dirt. I glanced and then looked away. "Are you all right?" I yelled.

Pil was on her hands and knees.

I knelt beside her. "Pil! Are you hurt?" I didn't see any wounds.

She shook her head.

There were many idiotic things I could have said then. The one I chose was "I still have my lizard!" I held out my closed hand.

Pil shifted to sit with her back against the peeling wooden wall of somebody's house. "Mine's lost." Her face sagged, and she slumped as if a great stone block were pushing down on her. "I know it wouldn't have worked anyway. Hell, I know that it was just a foolish hope. I'm pretty sure now we'll die at the Bole."

"We won't! The Bole is a place of power, sure, but I've been there before, and it didn't kill me. In fact, I've been there twice, and it didn't kill me either time!"

Pil didn't laugh and didn't even look at me. "It almost killed you. Ella said so."

Last year, in an unhappy sorcerous ass-whipping by the gods, Pil lost most of her memories of our life together. She and I had since worked to regain them, but many were elusive or jumbled in her mind. We had discussed the problem with a considerable amount of focus and frustration, as well as disagreements about whether I should stop drinking while we worked.

We had at last agreed that the Bole was the best place to find help for her.

I nearly revealed to Pil what Undinaer had said about the Goddess of Life sending these assassins dressed like drunken street performers. But I stayed quiet. Trutch was the one who had messed with her memories. Knowing that Trutch wanted to kill us now could distract her.

Clearing my throat, I said, "Pil, the Bole is the place for memories. It's old magic. Memories and destruction. Oaths, curses, and foretelling." I grinned. "The Bole will fall on your problem like a hundredweight of bricks, and we'll skip away laughing."

I watched her face. Whatever had made her love me was in those memories she lost. I didn't know whether she truly thought getting me back was worth risking death at some dark, impenetrable place of power that was beyond good and evil. She might doubt it.

But I thought we were worth it.

Pil stood, took a deep breath, and pulled back her shoulders. "Let's go to the Bole then." She smiled. "I don't care if it's ancient and imponderable. If it refuses us, I'll . . ." She shrugged. "I'll throw dirt at it."

"What do you want to do with the demigods' magic weapons and boots?" I asked. "And the belt and bracers? And I guess that hat over there shaped like a clam. It looks too silly to not be magical."

Pil chuckled, but it didn't sound happy. She could bind magic into objects that would either preserve bodies or tear them to pieces. Her expression said she was in the mood for tearing.

She ran her palm along the white spear's shaft. "Bring everything."

I set my magic lizard free and picked up the singing black sword.

TWO

Pil used to say that in some ways killing hadn't changed me. When I was young, I tended to help people who had nothing and destroy merciless assholes, and that was still true. But she said I had always been a cynical, arrogant, murderous liar. When I could solve a problem either by killing or by peaceful methods, I usually chose to kill the malefactor. Sometimes I'd kill all their friends, just to be thorough.

I once told Pil that I handled problems this way because I was good at it. She didn't find that statement entertaining.

If anybody else had told me I hadn't changed much, I would have ignored them. But Pil once loved me. I needed to convince her that I had changed, maybe just a little, but enough for her to love me again when the time came.

I needed evidence. But I couldn't think of anything I'd done in the past fifty years that would convince even a table-licking drunkard that I had changed much.

After Pil and I vanquished the two demigods, we carried all their magical chattel back to our inn like chubby, well-pleased donkeys. She grabbed Kenzie, Pil's grandniece by marriage, and they began an inventory of the magical spoils.

Kenzie was a tall thin young woman from the island of Ir, my homeland. She let her red hair grow long and tolerably wild, and her skin was light brown. She had experienced more deadly or horrible events than most sorcerers her age. Now she began running her long-fingered hands over the captured weapons.

"This sword is lovely," she said, pointing. "The spear is boring as a turd."

Pil snorted. "Let me show you something, young lady. You see all these white runes, lines, and squiggles on the black sword? It's been enchanted to Krak's toenails and back."

"That sounds champion to me!" Kenzie said.

"But every such enchantment contains the potential for catastrophe. It's like building a tower out of kitchen tables. You'll be tall and mighty until a table slips, and then you'll be lying dead under a hundred broken tables." She handed Kenzie the white spear. "Find the runes on it."

"I don't see a one," Kenzie said after examining the spear from tip to butt.

"This is an unmarred weapon imbued with a single purpose," Pil said. "I don't know what the purpose is yet, but I will. This spear won't fail until it's physically broken."

Kenzie nodded, grinning as if she'd been offered a nice lamb chop. "Thank you, Granda, I'll be remembering that."

"What can I do to help?" I asked, hoping the answer would be nothing.

"What did you plan to do today?" Pil asked without looking up from the white spear.

"I thought I'd sail down the coast and back. Just so my boat doesn't feel unloved."

Pil smiled at me. It hit me like a battering ram made of feathers. She was a smallish woman with gray-streaked black hair and the vigor of somebody who fenced with the town guards for a couple of hours most mornings. Even when she wasn't smiling, she was the most beautiful woman I had ever seen. Maybe not everybody would have held that opinion, but it was true to me.

Pil said, "Two awfully wise men have been waiting in the

common room for an hour to meet with me over a ridiculous thing I don't care about, so could you take care of them? In a way that doesn't involve killing them? I don't find them that tiresome."

"Take care of them" was a mighty broad statement, so I felt I could deal with these men in just about any nonfatal way I wanted. A few minutes later, a knock came at the front door. I answered and welcomed them, smiling and standing in the doorway so they couldn't enter without running me down.

I promised these men answers in great abundance if they went with me to the nice alehouse up the street, the Bones and Noses. I promised to guide them safely away from the horrible alehouse down the street, the Right Crust, which was a good place to be robbed and killed.

I bought these stiff and learned sorcerers several rounds, told them some lies, and introduced them to some friendly ladies. Then I escaped to the harbor just before midmorning.

Soon I raised the sail on my little boat and unmoored it, which was an easy task in the harbor. I remembered my first week in the city and the hell I had with this boat.

In most cases, the city's pole-up-their-backside masters required that little boats like mine be pulled up on the beach. That left space in the harbor for bringing in ships with food, trade goods, and rich people. I didn't care to launch my boat alone every time I wanted to sail, so I'd approached the masters to rent a spot along the dock.

They bellowed as if I'd asked to moor my boat between their daughters' legs. I increased my offer to quite a handsome fee. They raised their voices, called me a barbarian, implied that they might run me out of the city, and gave their guards significant looks.

I smiled and complimented their wisdom and beauty, since I didn't want to make enemies. It's true that I drew my sword as I spoke, but that was only to make the guards think twice. The city masters must have been a timid bunch, because they shouted and fell back, ordering the guards to arrest me. Two of them ran out of the room.

Nobody died or was even hurt much. Pil had come walking with me to the meeting since it was such a nice day. As things were going to hell, she urged me aside, calmed everybody, and spent ten minutes securing a space for my boat. After five more minutes of chatting, she had arranged dinner that night with three of the city masters.

As we walked back to the inn, she held my hand. "I hope you don't mind me jumping in, but I wanted you to get what you want."

"That's awfully kind of you," I said.

"And I didn't want to leave with that room painted in blood, the city leaderless, and us forced to move away from yet another place."

We walked along for ten seconds before I said, "You may not remember that you love me, but you sure as hell remember some things about me."

Now I sailed down the coast until early afternoon. When I came about, I saw smoke on the horizon just about where the city should be. I began tacking back up the coast, and by late afternoon I was watching the city of Arborswit burn.

The whole town looked to be on fire, and I examined the disaster from a mile offshore. Standing in the bow of my little sailboat, I tried to pick out whether our inn was burning. If it wasn't, it would be soon. The whole city was built of old timber that would burn almost like straw.

I hated this city. I had never told Pil, but I'm sure she could tell. The narrow streets tangled like snakes, we ate fish every meal, and the brackish well was all the way across town from us. But my wife had demanded we stop wandering and rest in Arborswit for a while. I didn't argue since she possessed great moral superiority. I had been lying to her every day for months.

Pil disliked unneeded killings, and one of the helpful things about sailing was that I hadn't yet stabbed any annoying bastards while alone on a sixteen-foot boat. But when I saw the conflagration she was now facing while I had been playing on the ocean, my insides wilted.

The late sun threw shadows across the whole city, and smoke slouched above everything until the wind pulled it away. Of course, Pil was also a sorcerer and more capable than me. She'd eaten a demigod for breakfast this morning, metaphorically. She wouldn't need my help to escape.

That didn't sound convincing in my head. I said the words out loud, and they sounded even worse.

Hopping back to the stern, I hauled to fill the sail, even though the wind wasn't blowing from a helpful quarter. I cursed myself for sailing today, playing on the water like a boy.

I tried to steer a point closer to the wind to reach land sooner, but the sail shivered as I turned too close to the breeze. I let the boat's head fall off to my former course and grimaced. The wind from this quarter couldn't speed me into harbor. Tacking back and forth to the city would require a grueling age of work. The whole city could be a mass of fire by the time I arrived.

I considered the wisdom of spending magical power to change the wind's direction, at least for a short while around me. Power was measured in squares, an arbitrary unit set by the gods. Generally, a square was the power required for one major feat, such as bending open the hull of a big ship or enchanting ten trinkets and charms with useful spells. However, that was an oversimplification of the most outrageous sort.

Only the gods could provide power, and they made sorcerers suffer and dance like trained dogs to get it. Using power was never a light decision. I had come to the mainland with five squares of power, and I had almost four remaining. I estimated that changing the wind would require at least one-fourth of a square.

I didn't have to consider for more than a couple of seconds. Pil might be dying.

With my right hand on the tiller, I stretched my left into the empty air, pulling at my reserve of magical power. I spun some of it into four white bands and flung them into the sky in four directions.

The wind eased around from southwest to northeast, and my boat shot toward land. But I was worrying for no reason. Of course Pil didn't need me to help her! I'd probably rush through the city, find her already fled, and escape scorched but alive. We'd laugh about it in a year or two.

Or maybe we wouldn't. I ground my teeth and trimmed the sail to get a smidge more speed. I banged the side of the boat with my fist. I had spent much of the past two years believing that Pil was dead. The idea of her death had become a tender spot for me, like a cut that wouldn't heal.

The boat jerked so hard I fell to my knees. Then it ground to a halt, as if I had run her onto a sandbar. The wind still filled the sail, so I eased it down lest the mast be cracked.

When I peered over the side, I saw no sandbar, only water deep enough for a ship a hundred times bigger than my boat. I didn't have time to screw with whoever had enchanted this bit of the ocean, so I considered doing a reckless thing.

The likelihood of being torn to bits was real, but I decided to risk it anyway. I said, "Limnad, I want you," as if the person were sitting beside me.

Limnad the river spirit popped out of the ocean like a cork, close enough beside my boat to tweak my ear if she wanted. She'd be more likely to yank off both my ears and sew them over my eyes. Limnad appeared as a perfectly formed, unclothed woman with blue skin and hair. She was so unnaturally perfect that looking at her for too long was terrifying.

The ocean was rolling, but Limnad stood on the water as if she were standing on a rock. "Hello, Bib! You look like crap! Look at all those lines on your face! Although I don't guess you can look at your own face, can you? Here."

She reached toward me and opened her hand, producing a small frameless mirror. Then she rushed to the boat and held the mirror in front of my face. "Do you see? Look at yourself in all detail, Bib. You look repulsive. You should get more sleep. Without sleep, you'll get lines that make you look angry, or guilty."

"Thank you, Limnad, that's good advice. I need your assistance."

Limnad closed her hand, making the mirror disappear, and she smiled. "What do you need, Bib the sorcerer?"

"This water's been enchanted to hold my boat in place, and I need to be in the city as fast as I can."

"Ooh, interesting! Let me look!" Limnad plunged below the surface.

Limnad seemed to have forgiven me, which was a fine thing. The last time we met, she had flung me into the side of a building and threatened to kill me. This was better. I didn't need another enemy, especially a supernatural one.

A minute or so passed before Limnad's head poked up from the water. "Still looking!"

"Wait!"

She dove again.

Spirits tended to be excitable and easily distracted. She might be down there counting all the blue fish. I waited.

Three or four minutes later, Limnad rose above the swells with great majesty. "It's a puzzle. Why do you even want to go to that smelly city? It's on fire. It'll all be burned up by tomorrow morning!"

"Pil is over there, and I'm afraid for her. She may need my help to escape."

"Really?" Limnad stared at the city. "Yes, I can sense her there."

I tried not to raise my voice. "If the boat won't move, please carry me to the beach."

She shook her head. "Too close to a habitation of man. You know I can't go where men have built ugly things."

I raised my voice. "Carry me partway! I'll swim from there!"

Limnad gazed at me, chewing as if she were imagining how I'd taste. "You really are stupid. How did you get to be so old for a man? You should have been dead years and years ago." She leaned against the side of my boat and ran her hand along the top of the gunwale.

I jerked away from her. "You're the one who stopped my boat!" I murmured. "Why?"

"To kill you, that's why! And to play with you first." Before I could twitch, she rushed over, reached into the boat, and grabbed me by the chin. "Bib!" From her throat, my name was a guttural explosion of disgust, even though her voice was normally as sweet as a stream across stones. "I hope you've decided to die right now. If you haven't, this conversation will disappoint you!"

As a sorcerer, I had once bound Limnad to obey my commands. That enraged her, but the binding charm prevented her from hurting me while she was bound. Most bindings eventually destroy one or both parties, but she and I had managed to survive and even become friends.

That friendship ended when I took Desh, her lover, away to the gods' war, and he never came home. This had to be about Desh. It didn't matter that Desh died more than seventy years ago, most of which I spent in the Dark Lands not aging. Spirits like Limnad endured vast lifespans and could hold a grudge for centuries.

I tried to speak but just mumbled since she was about to crush my chin. I tried again, and she let go, pushing me away.

"Limnad, I know that Desh—"

"Don't say his name," Limnad grated. "You let Desh die." Tears ran fast from her eyes as she said the name, covering her cheeks in moments.

It wasn't quite true that I'd let Desh die, but the spirit didn't seem to be in a mood for fine distinctions. "Limnad, I know you like Pil, who is my wife now."

She glowered. "I pity her."

I nodded toward the burning city. "She is over there in awful danger. Let me help her."

Limnad cocked her head as if I was ignoring something important. "You are doubly stupid. No, I won't let you help her. That's why I'm here! To keep you from helping her! She's coughing now. Her throat and chest must hurt a lot."

"She'll die!" Those were the most obvious words I could have uttered. I shook my head as if that would help me think better.

Limnad smiled again. "If Pil married you, then she's probably hoping for death right now." The spirit plunged into the sea and shot up on the other side of my boat, throwing enough water to soak every part of me.

"She's not dying," I said, although a big, cold stone had appeared where my guts used to be. "You're just scaring me.

Limnad, if you agree to save her, then you can kill me. I won't try to fight or run." I said it in a light tone, but after a breath, I realized it really would be a good bargain.

Limnad bellowed, "I'm not lying to you! Bib, I can kill you whenever I want, with a bargain or without one!"

I shook my head and covered one ear against the enormous sound of her voice.

Limnad then said in a casual tone, "Pil is lying on the ground now with her face mashed into the dirt. Her eyes are closed, and she's not breathing too well."

I leaned toward her and snapped, "If you can kill me whenever you want, why haven't you already done it?"

"I don't know!" The spirit took a breath. "I've set out any number of times to make you into an octopus puppet with your entrails for tentacles, but I always get distracted." She smiled, and I shivered. "Now you have brought me right to you!" Limnad leaped into my boat as graceful as an otter and stood in front of me, her fingers making claws.

"If you kill me, please send someone to save Pil."

Limnad rolled her eyes. "For this to be your last few seconds of existence, you're awfully dense." Limnad lifted her head and gazed at the city. "She's almost gone."

"I don't believe you." I shook my head hard to convince myself how much I didn't believe her. "Pil always let you play with her hair when you wanted to!"

Spirits are cyclones of thoughts and feelings. Limnad shuddered. "Other people have hair! Pil didn't excrete pearls!"

I squinted.

"From her bottom, I mean!" Limnad's hands became fists instead of claws.

"Limnad, what can I do? What can I give you?"

She howled, "You can make Desh not die!" She fell to her knees and stared into my face, more terrible than a shark. "You can give him back to me." The spirit waited with her eyes wide, as if I might really be able to do that.

"I wish I could. I'd bring him back and throw a party."

"Bib, if I carried you to the shore right now, you might be able to save Pil. Maybe." Limnad pouted. "I'm not going to do that."

I couldn't do anything useful, so I drew my sword.

Limnad snatched it out of my hand, broke it, and threw the pieces in two different directions. She closed her eyes. "Ah, now she's dead. Something terribly heavy fell on her."

I sagged. "No, you're just saying that."

Limnad sagged in a mirror image of me. "I intended to watch you suffer and then kill you, Bib, but I won't do that. At least, not today." She shot out her hand and broke my left little finger. I yelped but held my breath when she cried out louder, as if she'd broken her own hand. She panted. "Stop it! You squeal like a bunny. Bib, I want you to anticipate the day I'll kill you." She began nodding and kept on. "It'll be bad. Being eaten alive by little fish will be the happiest thing about it."

Limnad poked my right knee with her forefinger. I heard a crack, and pain rushed up my leg. At the same time, Limnad shouted in pain. A thought hit me, and I said in a quiet voice, "It's not your fault either. You don't have to hurt yourself."

"Hah!" she called out, but without much force. Then she embraced me, and I thought I was about to be crushed. Limnad whispered, "You will grieve until I kill you. I lost Desh, and he's forever lost. Now Pil is lost forever too. You and I are the same. Only death can release us." She let me go and stepped back.

I plopped down on a thwart and lowered my head as I clutched my knee. "Well. That's a lot to think about." I didn't want to insult the river spirit, so I counted to five before looking up. "Limnad, just in case you're wrong, I'd like to go back to the question of saving Pil."

Her jaw fell open. "Here I am letting you live so that we can suffer, and you have the steam-hot nerve to ask for more favors? May garfish eat your soft parts!" Limnad's skin had turned a dark, shiny blue. "I can't . . ." She shook her head and dove into the ocean.

I hadn't hoped for miracles from Limnad, but I'd have appreciated her not destroying most of my hope.

The spirit surged out of the water. "Pil's dead, and you can't save her. If you can't stand that, go ahead and drown yourself, you turtle's asshole." She dove beneath the swells. Then my boat was released from its mystical, invisible sandbar.

I made sail again. My broken finger caused a bit of awkwardness, but soon the boat shot across the water toward the beach, and I watched the flames devouring Arborswit.

THREE

Ten minutes brought me to the beach. I stumbled over the boat's gunwale into the surf and limped up toward the dry sand, dragging at the little boat with my right hand. That strained my wounded knee too much, and with a sigh, I let the boat go. I didn't turn to watch the surf pull it away.

More than two hundred people stood or knelt there, sagging as they watched their homes burn. I heard cursing and crying. Some comforted others while the rest stood apart.

Four soot-faced city guards watched me—two with spears, one carrying a sword, and one with what looked like a post he'd yanked off a fence. All of them wore their brown hair long and had fluffy mustaches, which was the fashion in Arborswit. Some mustaches and hair had been partly snatched away by fire. One guard was bare-chested, and another had no boots.

A short, broad guard pointed his sword at me. "Hey!"

I pretended I hadn't heard him.

"Hey! Where are you coming from?"

"The ocean!" I rolled my eyes at two of his friends. "Before we discuss which ocean and what part of that ocean and how the fish taste there, I need to rescue somebody." I stepped to walk past them, but he shifted in front of me.

"Nobody's allowed into that damn catastrophe!" he said. "If you can't rescue somebody between here and that closest building, just get in your boat and sail off."

I feared I'd lose time if I thrashed these guards and whoever else chose to help them. Time was the most precious thing in the world just then. I stumped along faster and reached to loosen my sword in the scabbard. Then I snorted, remembering that Limnad had broken my sword. I turned to examine the flames. "Also, I need to report."

"No, you wait here! Don't move!"

I whipped around to face him, almost falling down. "Wait? There are ass-rotting pirates sailing in from every damn place—hell, popping up out of the sea, slaughtering his, hers, yours, and everybody's sailors, and maybe they'll traipse down here to murder a few soldiers next, so will I wait here? I will not, by Krak's ass! I won't wait here when every second means another of our comrades dead!"

The man wrinkled his graying brow. "Pirates?"

I stumped up the beach toward the city, not bothering to answer.

"What do you mean, report? Report to who?" the man yelled.

"Who do you think? To the commander!" I kept walking as they muttered, and I didn't look back.

I heard hoofbeats and glanced to my right. A man in a grimy uniform rode a black gelding right toward me. Maybe I'd have to kill this fool instead of talking him into submission as I had the others.

I needed the man's horse. The inn where we lived stood at the city center, and my knee would prevent me from making a brisk trip there on foot. I hesitated.

Magical power was risky to come by and beyond valuable. The gods traded power to sorcerers, and the things they demanded sometimes ruined the sorcerers' lives. I pulled a yellow band out of the air anyway and tossed it to settle on the gelding.

I couldn't make the horse do anything. But I could convince him of things that might not be strictly true. I planted the idea that the man on his back was really a wolf.

After five seconds of furious bucking and neighing, the horseman's butt bounced on the sand. The gelding reared to smash the man to death with his hooves, but I rushed to promise him that I could protect him from wolves, lions, bad water, and thrown horseshoes.

The horse trotted to me like a puppy, and I mounted. We galloped away before anybody could run over and stick a spear in my back.

I rode deeper into the city, down a long curving road, up two shorter streets, and around three corners. Not every building was swathed in flames yet, but nothing could save them short of a profound storm. Spinning another yellow band, I calmed the gelding against the fire that had begun reaching higher on each side of us. Bits of burning debris fell into the street.

When I rode down a street that seemed to almost turn back on itself, I knew I was close. I drew rein in front of the burning inn. It was grandiose to call the place a burning inn. It was no more than a collapsed jumble of blazing timbers. No man, woman, or sorcerer could survive in it.

I stared at the flames, wondering what to do. I wondered what to do if she was dead.

I took a breath, coughed on the smoke, and closed my eyes. Pil would of course escape this frolicking disaster without me! She was a powerful sorcerer, better than me, clever and harder to surprise. No simple conflagration could kill her, and she'd have taken the young people with her to safety.

That was all true, so why had I been sweating desperation to save her? I decided that wasn't a question to contemplate with my ass nearly on fire.

If Pil had fled, she probably had left a sign or message for me. I glanced around, but none was evident, and the gelding was snorting and sidestepping as my calming suggestion faded. I hated to spend power to soothe the horse again, but without him I wasn't sure I could move fast enough to escape the city.

A voice blared from behind me. "Most everybody went down that direction!"

I turned but didn't recognize the person speaking. He was close to the tallest man I'd ever met and broad enough to call the front of him a wall without sounding silly. His skin and clothes were heavily smudged, and his left sleeve was smoldering. He carried a thick metal-banded club in one hand and a limp woman who wasn't Pil over the other shoulder.

"That way!" the man yelled, pointing with the club. He waved the other big hand in front of his bug eyes and jerked his head toward the bottom of the street, then almost dropped the woman. "That's where most of 'em went." He coughed twice, wheezed, and in a voice pitched high for a man his size, said, "I'll bet you never thought you'd see Arborswit burn up like this, huh?"

"I never thought about the damn place at all."

"Got to get Wenda out of here before she smothers. Good luck. Don't be waiting around for the neighbors." The man trotted right past me. The woman seemed to weigh no more than a rolled-up blanket to him. Thirty feet past me, he called back without looking, "Are you Bib?"

Suspicion rushed through me. "Maybe."

"That small woman said I should tell Bib he ought to follow her down this way." He pointed again with his club. "If you're Bib, then I did my duty and I told you." He trotted on.

"Wait!" I patted my horse to soothe him as well as I could, and I urged the beast to follow the man at a fast but nervous walk. "Pil's alive? Is she all right?"

The man turned. "Don't know about a pill. I don't know whether that woman's still alive, neither. Stop!"

I drew rein. "For what? To cook my horse?"

The man then said the last words I expected to hear: "Asa, I bind you."

My body spasmed as something invisible clamped around my neck, as solid as an iron ring bolted to a castle. This ripe pile of flesh was compelling me to serve him by using my true name—Asa. It was the same damn thing I had done to Limnad years ago.

I shouted, "What? You nasty bastard! Shut up! If you clamp your mouth shut and don't say another word, I might let you live!"

My threat wasn't immediate. Once the binding started, I couldn't hurt this man in any way.

He opened his mouth.

"Don't say it!" I yelled.

"Asa, I bind you."

Both my arms snapped rigid when invisible bands seized my wrists. I knew that struggling was useless, but I couldn't help it. Soon he would bind my ankles too. Then he could command me five times, once for each band. After fulfilling all the commands, I'd be free. That included free to torture and kill him with profound creativity. "You ugly puddle of ooze!" I yelled. "Eat nails and glass, you runny pile in the whorehouse gutter!" I drew a breath to curse him some more. At this point I had nothing to lose.

"Asa, I bind you."

Pain screamed up from my right knee as both legs locked, pulled straight by bands on my ankles. I slid sideways off my horse and slammed onto the hard-packed dirt. The gelding bolted, and I hoped it was to safety. I gasped, then shouted, "You tower of goat filth! I bet you have family! You can be sure I'll find out. I'll kill them first and then torture you to death! How would you like to get impaled?"

The big man paused, peering at me. "Will you really kill my family?"

"Yes!" I shouted, probably with too much vigor.

"Naw, you won't."

No, I wouldn't, but I hated that he saw through me. The bands at last relaxed. I couldn't see them, but I could still feel them. I climbed to my feet with a sneer and threw the man a foul gesture.

"Let's start this partnership off with clear rules." The man pointed at a mass of flames behind him. "I could command you to walk into that fire."

I grinned. "You could, and I'd die. But you'd be visited by my friends, who are a rowdy lot. And some of them live in realms nastier than this one."

He shook his head and laughed, a gentle, rolling sound. "Come on." He dropped the woman, who landed like a pile of laundry.

"She was dead this whole time," I said, as if it would be new information to him.

"Handy prop." The man gave a crooked, squinting smile. Then he trotted down the street away from me.

As a bound creature, I was obliged to stay close to my master unless he specified how far I was allowed to stray. I followed him at a stumping run, trying to keep up. "It's not too late to release me!" I called out. "I killed the God of Death. You don't want to be next."

He called back over his shoulder, "Killed a god, huh? Well, I killed three. Two of 'em this morning."

FOUR

I t takes a lot more work to kill a god than to say you've killed one, or three, or all the gods plus two unicorns. I nearly said that to the trotting beef-slab of a man and then called him a lying son of a bitch, but I held still.

Instead, I snarled and limped behind him through the burning city, waving cinders out of my face and keeping my damn mouth shut. The big man didn't take the turns that I would have chosen, but he picked streets that weren't so smothered in fire as to kill us.

A bound creature earns no advantage by giving his master information. Every word he speaks is a chance for the master to figure out how to command the creature more creatively, or to heap on greater mortification.

But if I stayed silent, my smug, slope-browed master would at last get uncomfortable and feel that he must speak. Then each of his words could be a knife I might drive deep into him if I was clever enough.

So, this sorcerer would eventually speak words to command me, forcing him to describe how things should happen. Describing reality by using words is a ticklish business. A word can mean different things. Once commanded, I would act, making real things happen in the real world. I could obey his words in a way he hadn't intended, at least if I was imaginative.

If he said, "Bring me a beer," I might steal all his money, buy a brewery, create the perfect cask of beer, burn down the brewery to preserve the secret, and drop the beer cask on his foot.

Only a fool would bind a creature any smarter than a mop, and few sorcerers lived through a binding attempt. So this stone wall of a man was a fool.

But if I wanted to talk about fools, I myself had bound more than one creature in the past, including Limnad. And this sorcerer had sure as hell been sharp enough to surprise me. I shook my head, pushing away the notion that I might be even a bit more intelligent than the man who had bound me.

I probably couldn't outsmart him. I would have to employ raw cunning and spite.

The sun was dropping into late afternoon and smoke swept our faces at times, but I could see the man well enough. I doubted he was more than twenty-five years old, quite a respectable age for a sorcerer.

The big man turned in place. "I'm Margale."

"Wonderful," I said. "My mother's name is Margale too." I bit my lip for talking too much.

Margale snorted. "Listen to me. You won't let anybody know, by word, action, expression, emotion, or omission, that you have been bound. That's my first command."

I cursed silently when I couldn't immediately find a way to corrupt that command. But an invisible weight fell from my left ankle. Margale could command me only four more times.

"Now the good part," he said. "You will kill King Hale of Silvershanks in the most efficient way you can. Don't fart around about it."

I wrinkled my nose as if his command stank. "Silvershanks? The kingdom we're in right now?" I wiggled my right foot, which suddenly felt lighter. With this command, two bands were gone.

"You expected I'd say some far-off spot like the Dark Lands?" Margale winked. "You're too well-traveled to enjoy the pleasures of home, Bib. I have to accept that you're a smart man, and you must be looking to take advantage of any slip on my part."

He jumped right in front of me, lighter on his feet than I expected, and he stared down as if I was at the bottom of a hole. "We might run across some friends of yours soon. If you act like an ass, I will kill them all before anybody moves." Margale smiled the way he must have when he tortured insects as a boy.

"So Pil's alive?" I asked, feeling weak. "The small woman who told you about me?"

Margale shrugged. "I don't know. She could be deader than a banker's heart by now. But you should assume she's alive and not misbehave."

I pulled my knife and pressed the edge along the side of my neck. If Margale was holding Pil's life against my behavior, then I was a crushing weight over her head. I doubted I was capable of behaving like a good slave, so just by existing I threatened Pil's life.

I jerked the knife to cut my throat. I sliced myself pretty well but hadn't yet cut anything important before Margale shouted, "Don't kill yourself!" The knife fell out of my hand, and the weight on my right wrist disappeared. With hardly a pause, Margale went on, "Or harm yourself in any way until I'm done using you."

I paused, feeling for the weight of my left wrist to disappear. It didn't fall away, though. Margale's pause between telling me not to kill myself and telling me not to harm myself must have been brief enough for the whole mess to count as one command.

"Eat a bug," I said, bending to pick up my knife. I bit my tongue, then bit it harder before at last sighing. "I've got to ask this. How did you learn my name? My real name?"

"I really shouldn't say." He grinned and scratched at his tidy beard before striding down the burning street. "I got it from a sorcerer in the Hill Lands before I killed him."

"Who?" I limped hard to keep up.

"Doesn't matter. He tortured it out of an imp he killed. The imp had gotten it from the sorcerer Lessimal, who gave up your name to free herself, but the imp slaughtered her anyway."

"Wait. What?"

"Lessimal had traded some god-forged doodad to a monster named Kruppin to get your name, then she buried him alive under a church. I swear, knowing your name is more dangerous than eating poison. It worries me a bit, to be honest." Margale's grin was too gigantic for him to be all that worried.

"So you're the only one who knows my name now." I raised my eyebrows.

Margale's grin faded. "You don't want to make anything out of that." He turned to trot away down the street.

We seemed to be pushing beyond the thickest fires, and soon the buildings on each side were hardly burning at all. We entered the main marketplace, a big open oblong area that still had some unburned awnings. Margale waved at a few soldiers who waved back. Then he led me out of the city to join a small crowd of grimy people trudging east along a decent road. None carried more than a bag or two of possessions.

Arborswit lay in a great pine forest that ran all the way to the coast. That's why the city's inhabitants built using timber, and that's why most of the trees near the city had been chopped down. The woods grew thicker as we gained distance from the city. We followed a stream of people traveling into the evening with sunset someplace behind the burning city. Three other roads left Arborswit in different directions, and I imagined each one crowded with shocked and fleeing citizens.

I limped behind Margale, considering ways to pervert his commands and to make him waste more of them. That puzzle frustrated me, so I occasionally switched to other, more productive efforts like cursing. I cursed Margale with a rank thoroughness that would have made all the sailors I had ever known smile.

Margale paid no more attention to me than he did to the smoky breeze.

When I walked past a tree trunk thicker than I was tall, Limnad stepped out from behind it. She was easy to recognize. She glowed with a faint blue light, which caused everybody near us to cry out or run away. A hefty woman nearby stumbled off into the forest, begging the gods to know why fire and demons plagued her on the same day.

Margale stopped and faced Limnad, keeping quiet and relaxed. That probably meant he was terrified, or at least pretty damn scared. I had been the first time I met Limnad.

I stopped too. "Hello, good spirit."

Limnad laughed and rushed in a little circle around Margale, kissing him on both cheeks. Then she hurled me to the ground and put one foot on my throat, grinning. "Sorcerer, you fill me with happiness! This is the first time I've been filled with happiness in seventy-one years and four days, so good job!"

I calculated the years but really didn't have to. Limnad was talking about the last day she had been with Desh. I had left for the Dark Lands shortly after Desh died, and I spent over seventy years there. Then I had been back in the world of man for about a year.

Limnad wasn't waiting for me to do math. She cocked her head at Margale. "Now that you have bound Bib, we can take our time making him suffer. We could start with a simple thing like forcing him to rub nettles into his own eyes." She bent over and brushed my hair away from my eyes as gently as anybody who had ever loved me.

"Or we could make him cut off all his own toes and fingers—except for two fingers and a thumb to hold the knife!" Limnad went on.

Margale cleared his throat. "Those suggestions are fine, of course."

Limnad's face went blank. "We could make him kill his wife. That would hurt him a lot." Tears filled her eyes, and she shook her head. "No, we shouldn't get complicated." She smiled up at Margale and bubbled, "Make him eat his own foot!"

I coughed. "Pil's really not dead then?"

Limnad rolled her eyes at me. "I wouldn't suggest that you kill her if she was already dead. That would be silly. Now, hush." She shifted some weight onto my throat, and I gagged.

Margale said, "Spirit, those are good suggestions, really remarkable. But I already have plans for Bib. I can't reveal them yet, but I promise he'll suffer. When I'm done, he'll wish he'd been allowed to eat his own foot."

The spirit ran to Margale, almost too fast to see, and she stared up at his face with her body almost touching his. She breathed, "Are you lying? I hate liars. Bib's a liar, you know. I'll pull out a liar's liver and make him wear it like a beard."

Margale leaned away from Limnad but managed not to step back. If she wanted, she could tear him apart before he finished that step. He nodded hard. "I'm telling you the truth. Promise."

Limnad leaned in closer to Margale, even pushing her body against him. "I'm trusting you. And I'll be watching to make sure you hurt him enough. Well, I guess that means I'm not trusting you after all." She shrugged, and her blue hair floated above her shoulders for a moment before settling. "Just remember that you got yourself into this, sorcerer, and if I don't like how you handle things, I'll . . . I'll take Bib away from you, no matter how bound he is."

Margale nodded.

"Don't squander this chance to punish him. Be creative. But don't . . ." Limnad gripped Margale's face between her palms. "I guess you can kill him if you want, since right now you own him." She smiled and flowed backward toward me. "When you're done with him though, if you leave the remaining bits for me, you'll get a present!"

Limnad glanced at me, then lifted her chin at Margale. "Sorcerer, I don't know you and I don't like the way your nose sounds when you breathe, but a lot of people have tried to kill Bib. Animals too, and demigods, and dragons, and gods. So, think about that."

Margale almost rubbed his nose but yanked down his hand. "I understand." It didn't sound to me like he believed her.

"The spirits have decided that Bib can only be killed by somebody who loves him," Limnad said lightly. "So don't act like an ass." She raced away into the forest, disappearing in a moment.

"Come on, Bib." Margale tossed his head. "King Hale won't come running to you to get killed."

I jumped up and laughed. I didn't care what this man was planning, and hardly cared what Limnad thought, because Pil was probably alive.

Margale grumbled, "Congratulations on your wife not being dead yet."

I could just make out his face by the branch-filtered twilight. "Thank you! We should celebrate. Do you have anything to drink?"

"No, sorry."

"Never mind. I'll celebrate by being the most cooperative bound creature in history. I'm not asking to eat my own foot, but I'll do what you say and kill who you want killed. I won't even try to twist the meaning of your commands. It's a celebration!"

"Shit. I wish I'd given you a drink and avoided all those lies."

Some of the refugees had crept back to the road and resumed their trek, muttering and arguing. Margale pointed down the road. "You go in front, Bib. I don't care if you're . . ." He glanced around and lowered his voice. "I don't care if you are restrained, I don't trust you as far as I could sling my mother by the tits."

It wasn't a nice thing to say, but I'd heard much harsher, so I didn't comment.

Margale looked at his feet for a second and sighed. "Which isn't too far, since I'd never do something like that."

FIVE

As I stumped along through the late evening toward sunset, the wind swung around from behind us. Blankets of smoke blew out of the city, stinging our eyes and making us cough. Margale pointed for me to follow the road, so we waded east in a river of sad, battered people fleeing the burning city.

I said over my shoulder, "Are we just traipsing down the road, or are we looking for any particular thing?"

"Don't worry about it. Keep walking," Margale said.

"Are those two more commands?"

He snorted. "No. Go on and worry if you feel like it. If you don't want to walk in front, you could hang back and get dragged along fifteen feet behind me. It doesn't matter to me."

"I can't believe that it doesn't matter at all. You must have preferences." I had the sense that the man was getting tired. If I could prod him enough, he might screw up and give me two more commands before long. With luck, I'd be torturing him before midday tomorrow.

Margale ran past me at a fine clip. I jerked and then followed him. My knee had been hurting, but that changed. It began popping and hurting both.

"Slow down a little!" I yelled.

"Is that a command?" He laughed.

"Asshole. I'm going to start the torture with your teeth. I figure knowing the plan might give you comfort."

Margale laughed again but didn't slow down.

I followed him for a few minutes, then said, "I could be a little more cooperative if you help me find my wife."

"King Hale isn't going to wait around for any family reunions."

"Let me define that. By cooperative, I mean that I won't kill everybody you care about. Hell, I could kill all the people who have ever said something nice to you. Or I would, unless you command me not to do that."

Margale turned and stood facing me. "We established that you wouldn't kill my family."

"That was this afternoon, in the burning ruins. Back then I thought my wife might well be dead. Now it's nearing dark, my wife's probably alive, and I damn well want to see her to make sure."

"Huh. I don't know whether she's alive. But if she is, it wouldn't surprise me to spot her along the road sometime tomorrow."

It took me a moment to consider that. "You know where she is? She's alive?"

"I wouldn't say yes to either thing, since she's not standing here in front of me. As for tomorrow? If you don't make trouble, we'll find out about her then." He turned and jogged on.

I had no choice but to follow.

After sunset, an occasional person on the road carried a torch, which threw just enough light for people to walk without stepping on each other. We passed four villages in the darkness. At each one, a few of the refugees on our road stopped, in some cases flopping down as if that was where they'd spend the rest of their life. Yet the road was still crowded when we reached the first actual town.

Enward Township was lit by a fair number of torches and a few lanterns. I'd visited there a few weeks ago to buy vegetables fresher than the ones sold in Arborswit. That was my errand. I also intended to cause trouble, drink, and gamble while I was there. I didn't see why I couldn't have fun and buy vegetables at the same time.

Three or four hundred people lived in Enward, but far more trudged or clumped in the streets now. Even more spilled over into shops, gardens, and homes. Some people dug vegetables out of gardens, brushed off the dirt, and started eating them.

As Margale and I walked toward the town center, I saw three people squatting behind various trees. They must have hoped that a tree trunk as wide as their butt might hide their defecation from hundreds of other people. We slowed to an impatient walk when we reached the heaviest crowd.

A few torchlit faces caught my attention. "Margale, not all of these wretches look sooty or burned. Some just appear exhausted and beaten. Where do you think the exhausted ones came from?"

"Someplace inland." He shrugged. "Towns are being destroyed all over the kingdom. It's the evil of King Hale."

"I'll need a more specific explanation than that."

Margale grunted. "Hale is fighting an unjust, wicked war. He's losing, but he won't admit it. Says he'll see every soul in the kingdom dead, children too, before he surrenders. He's a malevolent bastard. You should be proud to assassinate him."

"Why don't you do it? It doesn't sound as if you like him much."

"I'll be busy making sure we get out of there alive." Margale said that with no inflection, so I didn't suppose it was a joke.

"I haven't heard a damn thing about this war! Did it just start?" I asked.

Margale shook his head. "It started about the end of spring. It reached this side of Silvershanks just recently. These people probably didn't believe there was a war."

It was possible. Even among town-dwellers, most people never traveled more than a few miles from home. Whatever was happening forty miles away might as well be happening on the other side of the world. A few travelers and sailors would have brought news of the war, but those people were strangers. Nobody could trust a stranger. Whatever they said would be a lie, as sure as sheep were soft.

But no, that didn't make sense. I had been living in Arborswit for two months, and if anybody, even a stranger, had said the word *war*, I would have politely asked about it and bought him drinks until he was too pickled to lie.

Nobody had mentioned war to me. Margale was trying to trick me about something.

Halfway through town, I spotted a tall skinny man on a side road holding up a loaf of bread as he walked toward us. He handed it to the closest refugee, a man who hugged the loaf like it was a baby. A square woman with a hard face held a torch and an enormous basket full of loaves. The skinny fellow grabbed another loaf from the basket and gave it to a sooty, muscular young man with fashionable brown hair.

"Me!" a woman yelled, pushing toward the couple.

"Me first!" a boy shouted.

"Oh shit," I muttered.

In a few seconds, everybody within yelling distance was struggling toward the bread, shoving and dragging other people out of the way. The baker handed out bread in a frenzy for several moments until somebody grabbed the basket away from the woman. The pair backed away with big eyes and slack mouths. Somebody grabbed the man's arm and begged for more bread.

Two unkempt, sagging men who looked like farmers ran over to save the baker and his wife. Within a few seconds, the farmers had been dragged down, but that distraction let the baking couple run off the street. Then they were trapped by refugees running from that direction.

"Come on." I pulled my knife as I pushed toward the trouble. When I had limped fifteen feet, I jerked to a stop as if a cord was tied around my waist.

"No," Margale said. "We have other problems."

"You're going to have a problem with me if you don't change your mind!"

"Forget it."

I fell on the ground and lay on my back, legs and arms in the air. "Either you let me help them, or I'll make you drag me all the way to King Hale's feet. Or you could use a command to stop me from doing that, I guess."

Margale ground his teeth. "All right then, I'll help."

We pushed through the crowd to the fallen farmers. I kicked and shoved people freely so that I could get past without stabbing them. Margale's club was tied to his back. He used his size and his open hands to move people. I saw him pick up one woman and throw her at another.

The farmers had been stepped on and bruised but not broken. By the time we reached the baking couple, the crowd around them had realized they didn't know what they were doing or really what they wanted anymore. About half of them had turned to bitch out the others for scaring the baker. He and his wife were hurrying away when we arrived, so we didn't have much to do.

"I guess we're heroes," Margale said. "Without us, everybody might have died."

"Yes, they might have!" I snapped, even though I didn't disagree with him. "You don't know. You have no more imagination than a dead bird in a ditch. Go home. I'll kill King Hale without you."

Margale made a face and pushed through the crowd again, motioning for me to follow.

Some refugees had stopped in Enward. Others must have traveled north by the road to the coast. Margale and I walked eastward but soon saw people grumbling as they trudged back toward the middle of town.

Four spearmen in peasant clothing stood at the eastern edge of town.

"Go back," said a tall but stooped older man. "Nobody goes this way. It's not allowed."

A dozen men and women had walked this far along with us. They began throwing weary arguments and insults at the spearmen.

The old man held up a hand. "Call me a turd-sucker if you

want to. Maybe you've got the right. The king says to close it, so we close it."

A boy shouted, "Why? Why's it closed?"

The old fellow nodded at the boy. "The king didn't explain it to me when I was having breakfast with him and the head priest and the general of all his armies. I'll ask him for you when we retire for drinks tonight."

That might have gotten a few chuckles in regular times, but not tonight.

"Go north or go back. Be happy you ain't dead," the old man said.

Margale walked toward the man, holding up both hands. I had to follow, so I noticed light glinting off a buckle Margale held out to him.

After examining the object under a torch, the old man nodded to Margale. "Go on. Kill some for me."

Margale led me onto the darkened east road as the refugees complained behind us.

Once the torches were a good ways behind us, I said, "So you're a king's officer now. Or maybe a messenger."

He shook his head.

"Scout?"

"I'm not a scout. But the man I killed two days ago was."

The woods and their pine odor thickened as we walked on a deserted road. We had drifted several miles inland, and I couldn't smell the salty ocean air anymore.

Two hours after we left Enward, my knee started throbbing harder. "When the hell will we get to the king? And can we get a drink before I stab the son of a bitch in the heart?"

"Impatient?" Margale asked. "I've noticed that when you're in pain you get that way. Or when you're mad, or tired. You're kind of like a toddler."

"That's your opinion? You and my wife might get along, if I weren't going to torture you to death for binding me like I was some nasty little thistle spirit."

Margale waved me away as if I were no more than a mosquito.

Not long after moonrise, we met sixteen men and women shouting as they hurried toward us. A few carried torches. They looked about like most of the refugees I had seen since Arborswit— dirty and unkempt, with faces tightened by fear.

"Bandits!" they shouted as they ran toward us. "Robbers! Murderers!"

"Makes sense," Margale muttered to me. "The whole world's being pounded like rats in a sack. Banditry would come next."

Most of the people talked over each other until an older man with shaggy gray hair spoke for everybody. "There's killers and thieves around, twenty of them. Thirty! We found two whole families killed, stripped off, and fingers cut off for the rings. Just evil."

A teenage girl spoke up. "And they found us too!"

Shaggy Hair scowled at her.

"How did you get away from these bandits?" Margale asked. "It seems sloppy of them."

"We have nothing," Shaggy Hair said. "They can't rob you unless you have something, and we don't, so they didn't." He stared at the ground. "They could hurt us though, so they did that instead."

One of the men nodded. His face was more bruise than skin. Several of the women looked away.

"Where are these raw bastards?" I asked.

"Bib, this isn't our task," Margale said.

"Well, if it's not, then our task isn't worth a damn!"

"Take hold of yourself. You're a man of learning. Act like you learned something."

While Margale and I argued, the refugees backed away from us.

"Do I have to threaten to get dragged across the kingdom on my butt again?" I yelled.

"Only if you do it naked," came a man's voice some distance off the road behind us. "Take off your clothes. Or die. Of course, that's implied."

I glanced at the poor refugees on the road. They had edged around so that Margale and I faced sort of north. Now they had withdrawn up the road, and each of them held a weapon. Most were armed with clubs, but I saw two spears and a hayfork.

I turned to look south. Just inside the tree line, thirty feet away, six men stood pointing crossbows of various styles and in different states of disrepair. Two other men stood apart, each hanging onto a bound child and holding a knife to the child's throat. They were all decently lit by the almost-full moon.

One of the men, a gaunt middle-aged fellow with a block jaw, shook the little girl he was holding and yelled, "Off with the clothes, you fine gentlemen. You haul 'em off and then skitter on down the road with your balls dragging, or you can wear 'em while we shoot 'em full of bolts. And don't think about fighting us, unless you want to see these two beautiful children get their throats sliced up."

Margale whispered, "I'll deal with the crossbows and the ball-draggy man. You kill these here on the road."

"Wait. These are bad times—"

"You don't mean to let them go, do you?" he whispered with a scowl.

"Hell no. Ball-draggy Man and his friends there have to die, but I bet these people on the road are only kind-of guilty."

"Stop whispering!" Ball-draggy Man yelled.

I smiled at him and kept whispering. "These folks here are just being used."

Margale whispered, "They're complicit. That means just as guilty as the others. Screw them."

Ball-draggy Man shrugged. "Whatever you want."

I judged that I had a couple of seconds to act before he ordered us killed. The crossbow bolts were made of steel. I could do sorcery spinning on my head for a year and not affect steel, since it had never been alive.

On the other hand, the crossbows were mostly wood and under great tension. If I spent a little power, I could weaken the wood in a moment. Then the crossbows would fly apart before they could be fired.

With immense efficiency, I spun six red bands to drive rot into the crossbows. They would do their damage almost instantly when I hurled them.

Then my spirit was pulled up through the top of my head, and I left my body behind.

Some god was hauling me to the Gods' Realm to trade for power. Or maybe they wanted to chat and tell jokes. More likely they wanted to yell at me and try to terrify me into making some obscure but fatal mistake.

SIX

No time passes at home while a sorcerer is in the Gods' Realm, so I wouldn't be slaughtered while exchanging insults with the God of Death, or whoever wanted me. But returning from the Gods' Realm could be disorienting.

I had great experience in sorcery, but there was a real chance I would fumble away those six red bands when I returned. And I might not be able to pull six more and fling them before Ball-draggy Man said, "Fire."

After two seconds of profound darkness and a stab of nausea, I arrived in the gods' trading place. I stood on a patch of common brown dirt. The gods considered everything else in their realm far too nice to be touched by a sorcerer's awful feet. The dirt patch was a cramped pen, and sorcerers were like lean nasty chickens that the gods squeezed eggs from until they were empty and could be eaten.

In the trading place, the gods asked sorcerers to do things in exchange for magical power. A young sorcerer's first trades always seemed reasonable, or even good. Later, the gods would demand that the sorcerer do questionable things, or perhaps horrible ones. The sorcerer might lose things or people he loved, have awful things done to him, or be required to kill others.

Why would a sorcerer agree to that insanity? A lot of people have answered that in different ways. Some say we're addicted to magic. Others believe we make bad trades when magic is the only way to save someone or something important to us. I have spent a lot of years thinking about this question. I've decided that without magic, a sorcerer is as powerless as anybody else, and great will is required to accept being powerless.

But hell, even with magic, sorcerers are powerless to change most things that matter. I once stopped a war between the gods and their eternal enemies, which I thought was a fairly good day's work. But I had merely inconvenienced them. They returned to warfare as soon as they could do it without looking foolish.

In the trading place, a breeze cooled my skin and the air smelled like electricity. Most sorcerers could only perceive what the gods wanted them to hear while in the trading place. I could see and hear everything, even the things I wished I could forget. The first time that happened, I thought it was because I was far older than most sorcerers. But Pil was much older now than I had been when my "trading eyes" opened, and she had never developed that ability.

I faced the small forest, which seemed different every time I visited but was always familiar. Today the leaves were brilliant red, almost hard to look at, and the tree trunks looked black. Something big and white stalked among the trees, and I saw two more of the creatures farther away rushing toward one another. They smashed together with enormous roars, deep and round. Two breaths later, they drifted apart, growling and snorting, having knocked over two trees.

Something above me screamed, and I scanned the sky. Dozens of falcons, hawks, and eagles soared in the sunrise, each one trailing colored streamers. A hawk was falling to earth while another flapped away in victory. Then a falcon streaked down on an impressively plumed eagle. The falcon punched the eagle as it hurtled past, and the eagle tumbled out of the sky.

"Holy shit," I muttered. This was not how the trading place normally behaved.

A light blinded me for a moment. When it faded, I looked in

that direction. The usual endless field of flowers grew there, with deep green leaves and pale blue petals. That would have been comforting if each flower wasn't sending a shaft of brilliant light as far as I could see. Most shot into the sky, or at least above my head. But when the wind ruffled the flowers, some bent far enough to shine their rays flat past the horizon.

Thunder crashed loud enough to drive me to my knees, and lightning ripped across the sky, even though I couldn't spot any clouds.

A woman's bouncy voice said, "Hello, Murderer."

I finally turned to the massive gazebo where the gods sat and mocked sorcerers who fancied themselves wise. Normally it was made of white marble. Today the entire thing was gold.

The woman went on, "You're right to say 'holy shit.' That's . . . so well put. I've missed the way you say things."

"Mighty Gorlana!" I said, standing to face her. "How's the mercy business?"

Gorlana, Goddess of Mercy, lounged on a bench on the lowest level of the gazebo. Waves of blond curls fell loosely around her heart-shaped face, which was ideally beautiful, and draped across her bare shoulder, which was equally ideal. Her long sapphire gown clung strategically to her body. It revealed an uncomfortable amount of leg and a disquieting expanse of bosom. She wore jeweled rings of various designs, some puzzling to look at, on all her fingers, along with four necklaces, nine earrings, three diamond hairpins, and five toe rings well displayed through her delicate silver sandals.

Most goddesses created some type of glamour to produce awe in men who looked upon them. Effla drove men almost insane with desire, for example. Gorlana didn't produce any effect like that. I had asked her about it when I was young.

She'd answered, "Do you think I need tricks?"

Now Gorlana said, "Mercy isn't a business! It's a gift. A blessing."

"A thing you're much more likely to grant to people who can afford an emerald tiara."

She waved her hand with a wisp of a smile.

I pointed up and glanced around at all the brutal activity. "What the hell is all this?"

She pursed her perfect lips. "It's a celebration. Today is the anniversary of the day Ever-Victorious Krak, Father of the Gods, led us to drive the Void Walkers out of the Dark Lands."

I waited for more, but it didn't come. "You're kidding."

Gorlana widened her eyes and gave the tiniest shake of her head. "I needn't have said 'led us to.' It could have been 'Ever-Victorious Krak, Father of the Gods, vanquished the Void Walkers and drove them out of the Dark Lands.' That would have been more accurate, according to some very wise and powerful gods."

I muttered, "That's not the way I remember it . . ."

"Well, I'm not sure that matters! After all, I hardly remember it at all because I was busy dying. I owe my life to the one who vanquished the Void Walkers and drove them away. Which is Father Krak, of course. The one who drove them away." She blinked at me and smiled with the charm of a goddess.

I was the one who had convinced the Void Walkers to withdraw, which wasn't anything like vanquishing them. Krak had contributed his severed hand to the effort. Then he waited behind his lines, probably wishing he had his hand back so he could slap some of the complaining gods with it.

That certainly wouldn't be how the Father of the Gods remembered it.

I nodded. "I understand, Mighty Gorlana."

"I hope you do. I do not forget. Murderer, sometimes I feel a teensy bit nostalgic when I look back on the years that I owned you."

"Then why did you sell me to Harik?" I snapped.

She raised her eyebrows.

"Your Magnificence," I added.

"There were reasons, not that I have to explain myself to you! But . . . it was becoming clear that you would solve most of your problems by sticking something pointy into another person, and Harik was the God of Death, after all."

"All right," I said with a little sigh. I thought I had forgiven

Gorlana a long time ago for selling me, but my clenched jaw told me I hadn't. "When I killed Harik, why didn't you claim me then? You let me be taken by that oaf, Baby Harik."

Gorlana paused, and I couldn't read her expression. "I have a proposition for you, sweet Murderer. I bet that you can refrain from killing if you want to. You can be merciful."

"I'll be honest, Mighty Gorlana. I would like to be merciful, but that doesn't sound like me."

"Hah! It doesn't sound like the things you've done, but that's not the same as who you are. I propose this: You will fight many foes soon, and I bet you can defeat them without killing them all. You can kill fewer than you spare."

"That's a whimsical thought, but I don't think it too likely. What do I get if I perform this almost unbelievable feat?"

"Well, I get you. You will get . . ." She hesitated. "You won't belong to New Harik anymore. You will belong to me again. Admit it, your life was far more pleasant when I owned you."

"I can't deny that. Belonging to Old Harik was worse than belonging to a farting hyena. But Baby Harik already owns me. I don't see why he would agree to participate."

A brash, nasal voice rose from deep inside the gazebo. "I've already agreed, Murderer. Old friend." The new God of Death strolled into view wearing a well-cut black suit. His face could have been called plain if his nose hadn't been broken more than once. He was bareheaded and beardless—beards were out of fashion in the Gods' Realm at the moment.

Propped over his left shoulder, Baby Harik carried a five-foot-long war hammer. Blue and yellow fire consumed the weapon's head. The flames filled a space as big as a watermelon, smoking and flinging sparks.

I glanced at Gorlana. She turned away from Harik and stifled a laugh.

"Damn, Baby Harik, that thing's bigger than you are!" I said.

Harik grinned, showing slightly crooked teeth. "I reached an understanding with our boy Fingit, and he agreed to build a weapon to my specifications." Baby Harik balanced the hammer, which must have weighed thirty pounds, on the tip of his little finger.

"It's bigger than anything I've got," I said. "So, you greasy, gutter-sucking ringtail bastard, why would you get involved in Gorlana's fun? I don't even think you like fun."

"Because if you fail—that is, if you kill more than you spare—then you will come to the Gods' Realm to be my servant for, oh, a period of time we'll work out later."

I laughed, even though I didn't feel like laughing.

"Wait before you toss this deal on a heap of trash," Baby Harik said. "If you participate, we will each give you two squares of magical power now. That's no matter who wins." Gorlana nodded.

I considered the deal. Four squares of power, two from each god, were enough to do significant damage, or to help a lot of people depending on how a sorcerer felt about things. I had less than two squares now, a sadly meagre amount in dangerous places like these. But it was a ridiculous proposition regardless. I made a show of looking behind me. "Your Magnificences, I had to check whether I was about to be ambushed while stunned by the stupidity of all this."

"There's one more thing, and it's terribly serious," Gorlana said. "You and the Knife have worked hard, so very hard, to reclaim her memories and restore her love for you."

When Gorlana mentioned the Knife, which was the gods' name for Pil, my mouth went dry. "We don't need your help. It would probably hurt us anyway."

"Don't think that way," Gorlana said. "No matter who wins, at the end of the contest, I will give you a charm. It will make her love you again, never mind this lost memory business. It won't be some false village-dabbler love trinket, either. It will use my godly power to restore the love you had."

Baby Harik stepped in front of Gorlana. "How can you turn that down, eh? I don't even like the Knife, and I'd take that deal."

I knew that I should turn them down, but I had to ask a question. I said slowly, "So I wouldn't get the charm until the contest ends. When will that be?"

Baby Harik stared down at me. "According to various agreements made between several involved parties, you may not know when the contest will end. You'll be told when it starts and told when it's over."

"Hell no!" I pushed back toward my body in the world of man, but Gorlana snatched me.

She said, "Wait a moment! I believe that being called the Murderer does not force you to kill all the time. You can wound people or terrify them. I have faith in you. Don't throw away this chance!"

"And I believe you'll kill the dumb bastards every time!" Baby Harik said.

"The answer is no!" I yelled louder than was appropriate for addressing gods.

Gorlana sat up straight. "Well, who knows? This offer might pop up again."

Baby Harik added, "If the contest ever starts, then it's already started."

I squinted at him. "What?"

Gorlana said, "If we offer this again later and you say yes, then counting the enemies you kill versus those you spare will start . . ."

"Now!" Harik said. "Right now."

I waved both hands at them. "That seals it! This whole deal is too ignorant to participate in."

Both Gorlana and Baby Harik stared at me without much expression. They were still at it when I pushed myself out of the trading place and drifted back toward my body.

SEVEN

When sorcerers leave the trading place, gods often like to hurl them back into their bodies, sometimes so hard the sorcerer is knocked down. But I was leaving the trading place at my own speed, giving me a fine chance of hanging onto those red bands. I could do nasty things to crossbows before they punched holes in us.

I did not do nasty things to all those crossbows, however. Just as I arrived, the ground under the crossbowmen rippled and snapped like a sheet being straightened. Four of the men fell, and three of those fired away into the woods to terrify some rabbits and squirrels. The other two men twisted and swayed but kept their feet. One of them fired, putting a bolt straight through his left foot.

I spared an instant to appreciate the fact that Margale must be a Bender, the type of sorcerer who can drastically reshape anything that's never been alive. That relieved me. I had suspected he was a Burner, who can cause things to combust with fantastic heat—as long as those things aren't living flesh.

Two crossbows remained dangerous, so I flung two bands to rot them. The weapons flew apart under the strain. I ignored the ones that had already fired. This tussle would all be over before their owners could recock and reload.

I had four red bands left with nothing to do, and they wouldn't wait around long for me to command them. Ball-draggy Man and one of his friends were pressing their knives to the throats of two children. Each knife handle was made of wood. I could shatter the handles and drive splinters into each man's palm and fingers, but doing it without hurting the children would be a trick.

I hate sorcerers who wave their hands around, hoot, and bellow like a moose when performing a sorcerous feat. It's like shouting, "Hey, I'm a sorcerer doing some magic you may not like! This would be a good time to hurry over here and kill me!"

However, in this case I employed some considerably intricate gestures to make sure the wood exploded only where it touched the hands of those awful robbers. Ball-draggy Man and his friend both screamed and bent over their bleeding hands.

These two wounded bastards had threatened to kill the children, who were rushing away like terrified geese. These two had to die. I didn't have strong opinions about the crossbowmen. Maybe I could just wound them, set them on the grass, and terrify them a bit. Once they got done crying and apologizing, they might go on to do more useful things than loiter in the forest to steal from people.

I stabbed Ball-draggy Man in the kidney with my knife. He gasped and fell. Two seconds later, I cut his friend's throat as he was explaining what a huge mistake this all was. Then I turned back to the crossbowmen.

Three of those men were scattered around, not moving. The other three were up and staring at Margale as if he were a great hairy serpent. He swung his club two-handed and smashed one of the men in the chest. The air exploded out of him as he tumbled more than ten feet and landed limp in some tall, unruly grass.

I rushed to subdue the last two men. I had turned down Gorlana and Baby Harik, but they were counting every death and capitulation. Just in case I changed my mind, I needed to stack some of my enemies in the "survived" pile. Otherwise, I might become buried in dead foes with no possibility of catching up.

But as I limped toward the fight, Margale swung his club back the other way, slamming it into the next man's back. I heard bones breaking, and the man skidded onto the road, his arms and legs flopping.

I grabbed the last crossbowman's arm and pulled. Margale snatched his other arm and yanked at the same time, making me stumble. Then he stepped between the man and me, forcing me to let go of the fellow's arm or get knocked flying by Margale's enormous ass. I was unable to stab my master, so I backed away.

Margale punched the man on the side of the head with his fist. The man's skull produced a loud unhappy cracking sound. He collapsed onto the grass lightly, with surprising grace for a man who was already dead.

"Damn, Margale," I said, cleaning my knife. "I wanted to question one of those boys."

"Why? They're just lousy bandits. They're less interesting than a butter churn. Or my sister's husband." He curled his lip.

"All the same, if somebody else threatens our lives, let me pound and capture a few. They might surprise you with what they know."

Margale frowned and refused to agree to any such thing.

The refugees gathered in a clump, shuffling but not running. Shaggy Hair approached us with shaky steps. "Thank you! You saved little Temra and Pepp! If you hadn't come along, I just don't know." He shook his head, sending his thin hair whipping back and forth. He smiled at us, showing less than half the normal complement of teeth.

These people hadn't tried to kill me, or at least, they hadn't been too obvious about it. They were a weary, sad bunch, and I couldn't consider them enemies.

"Be quiet!" Margale pointed his thick finger at Shaggy Hair. "You're all part of their gang. You're the bait. You're as guilty as they were."

"Oh, we can let them go," I said. "Those hard men are dead. Without them, these people won't cause trouble. They're not clever enough."

"What if they meet some more hard men? There are tragedies

all around, which turn good people into murderers." He lowered his brow at me. "Maybe that's what happened to you."

"We'll be good!" Shaggy Hair cried out. The people behind him nodded and muttered as they edged away.

I couldn't attack Margale, which limited how I could help these people. I had no red-hot urge to save them anyway. Margale was certainly right about their guilt. But they were helpless, or the next thing to it, and killing them seemed like a foul turn.

"I suggest you run, folks," I said. "Chasing all of you would be a trying task, and Margale here has business down the road. Some of you will probably live."

By the time I finished, all of the peasants had changed from dejected ass-draggers into scrambling people desperate to live. They each made their best speed across the road and ran for the trees.

"That was foolish," Margale said. "Although . . . you gave them a little hope, which is a gift, even for a moment."

The clothing, hats, and shoes of all the adults running off flared with white heat, almost too bright to look at, and burned away in a moment. Men, women, and any children too close to the adults, shrieked and ran a few steps. Then their blackened, smoking bodies collapsed and lay still.

The five surviving children stared and stumbled away from the charred corpses.

I didn't display as much outrage as I might have. Any outrage would have to pierce my great shock at what Margale had just done. I stared at the man. He tried to hold back a grimace but failed. Then he looked around at the bodies.

A sorcerer could have only one ability, but Margale had just demonstrated two—Bending and Burning. The idea of "only one ability" was so fundamental that I had never heard any other possibility discussed except as a joke. My teachers had never let slip any hints about it being a real thing, and most of them were a chatty bunch.

So, it couldn't be what it looked like. I scanned the road and the trees, looking for a second sorcerer hidden someplace. I didn't see her or him.

I allowed myself to flirt with the idea that Margale might be both a Bender and a Burner. I didn't know how it could be possible, but I did know one thing. I wasn't going to acknowledge that there might be anything special about the bloodthirsty son of a bitch. He could explain himself if he wanted.

"Dammit!" I shouted at Margale, glaring. "Damn you for a bloody-fisted, stick-up-your-ass murderer of the mostly innocent! I don't guess you've ever slipped and done something wrong, have you?"

He shrugged. "When I bound you, I didn't command you to keep your mouth shut. That seems like a pretty big mistake now." He laid his bloody club across his shoulder and marched on up the road, ignoring me, the dead, and the crying children. I hurried to keep up with him.

I needed information that no human could give me. I hated going to the gods with a mere question. It felt like I was a gawking peasant asking for directions to the privy. But I didn't see an alternative. I fell behind Margale the full fifteen feet I was allowed at this point. I didn't want him sensing that I was headed to meet with the gods. He might grab on and come along.

Lifting myself up through the top of my head, I called out, "Mighty Gorlana, I come to trade!" I didn't really want to trade, but I'd have to give up something to learn anything, even with the Goddess of Mercy.

I arrived at the brown dirt patch in the trading place. Everything around me looked just as I'd left it minutes ago—a crass symphony of light and savagery.

Gorlana smiled at me, sat on a bench, and leaned forward. I smiled back at her. "Your Magnificence, have you enchanted your gown with divine magic? That's the only thing that could keep your formidable breasts inside it."

"These things?" She waved a hand in front of her chest. "I can choose whatever form I want to show mortals like you. But they are nice, aren't they?" She dimpled for an instant. "I didn't think you'd change your mind so soon, dear. You only need to say the words, and then you'll have accepted our agreement."

"Oh, I'm not accepting. If Baby Harik's involved, then it has to be viler than whatever you can squeeze out of a cow that's been dead a week."

Gorlana's nostrils flared. "I offered you three nice things. You can have the power right away. You can be sure about love once the trial is done. And you can belong to me again, which you must agree is the most important thing!"

"Why do you want me back?"

"You're funny. No, not like that. I mean it's entertaining to watch you try to be amusing."

I took a breath. "I realize that you're a goddess and don't have the failings of mortals, but that sounded like a lie," I said.

Gorlana grew still. The white things in the woods went silent. Every predator bird in the sky swooped and landed on the gazebo's roof. Then they stared at me.

I said in a much smaller voice, "However, my hearing has become less reliable in recent years."

Gorlana smoothed her gown. "What do you want, Murderer?"

"I would like one question answered."

She motioned with a graceful hand for me to go on.

I stopped myself from clearing my throat. "Is Margale, the sorcerer traveling with me, both a Burner and a Bender?"

"That sorcerer with whom you're traveling? You mean the Avalanche?"

"The Avalanche?" I resisted the urge to widen my eyes and add *Really?*

The gods always gave sorcerers names and would use only those names when speaking to and about them. I had overheard the gods talking to or yelling at each other quite a few times. They had never used a sorcerer's regular human name.

Even the cleverest sorcerers had never figured out how the gods determined those names or what significance a name had, if any. The gods named me the Murderer, and I thought it was mighty obvious why. But I had known sorcerers named Feather, Anvil, Nub, Freak, Knife, Farmer, and others. Those names might or might not mean something understandable by men.

I felt certain that the gods' names for us had nothing to do with destiny. If the gods could see the future, they wouldn't do some of the stupid shit I've seen them attempt.

But the Avalanche? He might as well have been named the Imponderable Obliteration of Everything You Love.

I smiled at Gorlana and waited.

"No," she said. "I won't tell you unless you agree to this contest."

"Instead of the contest, how about we get attacked by lions at some point?"

"So that you can charm them to ignore you and eat the Avalanche? I perceive that you're not serious about this, not at all."

Gorlana flung me down into my body. I stumbled and cursed my sore knee but didn't fall.

Margale said over his shoulder, "Either you tripped over a frog, or you've been talking to gods, Murderer." He paused. "How is Gorlana, anyway?"

"Unhappy. She's thinking about sending lions to eat you."

He laughed and picked up the pace.

Somebody was telling Margale about me, my movements, and my deals with the gods. The obvious suspect was Baby Harik, but I couldn't rule out any of the other gods.

Before I could kill, or overcome, Margale, I needed to find out what sorcery he could actually perform and who his divine allies might be.

Margale turned to face me, walking backward, and yelled, "Hurry up, Bib! If we rush, we can find out before sunset whether your woman escaped the city."

EIGHT

The moon rose toward midnight, and I still hadn't seen Pil. In my imagination, Margale would point her out from the road, as if she were a colorful bird that he was sharing with me. I realized that I was tired, and my mind was wandering.

"To hell with that shit," I muttered. I breathed deep in the washed-out darkness and focused on the back of Margale's soon-to-be-tortured-to-death head. That revived me.

At last, we rounded a curve and saw four lanterns on a building beside the road not far ahead. Two people stood in front of this moderately large structure. I assumed it to be an inn, a tavern, or a stable. Travelers would be pleased to find any of those along the roadway.

Margale broke into a run toward the building. That forced me into a wobbling run. One of the people, a fair woman of average size, sprinted and jumped at Margale. He seized her in a fierce embrace and laughed, lifting her off the ground and spinning around with her.

I bent to massage my knee. The other person out front, a bristly man wearing a steel helmet, grunted, "H'llo Bib. I've shit out things that looked better than you."

"Is Pil all right?" I stalked-dragged toward him, my hands out to grab his shirt.

His shoulders twitched as if he was about to shrug, but he frowned instead. He bellowed, "Your Ladyship, you might want to look at this thing here in the dirt!"

This man was a soldier named Grinder who was traveling with us. From the way he called out to Pil, who he sarcastically called Her Ladyship, I couldn't tell whether she was inside the inn, somewhere outside, or just within earshot drawing well water.

The man was an asshole.

I backed up as far from Margale as possible so I could see Pil coming out the door or from around either of the inn's front corners. I almost shouted at Grinder to tell me where she was, but she sure as hell wasn't within fifteen feet of Margale. If Grinder told me where she was, how could I explain not running to find her?

Margale was an asshole too.

Grinder was edging toward Margale, who was still embracing the woman. The soldier leered at them from ten feet away. Maybe he thought that showed discretion. He scratched his bristly beard with one hand and pushed back his bent iron helmet with the other.

Pil ran out the inn's front door, her long dark hair wet in the lantern light. She wiped her hands on her trousers as she ran and smiled at me. Her smile had charmed a lot of people over the years, and it had sure done the job on me.

Grabbing me, Pil's words bubbled out. "Don't you think I was worried, because you've shown up after worse than the world burning down around you, but I'm happy you didn't make us wait here for a week. I got your note." She squeezed my shoulders and then turned my head with her fingers. She winced and touched the cut on my neck. "Talli said you were right behind us, that her friend would bring you along, so I'm happy he was honest, and . . . Krak's thumbs, he's huge!"

"What note?"

"The one you sent saying to meet you here. Talli brought it." She nodded toward the young woman who was now whispering with Margale. "How do you know her?"

I didn't want to share too much before we could talk where Margale couldn't overhear. I hesitated and then lied. "She owes me a gambling debt. She can't throw dice worth crap."

Pil raised an eyebrow at my lie but nodded. She whispered, "How did you know about the fire in the city?" She hesitated. "Did you start it?"

I whispered back, "That hurts. Do you think I'd set a fire that killed so many and beggared more?"

Pil said, "Of course not," while at the same time her head made a tiny nod. It was probably subconscious. "If you hadn't warned us, we might not have escaped." She drew a breath to keep talking, but instead she grabbed me in a hug.

I wasn't going to interrupt that, and it went on for as long as she wanted. When she stepped back, I said, "Do you still have this note?"

She reached into a pouch for a piece of parchment folded twice. "It's written in your hand." As I unfolded it, she said, "It smells like you."

I raised my eyebrows.

She said, "After fifty years, I know what you smell like."

The words looked as if I had written them. So Margale burned the city and forged this note to make sure the people I liked would escape. I tried to glance at Margale, but the binding stopped my head as if my cheek had smacked against a wall. Of course, looking at Margale right now would be like pointing at him with a great red arrow bearing the word *malefactor*.

I sighed. "I have spoken to Gorlana quite a lot lately. Maybe this note was her way of being merciful and saving your lives."

Pil held still for several seconds. "Really?" The word was a dagger of sarcasm.

"Probably not." *But it's all I can think of right now.*

Pil leaned in close to me and whispered, "What's wrong? Why are you lying?"

Grinder saved me by sauntering over beside us. "Sorry to break up all the smooching and groping."

Past Grinder, a squat woman with pinched eyes and thinning

gray hair glared at me from the inn's front door. "I got rooms for them kind of frolics, you two. Out by the road ain't proper." She wrung out a gray cloth as if it were my neck.

Grinder smirked but didn't look back at her. "If I'm going to be a messenger and a guard both, it would be fair to pay me more."

Pil looked away from the guard, trying not to laugh.

I had insisted every morning for two months that Grinder be fired, but nobody listened. It was partly my fault we had to deal with him. Kenzie was a sorcerer too, and I had once told her that the best way for a sorcerer to defend themselves in battle was to hire a few stout soldiers. I also mentioned something about paying for drinks and whores for the ones who lived.

Kenzie and her husband, Vargo, had shown up on the mainland a few days after Pil and I arrived, arguing with each other even as we opened the door to them. The issue seemed to be that Kenzie wanted to be there and Vargo wanted to go home, but they went at it as if their lives and the destiny of all the people who walked this road were at stake.

Kenzie, who was already a capable sorcerer, then demanded that I teach her everything I knew about sorcery. Telling her to go to hell would be awkward since I really had promised to teach her, but when I made that promise I thought I might be dead soon. The promise had been nothing but a kind gesture.

Kenzie didn't care and had presented herself, ready to absorb knowledge. After her first lesson with me, she hired Grinder to protect her. His job was to stand in front of her in battle. Since no battle was happening at the moment, he must have felt that getting drunk and passing out before sunset would be all right.

Kenzie had chosen the man herself, so she wouldn't admit that he was a piece of crap in a bad helmet.

"You work for Kenzie," I told Grinder. "Ask her about a raise. But be nice. Last week, she learned how to make a man's willy turn to straw."

Grinder backed off a step, realizing that I must have taught Kenzie that trick—which was a thing neither she nor I could actually do. Grinder stuck out his jaw. "I'll ask her. Probably having sweaty up and downs with that glum husband of hers."

He swaggered back to the doorway, asking the innkeeper, "Old Mam, where's the boss woman?"

The woman raised her voice toward me. "In a room proper for her activities!" She stepped aside to let Grinder pass, saying, "You're a horrible young fellow, aren't you?" as she patted his arm.

He chuckled and stepped inside.

"Well, somebody likes the grimy weasel," Pil whispered.

I bent to kiss Pil. She didn't truly pull away. She only turned her head a bit and looked at my chest, which made kissing her more awkward than cracking a walnut with your tongue. I gave up on kissing, squeezed her again, and let go.

Pil cleared her throat. "We're close to the Bole now. I mean, it's just a couple of days from here, right?"

"It is, although we may need to make a little detour. Nothing of consequence." *I just need to go commit regicide*, I didn't say. "And after we bring back your memories, we can go hunt dragons!"

If I expected Pil to smile at that, I was a fool. She grimaced, turned away, and called me something nasty under her breath. I had enticed her to the mainland by promising we would find and study dragons while we looked for her memories, and that had been telling her the most awful sort of lie.

We had both seen dragons, and seen them up close, so the promise might not seem outrageous. But I didn't know where any dragons were and had no way to find them. I had lied to her because the Goddess of Life was forcing me to leave for the mainland, and she assured me that if Pil didn't come along, I would never see her again.

The promise of dragons was what convinced Pil to come with me rather than stand fast at home. Well, when she remembered everything, maybe she'd recall that she loved me—even when I told her the most awful sort of lie.

I smiled a little too big. "All right, then . . . we'll talk about dragons later."

Pil shook her head. "Maybe we should go to some place of

power besides the Bole, such as the Deeper Spring, which I think lacks the Bole's . . . well, malevolence."

"But it's not as powerful."

"What about the Six-and-a-Half Stones?"

"I've been to the Bole, and it's the right place. Don't give up!" I held my breath because the closer we got to the Bole, the more often we had this argument.

"We don't even know what we'll do when we get to the Bole! Do I chant, or stick my head in the water? Hold my breath? Throw dirt at it? Throw dirt at you?"

"We'll figure it out. We're very smart."

Pil walked back inside without commenting.

A few seconds later, Margale loomed beside me. "Dragons? Really?" When I didn't answer, he said, "You can't promise ladies they'll see dragons if you can't show them dragons. And there aren't any dragons. No wonder she wants to stomp a mud hole in your ass."

"Stay out of it!"

Margale shrugged. "You have to be truthful with ladies. If you win them over but you've done it with lies, what have you really gained?" He coughed and glanced back at Talli. "I understand the rooms are all full. Unless you can make peace with your woman, you'll sleep in the stable." He whispered, "But don't go too far. I'll allow you two hundred feet—for now." He snickered as he and Talli walked into the inn holding hands.

I felt the crazy urge to tell the man that of course dragons existed, even if almost nobody had seen one and lived through the event. I had seen dragons, discussed philosophy with them, played with their babies, and in some cases, killed them. Margale didn't need to know any of that, of course.

Even with all the smoke in my nose, the stables smelled foul. A great elm tree stood not far behind the inn, so I lay down under it and considered five probably impossible ways to kill Margale.

I heard the inn's back door open, and I sat up. The old innkeeper was stomping toward me.

"You're sleeping under my tree," she said in a flat voice, and she held out her hand.

"I suppose I am. What's the rent for soggy ground under a mighty unattractive tree?"

"Six bits."

"I think I heard you say one bit." I fished in a pouch and passed one copper bit to her.

She stuck out her jaw. "Fine, but only if you're on your feet and out of here by sunrise."

I flopped back down and fell asleep within a minute.

My eyes blinked open when I heard a hissing sound. I realized I had heard it more than once before I woke. Easing my knife from its sheath, I rolled over, scanning the area for hissing things. The moon hung orange over the horizon. The sky was beginning to lighten on the other horizon. The inn's front lanterns threw just enough light to show that no one was standing near me.

Rolling to my feet, I faced the other side of the tree, but nobody was there either. I lowered my knife and turned all the way around.

"Hssst!" came from straight above me.

I looked up and jerked when I saw a dragon's head the size of a healthy boar. The dragon's neck stretched straight up into the darkness of the treetop. I backed up a few steps but then held my ground. If this creature wanted to kill me, it could have burned me up while I was spinning around like a moron with my knife in my hand.

"Hello, Chartreuse," the dragon murmured. "You sleep like a dead cow."

"Hello, um . . ." I had known two baby dragons who called me Chartreuse. They were Praxis and Chexis, and now I had an even chance of guessing the right name. "Hello, Chexis."

"You do remember me!" Chexis squeaked in a less than dragon-like way. Then he lowered his voice. "Of course you remember me. I was a memorable baby."

"Sure, that's right. Where are your mother and brother?"

"That wouldn't be a wise thing to say." The dragon slithered out of the tree with hardly a rustle and stood in front of me, stretching more than thirty-five feet long. His head stood three feet above mine as he said, "In fact, telling you that would be idiotic. You kill dragons!"

I defended my actions by saying, "Um."

Chexis lowered his face until it was a foot in front of mine. Grimy smoke drifted out of his nostrils. "I want to talk to you, Chartreuse. Why did you think you could murder dragons with no consequences? Keep in mind that consequences might include getting burned up or eaten."

Chexis sniffed and then puffed thick gritty smoke into my face.

NINE

The young dragon Chexis gazed into my eyes from a foot away and waited.

I managed not to step back. "You're right, I killed dragons. I killed one to save you and another to save myself."

"Couldn't you have only killed the important one? The one who was trying to hurt me?"

"I didn't think of that."

"Chartreuse, saying you're not smart enough isn't a good excuse. I suppose it's the best you've got, isn't it?" He growled at the ground. "Chartreuse, you mustn't kill dragons. You have to understand that killing dragons is a very bad thing to do. Do you understand that?"

"Yes, I understand, Chexis."

"Are you sure you understand?"

"Oh yes."

I had only been able to slay those dragons in such a fine, heroic manner by using the God of Death's sword. That weapon was gone now, and the worst harm I could do a dragon would be hurting its feelings. Chexis sure as hell didn't need that information. "Chexis, you should probably call me Bib."

Chexis twisted his lips. "Well, that's a boring name! Do you really want me to call you that?" The patch of grassy black tendrils on his forehead stood straight up, and he started talking faster. "I could call you Syrtax! That's a great dragon name. It's very elegant! I don't mind if you have a dragon name, but don't tell anybody else."

"Thanks, I'll stay with Bib."

His forehead patch fell forward. He lifted his head and waited a few seconds. "That's smart. If you have a dragon name, everybody will be disappointed when you're puny and can't fly or breathe fire. You shouldn't create confusion."

"That's settled. Is your family well?" I winced. I was making conversation with this dragon as if he were the neighborhood shoemaker.

"Thank you for asking. They're perfectly well, since you're not there to stab them to death."

"We can all celebrate that!" I let my smile drop. "You hunted me down, Chexis, which likely was a tedious effort. I'm pleased that you did, but you found me for a reason, other than teaching me not to kill dragons. What is it?"

I figured Chexis would want to know how I killed those dragons, or whether I could find his family a safe place to live, preferably one with lots of unattended sheep, goats, and yaks. He might have questions about his infancy. I had been his nanny for the first few weeks of his life.

The dragon surprised me by saying, "My brother doesn't remember you."

I pursed my lips but didn't comment.

"But I remember you. I remember everything, including all the songs we sang. Singing is a horrible thing to teach a baby dragon. You should walk around apologizing to everyone for doing that." Chexis flicked out his tongue and shook his head like a wet dog drying off.

"You sang 'The Sailor's Five Whores' better than my father. I was impressed." I couldn't make out what Chexis wanted from me. That was a little disturbing, since he was an invulnerable magical creature that was smarter than me. "Why was it so bad to teach you songs?"

Chexis stretched out his neck and sniffed me. "You reek. There's something wrong with you."

"The stable is right over there." I nodded toward it.

"That's not it."

"I ran through a lot of smoke yesterday."

"No, that's the only thing making you bearable."

I held still and didn't meet the dragon's eyes. Margale's command wouldn't allow me to give any hint that I was bound. But if this magical creature could figure out my situation on his own, then I could stay true to my command while Chexis stomped Margale into a bloody lump.

The dragon pulled back and stared at me for a few seconds. "Oh, maybe your head hurts, or maybe you're hungry. Where are your turkeys?"

I blinked a couple of times. "I . . . I didn't bring any with me. Why would I want turkeys?"

"All I ever saw you eat was turkey. You charmed them to fly in from the ceiling. It was the most interesting thing you ever did. Was that the pinnacle of your life? I guess it might have been."

"Those were geese, son. Don't feel bad for skewing the memory. You were just a sliver of a dragon."

By moonlight and lantern light, I could make out many details about how the dragon had grown. He was about half the length of Red, his mother. His teeth were half as long as my hand. He could kill me with one bite if he wanted.

"Not turkeys. Other fat birds, then." He didn't sound upset that I had corrected him.

"Chexis, how have you grown so big? You're not much more than a year old."

He snorted, and the air warmed up as smoke wafted from both nostrils. "Bib, you are the last creature in existence who should comment on how old somebody should look."

I chose to ignore that, since it was the truest statement he could have made. I spent seventy years in a nasty realm where people didn't age, probably so they could suffer longer. Pil spent almost fifty of those years with me. Now she looked like an energetic, healthy woman of forty who had always been beautiful, while I looked like I was forty-five years old and had been stomped on by bulls for forty of them.

In reality, Pil had been alive for eighty-seven years, and by my best guess, I was a hundred and thirteen.

"Chexis, you still haven't told me how I can help you, but whatever it is, I will probably agree, since I'm practically your uncle."

The dragon rushed to scoot away from me, tripped on his tail, and skidded backward on his butt across several feet of grass. "Don't say that!"

"I was only having fun with you," I said, standing so rigidly I nearly vibrated. "Just joking."

"Don't joke about that!"

I waited for a couple of breaths. "All right, I didn't mean to offend you. What's the matter, son?"

"Sphynthor says that I'm—"

"Excuse me, who?" I leaned forward, as if that would let me hear a damn bit better.

"Oh. That's Mother's name. Not her real name—I'm not going to let you charm her with that. It's her everyday name. She only used Red for a special mission."

I waited.

"Yes, the mission to devastate this world, kill most of its people, and remake it into a dragon paradise."

"Sure. Are you angry that I got in the way of that?" I asked.

Chexis stood up and shrugged, a movement so human it startled me. "No. I don't know what a dragon paradise would look like."

"I guess there'd be yaks."

"I guess. Sphynthor gave me permission to explore the world." Chexis didn't react to my pathetic yak joke.

"I'm honored that you came to visit me while you were out exploring." Just after I said it, I realized that his visit really had touched me.

His head-grass swept back, lying almost flat. Chexis said, "Chartreuse . . . Bib, I mean. Dang it, I'm going to call you Syrtax. You secretly want me to. You're just afraid that you don't deserve a dragon name. How many men can say they have a dragon name given to them by a real dragon?"

"I wager I'm the only one."

"See?"

"See what?" I asked.

"Syrtax, I want to tell you the truth. Well, that's wrong. I want to tell you some of the truth."

"That's fine," I said. "I do that sort of thing all the time. Spit it out."

Chexis worked his jaw, and I thought I had chosen my words poorly. But in a strained voice, he said, "Sphynthor didn't allow me to go. She suggested I go away for a while. She very firmly suggested it, using claws. She thinks that I'm too . . . mannish. What do you think about that?" He dropped his head for a moment but then stared hard into my eyes.

I got the sense that I'd better not give the wrong answer here. "I don't know what 'mannish' means."

"Syrtax . . . when I was a baby, did you do something to me to make me too human?" He rushed on to say, "To be clear, *too human* would be *human in any way at all.*"

I started to reach to pet his nose, but I held back from such insanity. "I can't see that you're human, Chexis, not even a little. You're terrifying me just by standing there."

"Really?"

"Really. I'm not lying." And I wasn't. "But what did Sphynthor mean when she said 'mannish'?"

Chexis's head drooped. If he'd been a boy, I might have thought he was about to cry. But he was a dragon, and this behavior might mean he was about to eat me.

He said, "I don't know what she meant. There was too much clawing and biting to ask about etymology."

My brow furrowed, and I blinked.

"Oh no." Chexis sighed. "You're stupider than I thought. Well, maybe it's instinctive . . . I mean, maybe you're born with this knowledge."

I didn't hesitate. "It will take a little thinking and research, but I'll be able to tell you what she meant by 'mannish.' Give me a few days." If I kept Chexis nearby, maybe he'd sense that I was bound and then bite Margale into three or four pieces.

The inn's back door opened and then slammed shut. Chexis shot into the air in a thunderclap of translucent wings. The dragon had swept around out of sight by the time Grinder reached me, carrying a lantern.

"Gonna rain?" Grinder was holding out a palm and glancing at the sky. Then he slapped his leg and sneered at me. "I was hoping you'd still be on your damn belly asleep so I could kick you a couple of times. That big mountain of a raw-ass bastard has bought horses for us." He jerked his head toward the stable. "Get to saddling, you stumpy old fart."

I knew that Grinder was a brutal thug, but he'd never said a hard word to me. But when he'd seen me arrive tonight, a gray-haired man limping and breathing hard, only to be exiled to sleep on the ground, he must have decided I had become prey.

I no longer answered every threat and insult with murder straight away, at least most of the time. So I didn't expect to have Grinder on the ground with my knife pressed against his throat in a few seconds. Grinder had expected it even less.

"I'm sorry, damn you!" Grinder choked out, flailing his arms and legs. "Don't kill me! In all the gods' names, don't!"

The lantern had broken, the spilled oil was burning on the dirt, and pain had spiked in my broken finger. I snarled, "I might have spared your life, but you had to bring the gods into this."

Footsteps and voices approached from the inn. The innkeeper was charging toward me, holding a heavy pan over her head. "Stop that! Don't hurt him!"

Kenzie snagged the woman is if she were a chicken while she shouted, "Bib! Let the man live! He doesn't know better! He has hardly a brain! At least wait for me to hire a couple more before you kill him!"

I glanced up, ready to smile at Kenzie's sorcerer-like practicality. She carried another lantern, which she shook at me. Her husband, Vargo, stood beside and behind her, nodding at me and making stabbing motions.

I decided not to kill Grinder, as a favor between sorcerers, but I couldn't just let him go. I glared into his face and yelled, "Sorry, Kenzie, it's too late. My blade has been unsheathed and must drink this idiot's blood. Do you want to say goodbye to this worthless, cross-eyed slave to petty cruelty?" I looked up again before the soldier could see me grin.

Pil stood motionless beside Kenzie, and she wasn't grinning. She said, "Bib, spare him," as if she was telling me not to play in the chamber pot. When I lifted my knife, she turned back toward the inn, but not before I heard her say, "Why did I ever want this?"

TEN

I ran to follow Pil inside, stumbling worse than a crippled duck. Before I reached the door, I rooted out a bit of dignity for myself and limped inside like a prince of sorcerers, if there were such a thing.

Just through the door, I jerked to an awkward stop.

Pil was waiting for me right inside. "Is this the kind of thing I'm trying to remember about you?" She said it calmly enough, but she put me on the defensive like I was a boy facing a gang of other boys he'd betrayed.

"I wasn't really going to kill him. I merely scared him to mend his behavior."

Pil surprised me by patting my arm. "I don't know that I can believe you, since you're a lying bastard, and I know why you're that way, but knowing doesn't make up for being lied to all the time."

"I'm not lying." I looked down because of the stupidity of that statement. Prevarication was one of my failings, and Pil knew it. But she also knew that I wasn't a wise sorcerer or even a powerful one, so I thrived by being a sneaky one.

Pil said, "Somehow I imagine it mustn't have been so bad in the Dark Lands when it was just two of us, and monsters might charge in to kill us at any moment." She shrugged. "I wish we were at the Bole already and could stab all this lost memory business in the nuts." She took my hand with the broken finger, and I sucked air.

"Are you hurt? Did you pound some bar too hard?" She grinned.

"I got it from Limnad when she told me to go play in an avalanche."

The inn's back hallway was dim but bright enough for me to see her swallow.

I said, "She prevented me from reaching the city while telling me all about how you were being burned to death. Once she told me you were dead, she let me go so I could see for myself."

"Oh. I'll bet she just wanted to torment you." Pil shrugged. "I occasionally understand the urge. Since neither of us is dead, I'll put Limnad's frolics out of my mind for now. Maybe Kenzie will fix your finger if you're nice to her. Nicer than you have been."

Margale poked his head into the hallway and shouted, "It's getting light! Saddle! Ride now! Eat and make love later!"

Pil, less than half Margale's size, squared off with him. "Keep your tone pleasant or at least civilized, you crumbling hillside. We have tasks and won't ride off until we finish them."

I noticed Pil slip two fingers into a pouch on the back of her belt. Whatever she pulled out might cook Margale like a squab. I also saw a small stack of firewood against the wall begin smoking.

Margale was a Burner then, but I had never seen one with so much control. Most Burners could either turn things into white-hot obliteration or retire for a quiet drink, with nothing in between.

If Pil and Margale fought, an awful lot of screaming destruction was about to take place in this hallway no bigger than a couple of wagons. I would be the innocent onlooker, and I knew what happened to them.

I said, "It's best if Kenzie heals me, Margale. If I'm all stove up, I might not perform well should somebody need to be killed." From behind Pil's back, I lifted my eyebrows twice at the man.

Margale bit his lip but nodded. "Do it as fast as you can."

When he had gone, Pil led me into a room with a tall bed. Kenzie was waiting there.

Kenzie took my finger with an admirable touch of gentleness. Healing never treated the healer well. "This is not so bad. Your guts aren't all hanging free. That's my standard for serious wounds with you, Bib."

I nodded. "Thank you for doing this, Kenzie. I don't know what it's costing you, but you're generous, regardless."

"I'll fix your knee too. It's broken twice over." She glanced up at me, but I didn't explain how it had happened.

Kenzie went about putting my finger back in order by pulling bands and sheets of power to reshape my body. Once, I had been able to heal this way, but I gave up that power long ago.

"Pil, Margale is a Burner," I said.

She stuck out her jaw. "I saw the smoke. It's unfortunate if we have to fight him."

I said the next part really fast. "He's a Bender too. I saw him do it myself."

Pil laughed. "He fooled you somehow."

"I don't think so."

"Has he actually told you he's both Bender and Burner?" Pil asked.

"No."

"Have you questioned him about it?"

"No." I was starting to feel like a boy again.

"Can you think of a way that *you* could make people think you're both a Caller and something else?"

"Sure. I could have an ally in hiding." Now I was feeling like a stupid boy.

"I'd say that's a much more likely explanation, so let's stop assuming Margale has impossible abilities and start looking for his sneaky friend. Or better, let's leave. Whatever direction he rides in, let's ride in a different one, because we can circle around to the Bole, you know."

I cursed silently. I had to go where Margale went. How would I explain that to Pil and the others?

Before I could come up with some ringing great lie, Pil went on, "I made you a present, Bib."

That pulled all my attention away from lying. Pil was a Binder, adept at working magic into physical things, and seventy years of careful practice had made her damn good at it. Most sorcerers die young, but Pil had followed my advice to never trade for power when the trade was likely to change you. Also, she had lived almost fifty years in the Dark Lands, where power couldn't be acquired and there was no temptation to make foolish bargains.

Pil reached under the bed and pulled out something long, thin, and wrapped in cotton cloth.

"I hope you enjoy it," Kenzie said, still working on my finger. "I hauled the benighted chunk of iron on my back when flames chased us, sucking the smoke all the way here."

Pil ignored her and unwrapped a plain-looking sword. In fact, it was ugly—bent and pitted. She said, "Desh taught me the value of making things look unpleasant."

"Thank you, Pil, this is kind," I said, as she handed me the sword.

"I know you hate naming weapons, so I just named it in my head." She smiled and started talking faster. "It's the cousin of a sword Desh once gave you, although I admit without any boasting that I've improved upon it. It is powerful in the thrust but less so in the cut."

My stomach got queasy.

Pil's smile was growing bigger. "If you beat an enemy without killing him, your vigor will increase, at least to a point, but if you kill enemies then your vigor will fail bit by bit until you return to your normal self. You won't become weaker than normal, and you'll return to normal a while after you stop defeating enemies."

"Pil, I don't want to throw doubt on a gift, especially an enchanted one, but the sword Desh gave me shattered at the worst moment and stabbed me in the neck."

Pil held up one hand. "But that happened because the sword's power was profoundly at odds with your nature as a killer! This is the improvement I made, you see. It resists destroying itself even if your nature and the sword's clash."

"Resists?"

"Nothing can be certain, you know that." She put her hands on her hips. "Dammit, how many magic swords do you have right now?"

"None."

"Then shut the hell up and take the thing!"

I nodded, said, "Thank you, dear," and buckled on the sword.

During that argument, Kenzie had moved on to healing my knee. My finger felt as good as it had yesterday morning. Kenzie hummed a little. Pil and I sat silently on the bed, but it didn't feel awkward.

"Done," Kenzie said.

"Are you sure? It still hurts," I said.

Her cheeks grew red. "Do you think to question my skill?"

"Who's the one who journeyed here so I could teach her about magic?"

Her cheeks reddened. "Fine!" Once she put her hands on my knee, she said, "Oh, you're right. Well, you must see it's a small mending." A few seconds later, she said, "Done! I've fixed up that knee properly."

"Kenzie, it still hurts," I said slowly.

"Shit! Balls and perdition!" She put her hands on my knee again. "It was healed up in a fine way just moments ago. It's gone off again now. I'll beat this thing with a stick."

I shook my head. "No, don't. Your teachers probably never mentioned this, but I know what's happening. Did you ever wonder why sorcerers don't heal themselves or rich patrons into immortality? Restore failing hearts? Cure their weak eyesight?"

Kenzie shook her head slowly. "Well, sorcerers don't get old. Mostly."

Pil caught her breath.

I said, "A body can be healed only so much. If I had died when I was twenty-two like a good sorcerer should, this would never have come up. But I'm old, I've lived hard, and I've been healed to hell and gone for years."

Pil grabbed my arm tight, as if I might float out of the room if she didn't hold me down. Kenzie stood up, squinting.

"Kenzie, I doubt that healing me will fail consistently," I said. "But eventually it won't work on me at all." I stood and walked to the door with just a brief twinge and hardly any limp. I smiled at Kenzie. "Don't feel that you've failed, because you haven't. See, it's not so bad."

I walked back to the bed and then to the door again. It really wasn't bad. It was just bad enough to help a truly skilled opponent kill me.

ELEVEN

I firmly believed that Pil was the best sorcerer alive. I realized long ago that she would be a better sorcerer than me. When she wasn't more than a girl, long before we married, she gave me a magic walnut.

Nodding, I thanked her, dropped it in a pouch, and blew on my fingers to warm them. Then I kept on peering over some frigid rocks, puzzling about how we'd get past fifty men guarding a squid-dick hooligan who called himself "Baron Wolfpack."

Pil reached up to slap me on the shoulder. "You son of a bitch, you didn't even look at it!"

"I apologize, Pil. I'm rude and not worth the air it would take to blow my nose. I'm sure it's a fine walnut, full of clever magic."

"Someday somebody is going to stab you for being an ass, and maybe it'll be me."

In fact, Pil did stab me in later years, more than once, and she didn't screw around about it. Both times, I almost died. We had the most colorful history of any married couple I could think of.

"I'll have to stab you later," she had said, "because I have solved our problem with those guards."

"That tickles me." Although I wasn't too excited, I asked, "How?"

Pil had already snatched the walnut back out of my pouch and held it in front of my face. "This grows walnut trees."

I bit my lip and considered whether she was joking. "Yes. More than one?"

"A whole forest! Well, a tiny forest."

"Fine sorcery." I smiled and was now getting excited. "We can sneak past these boys if we have a nice stand of woods that appears for no reason. How fast do your trees grow?"

"Fifty feet tall in ten seconds." She tried not to grin but couldn't help it.

My eyebrows shot up. "Pil, that sounds like it would take a vast amount of power. May I ask how much time you spent making this?"

"I worked on it for two days, but that was several weeks ago aboard ship." She shrugged. "I thought we might need something like it eventually. It doesn't just grow trees. One tree will grow directly under each person."

I stood straighter. "Driving the limbs and branches up through each man's body?"

"Flinging guts and gore in all directions, you mean? No, that's the way you'd do it. The men will be captured in the limbs and hoisted unhurt high in the air." She mimed it, using one arm for the tree and the other hand for a man, fingers flailing. She made tiny sounds of distress. "No blood, but maybe some puke."

I examined Pil's face as I tried to calm a sick feeling. "I know I don't have the right to question you, but damn it to Lutigan's fourteen shortest whores, I worry about what you've been giving up for all this power."

Pil laughed. In spite of everything, she sounded so happy that I almost laughed with her. She said, "It's not all that bad, because ten seconds after the trees finish growing, they'll dissolve into sawdust and splinters, and trees that exist for just twenty seconds don't require a lot of power."

"So . . . each man will then be dropped about forty feet to the ground. Will there be blood then?"

Pil winced. "No magic is perfect. You know, I wanted to bring in waves of crows for atmosphere, but that would just be vanity, wouldn't it? Who could justify the cost?"

Ten minutes later, when Pil wielded the magic walnut, her plan could have gone wrong in a thousand different ways. But it all worked the way she said it would. I knew then that Pil would far surpass me as a sorcerer, if she lived.

For that reason, I felt a bit foolish at the inn examining both edges of the enchanted sword she'd just given me. I couldn't stop myself, though. It looked dull, nicked, and bent, as if I had beaten an anvil with it for an hour.

Pil said, "Take off your clothes," the way she might say, "Eat your soup."

I glanced, but she wasn't smiling.

"Take your clothes off! Every stitch! Kenzie, you too." When we didn't start hauling off clothes right away, she glared and pressed her lips together.

Kenzie and I stared at one another. Neither of us undid a single tie.

"Hurry!" Pil said. "That big, bumbling hippo may burst in and demand we sprint down the road, saddling our horses as we hop on one foot, and since he's a Burner, I don't want to fight him just yet." She held up a tightly tied bundle of clothes, shook it, and grinned before hurling it at my chest. She followed it with a pair of boots.

"If you're too grand and mighty a sorcerer to wear clothes that refuse to burn"—she peered at a similar bundle before tossing it to Kenzie—"maybe Grinder will want them."

"They're charmed against fire?" Kenzie asked with a blank face. "If Margale's a Burner, well, how could you know we'd need this thing? And where are the fire-shedding clothes for Vargo?" She ran toward the door, I suppose to call her husband, but Pil grabbed her arm.

"I'll get Vargo. You get those sooty, nasty old clothes off. As for how I knew, we came here looking for dragons," Pil said in an airy way. "When dragon-hunting, clothes that won't burn up would be a reasonable precaution, right? So it's a good thing I had time to finish them in Arborswit before it deflagrated." Pil turned toward me like she was training a crossbow, and now her brows lowered. "Of course, we haven't seen any dragons yet. You probably lied about them, Bib, and I bet there's not a dragon within a thousand miles of here."

I looked at the floor and managed to stay silent. I began undoing the ties on my jerkin and turned my back to Kenzie.

Pil ran out of the room and returned in a minute with Kenzie's husband, Vargo, who was a medium-sized young man, sturdy, and balding. He had a strong chin and a nice-looking face. He arrived just when I had shed all my clothes but before I had put any on.

"What the dying hell?" he almost shouted. "At least put on a shirt!" Pil handed him a bundle and told him what to do with it. She was his great-aunt and might have spanked him as a boy. Now he shut up and obeyed, as if his granda might beat him again.

The bundles included belts, hats, gloves, scabbards, and small pouches. Just as I had my pants on, Pil's head came up. "Horses. At least six or seven. Maybe more."

I didn't hear a damn thing. But I didn't doubt her.

"Are they getting closer" Kenzie asked.

Pil tilted her head and told Kenzie evenly, "Hm. I didn't hear them a few seconds ago, but I hear them now. What do you think?"

Kenzie didn't answer. In my imagination, she was blushing.

Now I could hear the hoofbeats, and those horses were running at a gallop. I pulled on my boots next. I could fight, run, and flee just fine without a shirt, but trying such things barefoot was an aggravation. I buckled on my sword belt, ran through the inn, and strode out front, holding my sword as if every man in the kingdom should be terrified of me.

Margale and Talli stood straight and relaxed as they faced twelve armed horsemen wearing the blue uniform of Silvershanks. A severe young barefaced man with cropped hair raised his ragged voice. "Odds are you're a brace of traitors and murderers." He nodded toward me. "The graybeard there too. I'm ordered to capture you, but I'd prefer to kill you and to take a lot of time doing it. Hundreds are dead in Arborswit. We followed the trail you left." He spit on the ground.

Kenzie appeared in front of the doorway, carrying the pure white spear. Grinder pushed her aside to jump out and stand in front of her with his sword drawn.

The other soldiers, all of them older than their leader, growled, muttered, and cursed us.

Margale said, "You have it all wrong, sergeant. We didn't hurt anybody, and in fact, if we hurt your people, it would stop us from carrying out our mission. We're traveling—"

"I don't care to hear it!" the young man shouted. "You're killers and criminals. Throw down your weapons or die where you stand!"

"I thought you were going to torture us," I said.

"I am!"

"Well, how can we die where we stand if you intend to torture us to death? Do you know some methods of torture where we stand in one place until we die? I'd like to know about them, for the sake of curiosity, if nothing else."

I glanced at Margale. He was staring at me with his mouth open.

The young soldier screamed, "Don't try to be funny with me! Surround them!"

The horsemen couldn't truly surround us. Our backs were to the inn and its door. We could retreat that way if necessary. They did form a semicircle around us, and they did it with fine discipline.

Margale said, "Forgive my idiot servant, sergeant. We are part of the delegation from Her Majesty Apsel, Queen of Havenswit. We're expected to visit your king within two days to reach terms for ending this war. If you don't want to escort us there, at least don't delay us."

"You're from Havenswit?" the young man breathed. Then he shouted, "Now I know you're tit-dragging criminals! Kill them all!"

The sergeant's men snapped to follow his order, and he possessed great natural authority. He did not possess much experience fighting next to buildings. Half his men were armed with swords and had a hard time getting close enough to fight us unless they dismounted. The others were armed with spears, which gave them reach, but once they tried to pierce us, their horses either came to a halt or had to turn away, which left the riders' backs exposed.

Being on horseback had been their greatest advantage, but suddenly it became a huge handicap.

I blocked one spear and yanked another to pull the horseman off balance. Then I ran past that man, feeling the little stick in my knee, but it didn't slow me. I reached a man who was dismounting and sliced the back of his neck before he could raise his sword. Anybody who felt that wasn't sporting could suck rocks. Losing meant death, and fairness had nothing to do with it.

The fellow whose spear I had yanked was turning his horse to reach me. I sliced his leg, but not deep enough to kill him. A little wave of energy passed over me, and I felt just a bit stronger. The horseman rode away from me.

I didn't watch Talli and Margale, but glimpses and curses gave me the sense that she fought like a blade tied to a whirlwind, while he was an avalanche, too overwhelming to resist. When a horse near me cantered away, I spied the young sergeant who had been standing on the other side of that horse from me.

The sergeant made a fast advance behind his sword's point, feinted a thrust at my head, another at my belly, and then slashed at my sword arm. He was skilled, especially for his age, and he looked surprised when his sword arrived, and my arm wasn't there. I tried to disarm him, but he slipped away.

He reset himself for the next pass. That showed he was accustomed to training yards and formal duels. In a real fight, there is no resetting and there are no passes. As he paused to collect himself, I cut him across the skull and face, just missing his left eye. With a regular sword, I might have killed him, but Pil had enchanted this blade to have a devastating point yet not so sharp an edge. He dropped his sword and staggered away, holding his face. I felt another wave of energy.

Pil had run around one side of the inn and Vargo around the

other, both with weapons drawn. Now the horsemen found themselves surrounded. Two retreated at a gallop, one of them pausing to pull the wounded sergeant up behind him. The one whose leg I had sliced was already riding away with a companion. The other eight lay dead or wounded, some grievously.

That wouldn't do. The sergeant and his boys would hurry off to report their failure. Whoever they reported to might send fifty men, or a hundred, after us next time. I needed to kill these four fleeing soldiers before that happened.

I mounted the closest horse, sword in hand. As I wheeled the stallion, Pil shouted, "No! Don't chase them!" I didn't pause to explain, because she knew exactly what I intended to do and why.

As I galloped away, a lousy thought hit me. Yesterday, Margale had given me permission to stray as far as two hundred feet from him. He had never corrected that, but maybe now he'd whisper permission for me to go kill our common enemies.

I hit the two-hundred-foot mark at a gallop, and my horse never faltered. However, I was yanked off the back of my mount as if linked to a chain. I rolled as I hit the ground but still smacked my elbow hard.

"What the hell was that?" Vargo asked, walking toward me. Nobody else was talking, but everybody stared. In the back, Margale grinned at me but rubbed his face to wipe that away.

I shook my head, pretending I was dazed. "I . . . it was an evil spirit. Well, a cranky one. I pissed off Limnad to hell and gone yesterday. She's probably softening me up before she feeds me to some wet nasty thing."

Everybody muttered and exclaimed over that. Margale gave me a tiny nod. I could tell that Kenzie didn't believe me a bit, but she didn't argue.

Pil narrowed her eyes at me but didn't comment either. She grabbed my arm and held it tight. "I'm glad you didn't go murder them."

"I'm glad that fact brightened your day. You don't have to be sad for them and their short wasted lives."

"To hell with them. When you do that kind of thing, I'm sad for you."

"And I'm sad for you, Pil!" Vargo glared at me. "He's a liar. Murderer! Bib, the idiot drunkard! You're better off not loving him!" He nodded at me. "Sorry, Bib, but it's true."

Kenzie leaned toward her husband. "That's no use, is it? I've tried to reason with her, but Granda . . ." She stared at me and sighed. "I can love you as my teacher, Bib, but you're no man to be in love with."

Pil walked away instead of defending me.

"Well, hell," I said. "I'm the only one around here who's happy, and I just fell on my ass."

"You're not the only one," Margale said. "I found that pretty enjoyable. Let's chase down a few more activities, Bib, and see how happy each one makes you."

TWELVE

Pil demanded to know why I wanted to go with Margale, so of course I lied. I said he had asked us to ride with him for a while. That was almost true. Margale had given me an irresistible command to go with him until I was a sword's length away from King Hale. Technically, that was kind of like asking.

I also told Pil that a small detour would give us time to mentally prepare ourselves for the ordeal at the Bole. That was a great honking lie, because I was ready to dangle my feet in the Bole's waters in an instant. I didn't want to wait anymore, and I doubt Pil did either.

To finish off, I told her that it would be mean and rude to refuse Margale's invitation, since he and Talli had saved Pil and the others. Actually, I intended to torture Margale at the first opportunity.

Pil didn't challenge my lies. However, she frowned and stared at the stable wall for a while.

We had been riding behind Margale as he rode for an hour or so when Margale's friend, Talli, rode up beside me and shouted, "Tell me three fun things that I've never heard of."

I hadn't spoken with her yet or even thought much about her.

The dragon, magic sword, unhappy wife, and busted knee had all occupied my mind.

I strained a bit to make out her words, since Margale was leading us at a sharp trot. Talli reminded me of a young girl I once knew named Yita. They both had black hair, dark eyes, and olive skin. But Yita had been thirteen years old and sturdy. This woman was about twenty-eight, sturdy, and voluptuous.

Talli wore serious, plain traveling clothes, but under the tunic she wore a bright yellow silk shirt with a ruffled neck and embroidered cuffs. I considered that for a moment. That intense yellow was impossible to achieve with natural dyes. The only way to get it was to craft it using magic.

What other bits of magic was Talli carrying? Everything she was wearing and every trinket she had strapped onto herself might be enchanted. She could be like a walking place of power. It wasn't impossible. Hell, Pil had charmed all of my clothes against fire, including my smallclothes.

Was Talli a Binder who crafted her own magical shirts, weapons, and underwear?

Talli watched me, waiting, so I put speculation aside. "Fun things? I might have told you some fine ones if you were polite and respectful. And if you introduced yourself."

"Oh fine. I'm Talli. Polite? Nobody ever laughed until they peed while being polite." She gave a fine, wide smile, showing almost white teeth before leaning forward to shout at Pil, who was riding on the other side of me, "And respect isn't what we really want, is it?"

Pil answered, "I don't know. I respect you for helping us escape the fire."

"Good!" Talli squinted at me. "He's a little worn, but do you mind if I use him?"

Staring straight ahead, Pil opened her mouth and then closed it.

"Obviously he belongs to you, but I thought things might be getting a little . . . I don't know. Tedious. Pil, admit it, you might want variety. Or just a rest."

Pil waited, but I didn't want to speak and get in the middle of this. Finally, Pil gave me a hard look. "He doesn't belong to me.

Technically he does, but things are complicated. So he can do whatever he wants." She looked away.

I ground my teeth.

Talli laughed. "Don't look so pissed off. I was just having fun with you. Pil, I don't want him!" She looked from Pil to me and back. "Maybe you don't appreciate him as much as you could, do you?"

"Maybe I don't," Pil said. "What has Margale told you about Bib and me?"

"Nothing! I get to find out all about you on my own."

"What can you tell us about Margale?" I asked.

She leaned back with a small smile. "I don't talk about him behind his back."

"So what's this war all about?" Pil asked. I glanced at her and nodded that I liked this line of questioning.

"Oh, the war!" Talli's mouth and eyes drooped. "This awful war has to end. I've seen the . . ." She rubbed her eyes with the back of one hand. "Damn that greedy son of a bitch King Hale! He has mines, gold, and silver, but this is a hilly kingdom." She nodded ahead at some hills ahead of us. I figured we'd be in them before dark.

Pil said, "Hard to pull ore-filled wagons across those rocky slopes."

"Right! But a wide river runs through the kingdom of Havenswit, just east of here. They ship everything from sheep to shirts down to big cities, which are a hell of a lot more entertaining than this wilderness."

Talli shook her head and then pushed her loose black hair back from her eyes. "King Hale attacked, and Havenswit suffered. But Queen Apsel's army drove them the hell back over the border. Margale is one of Queen Apsel's retainers. The most important one, if you ask me. He expects this war to be finished in a month."

I smiled at Talli. "That's quite a bit of knowledge, and I thank you for it, Talli. I may have to stay up all night thinking about it."

Talli smiled at Pil with her eyes crinkling. "Don't spend too much time thinking! Where are my three fun things to do?"

I hadn't expected she was serious about that. I cleared my throat. "Visit a spirit in her home. Bring a gift."

Talli nodded. "I'll do it tomorrow."

"Play with baby dragons."

She snickered before clearing her throat and sitting taller. "I'd have that carved on my tomb if I did it."

"Marry somebody who's tried to kill you at least twice." I shrugged as if I did that every day before breakfast.

Talli laughed until she rubbed her eyes again. She called past me to Pil, "Thank you for letting me play with you a little! I like him even more than I did when I heard he calls himself Bib."

When I first went to the Dark Lands, Pil had stayed behind, and she told stories about me. They had been told and retold all these years, and by now people saw my life as a warning about all the things a person shouldn't do. That included lying, theft, murder, drinking, jealousy, cheating, and general misbehavior. The name *Bib* had come to mean a vile person who did all those things. It was a foul insult, and nobody named their child Bib now.

When Talli had ridden on, Pil said stiffly, "She's a sweet girl. Probably a murderer, but we can't hold that against her, can we?"

I examined Margale's back from where he was riding three horse-lengths ahead of us. As I watched, he shook his head a bit, and his shoulders lifted as if he was sighing.

When we halted at midday for a short break, we found that none of my group had brought much food. This trip had been a rushed affair for us, either chased by fire or dragged along by Margale.

Talli laughed at us. "Don't you know how to travel? Have you never been away from home? Does your mother cook all your food? I'll throw dice with you for some of ours. I'll hazard a crust of bread if you put up two silver nobs."

"You chest-heavy cow!" Kenzie yelled. "Two coins of silver can buy ten dozen loaves and a keg of beer!"

"Really?" Talli looked around. "Where are these ten loaves you're speaking about? Off behind that tree?"

Kenzie took a step toward Talli, gripping her spear. "Don't play funny with me, you dripping twist!"

Talli didn't seem concerned about being threatened with a pure white spear. She laughed as she skipped back away from Kenzie.

Vargo groaned. "Stop it! We're going to starve, and I have to listen to this."

Kenzie wheeled toward him with her teeth bared. Then she looked away and blushed.

Margale stepped in. "We can share. It's best for everybody." He nodded toward Talli, who laughed until she snorted. She began combing her hair with her fingers.

"Talli, please get the food," Margale said. "I'll stay with our guests." He eyed Kenzie's spear.

"I'm not digging in your nasty saddlebags," Talli said.

"Dig around in your own! The food's packed there."

Talli looked at Margale with a blank face. "You were supposed to bring the food. Weren't you?"

Margale drew a deep sigh.

At least we'd brought plenty of water and weak beer.

"Maybe we can pass a town this afternoon and buy food," Vargo said with some hope in his voice.

Margale shook his head and then scratched his beard. "Nah, there aren't many habitations in these hills other than mining towns, and we won't reach those until tomorrow. Who would want to live here? You can't farm worth a damn, and your kids would starve."

Kenzie gripped Vargo's shoulder. "At least the weather's nice . . ."

Margale scowled. "Don't talk that way. It invites bad weather."

I said, "Oh, I can guarantee we'll have beautiful weather the rest of the day."

At sunset we gathered wood and brush, built a fire, and sat around drinking beer. Pil took first watch. Everybody was tired, hungry, and grumpy. Our conversations floated on a sea of sarcasm and spite.

The bright but waning moon had risen clear just after sunset, so we had a nice bit of moonlight.

I spotted the stranger first, walking out of the scrub trees at a measured pace. I stood to face him with my hand on my sheathed sword, and everybody else looked that direction.

"Hello, you people!" the man called in a deep, happy voice. "I want to come and sit next to your fire. I'm a guest! I brought food to put in your fire, and then we can eat it together!" He held up two great, bulging burlap sacks and shook them. "I'm not here to murder you! I know you like to murder people, but I'm your guest!"

Pil charged out of the stubby trees and stared at the stranger. "I don't know where he came from! I'm sorry!"

The man kept coming with steps that appeared tentative. He didn't seem to be carrying any weapons. "You're apologizing to me, nice woman, but you shouldn't. I haven't told you my name yet. My name is Tem. Now you can say, 'I'm sorry, Tem, my guest.'"

He stopped, but none of us spoke.

"Darn! I mean, I'm Tem Hollicoxe." He smiled and nodded around at us. "Now we can put this food in your fire and eat it!"

I hardly paid attention to that statement. Margale was one of the biggest men I'd ever seen, but Tem was half a head taller, with shoulders and arms so enormous they seemed unreal. I wondered if he was one of the gods' servants, a kind I had never seen.

When none of us answered, he kept coming. He stared at his feet to walk through some fallen branches, when he could have walked around them. He got past them, grinned, and tripped over something I didn't see. He fell right on his face. He didn't try to turn his head or break his fall in any way.

Tem jumped up and rubbed his nose, which was streaming blood. He smiled again and shrugged. "That was embarrassing. It could have been worse, though, when you think about everything that could have happened." He stared straight at me and gave me the most exaggerated wink imaginable.

I closed my eyes. By Krak's radiant ass, it was Chexis.

THIRTEEN

(CHEXIS)

My dinner with Syrtax and his companions was everything I could have hoped for, although I shouldn't have been surprised. I had known it would be a success. A realm in which a man outwits a dragon is a realm in which rabbits hoard things and eat cows.

Human lives are so wretched and so stupid. I pity them for their suffering. It would be so much better if they'd go someplace where I never have to know they exist. At the very least, they could live in tunnels where I'd never have to see them.

After the humans greeted me in their primitive way, they brought me to their fire, which is the center of social activity. They made me their guest, and I was a good one. I was probably the finest guest they'd ever invited to a fire, or to any other place. I made a subtle human expression with my eye to warn Syrtax not to interfere with me.

I'd planned this evening because I didn't want to wait for Syrtax to answer my questions. I would be human for an evening and do human things with humans. Then I'd have confirmation that those things are indeed human things. I'd know what they felt like. I could avoid ever doing them again, and then I could go home.

I had changed shape only twice before, and this was my first time shifting to a human form. I was shocked by the stench that comes with being human. I always thought they must sleep in a nest of their own spit and excrement, but I guess it's just the way they smell all the time. Maybe that's why they don't live in tunnels.

For one month, I had been spying on humans in their nasty little houses and towns. It was much easier than I expected! I spied on them at night, hiding in places like barns, up in trees, and in the shadows behind buildings. I wandered around on a lot of roofs, and nobody ever heard me, since I'm a thousand times quieter than any human ever born. Sometimes people walked past when I wasn't all that well hidden, and they never saw me. I think humans don't expect to see a dragon in their town. When they see one, they think it's something else.

Although I spied on humans, I didn't learn much, because the town people were as ignorant as buttons. I found that I liked real buttons, though. I had begun hoarding, and I collected a fine hoard of buttons in lots of different sizes and colors. They were more satisfying than coins. Gold is sort of boring.

I learned that humans like big things. I heard people talk about that a lot, so I became a big human. I was far larger than the biggest of these humans, so they liked me as soon as they saw me! When I hurt my face, and it really hurt, the woman with big hair wiped the blood off and put my nose back where it should be. That hurt more than falling on it.

In the towns, I had made a list of what humans like. The list didn't have much coherence. In fact, it didn't make any sense to me! But I didn't want to wait around for Syrtax while he wasted time eating pig and putting cloth on his body. It was time to act.

Yesterday, I'd located Syrtax and hidden in a tree while he was sleeping. He's hard to wake up. Maybe it's because he's scrawny. He seemed big when I was a baby. I talked to Syrtax briefly, and I couldn't have been more disappointed if he'd answered by chewing up coal and spitting it at me. I don't think he knows much. He promised to get answers for me, but it would take a few days. What a ripping lie! Since he was spouting untruths at me, I should have asked him to tell me a nice story about raccoons too.

That wasn't the big problem. Syrtax had been charmed in some fashion. I didn't say anything because he's a sorcerer, so he probably knew about the charm. He might be fine with it. I have doubts.

I couldn't count on him, then. Probably, I couldn't. I wouldn't tell him that, though, because I might really want something from him later, and I didn't want him sulking around with his hurt human feelings.

My opening ploy was to ingratiate myself with the humans by being their guest. Guests have a special status, at least for one night. After that, they should leave. It's complicated, like all human things seem to be, but my tactic was brilliant! They gathered around me and listened with great care to everything I said.

Guests bring food. Earlier I had stolen a little sack of bread from a cart while I hid behind a couple of big bushes. I don't understand bread. Humans want to grind up weeds, shape them like something that comes out of their bottom, and eat them. The sack held nineteen bread-turds.

Humans usually don't eat just one thing, so I brought along some black birds I found lying on the ground. I also brought the bugs that were eating the birds, which I thought was considerate of me.

I remembered that Syrtax liked geese, so I caught ten of them. They honked and attacked me like tiny dragons! I didn't remember them biting Syrtax as often as they bit me. Geese must love humans. I stuck them all in a sack, but they wiggled and screamed and were so annoying that I stepped on the sack.

When I brought out the food, some of the humans went almost mad. I didn't know humans liked to eat so much. That was new information. Some of them squealed and jumped in place like they had to urinate.

The humans did some things to the geese that seemed confusing, then they put them naked in the fire. Everyone sat staring at the geese or at me.

I had a little trouble remembering what humans normally do

while their food is in the fire. Sometimes they sing, but once in a while they pray. Inspiration hit me, and I did something I hadn't thought about before. I had only ever heard Syrtax singing, but I was too clever to just sing one of his songs. I decided to sing but make it a song about man's relationship with the gods. I considered what I'd learned about humans and gods. Then I created a song that all the humans would love.

> *I pray to Krak for guidance,*
> *I pray to him all day.*
> *I wish that he would listen,*
> *I have a lot to say.*
> *I'm off to crush a kingdom,*
> *And they'll get really mad.*
> *I hope that it's the right one,*
> *Or I'll feel awful bad.*
> *I was born to be a killer.*
> *It is my destiny.*
> *And when the dead surround me,*
> *It fills Krak up with glee.*

I looked to see what Syrtax thought, but he turned away and looked at the ground. His mate grabbed his arm, which I would have found rude. As I watched them, I felt something odd happen to my face, probably a nasty human thing like sweating. The feeling went away, and I saw that my song was a brilliant success.

Everybody sat, too moved to say anything. Then one of the men, the one with the steel bowl on his head, began smacking his palms together. That's how I knew they loved it. It must have been his job to speak for everybody so that no one else had to hurt their hands showing how much they loved my song.

Then the man with the steel bowl on his head walked up to me, and I waited for him to praise me. "That was the worst damn song I ever heard. It ain't even got a girl in it."

That surprised me, and I didn't understand the relevance of his criticism. It was a puzzling situation, and I wasn't sure what a human would do in that situation. From what I had observed in the towns, the right response would be sticking a piece of metal in the man's chest. But I hadn't brought a piece of metal with me. I felt sure I was strong enough to beat him to death, but that might be rude after a meal.

Things were getting complicated, but I was handling it.

I said to the man, "I understand what you're saying. I'll keep it in mind."

He made a sound with his nose and kicked dirt on my shoe. Then he walked away.

The woman with big hair said, "I'm sorry, that was impolite. He doesn't know any better."

I shrugged, which felt nice. Both dragons and humans shrug in the same way, and it means about the same thing. I said, "Is it time now to tell stories about all the people we've copulated with?" I silently called myself a bad name because I had sworn not to ask anybody what to do. A human would know and just start telling his copulation story.

Syrtax said, "We're passing that by for tonight. Sorry."

That pleased me, because I had no idea what I was going to say. I took off my shirt. "Where's the water? I have an unpleasant amount of dirt on me."

"We didn't find any water here, and it's too heavy to carry with us," Syrtax said. "We'll bathe twice at the next watering hole."

"All right." As I put my shirt back on, I tried to think of a way to tell Syrtax to stop talking. He already knew I wasn't human. If the others figured out that I was a dragon, they might do things that weren't normal for humans with a guest at their fire.

They might try to kill me. When I wasn't in my dragon shape, I could be hurt or killed like any other creature.

I glanced around and saw some horses. Horses are very important to humans. I said, "You have beautiful mounts." I walked to the beasts, proud that I had used the word *mounts* correctly. I petted the biggest one on the neck. Then I scrambled onto its back. That was a lot harder to do than I'd expected.

"Stop that!" the big man shouted, as he ran around the fire toward me.

I sat contemplating how to make the horse run.

"I said, stop that!" the big man bellowed. His shout scared the horse, which ran.

"Thank you!" I yelled over my shoulder.

The horse ran for nine seconds before a wall of dirt appeared in front of us. The horse stopped and reared. I fell off its back.

I had done every human thing on my list, except for washing dirt and talking about copulation. It was time to end the evening.

The humans were chasing me and shouting. I ran away at an angle, passing a few small fat trees. Once I had a lead, I changed back to my dragon form while running. I did it in just a few steps. Shreds of human clothes fell off my body, and I flapped my wings just enough to clear the trees. I skimmed over the forested hills, thinking about how perfectly everything had gone. Even falling on my nose had just made them like me more.

I had been an ideal human. I knew things and behaviors to stay away from now.

Almost without deciding to do it, I flew circles above the hills until the moon set. Then I flew back to the humans' camp in heavy darkness.

I found Syrtax standing a short distance away from the others, so I landed and crept up on him almost silently. "It was perfect, wasn't it? Tell me how perfect it was." I didn't really care what Syrtax thought, but he was human, so I might as well get his confirmation and praise.

"Son, I don't want to hurt your feelings, but after you left, we all tried to guess what you were. Nobody guessed human."

I stood still for what seemed like a long time. When I'd flown here tonight, my spirit felt powerful. Now I felt weak and alone. I wanted to curl up someplace dark and sleep for a long time. But I couldn't bear the idea of looking weak in front of Syrtax.

I flicked my tongue. "Did I do anything like a human? Anything? Even one tiny thing?"

"You brought food and you made yourself welcome. Those are two pillars to build upon."

I hissed. "I don't want to build on this stuff! I want to not do it!"

"Oh," he said. "Chexis, after you sang your song, which I thought was excellent, why did you start crying?"

I gave the man one slow blink before growling, "What? I didn't do anything so horribly human as have water leak out of my face! I can't imagine what that would feel like."

"Maybe it was a trick of the firelight, then."

I put my nose a few inches from his. "Look, I don't want to be mannish. I guess I don't know what that is, but I don't want it anyway!"

Syrtax backed away. "Aren't you a little happy, son? You didn't behave like one of us awful humans on most of those things."

"I didn't behave like a dragon, either! Those were things a dragon would never do." I surged forward and lifted my head to loom over him. I couldn't afford dignity right now. "Syrtax . . . Syrtax, help me."

"I'm working on it. It will just take a few more days."

"I want you to help me right now! Who's not letting you help me? I'm more important than they are. I'll eat them."

Syrtax made an expression with his face, but I didn't understand most of what humans do with their faces. What kind of horrible thing had I really done with my eye when I tried to signal him?

Syrtax said, "Chexis, I have made commitments." He looked toward the sleeping humans.

"Are these commitments more important than me?" If he said yes, I would bite him in two, or at least nip him hard.

"All are important in different ways. Please understand."

I snapped my wings and launched myself into the air, paying no attention to the great boom they made. Syrtax was going to be sorry he hadn't said that I was the most important.

FOURTEEN

After Chexis gathered up his hurt feelings and flew away, I strolled back to camp to get a few hours of sleep. I hoped I hadn't misjudged the young dragon, but he wasn't my deadliest problem at the moment.

When I realized what I had just been thinking, I stopped dead beside a fat and prickly bush. I cursed myself in a whisper for thinking I could judge any dragon at all, no matter how old. I had spoken to Chexis as if he were a boy who wanted to go riding on a sunny afternoon, and I was telling him I had to fix the roof first. That was a mighty casual way to approach an invulnerable eater of meat.

"He's not a baby. He can kill me with one bite." I whispered it out loud to impress upon myself there should be no screwing around with dragons. Whenever Chexis returned, I had better have more useful things to say than *Sorry, you're not important enough to pay attention to right now.*

I lay down ten feet from Pil and closed my eyes.

It was still dark when somebody kicked me awake, their boot whacking against the sole of mine. I rolled to my feet fast with my hand on my sword. It was still dark, and light from the coming sunrise hadn't touched the horizon yet. I rubbed the sleep out of one eye and recognized Kenzie by her vague outline against the stars.

She grabbed my hand and led me away, far enough for our voices not to wake anybody.

"Damn, Kenzie, you may be young and made of steel, but I'm over a hundred years old. I don't need so much sleep, but if I don't slow down and rest, I get droopy and mean."

"You've not taught me a single bit about magic, as is your duty, for three days," Kenzie snipped, patting my hand so hard it stung. "I'll not allow this to go on. If I don't chase you with a broom about this, you may look around and decide that our bargain has flown away like a sparrow."

"I hear it," I grumbled. "If the bargain tries to fly away, you'll whack me with a broom. Let's talk about magic, then, and try not to yawn. What do you want to learn?"

"Power."

"The gods give you power in exchange for making your life hell until you die. I'm going back to bed. Dirt. I'm going back to dirt."

"No." Kenzie didn't let go of my hand. "I already know that hell and death stuff, and more besides. I want to know how to create the strongest magic I can using the tiniest possible dusting of power."

I said, "Well, you chose a worthy subject. Sit down so I can educate you without sore feet. Listen now, because you'll probably never hear this again. The bigger the magical endeavor, the more power is required. Pulling together a vast thunderstorm is more expensive than calling a nice rain for your garden."

"Oh, and ice is colder than water, and a horse's ass is bigger than yours. A little," Kenzie told me in a voice just short of a sneer. "Tell me something new!"

"Did you know that patience is one of the foundations of sorcery?"

Kenzie slapped my knee in the dark. "That's not what you told me last month. You said the foundations are courage, deviousness, perseverance, mathematics, and charm."

"I forgot patience. Stick it in between mathematics and charm."

After a long pause, Kenzie breathed, "Are you teaching me crap that you just make up when the time comes?"

"If I am, what does that mean?"

This time she was quiet for a good half minute before saying, "I should always be the one who declares what reality is today. And convince everybody else."

I snorted. "You really can be taught. Darling, if you don't remember anything else we ever talk about, remember that. Back to power and spending less of it. The most basic method is enchanting things to do what they already want to do. Don't go against the nature of a creature or a thing. Wood that's dead wants to rot, not grow. Dogs want to eat, sleep, make new dogs, and play. It takes a lot of power to convince a dog to swim a fast river."

"Noted."

"Second, you should, whenever possible, touch whatever you charm or ensorcel."

"Ensorcel? Really? That's a fancy word," Kenzie said.

"Hush. I want you to absorb my wisdom. Absorb the hell out of it."

Kenzie giggled, reminding me that she wasn't much older than a girl.

"Touching something often makes a spell much less costly, so do that if you can safely," I said. "Also, time is another good way to lower the cost in power. If you want to charm a bunch of trees to shake when an enemy comes near them, you'll spend less if you take a few hours to set that up. If you have to do it all within a few minutes, you'll be bleeding power."

"That makes sense, sure."

"I know it does." I smiled, which she couldn't see, but I bet she could hear it in my voice. "Another aspect of time is how long the magical effect lasts. Here's a sneaky one: You can heal somebody, but it doesn't have to last. After a certain number of hours or minutes, the wound returns as if never healed. But you didn't burn nearly as much power."

Kenzie gasped. "That's just . . . repulsive."

"Maybe. What if somebody is dying and you don't have enough

power to save their life? Maybe you could heal them for just a few hours using the little power you have and try to trade for more before your temporary healing fails."

Kenzie didn't comment.

"Now, let's talk about some fairly subtle techniques. Only Binders use them regularly, but other sorcerers can employ some if they're clever. The first is payment by other than power."

"That gives me a little shiver. Why is that?"

"I'll explain it, and then you can tell me. A Binder could make a pair of silent-walking magic slippers using less power if she accepts something bad while making them. She might have an appalling limp for a week to offset some of the power she needed. Or a bad thing could happen to the person wearing the slippers. Maybe he trips three times a day or can't run fast while wearing them. But nobody can hear the slipper-wearer coming. A Binder can make all that happen and for less power."

"How would a Caller like us use those things?" Kenzie asked. "We don't make slippers."

"If you call an ice storm, you could also require that you'll slip and fall on your ass twice during the storm. You'd save a little power, although it would be tricky to accomplish. Or you could accept that the sun would shine off the ice and blind you once before it melted."

Kenzie didn't say anything.

"Have I drawn back a curtain and stunned you with the complexity of the sorcerous world?"

"No!" She cleared her throat. "Maybe."

"Hold on then, I have two more. They apply to Binders only, or at least I can't think of a way we could use them. First, if a Binder is creating a magical object, like a sword, better quality materials lower the cost of enchanting. Or allow a stronger enchantment for the same cost. It costs less to enchant a fine steel sword to be extra sharp than to enchant a stick to be just as sharp. But with enough power, it's possible to enchant either one to cut equally well. Of course, the knife would last for years while the stick would break after a minute or two.

"Second, maybe the soon-to-be-magical object will be used by a specific person. If that person is involved in the enchantment, less power is needed. This can be extreme. If Pil forged a sword just for you, it would be cheaper, or more powerful, or both, if you got involved in creating it. You could hammer it for a while."

"I've never thought of that, but it doesn't sound extreme."

"Or the bucket used for quenching the hot blade might have your blood in it. Not a whole bucket of your blood, of course. Maybe a big flagon. Or—"

"That's enough! I'd like to never know what you were about to say. Bib, how have you used these more subtle techniques?"

"I've never used a damn one of them."

"Bib!" she shouted. I heard somebody moving around in the camp. "Why did you tell me all this, if it's untested crap?"

"Oh, it's been tested. I didn't figure it out. Pil did while I was running around killing things. It took her ten, or maybe twelve, years to fully test and understand it, but I couldn't have done it if I'd had a thousand years and a hundred assistants. She's a damn genius."

I didn't say that Pil had then spent a month spoon-feeding me the knowledge she had taught herself. And I had just given Kenzie the basics in less than an hour—much less. I once encouraged Pil to write a book about it all, but she refused. She wasn't convinced the knowledge would help people more than it hurt them.

We picked our way back to camp, stepping quietly. I lay down on my dirt bed and slept about an hour before we were up and preparing for the day.

Morning came in gray, breezy, and spitting drops of summer rain. I had sweated like a farm animal the day before, so the cool wind was like a holiday, apart from the binding, and the assassination, and so forth. Margale pushed us at the fastest pace so far, and I wondered whether we were closing in on his objective.

As we clopped along for the next three hours, the fat bushes became shorter fat bushes and then disappeared altogether. We gradually climbed into the hills. At first, they were gentle, but soon they grew steeper. Conversation became more challenging than it was worth.

Late in the morning, I spotted a strand of smoke rising from someplace ahead of us. We couldn't see the source because of the hills between us.

I pointed it out, and Margale called a halt. Still mounted, we gathered where everybody could hear.

"That's coming from one of those squidgy little mines!" Vargo shouted.

Margale pointed at Vargo. "Is it? Did you grow up around here? Have you even passed through before?"

Vargo shook his head. "No and no, but I have a grand head for distances and can read a darn map." He held up a yellowed sheet of parchment bigger than his face. "I bought it from a sad and moaning fellow who was bad at throwing dice."

"It's probably a fake, so shut up!" Margale yelled. "I'm done with your puppy dog yapping!"

Vargo started folding his map without taking his eyes off Margale. "Not so fake as a man who claims we're clopping down the road all friendly while he pushes us as if we were marching to war."

Instead of answering, Margale turned his horse and trotted away from us, toward the smoke.

Pil rode up beside me. "We've been polite and grateful to this grim, horrid boulder. Let's leave him. The Bole lies northeast."

I turned to say, "Let's wait until tomorrow morning," but no sound came out of my mouth. Apparently, anything I could say might give away the secret that I had been bound. I managed a tiny shrug.

Pil lowered her voice so that I could hardly understand her. "Is something wrong?"

I couldn't even shrug.

"Are you mad at me? Or is it something magical? Are you sick?"

I couldn't gesture or even look at her. Maybe my face would have given everything away.

Pil edged away from me, grumbling and slapping her thigh. I really had expected her to figure it out by now.

Margale kicked his huge horse into a canter and continued down the road toward the ribbon of rising smoke. I urged my horse to follow, lest I be dragged out of the saddle.

I tested my voice quietly now that Pil was farther away, and it seemed to be working. I yelled, "Margale, why don't I—" Then my mouth closed again. I was doing a piss-poor job of defining everybody's reality today.

Fine, so I couldn't talk worth a damn. I could make myself understood some other way. I examined the clouds and figured I could pull together a small storm in about ten minutes.

But if I did, the energy cost would be high. Well, higher than convincing a few sheep that a man was a pile of grass they should knock down and nibble at for a while. If I pulled together a storm every time I saw rising smoke, by year's end the gods would own me down to my knees.

Pil, Kenzie, and Vargo rode abreast behind me, but I couldn't hear what they were saying to each other. I thought for an instant about cutting the word *help* into my palm and holding it up where they could see. The moment I thought that, my hands locked as if they were marble.

We topped the hill we had been riding up. Just three hundred feet away, two small buildings were burning and throwing off dark smoke. Three men fled from a building and ran across the road, chased by eighteen soldiers on foot. Three horsemen held back.

"We should save those men!" I yelled at Margale, surprised that I got those words out.

"What if they're wicked and should be hanged?" Talli asked.

Margale drew rein. "Those are Queen Apsel's soldiers doing the chasing. Let them tend their business. We'll wait."

"To hell with that!" I rode my horse past Margale at a canter, calling back, "Stop me, if you can afford to!"

"They're more than two hundred feet away, you half-wit!" he yelled.

Pil and the others were shouting after me. Almost two hundred feet down the road from Margale, I halted. He was right; I couldn't reach those soldiers with weapons. But they were within easy shouting distance.

I yelled, "Hey, all you squint-eyed, hairy tumors wearing ugly-ass uniforms! Or are you wearing the queen's old ass-wiping rags? Everybody knows that her army has the saggiest tits in ten kingdoms. Just pull up your shirts and confirm it for me. Do women laugh at you? You can't say? Because no woman has ever let you repulsive, gopher-brained, snails-for-balls, eternal shame to your daughters and sons even get near her tits! Do I have any little part of that wrong, you cringing pots of pisswater? If I do, come over here and set me straight!"

I had their attention, and they weren't happy. The binding hadn't stopped me from heaping abuse on them, so I went on.

"You have the brains of a busted flute! You've got busted flutes between your legs, too. You're a damn symphony of inadequacies and revolting habits! At your birth, your fathers bent their heads and cursed you, themselves, your mother, the neighbor, your ancestors, and the damned-to-Krak dog because you had arrived to drive a dagger of shame—"

I was dragged off my horse by the binding charm. I had been waiting for it and rolled when I hit the dirt, coming up on my feet. Margale was trotting his horse away from the soldiers, but he was too late. They roared and ran after me, shouting vile threats. One man with a carrying voice yelled that he'd pull out my guts and feed them all to his hogs.

"Damn! Damn, damn, damn it!" Margale shouted. I hoped he was worrying about how mad his queen would be if he killed her soldiers.

Margale turned his horse to better witness the nightmare running toward him. I ran away from the nightmare, making a nasty gesture behind me.

Without halting, Margale called out to me, "Bib, defend . . ." He stopped before the command was fully out of his mouth. Then he glanced at Pil, who was watching him. "I mean, everybody should watch each other and be careful." He glared at me.

Pil examined Margale for a moment, and then her eyes flicked back and forth between Margale and me. But her horse started stamping, and she had to calm it while she drew her sword.

"It's all right!" I yelled at her.

I ran toward Margale and didn't worry too much about the infuriated soldiers behind me. I planned to run right past him, and keep going, unless he wanted to use a command to stop me.

FIFTEEN

As I ran toward Margale, leading the pissed-off soldiers straight at him, I hadn't forgotten about the three fleeing men. I might try to help them if it was practical, but mainly I wanted to force Margale to give me another command. Maybe it wouldn't work. But if I persisted in doing the most dangerous and unhelpful things I could think of, he'd either have to waste a command to stop me or suffer whatever hell I stirred up.

I sprinted toward the gap between Margale and Talli. Once I was past, they'd be forced to fight the queen's soldiers. Nobody was going to interrupt a frenzied charge to ask Margale whether or not he was my friend. Those men were chasing me, the low, foul-mouthed denigrator of the worthy. They were the worthy. I was the absolute definition of unworthy. Even dogs must hate me.

But I felt sure they wouldn't mind swarming Margale too.

When I reached Margale's stirrup, his hand shot down and grabbed me by the collar. I stopped with such a snap my feet almost came off the ground. Still holding me, he slid off his horse and said, "Bib, do you think we're in a good place to face them?"

I didn't answer and didn't care what he thought. Once the

fighting started, he'd let go, and I would run the hell away. Margale could make a stand that would gratify any hero who ever had a statue.

Margale lifted me so that only my toes touched the ground, and he dragged me two steps toward the mob. Then he bellowed, "I have him! I have him right here!"

I realized what was happening an instant before his fist slammed into my cheek. It felt as if he had dropped one of those hero statues on my face.

I sagged, but Margale held me up for a couple of seconds. I heard Pil shouting my name. When Margale released me, some part of me thought we might all flee. I hoped somebody would throw me on a horse, because my knees were working only part of the time.

Margale hadn't let go of me so we could run away. I had been overoptimistic to think that. I turned to spit blood at him, but I found his hand there instead of his face. He slapped me with one hand and punched me in the stomach with the other. I lost all the air inside me.

Vargo tried to shove his body between Margale and me, but Margale brushed him away like he was an ant on the kitchen table.

The soldiers were cheering and pretty damn close to us now. I thought Margale was done hitting me, but my ribs were standing there with nothing to do but get punched. Margale slugged them with his right fist. I suspected he could have hit me harder and broken them, but I staggered and dropped to my knees anyway.

Margale grabbed my collar again, stepped forward, and held up his other hand for the soldiers to stop. They slowed but didn't quite halt.

Margale shouted, "He's a disrespectful wad of hair, isn't he?"

The soldiers' shouts sounded happy and vicious.

Margale slapped me again, this time so hard I thought my eye would fly out of my skull. "I'll take him with me and teach him to respect brave men like you!"

The shouting became less happy.

With my other eye, I saw that the soldiers had stopped twenty feet away. Talli had dismounted. She and Kenzie were shoving and kicking each other to stand closest to me. Pil stood on the other side of Margale, spewing curses and threats.

My desire to hurt Margale had grown huge, but I couldn't attack him. I couldn't hurt his body, but if he loved Talli, then it would sure as hell hurt him if I killed her. I eased my knife out of its sheath and held it reversed, the blade hidden along my forearm.

The soldiers shouted wild arguments about why they should be the ones to deal with me. Margale dropped me and held up both hands. I sank to my knees. "Men, I will teach him respect, and when we reach Queen Apsel's palace, I'll lock him in her dungeon."

The murmuring was uncertain.

"And I'll torture him!"

That drew some cheers.

"And when the queen hears what he did, she'll want to yell at him herself, and maybe spit on him."

That sold the soldiers on Margale's plan. They could degrade me and torture me themselves, but the queen wasn't here to spit on me. I saw some nods as the soldiers drifted back toward their mounted officers.

"Bib, let me help you up," Talli said. She was standing right beside me. Kenzie was on the other side of her, bent down and rubbing her shin. I turned a little to get a smoother thrust into Talli's heart when she reached for me.

"No!" Margale snapped. "He wanted to play the ass, did he? It'll be fair for him to drag his own ass up on his horse! Which is halfway up that hillside." He pointed.

Talli marched past me to face Margale. "You didn't need to hurt him that way! There must've been other things you could do."

"None that were as much fun," Margale said, with a tiny grin.

"You rotting asshole!" Talli yelled.

"That was a joke. We had a bunch of options." Margale began ticking items off using his fingers. "We could run. We could fight. We could bribe them. We could threaten them if they believed the threat. Or we could join them, which is what we did."

"You think you know everything!" Talli turned her back to the man. "Well, maybe you do know everything. But you don't have to show it off!"

"I chose the option that gave us the best chance," Margale said.

"Chance for what?" Talli shouted.

"Chance to keep you alive."

"Bullshit!" She stuck a finger in Margale's face. "You're trying to convince me that when you beat the ever-loving hell out of him, it was somehow my fault. Well, to hell with that! I don't have blood on my hands and busted knuckles."

The woman bent to take my arm and help me up. I could not have had a more perfect target, but I hesitated and didn't strike. There was something wrong with Talli, if she loved a man like Margale, but I couldn't kill her. The same argument could be made about Pil, because she had once loved a man like me.

Margale had pounded me hard, but he'd chosen his targets with care. I was bruised and a little bloody, but he had left me fit enough to kill a king or two. Neither he nor Talli offered to catch my horse, which had indeed frolicked halfway up the hill. I staggered in that direction, not as hurt as I was letting on.

Vargo cursed Margale with sharp, colorful words and ran to fetch the horse for me. Kenzie examined my injuries, Pil stood guard over me, and Grinder wandered around sneering at things.

"That was almost a real shitstorm," Grinder snorted, winking as he walked past Talli. She ignored him.

Everybody watched me drag myself onto my horse. Although I wasn't broken, the beating had left me so sore I felt like a puppy climbing up on a tall chair. Peering at Margale, I muttered, "A subtle bit of sorcery."

The big sorcerer came close to smiling. "It didn't even require magic."

"The purest form." I smiled and rode close enough to converse with him privately.

If we stayed on this road, soon every mile would put the Bole farther away instead of closer. It was time to avoid that, if possible. I leaned toward Margale. "You may have had fun back there, but it'll get less amusing fast if I do that kind of shit every mile between here and King Hale."

"It hurt you more than me." Margale winked.

"Really?" I glanced at Talli. "Tell me that again after the two of you lie down tonight. In fact, she and I can commiserate about what a bastard you are. You'll have to waste a command to keep me from making Talli hate you by the time we get to Hale's castle. She's halfway to hating you now."

Margale clenched his teeth and looked at Talli, then back at me.

I said, "I'm an expert on making people hate you."

"Huh, I'll bet you are. What are you thinking, then?"

"Pil and I need to visit a spot northeast of here. It would take us a day or so to get there, tend our business, and return to this road. Let us go there."

Margale snorted. "Of course. Maybe you'll stop on the way to stab my mother in the throat and burn down the house I grew up in. No, I'm not sending you off by yourself!"

"But—"

"And I'm not coming along so that you get an extra day to trick me into giving you more commands!"

"I won't try. If you allow me to go, I won't try to trick any more commands out of you until King Hale's capital is in sight."

Margale frowned and shook his head.

"Admit it, I've almost tricked commands out of you four times. If you agree to this small detour, I'll stop all that. That will make life after Hale's death a lot more certain, right? Hell, we might both live through this."

The big sorcerer chewed his lip with his brow wrinkled. "This has to be a trick. You're lying, of course."

"Margale, here's the truth. If we make our little side trip, I get my wife back. If we don't, I've lost her forever."

For an instant, I pictured Margale rolling his eyes and then turning Pil's saddle into a white-hot column of flame, but I pushed that image aside. Margale struck me as a man awkwardly devoted to love. Maybe perversely devoted, but still devoted.

At last, Margale nodded. "No more than a day."

"Or so. Make it a day and a half."

The big man hissed. "One and a half, then. But if I think you're trying some damn trick or laying a trap, I'll kill Pil, Kenzie, and that sour-mouthed fellow before you can pick your nose."

"There's one condition, though," I said.

Margale's eyes widened, and he reached for his club.

"Wait! Pil is in charge. She has to be in charge all the way there and back to this road."

"No!"

"Don't you think she'll be suspicious if you take over with no explanation? She may realize I'm bound and try to do something about it."

Margale opened his mouth and then hesitated to examine Pil. He swallowed, and I wondered whether he respected her prowess enough to be a little bit afraid of her.

"She's an excellent leader, better than you or me. Hell, she may save your life!"

"If we do this, you'll give me no trouble," he growled. "Right?"

"I swear, no trouble. Not until I see Hale's capital. Then you can expect every bit of trouble I can throw at you or under your feet."

Margale nodded, and I turned toward Pil to call out, "Margale and Talli will ride with us to the . . . to that interesting place we talked about."

Talli's eyebrows rose over her round eyes.

Pil shouted, "What?" so loudly that her horse and two others started. "After he beat the shit out of you?"

"That was fair. I admit it. Riling up those soldiers and dumping them on him was a nasty trick. And how many sorcerers have you fought against and later ridden beside as comrades over the years?"

Mouth open, Pil examined the horizon all the way around as if looking for whoever was making the world crazy today. Then she said, "Fine. Just fine. If any bears or demons wander past, ask them to join us too. Come on." She turned her mount's head and pushed it into a canter northeast, down the hill.

I intended to keep my word to Margale and not conjure up trouble. But the Bole could be a dangerous place. Maybe something unnatural would squash him or tear off his head. Or breathe fire on him until he died.

SIXTEEN

I rushed to follow Pil into the valley. Sunset wasn't far off, and I didn't care to struggle along searching for her if she decided to ride all night.

Rushing turned out to be a wasted effort. Pil had halted beside a great lump of rock two hundred paces down the hill, where she was pointing, glaring, and speaking sharp words to somebody hidden from my sight.

When I rounded the rock lump, I saw three people who had been concealed. They resembled the three men I'd saved by distracting Queen Apsel's soldiers.

One was a tall heavy man with a red face and a fringe of graying hair. He wore stout leather armor over a brown shirt. He was pointing a sword at the air above Pil's head. As I arrived, he raised his voice. "Of course we wanted to come here! We came here to get our hearts broken. Is that why you're here? If it is, well, Fingit rejoice that you're in the right damn place!"

He pointed behind him without looking. The body of another man lay face up with his hands crossed over his chest. He had been a bit younger than the gray-haired smartass. The body wore similar leather armor and also a leather cap. I could see by the blood staining his legs and the ground under him that he must have fled until his body gave out here.

The third man turned out to be a woman, young but old enough to have had a child or two. Instead of children, she had a fine bow and was aiming an arrow above Pil's head. She stood taller than most women, and a thick vest of undyed wool covered her torso. Her long brown hair was bound behind her shoulders, and the arms of her pink shirt had holes in them. She stared at Pil without emotion, but tears had run down her face, which was flushed.

With a firm jaw, Pil said, "I'm sorry, sir. He was . . . your son?"

"My brother."

"I'm sorry your brother's dead, but I can't wait here while you bury him."

The man raised his voice, "But you've got a spade!" He pointed at the side of Pil's saddle.

"It's just a little one," Pil said.

The woman spoke up. "It's longer than our fingers. Why do you need it so bad? Do you plan to mount it and ride down this hill on it, bumping your butt all the way?" She glanced at me and then looked harder. "You're the crazy fellow with the nasty mouth. I wish you'd come along two minutes sooner."

"I could have come along two minutes later." I shrugged. "Then you'd all be dead."

Margale, Kenzie, Vargo, and Talli rode up behind me. Pil held out a hand to command them to stay quiet and be still. None of them seemed about to defy her, which perversely aggravated me.

I spoke up. "Vargo, Kenzie, what do you think about this situation? You ought to have a say."

Pil stared at me, her eyes and mouth wide.

Margale snorted back a laugh.

"Are you soldiers?" Kenzie asked, ignoring Margale.

"We are!" the man snapped. "The best damn soldiers in the four kingdoms."

"Except for those who chased us out here and killed poor Lemlin," the woman said, gazing at the body for a couple of seconds.

"That doesn't count! It doesn't count at all!" the man shouted.

"Why doesn't it?" the woman shouted back.

"We was overrun—"

"I know, outnumbered a dozen to one," the woman muttered. "Nobody gives you a prize for how bad you're outnumbered."

"Speak up!" the man yelled, cupping an ear with his free hand. "Don't whisper behind my back!"

"You're deaf, you old bastard!" she yelled.

"Don't talk to me like that! I'm your father. You've got to respect that!"

"Fine, I respect you more than my pig." The woman tossed her head before glaring at Pil. "Now, what about that spade?"

"Pardon me," Vargo said, breaking in. "Do you mean you respect your father more than you respect your pig, or does your pig respect your father more than you do?"

The soldiers glanced at each other, then turned to train their weapons on Vargo.

"Wait!" Kenzie shouted. "Do you want jobs? As my bodyguards?"

"Are you sure?" Vargo asked her.

Kenzie shushed him. "I'll pay you the standard wage. Two silver nobs a month. Each."

The man chuckled. "You're a laugh, yes, you sure are. For that much, you could hire six of us. Each."

Kenzie turned to stare at Grinder, who coughed and looked away. She said, "Somebody told me that was standard, so it wouldn't be fair to offer you less. What are your names?"

The woman lowered her bow. "That's Pocklin. I'm Grik. We accept on one condition: help us bury my uncle here."

"No, we can't," Pil said.

Margale nodded. "Really, who has time for that crap?"

Kenzie ignored them. "If you work for me, of course we'll help you bury him. It wouldn't be right not to."

I said, "They can't keep up with us, Kenzie. They're on foot."

"Leave that to me." Kenzie dismounted. I noticed her left hand make four quick finger movements, almost certainly magic. She went on, "Pil, hand me that spade." There was no hint of a request in her words. It was all command.

Pil sighed and dismounted. "It's here, strapped to my saddle. It's tied tight, so let me." Pil seemed to do no more than rub the knots between her fingers, and they came loose. "Here."

Kenzie took the spade and tossed it at Grinder. "Start digging. And don't whine."

Grinder didn't whine, but with every shovelful, he cursed under his breath.

By this time, the sun was touching the horizon.

"We'll make camp here," said Pil.

"There's still light!" Margale barked. "Daylight! We could ride for hours by the moon!"

"That's true." Pil rubbed her chin and pointed at the horizon. "Why don't you tell us how the moon looks when you're riding under it fifty miles that way?"

Talli giggled.

Margale raised an eyebrow but didn't comment.

There were no trees, which meant no fallen branches, which forced us to make a cold camp. At just about full dark, while Grinder was covering up Lemlin, I heard hoofbeats and drew my sword. Two saddled horses with no riders trotted into camp and joined our other mounts as if they were all family.

Kenzie smiled at me. "Bib, my guards don't need to walk. Those soldiers you yelled nastiness at were stout enough to bellow and chase you, so I took these mounts from them. They have feet to walk on."

Vargo took the first watch. I had to sneak past him when I hiked my limit of two hundred feet away from camp. I wanted at least that much distance in case Chexis chose to visit. I knew the dragon to be stealthy. We might be able to chat without waking anybody if we were both careful and lucky. Also, if Chexis wanted to breathe and bite me, maybe from this distance nobody at camp would be in danger. Well, not as much danger.

Oh hell. If Chexis wanted to kill us, we'd all die. I might as well squat in the middle of camp, chat with the others, and wait for him there.

But I didn't do that.

Twice during these past nights, the young dragon had crept up on me. With my poor hearing, I couldn't expect anything different tonight. So, I began turning in place at a painfully slow speed. If Chexis was creeping along in an effort to be unheard, maybe I would see him, or evidence of him, as he approached.

I had been spinning and peering through the cloud-filtered moonlight long enough to feel like an idiot when I spotted movement in the direction opposite camp. I couldn't imagine how something as big as a dragon could remain unseen walking across the bare rocks, but it appeared to be possible.

Chexis was creeping, belly down like a snake, taking advantage of the curves and crevices in the rocks. His glowing wings were folded away, otherwise I could have seen him from a quarter mile off. As it was, if I hadn't been looking for him, I would never have noticed him.

When the dragon had come within fifty feet of me, I said, as if chatting at the dinner table, "Good evening, Chexis. The moonlight is lovely, isn't it?"

Chexis froze, then stood and raised his head to its full height of ten feet. "That's not fair. You're not supposed to hear me. I can't shock and terrify you if you hear me coming."

"I didn't hear you, I saw you."

"That's even worse." He writhed toward me, his claws scraping on the stone like a four-ton lizard.

"I'm sorry, son. I didn't mean to ruin your entrance."

"You didn't ruin anything." Chexis tossed his head. "I'll go ahead and terrify you now." The dragon produced a growl from somewhere deep in his body, not loud but full of menace.

I shuddered and stepped back.

Then smoke that smelled like burned meat billowed from Chexis's nostrils. When he opened his mouth, I saw yellow and blue fire, as if a forge were somewhere in his throat. He exhaled but didn't spout flames. The forge in his throat grew bright, and the smell of burned meat slapped me like half a charred ox.

I staggered backward another step but then held my ground. "That did it. Good job."

The dragon's fire and smoke died away, and he lowered his head to stare into my eyes. "Now that you are sufficiently terrified, we can begin negotiating."

I rubbed some soot off my cheek and managed to smile. "What do you want to negotiate about, my young Chexis?"

"You will help me learn to not be human, and you'll do it right now, and don't fool around with any other stupid humans, or I'll crush you with my foot." Chexis twisted the front of his body so I could see him lift the foot he was referring to. It had four claws, each longer than my hand.

I rubbed my palms together. "Chexis, that is an interesting offer. But I wouldn't be doing you any favors by accepting. You don't want to be human. I understand that. But your way of negotiating is a bit unfocused. Sometimes humans negotiate this way, and sometimes they don't. You wouldn't learn anything if I agreed to negotiate in this fashion. It would just hurt you."

The dragon held still for several seconds. "Yes, you're right. I have listened to a lot of humans, and they negotiate in a lot of different, annoying ways. I heard one of them stick a piece of metal into another and then shout, 'Get out of my house, you staggering dick!' That was a very effective negotiation."

"But harsher than normal."

"Was it?"

I nodded. "Usually, negotiation doesn't go so far as stabbing with knives. It often happens that each side gives up something of about equal value."

Chexis waggled his head up and down in what I guess was a nod. "Equal value. You mean, they both stab each other with a knife at the same time."

I smiled, wondering how this was going to end. "Knives. That's one example. Another is giving somebody a bottle of wine in exchange for a loaf of bread."

Chexis slapped his tail against the ground. It sounded like a charred side of ox being dropped from eight feet. "No! I have never heard anybody engage in such a simple and friendly negotiation."

"I'm sorry, I didn't explain it well. They would both call each other bastards, and a wine bottle would be thrown."

The dragon blew out a breath, producing a few curls of smoke. "That seems more likely. People should be like mice! All mice are the same! Maybe I should bite the arms off every human I see so they're all more alike."

"I'm sorry to tell you this, but some humans behave in just about the way you're describing. They cut off parts of other people, especially their heads. Or sometimes they burn other people or stick poles inside them. Indiscriminately taking off people's arms is one of the most human things you could do."

"Well, what's the least human thing I could do?" Chexis cried out. It hurt my ears because it was so loud. It also hurt because Chexis sounded so frustrated, and I felt a little sorry for him. I glanced back, wondering if the cry had woken up the entire camp. Maybe not.

"The least human? Asking for exactly what you want. As opposed to giving another person something and then just hoping to get what you want. Maybe not telling the other person what you want or even that you want something." The latter behavior was as human as could be, and I'd rather convince Chexis not to engage in it.

Chexis paused, and then said, "I see. That's stupid. I wouldn't have guessed that even humans are that stupid."

"Mostly they're not, but even humans behave that way once in a while. Let me suggest something that's better. It's hardly human at all. I'll offer to help you right now. Hell, I am helping you right now. But I'll ride with you tomorrow, away from everybody else, and help you some more. I'll help you every chance I get. All I ask in exchange is a very simple thing that I doubt will help anybody much. I want to introduce you to my friend, Margale."

The dragon looked away and sighed.

"I'm asking for almost nothing. It's nearly like you getting everything you want and only having to give me a puppy."

"Margale." Chexis stared at me. "You mean the sorcerer who has bound you to do his will."

I stopped breathing.

"No, I won't kill him for you," Chexis said, sniffing. "I like that he keeps you off balance. Think of something better for when we talk in the morning. Think fast. Sunrise will be here soon."

The dragon launched himself into the sky in a thunder of translucent, glowing wings.

I whispered, "Son of a bitch." I had once again had the gall to believe I was as smart as a dragon. I trudged back to camp, shaking my head and hoping for a few hours of sleep.

In the morning, I sat right up when Grik kicked me awake, but I couldn't stop yawning. I hadn't aged in the Dark Lands, but I was sure aging now.

Just as I reached my feet, a man screamed in ripping cold terror. Chexis had just arrived and was standing motionless in his dragon glory. I saw Pocklin backing away from Chexis so fast he tripped over nothing, then used his elbows and feet to keep fleeing while belly up. He never stopped screaming.

Grinder sprinted away without a sound.

Grik reached for her unstrung bow, dropped it, and drew her sword. She advanced across the camp toward Chexis. I immediately reclassified Grik as one of the bravest people I had ever met.

Margale backed away, snatching his club off his back as he put other people between himself and the dragon. He was breathing fast, but he seemed to be examining the creature before he acted. Talli retreated beside him.

Pil, Kenzie, and Vargo stared at the dragon without moving. They had all seen dragons before. In fact, they had been threatened by dragons much more horrifying than this one.

Chexis ambled across the camp toward me. Grik swung twice, striking the dragon on the neck and the nose. Chexis ignored her, and she threw herself aside to escape being trodden upon.

When Chexis reached me, he lowered his head to the ground and opened his mouth. A gray short-haired puppy the size of a ham rolled out. The little dog shook itself, barked once at the dragon, ran to me, and peed on my boot.

Chexis rumbled, "Syrtax, now you will give me everything I ask for."

SEVENTEEN

I ignored the puppy jumping on my leg, and I nodded at Chexis. "Your offer is fair, son." Since there was nothing I could do about it, I might as well say it was fair. "I'll give you all you want, but I ask one favor."

Chexis lifted his head. His forehead's patch of tendrils stood straight up. "Favor? I don't think so, Syrtax. I'm not sure what you mean by a favor, but it sounds shifty."

I smiled and shook my head. "A favor is something that costs you nothing to give, but it helps me. If you decide not to give the favor, it will hurt me. Granting the favor makes me grateful and liable to do a better job of meeting my side of the bargain."

"You mean you won't do the best job you can for me unless you get this favor? That just sounds sloppy. Lazy and sloppy. Maybe instead of bothering you, I should ask this puppy to help me. While he's doing that, I can kick you and whack you with my tail."

I gritted my teeth, hoping that Chexis would think it was a smile. "Please? It's a tiny thing."

Chexis yawned, showing his whole disquieting array of teeth. "Tell me about this favor. I'm probably going to say no, so don't spend a lot of time describing it."

"Pil and I want to travel someplace today. It's very important to us. I'll ride beside you all day to help you." Inspiration hit me. "In fact, you can travel with all of us to ask questions and observe our antic behavior."

Vargo and Kenzie began babbling objections. Pil's head dropped forward into her hand.

Margale stepped closer, and I saw that he had put away the club. "Dragon, does Bib belong to you?"

"Yes, of course!" Chexis snapped before glancing at me. He paused. "But not in any way your limited mind would understand, sorcerer Margale."

Margale squinted at me.

"Don't look at him!" Chexis lifted his head above ours. "You understand me, don't you?" The dragon pushed his face to within an arm's length of Margale's. "Yes, I know who you are, and I know what you've done."

Margale held entirely still except for swallowing once.

"But human affairs are too ridiculous for me to think about much," Chexis said. "You're always murdering each other and wearing clothes and eating things that come out of the ground. I really can't get involved." He blew a stream of black smoke into Margale's face. "I really can't."

Margale coughed. "That's a wise policy, I'm certain." He shifted his eyes toward me. I shrugged a little.

The dragon asked, "What's a human thing you like to do, Margale?"

The sorcerer took a deep breath. "I write poetry."

"Ooh!" Chexis sat back on his haunches. "Recite for me!"

"I've never written anything fine enough for a dragon to hear."

"Oh, that's probably true." He turned back to me, as if Margale and his ancestors back five generations had never existed.

Margale shook his head, stood straight, and backed away toward his horse. He seemed calm, but I noticed one of his hands shaking.

Chexis said, "I suppose I can give you this favor, Syrtax. Where do you want to go?"

Pil spoke up, grinning. "Northeast! Thank you! Give us a few minutes to saddle our horses."

"Wait!" Chexis boomed loud enough to scare the horses. Everybody except the stamping, rearing horses froze. Then Vargo, Pocklin, and Grik leaped to keep the horses from bolting.

"What is it?" I asked. "Is there some rite we missed?" I tried to grin. "Does somebody who's not me need to sing?"

"Yes, you forgot something, but by Ceslik's wiggly tongue, don't sing. Syrtax, you didn't name your little dog." The dragon said it in a tense, grinding voice, as if I had forgotten to feed my baby for a week. "Every creature must have a name! The lowest beings might be named Food. Some really low ones could be named Syrtax. But all creatures must be named." He stomped the ground with one foot when he said "must."

"That's fine knowledge to have, thank you." I wondered how close we had all just come to being mangled.

Chexis slithered toward me and lowered his voice. "I shouldn't have let you eat those geese without naming them first. I'd have stopped you, but I hadn't become a civilized being yet."

"A civilized dragon," I said without thinking too hard.

The dragon chuffed at me the way his mother had before she breathed fire. I didn't feel much confidence in my fire-shedding clothes just then.

"A dragon, which is the most noble of all civilized beings," I added.

Chexis shocked me by hanging his head. He muttered, "You shouldn't poke fun at me, Syrtax." He sounded more hurt than angry.

"I'm sorry. I won't."

I considered the question of dog names. I had never owned a dog, although I had been friendly with several. I lived such an outrageous and perilous life that any dog of mine would risk destruction every moment it was with me. Owning a dog would be mere cruelty.

However, I wasn't going to turn away a gift from Chexis. I had learned from the young dragon's mother that dragons revere their ancestors, and she had spoken of the hero Beymarr with special affection. But if I named the dog Beymarr, Chexis might think I was mocking his mother.

I picked up the dark pudgy short-haired creature, rolled him on his back, and scratched his belly. The little beast grunted and wiggled.

Margale spoke up with great solemnity. "You should call him Spot."

"But he doesn't have any spots," Chexis said.

"It will amuse his friends and confuse his enemies."

Spot writhed in my arms until I put him on the ground.

Chexis produced an enormous hissing noise and began shaking his head like a wet hound.

"Run!" screamed Grinder, who had just returned from his earlier bout of running away. Everybody else retreated.

"Wait!" I cried, raising both hands. "Don't be afraid. This is how dragons laugh."

Chexis laughed again. "I didn't realize how funny you humans are! I hope a few of you are alive when I'm done with you. I can make you my pets."

I carried Spot to my horse and glanced inside a big leather sack tied to my saddle. I didn't see anything inside that would keep me from dying. I dumped it out and hung it from one shoulder to lie against my chest, then I stuck Spot in it. He howled for a minute before quieting down. The next time I checked, he was asleep.

Kenzie led the way north through occasional cool morning showers. The hills became steadily less steep as we rode. Occasional scrub trees ten or twenty feet tall appeared.

I soon dropped back to join Pil and the dragon, and he didn't run me off. In fact, Chexis questioned me about what humans do. I answered as honestly as I could, which meant that my answers often made no sense, because human behavior usually drowns logic like it is a baby rat. I knew that the dragon wasn't happy with my performance because he kept telling me how awful and useless I was. Sometimes he snarled at me to make his point.

During a lull in the conversation, Pil shifted to ride beside me. She met my eyes and mouthed, *Holy crap! That's a dragon!*

I mouthed back, *I know! You're welcome!* I made a tiny bow from the waist.

Chexis rumbled, "Stop talking to each other. The only important thing is my problem. You have your favor. How long have—"

Pil interrupted, "Why aren't the horses scared of you now?"

Chexis paused before answering her. "They are. I'm surprised their little hearts haven't burst."

I examined Pil's horse. The creature's eyes showed a remarkable amount of white.

Chexis went on, "I'm making them behave for you and not show their fear. Otherwise, I'd have to listen to you whine all day about having to walk."

Pil grinned. "That's amazing. I'll bet that makes things convenient when hunting."

Chexis blew a few wisps of smoke. "You couldn't imagine how much it helps. Sheep aren't so bad, but goats leap back and forth, side to side, jump up and fall down. If we allowed them to keep that up, we'd never have time for anything important."

I opened my mouth to ask what was important, but Pil cut me off.

"Do you learn to hunt, or are you born knowing how?" she asked.

"A dragon's predatory skills are unparalleled. Our senses are so powerful it sometimes appears that we can see the future. Our claws can crush stone. If we want to eat an animal, it has no chance of escape. It should just lie down and not exert itself. We even hunt and eat humans." Chexis tossed his head and chuffed twice.

Pil gazed at the dragon with a tiny smile.

Chexis stared back at Pil. Neither looked away, and the tension drew tighter than a harp string.

At last, Chexis muttered, "Fine! I may have been given some advice on my first hunt. Advice of a very general nature." He raised his voice. "Not every creature is born knowing how to hunt. I'll bet your revolting parents had to teach you."

Pil nodded. "Yes, they did, and you know, I think Bib must have been your first hunting teacher when he pulled goats around for you to chase." Pil tossed the dragon a warm smile. She shifted it to me for a moment, then back to Chexis.

The dragon glanced at me. "Goat Drag."

In their infancy, Chexis and his brother sometimes sat on goat carcasses while I ran around the cavern, pulling them by ropes. We called it Goat Drag. I now said, "Goat Drag was fun, wasn't it?"

"Oh yes!" the dragon squealed, producing a thin column of smoke. Then he lifted his chin and popped his wings once. "I mean, it was amusing at the time. For a baby dragon." He slowly blinked at me with both eyes, which kept me quiet. I hadn't seen a dragon do that before and had no idea what it meant.

When Chexis didn't shout or maul me in the next minute, I asked something that had been bothering me. "When I left you and your brother, you said you'd be sad when you ate me. Did you get past the idea of eating me? Did you eat somebody else instead?"

The young dragon stopped and stared down at me from his full height. Pil and I halted so that we wouldn't ride on without him.

I waited about fifteen seconds, but Chexis didn't answer.

"That was mere curiosity," I said with a lot more nonchalance than I felt. "You don't need to tell me if—"

Chexis raised his voice. "Why are you asking me that? Do you plan to kill me?" He chuffed again, and more smoke billowed from his nostrils.

"No, son, I'm not thinking of killing you. I'm just curious, because if you decide to eat somebody, maybe I can help you find a tasty candidate."

"That's an awfully polite offer," Chexis grumbled, as if I had offered to kick him in his dangling hind parts. "Syrtax, go ride ahead and catch up to your friends. I'll follow with this human." He jerked his head toward Pil. "She'll answer my questions."

"All right," I said. "Vargo can tell Spot and me stories about his family's candle-making business. We might cut our throats from boredom, but it'll be a fine test of our will to live."

Pil waved and smiled at me. "It'll be fine, Bib. I think Chexis and I are getting along quite well."

I kicked my horse into a canter without answering Pil. I had begun thinking of Chexis as my dragon. I had let him chew on me when he was a baby. He had come looking for me, not for Pil. I cursed them both just loudly enough for them to hear me, but not so loudly I couldn't pretend I'd been cursing the weather.

Pil laughed, and Chexis rumbled as we entered a land of shallow but steep-sided hills. We rode along the bottoms of brown gritty ravines no more than twenty or thirty feet deep. It seemed like the sun struggled to climb in the sky.

We passed the last hill before midday and rode onto a sandy plain. We faced a stand of tall pine trees not far off, covering an area the size of a sad little village. No other trees grew within sight.

I had seen these trees twice before. The first time was when the old God of Death demanded that I swear an oath promising to kill for him. The second time was when I helped my daughter, Manon. She was committed to throwing the God of Death's book into the Bole. I prevented it from being burned to a cinder once she threw it.

My teachers had told me that the Bole was a place for oaths, compulsions, beginnings, and endings. I knew that was correct, because I had carried out uncounted murders for the God of Death, and later I killed him. I'd saved my daughter at the Bole, but later I'd stabbed her to death. The book might have brought her back, but I'd dropped it off a cliff, leaving it, and her, behind.

The Bole didn't ruin everybody, but it ruined enough. Yet it was a place of power, and we needed power to bring back Pil's memories of me.

"What is that place?" Chexis asked the question of nobody in particular.

Pil said, "Oh, that's the Bole."

"I've heard of it," Margale said. "I didn't know it was here. Huh. That's an oversight on my part, eh? The Bole."

The air around us was still, but with no warning, the trees began whipping and swaying like a gale was blowing.

"Maybe you shouldn't say its name," Vargo muttered.

"We're not going there, are we?" Chexis's voice trembled a bit.

"Pil and I are going," I said as I dismounted. "You can stay here and play games. I hear riddles are nice."

The dragon's wings popped behind me. By the time I looked around, he had climbed a hundred feet into the air.

Pil reached over and grabbed my hand, then she led me toward the Bole.

EIGHTEEN

By the time Pil and I walked toward the Bole, a haze had drifted in, softening the hot sunlight from above. A pure, still lake surrounded the Bole, turning it into an island. It wasn't much of a lake, really. No more than fifty feet separated the island from the outer shore at any point.

Pil squeezed my hand tighter as we stopped at the water's edge. She had never been to the Bole. "Is there a bridge? Or a boat?"

I shook my head. "We'll wade."

"It looks thirty feet deep!"

"That's deceptive. Come on."

After four steps, the water hardly reached Pil's knees. However, it came up to my chin.

When I stopped, she raised her eyebrows at me. "Maybe the Bole doesn't want you to come back, or it doesn't like you. So do you want to keep going?"

"We've come this far."

"Right. I'm not turning aside," she said, "but if you have to go back and tell riddles, I'll understand, because this whole venture would seem awfully silly if you drown on the way there."

Some god snatched my spirit up through my head with such

speed I might have vomited if I still had a body. I waited to appear in the trading place, but everything remained dark.

Gorlana's voice came from the blackness. "Murderer, you can have one more chance. Accept our offer. Show mercy to your enemies."

Baby Harik's voice cut in. "No! Kill the ever-loving pig flop out of them!"

"Thank you so much, New Harik, that was helpful," Gorlana snipped. "Now stay on your bench as we discussed. Murderer, if you say yes, we'll give you four squares of power now, no matter how many people you do or don't spare."

I was tempted to agree just to get the power. I had fewer than two squares left, hardly enough for a real crisis. When a sorcerer finds himself in a dire spot with too little power, the gods will squeeze every possible burden and horror out of him.

The offer tempted me but didn't convince me to join their divine, petty games. "I don't need more power just now, Your Magnificence," I lied. "So no thanks. And no thanks to you too, Baby Harik, you blundering lump on the very ass of godhood itself."

Gorlana might have giggled, but I couldn't be sure. Then she said, "Let me remind you, Murderer. When our contest ends, I will give you a charm to restore the Knife's love for you, just exactly as it was. I am the Goddess of Mercy. You know that I can deliver real love without tricks or falsehood. She would never know the difference. Really, there would be no difference."

The effort Pil and I were engaged in was chancy. Maybe it could be called desperate. If Gorlana delivered on her promise, as she was known to sometimes do, that would help Pil and me without danger of being ruined by the Bole.

But no matter what Gorlana said, I'd be tinkering with Pil's mind and memories. I had tried that in the past, and it had gone poorly.

"I must say no, Mighty Gorlana."

After a pause, Gorlana flung me back into my body.

I stumbled forward, and the surface rose above my mouth.

Looking up, I spat out some water. "All right, I'll swim. I think this has to be done by the two of us together."

"Don't swallow any of that mystical, ineffably enchanted water of power. It might turn you into something," Pil said.

We dropped hands so I could swim. After two strokes, something began stinging my neck and hands. The stinging grew sharper every few feet, and it spread to the parts of my body covered by clothing. I gritted my teeth and swam faster.

When the stinging reached my intimate areas, I shouted, "Trutch and Fingit kick this place in the balls and stab it in the ass! Damn this son of a bitch!"

Pil, who had already stepped onto the shore, asked me what was wrong.

"Snakes! Little water snakes! Or stinging bugs! Water wasps!" I gasped.

At last, I slogged onto the shore, slapping myself all over. Bloody pinpricks covered me everyplace I could see. "I hope you want to live on this island forever," I said, "because I may not be brave enough to try that swim again."

Pil laughed and took my hand again, paying no attention when I winced.

We kicked our way across a thick carpet of pine needles, fallen twigs, pine cones, and black dirt. Soon we reached a great gnarled dead tree in the middle of the island. It was unlike any type of tree I had ever seen in my travels, and I was better traveled than most. I could see the familiar dark hole, about the size of a person, in the tree's enormous trunk.

Pil and I stared at the hole for a few seconds before she said, "Do we crawl inside?"

I grabbed a pine cone and tossed it into the hole. It flared into sputtering flame as it fell. Nothing but sparks remained when it reached the ground inside the tree.

"All right. What do we do?" Pil asked.

"Since we're after your memories, I was hoping you'd have an idea."

"You son of a bitch! You haul me all the way here and don't

have a single flinking idea about what we should do? Maybe I'm glad I forgot you!"

"Wait! We can handle this logically," I said. "Your memories reside in your head, correct?"

"I'm not sticking my head in that thing! Your memories of me not remembering you reside in your head. Stick your own head in there."

"Nobody's sticking anybody's head anyplace, all right? Something has to pass into the Bole, so it should be something meaningful to both of us. Ideally, it should be meaningful to me because of you and also meaningful to you because of me."

"I created the fireproof clothes you're wearing, although they're not *fireproof*," Pil said. "Because anything will burn if you get it hot enough. Let's say they're fire resistant to an unreasonable degree."

"Fire-shedding."

"That's a fair way to describe them," Pil said.

I frowned at the pine needles and dirt under my feet. "Pil, did you enchant these clothes just for me? Did you care whether I wore this specific shirt?"

"Not really." She sighed. "I enchanted all the clothing and bundled it by size."

"I think that leaves one thing. This sword." I drew the sword she had given me. "The one that rewards me when I let my enemies live. You enchanted it for me to encourage me not to kill. Right?"

Slowly she said, "That's probably the best choice."

"You know that if we use the sword, the Bole will almost certainly destroy it."

"Let's find something else, then!"

"Like what?" I asked.

After a moment, she growled, "All right, fine! How do you think we should do this?"

"We'll both hold the sword and shove it into the Bole."

"Can't we throw it instead?"

"That would seem as if we're not fully committed, don't you think?"

Pil said, "If that's a factor, we should hold it by the blade. That'll show commitment, although we should wrap the blade in one of these fire-shedding shirts."

"I like that idea," I said. "Except we should use both your shirt and mine together."

Pil stared at the Bole for a bit. At last, she hugged me and turned away to take off her shirt. Considering the situation, her modesty seemed odd, but I didn't comment as I pulled off my own shirt.

Soon we both gripped the shirt-wrapped blade of my sword.

"Let's use our left hands," Pil said, "in case the Bole destroys any hand holding the sword."

"I'm sad to say that may be the best idea I've heard all day."

I positioned us and aimed at the opening.

I took a breath. "And . . . now!"

I shoved the sword and then felt myself thrown backward, my feet off the ground. I blinked and realized that orange sunlight was throwing long shadows through the trees. I had slept until late afternoon, if not sunset—of the same day, I hoped.

My head felt dizzy but didn't hurt much. My left hand made up for that. It felt like I had pushed it against a stove for a couple of minutes, but I couldn't smell burning flesh. But even as I flexed my fingers, the pain began to fade.

Before I could sit up, Pil grabbed me by the shoulders and shook me.

I tried to say something. My throat was so dry I just croaked.

"Bib. Bib! Bib!" Pil rasped, as she wiped my forehead with her hand.

I sat up and croaked some more.

Pil laughed. "I remember everything!"

I produced a dry chuckle and hugged her. It was pretty damn awkward, since we were both sitting on the ground. "How's your hand?" I whispered.

"It felt like it was torn off at the wrist, but it's better now. Aren't you happy I suggested using the shirts and our left hands?"

Pil kissed me once and then threw herself at me.

I was pretty sure it would be bad luck to make love beside an unfathomable fount of raw magical power that's neither good nor evil and which cares no more for people than it does for pine cones. But we did it anyway.

The next few days confirmed that doing such a thing was indeed bad luck.

NINETEEN

It wasn't yet dark when Pil and I rose to leave the Bole. Pil found our shirts beside the tree, scorched but without too many holes burned through them. I almost tripped over my sword, which was half-buried in the blanket of pine needles. I expected it to be a twisted chunk of steel. It hadn't been destroyed, but it wasn't quite the same.

The blade Pil enchanted had been slightly bent, as well as pitted and nicked. The metal was dull, and the leather-wrapped hilt was protected by a simple crosspiece. Now, I kicked the pine needles off the sword so Pil and I could examine it. Neither of us touched it.

"That's a good sight less ugly than it was this morning," I said. "Desh would be disappointed."

"It may not be the same sword. It's probably not," Pil said. "Somebody must have dropped it here when the Bole killed them."

I shook my head. "That's your mark on the crosspiece, which hasn't changed a bit. Neither has the hilt."

The blade had changed, though. The surface was a flat dusty black, except for the two sharpened edges. Those edges gleamed like raw steel. No mark or imperfection marred the blade.

Pil said, "Yes, Desh would laugh at us about this. I don't know what it means. Has the enchantment changed too?"

I shrugged. "Do you think it's full of evil now?"

Pil crossed her arms. "I don't feel full of evil now. Do you?" She waited, as if that was a serious question.

"I do not. Besides, the Bole's not evil, only powerful. And I'm sure as hell not going to leave a magic sword lying here in the dirt." I snatched the sword off the ground and shoved it in its scabbard to show how much I disdained the idea that anything around us was evil.

Dusk was gathering by the time we crossed the lake to the outer shore. I expected to swim and suffer, but the little lake allowed me to wade across unharmed.

"Maybe the Bole wants you to leave." Pil grinned and nudged my arm. "You're the annoying guest who pokes through every cabinet."

Kenzie, Margale, and the rest waited for us past the far shore. Margale had knelt and was petting Spot, but when I arrived, the puppy ran to jump on me. Chexis stood behind the rest with his head raised above theirs. It surprised me that he had returned so soon, since he'd seemed so upset.

While Pil and I dripped, Kenzie said, "If you hadn't swum back out by full dark, we were coming in to find you."

"No, we weren't," Vargo said.

Kenzie scowled at him.

He stuck out his chin. "It'd be too damn dangerous."

Kenzie had fought in more than one battle, and Vargo had fought alongside her. He knew the kinds of risks she would take, especially since she was a sorcerer.

"Where's Grinder?" Pil asked. "You can't trust him to go off on his own, you know that, or you should know that by now. Where is he?"

Everybody looked around.

"Maybe he deserted," Pocklin said. "He's a foul, nasty dog."

"He's not all bad—not all that much, he isn't!" Kenzie snapped.

"He's worse than syphilis," Vargo muttered.

Grik said, "I don't think he deserted. He wouldn't run off without this." She walked to Grinder's horse and patted its neck.

"Hell, who cares where he went?" Margale said. "One of us just got a free horse."

"I'm responsible for him!" Kenzie yelled. "Where is he?"

I caught Chexis staring at me. He glanced to the side and then back at me. If a man had done that, I would have called it furtive. Then he licked his lips so fast I almost missed it.

"Shit," I whispered.

I spent a few seconds adjusting to the idea that Chexis had probably eaten Grinder. The man was no loss, but I hoped Chexis hadn't enjoyed it too much. If he decided to eat the rest of us, we couldn't do much except run like mice.

Margale glared at me and cleared his throat.

"We should mount up and ride to King Hale's capital," I said.

"Why there? I hear it's a nasty old pit," Vargo said.

"And why ride all night to get there?" Talli asked.

"Oh, I meant we should leave in the morning." Margale frowned, but I ignored him. "I have an errand there. Nothing too important, but I'd like to be done with it."

"What about Grinder?" Kenzie asked.

"I imagine we'll see him again," I said. "We might not recognize him, though."

Chexis laughed by hissing and twisting his head.

Pil shrugged. "Fine, we'll camp, but in the morning, I want to discuss this idea of traveling to Hale's castle."

The plains were just about bare of trees, so we made a fireless camp again. Nobody suggested entering the Bole to gather wood there. Pocklin took first watch while everybody else prepared to sleep. I realized I'd been holding Pil's hand this whole time.

Before I could comment on it, the dragon slithered up beside Pil and me and said, "Answer some more questions for me."

"Fine," I said.

Chexis turned his head to look at me with one eye before gazing at Pil. "I don't want him to answer questions. Make him go away."

"No," Pil said.

The dragon jumped in front of us and spread his wings with a great popping sound. Both of our horses reared.

After I got done whispering to calm my mount, I said, "Pil, I don't mind falling back." *And not getting eaten*, I didn't say.

"Chexis," Pil said, "Bib can answer questions just as well as I can, and maybe better, so go ahead and ask."

The dragon lifted his head and drew a great breath. I glanced at Pil, who was trembling.

"I don't mind leaving!" I shouted. "I'll ride way the hell over there!"

"No," Pil said in a voice hardly loud enough to hear.

Chexis popped his wings twice, making two enormous bangs. Then he launched himself into the sky, his wings booming louder than usual.

"What did I do to make him dislike me?" I asked.

"He doesn't dislike you," Pil said.

"Well, he's sure as hell not singing and rubbing my tummy."

She laughed for a few seconds. "He doesn't want to look foolish in front of you. He'd be embarrassed."

"That's some pretty rank speculation."

"It's not. He told me."

"Using words? Not some eyelid flipping and tail thumping?" I asked.

"Yes, using real words coming out of his actual mouth, and you'll both be better off when he comes to terms with it."

I didn't know what to say to that.

Pil winked. "Maybe he thinks of you as his mommy."

Pil and I found a spot to sleep near the others. I suppose we could have wandered off to engage in some more sweaty frolics, but we were still near the Bole. Unfriendly things might find us, and we both knew enough to avoid being distracted in such situations. There would be plenty of time for amorous activities in safer places.

I fell asleep with Pil in my arms, wondering what to do about the man-eating magical creature that might consider himself my boy.

During the night, I woke each time the watch changed. The

bright moon was still high when Grik took over. It was reaching down for the horizon by the time Kenzie assumed the watch.

I woke when Kenzie screamed from some distance away. She cried out, "Ambush! Help!"

It was dark except for weak starlight. I rolled to my feet and drew my sword, trying to understand the situation. I couldn't see anyone but Pil clearly.

Before anyone could run to help Kenzie, Pil shouted, "Stop! Everybody stop! Wait for my orders! Vargo, run and help your wife. Pocklin, you go with him. Everybody else, stay close and watch the other directions!"

Vargo and Pocklin charged across the rough grassland to help Kenzie. I turned north and examined the flat darkened terrain.

Something stung my ankle, and it hurt like hell. Something else stung my left earlobe, and I heard buzzing. Three more stings came, jabbing into my neck, the back of my hand, and my left butt cheek, and I realized that some sorcerer had called these insects to assault us. If the sorcerer was crafty, he had invited some scorpions, snakes, and poisonous lizards too.

Pil knew all this as well as I did. She shouted over our cries and curses, "Follow me! Follow my voice!"

That was a wise response, since insects would usually be called to a small area in order to save power and concentrate the effect. I grabbed Spot and chased Pil's voice. As we ran, our horses began stamping, snorting, and neighing. Within a few seconds, all of them had galloped away.

I wasn't sure whether anybody else followed Pil. At least, none of our allies were close by when Pil and I skidded to a halt as twenty men came running at us, waving swords.

TWENTY

I rarely lose track of who and what is around me in a fight. Of course, I have to know those things exist first. In the dark, any number of things could exist without me knowing about them.

The force attacking Kenzie, Vargo, and Pocklin was somewhere off to my right.

I didn't know for sure where Margale, Talli, and Grik were. I had noticed somebody big running off to my left. If that was Margale, maybe Talli had gone with him. I had no clue about Grik.

Pil and I ran out of our campsite when the insects attacked. Some sorcerer, a Caller like me, was close by. He knew exactly where we were, because he had pulled those insects right to us.

The best way to retreat from these soldiers was back toward the campsite.

"Back!" I yelled at Pil. She didn't ask whether I was sure. We both ran back toward camp, which held my biggest weapon. The other sorcerer had created it for me. I just had to take it away from him.

I was already trying to steal the insects from him, pulling white bands one after another and tossing them at the mass of insects. I sensed a few poisonous serpents too, which made me smile. I immediately felt the other sorcerer react to me.

Whenever two Callers fight and one of them summons things, taking control away from the summoner is often a good tactic. For example, if the summoner has spent a lot of energy to build up a ferocious thunderstorm, taking it away from him is a good way to conserve power. It's also demoralizing as hell for the sorcerer.

The means of fighting for control depends on the sorcerer. The most elegant approach is understanding the target so well that mere power can't overcome your control. The more common tactic is brute force, piling on more power than the enemy can afford to spend.

Sorcerers who aren't particularly powerful nor wise, like me, might prevail if they can throw power fast, like a volcano. They can win quickly and conserve energy if their enemy can't keep up. I think of it like fighting a man who's throwing punches and you upend a bucket of bent nails and scrap iron on him.

I had about eight times as much experience as any other sorcerer alive except for Pil. Bent nails and scrap iron were my friends.

The mystery Caller in the darkness threw a well-placed band to keep control of his insects. I answered with five white bands in two seconds. That did the job, and I imagined him cursing as the insects forgot that he existed.

As Pil and I ran through the campsite, I distracted the insects by reminding them that it was nighttime, when all good insects should be still and quiet. Once we cleared the campsite, I planted the idea that everyone who entered the camp was eating all the insects' food and destroying all their spawn.

For a moment, I heard weapons clashing from Kenzie's position. Then the soldiers chasing Pil and me ran into the campsite. Their screams and profanity drowned out every other noise.

Pil pointed right, and we shifted right between these suffering men and Kenzie. I set Spot on the ground, since I had no safer place for him. This was why I shouldn't own a dog.

Men fled the insects, more or less the way they'd come. We

charged the closest ones. I thrust into a man's chest, but the sword didn't thrust as well as I expected, and he staggered away.

That perplexed me a bit. The sword shouldn't cut too well, but its thrust should have been devastating. If I defeated an enemy without killing him, the sword should have granted me energy. But it didn't this time.

I swung hard at the next man's leg to cripple him. The blade severed that leg and cut the other halfway through. As that man fell dying, a small wave of vitality washed through me.

I realized that the Bole had reversed the enchantments on the sword. I just had time to think that before three swordsmen converged on me under the starlight. I charged, which must have startled them. I made two cuts and a thrust, dodging their attacks as I did it, and I left two dead and one wounded behind me. With each kill, more vitality trickled into me. When I merely wounded a man, the sword took some energy away. That sealed it for me. The enchantments had been reversed.

I turned to kill an attacker on my right, but she yelled, "I'm Grik! It's me, Grik!"

"Fine!" I turned back to the regrouping swordsmen, planning to cut a path through them before they could attack again. Light flared over at Kenzie's position, and I heard men scream. It was the sort of magic Pil would use. I glanced around but didn't see her.

"Come on!" I yelled at Grik, and I lunged toward the closest enemy. With Grik on my right, I killed five men and wounded seven more by the time we came out the other side of the swordsmen's shattered formation. Grik had defeated three enemies on our pass through.

The swordsmen were running away now, and I didn't chase them. I let the insects go to save power, since I didn't think any enemies would bumble into our camp now.

Off to my left, the other direction from Kenzie, a great light flashed in the sky and then faded to a glow before dying out.

"There!" Pil yelled from not far behind me. I glanced back and saw her drop something. I supposed it was a useless trinket now that it had made light for her.

"There?" I shouted, looking out where the light had flashed. "Hell yes, there!" I made out at least eighty more men marching toward us. Grik and I ran to join Pil, Kenzie, and Vargo.

"Where's Poppa?" Grik asked, grasping Kenzie's sleeve.

Kenzie patted her hand. "He's hurt, but not so bad. His leg."

Pil asked, "Has anybody seen Margale?"

Nobody had.

Pil said, "Tell me later how shocked I should be. All right, Vargo, Grik, and I will lead them west. Bib and Kenzie, run south in the darkness and circle around. Hit them from behind before dawn. One of you call a storm for lightning, and don't let that damn Caller take it away from you! We'll make these men bleed until they decide we're not worth it."

Light flared from the east again. This time the enemy seemed to have lit torches. But I knew they weren't torches.

The sound of over eighty men screaming reached us. The fire-light showed the men running, struggling, and flopping onto the ground. Within twenty seconds, the fires were dying, and I couldn't see any men still on their feet.

"Damn it to Lutigan's swinging parts," Vargo breathed.

A light flared closer, and Margale walked toward us carrying a scarred-up copper lantern. Talli walked beside him, looking solemn.

"Happy to save all your lives," Margale grated as he panted a little. "Don't say thanks. That kind of, I don't know, cheapens it."

"All right, we won't," Pil said. "It strains the laws of existence to say this, but I'm glad you survived, Margale. Talli, it's good to see you alive."

"There's got to be a lot of survivors and wounded," Margale said. "We shouldn't let them wander around out there."

"I doubt they'll be difficult to subdue or run off after all this," I said.

"Mm." Margale looked around. Lights flared to the west and the south, some close and others out to several hundred paces. Screams reached us from both directions.

Talli's breath caught, and she stepped away from Margale.

"Krak! That's mere cruelty." Grik turned away.

I turned to Margale to call him a nasty, blood-licking jackal, but before I opened my mouth, I saw Margale change in an instant. One moment he was the brutal but casual sorcerer who had bound me. Then, with no warning, his brow seemed to become heavier. I looked hard and saw that it hadn't really changed, but it gave the impression of hanging above his eyes like a cliffside. He grimaced and then jerked before stretching taller and straighter.

I had seen this kind of thing once or twice. Margale was acting like a man who had just made a profound bargain with the gods, the kind that changes him deeply. I glanced at Pil to see whether she had noticed. She stared back at me, her eyes the size of hen's eggs.

In a dark, even voice, Margale said, "Bib!" He gestured at the ground beside him. "You can walk beside me for a minute." It wasn't a command. He had merely told me how far from him I could stray.

I walked along next to him as he strolled away from the others. He murmured, "Your little task is over. When were you planning to go back to the road?"

"At sunrise. After we catch the horses."

"Good. King Hale's audience will happen soon." Margale carried the lantern as he walked south, where some of the bodies still smoldered.

Shortly afterward, the sky began lightening toward dawn. Kenzie healed Pocklin's leg, since the wound would have prevented him from riding. Grik and Vargo began rounding up the stray horses, who hadn't run far.

I found Pil standing near the campsite and said, "The Bole reversed the sword's enchantments. I can cut through fence posts and cows and who knows what else now." I lowered my voice. "And it invigorates me when I kill. I know that's not what you wanted, but it's what we have now."

Pil closed her eyes and let her head sag forward toward the ground.

I said, "I'll try not to kill any more than I have to."

"I need to talk to you about something."

"This must be important," I told Pil.

She nodded but didn't meet my eyes.

I cleared my throat. "It's best to find out right away, even if it's something I won't like."

"You won't like it at all." Pil's voice was stuffy. When she looked up, her face was covered with tears.

I felt sick but said, "Go ahead."

Pil normally spoke quickly, but she rushed through this especially fast. "I thought I must have been missing some memories all this time, and I thought that because it seemed wrong that I didn't love you. It had to be my memories, and the Bole would give them back, and if I knew everything, remembered everything, I'd love you again."

"And you do remember everything. You said so."

"I know, but . . . there weren't any lost memories. That is, how can you know if memories are lost? There's just nothing where they ought to be. But how do you know they ought to be there? I have all my memories right now, but the Bole didn't give them to me. I had them already."

"But—"

"I just thought there had to be something wrong if I didn't love you. But I don't. I don't love you. I want to, but I just don't."

She couldn't have shocked me more if she'd hit me in the face with an iron.

"But you said you remembered everything," I said again, as if that would change reality.

Pil shook her head. "Listen! I already remembered everything. I wanted the Bole to fix things, and I know I acted like everything was all right, but I guess part of me thought if I acted like the Bole had done its job, then it would be true. I wanted it to be, but I guess it doesn't matter what I want." She shook her head and wiped her cheeks with her fingers.

I couldn't think of anything to say, so I watched her. It made no sense. Maybe she was sick, or maybe somebody had charmed her.

Pil spoke up again. "I wish I didn't have to say all this, but I need to be honest—"

"No, you don't. Honesty is for people with uncreative minds."

She laughed without much humor.

"Don't give up on the idea that if you act like it's true, it will become true."

"No, I need to tell you that when I left you in the Dark Lands, it was because I didn't love you anymore," she said. "That's what's true."

"Why are you telling me now? You could have waited."

Pil shook her head. "I didn't want to go with Margale, but I can see that you're going with the great, cruel oaf. And besides, every day I waited would have made it hurt more when I told you."

I didn't necessarily agree with that, but before I could pull together an argument against it, she walked away, dragging her feet with her head down. The sound of wind or maybe water rushed in my ears, and my voice sounded far away when I shouted for her to come back. It may have sounded far away for Pil, too, because she kept going. I followed her for a few steps but stumbled.

I sat down on the grass, and I realized with a bit of panic that I had known all along how this would end. I had told Limnad she could kill me as long as she saved Pil. Later I nearly cut my throat to save Pil from Margale's threats. People who know that others love them don't offer to do things like that.

I watched Pil trudge away. She didn't seem to be headed anyplace, just away from me.

Chexis swooped down, hovered for a moment, and landed near Pil. I watched her speak to him for a minute. Then the dragon sank down and curled on the ground. Pil lay down against the dragon's side, her shoulders shaking.

I watched them for a few seconds. All I could think to say was, "Son of a bitch! That's my dragon."

TWENTY-ONE

(CHEXIS)

Nothing these humans do makes a shred of sense. Any dragon who acted like them would be exiled.

Of course, I am being exiled.

I'm afraid that trying to stop myself from doing human things may be pointless. It's like saying, "Don't do crazy things." It's a bad strategy.

I'll just act like a dragon. I know what dragons do. I've seen it, and I have dragon instincts. If I act like a dragon really hard, then I won't have time to slip and do human things, no matter how crazy or sneaky they are.

I just need practice. Humans and human things had better stay out of my way!

This morning, I talked to Syrtax and his mate, and they wanted to explain more about how humans act. I wasn't that interested, but I didn't make them stop, because I'm a dragon. I can be whimsical and inconsistent if I want to be.

Syrtax's mate is more interesting to talk to than he is. She asks me questions about what dragons are like. He asks questions as if he already knows most of what dragons are like and just needs to learn the last ten percent.

What his mate asks and how she asks it also reveals a lot about humans. Well, I'm pretty sure it does. I need to terrorize a few other humans to verify what I learned from her.

I know one thing about being a dragon that I didn't know before. People aren't as tasty as I thought they'd be.

I ate the one everybody said bad things about. I ate him all up except for the steel bowl he wore on his head. I spat that out. I thought that the others might be glad he was gone, and I was right! Nobody went off looking for him, and nobody walked around mewling with water leaking out of their faces. That's awful, untidy behavior.

Maybe I'll eat a couple more humans. The first one might have been spoiled. I'll bet he ate bad food and then became bad food. I'm not done using Syrtax, so I can't eat him yet. I should probably eat him before I go home, though.

Maybe I could eat his mate next, but I do find her amusing. She's almost smart, like a puppy, or a whale. However, sometimes she says things that are so stupid I feel a little embarrassed, especially when she says them in front of Syrtax. I've started sending him away so she and I can talk without embarrassment. I know that's awfully benevolent of me, but dragons are mysterious and unpredictable, so if anybody doesn't like it, I'll just burn them to death.

I think I'll eat the other sorcerer's mate next, the man who complains so much about everything. It makes me want to fly down a canyon carrying him so I can fling him into walls. His mate will bear his offspring soon, so she has to be done with him. He'd just infect their children with his poor outlook. A happy outlook is important for babies. Syrtax always had a happy outlook when I was a baby, at least until he started killing dragons.

I dreamed that I killed a yak, then Syrtax sat on it, and I pulled it around. We had Yak Drag. That was a ridiculous dream. There's not a yak within a day's flight from here.

Syrtax and his mate went more insane than usual yesterday. They went to a tree that makes everything between here and the ocean vibrate. It made me vibrate when I flew over watching them.

I wouldn't touch that tree if Beymarr and Ceslik both threatened I'd get the Hundred Bites if I didn't. Then they stuck a magical sword in the tree. When the tree hurled Syrtax and his mate through the air, I said to myself that nothing good would come of that.

Later Syrtax was almost killed. A lot of people tried to cut him and his companions with swords. He cut and stabbed some of the men until some ran away. Then the tall sorcerer burned the rest to death. Syrtax was surrounded several times, and I thought he'd probably die, but he had good luck and stayed alive. Sometimes he's stupider than I remember him being when I was baby.

I don't want Syrtax to be dead, though. At least, not until I eat him.

I don't know why, but later Syrtax's mate became sad, and water leaked out of her face. It was hard to watch such stupid human behavior. The only reason I could think of for being so sad was that she'd hoped Syrtax would be killed, but he wasn't.

I flew down and asked her what had happened. She said some things that didn't make sense to me, and then water started leaking out of her face again. Instead of asking, I commanded her to tell me what happened.

"Nothing you want to know about," she said. Then she appalled me by applying snot to her arm.

I lowered my head to her level. "I'm here to learn about everything."

She shrugged. "I broke my husband's heart, and mine too."

She didn't say anything else, so I said, "That was careless. How long will you live now?"

"No, it's a metaphor."

That surprised me. I never considered that humans might know what a metaphor was. "Are you sure you mean metaphor?"

She smiled, even though the water and snot kept flowing. "Yes, I'm sure."

"Are you really sure? I don't think the songs Syrtax sang to me had even one metaphor."

She nodded. "I'm sure. A broken heart means that the most

important part of you has been pulled apart and can never be put back." The water started leaking faster, and she crossed her arms.

I stared over at Syrtax. He was sitting on the ground, watching us.

I had observed a lot of people during the past month. When this face-leaking happened, sometimes people held onto one another. In other cases, people hit each other, often in the face. Sometimes they used objects.

Syrtax wasn't holding any objects, so I assumed he didn't want to hit her face. He couldn't hold onto her, though, because he was sitting on his butt on the ground way over there. Syrtax did a lot for me when I was a baby. He saved my life once. I was a mysterious, noble, unpredictable dragon and could do a thing for him if I wanted to.

I lay down and curled up. "I'd hold you, since Syrtax can't do it, but if I did, I'd squish the life out of you. You can lie here, if you want to."

The woman stared at me with big eyes for a moment.

"If I'm doing the wrong thing and should hit you in the face instead, tell me that."

"No, this is the right thing." Then she lay down against me. "Thank you."

"Well, I'm noble and unpredictable. Don't get snot on me."

TWENTY-TWO

I sat on the ground for a while, watching Pil and Chexis. They lay on the dirt without talking, but Pil cried now and then. Spot jumped on me and ran around barking the whole time. I would pet him for a few seconds, then he'd run off to chase some dirt and scratch himself before coming back.

He needed real food soon, not the old bacon and salted beef I'd fed him so far. I thought about hunting and snares for a few seconds before my mind wandered.

Margale walked up to stand over me. "Are we leaving? Where I come from, we would already be riding."

Rage at Margale burned away my sadness. I craved his life. All of my thoughts turned to freeing myself and killing him. Torturing him was optional.

I stood, scooped up Spot, and grinned at the man. "I'm ready. Get on your mighty horse that shits like a herd of cattle."

He narrowed his eyes at me just as my spirit was pulled up toward the gods' trading place.

I had learned years ago that the Gods' Realm was in no way "up" from the world of man. They were different realms, and between them neither distance nor direction meant anything.

However, the gods had arranged for sorcerers to feel they were leaving their squalid homeland below and ascending to the radiant Gods' Realm.

They did it for the same reason they mandated that the Gods' Realm was always capitalized whenever anybody wrote it, while the world of man was never capitalized. The gods never missed even the pettiest opportunity to show their supremacy.

When I arrived, the brown dirt patch was covered in snow up to my knees. Snowflakes, thick and fat with water, hurtled nearly sideways, driven by a brutal wind. I began shivering within seconds. My eyes wept from the pain, and my tears froze halfway down my cheeks. My teeth ached with cold.

I couldn't see the forest or the field of flowers through the snow. Something in the forest was howling, and it didn't sound happy. I could just make out the closest edge of the gazebo.

"Mighty Gorlana," I chattered, "thank you for this fine weather. The days at home have been warm and sweaty lately."

Both Gorlana and Baby Harik stepped to the edge of the gazebo and stood as far apart as possible. Snow had settled on Gorlana's head like a crown, and ice chips covered her gown like diamonds. Baby Harik's black suit remained untouched by snow or ice. It was hardly ruffled by the wind.

"Damn fine job, Murderer," Baby Harik said, smiling to show his slightly crooked teeth. "You've killed quite a few more than you've spared. Keep up the fantastic work!"

Gorlana sighed with great subtlety, but I noticed it. "We're making you this offer a third time now, Murderer. I have faith that you have a shred of mercy buried inside you."

Baby Harik laughed and leaned toward me. "This is your last chance."

I opened my shivering mouth to tell the gods to bite me in a bad place. Instead, I said, "When will the contest end?"

"You can't know that." Baby Harik sneered. "You might manipulate the results! You know better than that."

"You . . . Your Magnificence, your predecessor . . ." I blew on my hands to get a little warmth on my lips. "Your predecessor, that pin-dick, lizard-faced cheese wheel of a god with the brains of a gnat and the morals of a turd pie . . ." I drew a breath and wished I didn't have to. "He screwed me with this 'you may not know' crap. I won't get into that kind of deal again."

Gorlana said, "Do you see how she weeps?"

"What?"

"The Knife. She wants so badly to love you. Helping her would be a gift. A mercy." Gorlana held up a huge garnet on a golden chain. "You'll get this at the end of the contest, no matter what. It will help her love you again!"

I said, "You mean it will make her do it."

"No, it only works if it's what she truly wants," the goddess said.

"That's a dumb restriction, if you ask me," Baby Harik said.

Gorlana ignored him. "And of course, you'll get six whole squares now!"

I shook my head, not wanting to open my mouth. I was shivering so hard I thought I'd bite my tongue.

Gorlana glanced at Baby Harik, who paused and then nodded. She said, "We'll tell you this much. The contest will end within a month from now. That means it could end any time between one minute from now and thirty days from now."

I foolishly allowed myself to consider it. One month wasn't a horrible length of time. I knew I could defeat enemies without killing them. I had done it before. Gorlana would own me then. She was a goddess and therefore horrible, but she was a thousand times better than that ass-stain Baby Harik.

Most important of all, when I used the charm, it would only make Pil love me if she wanted to. Based on how hard she'd been crying into the dragon's shoulder, she must want to.

I closed my eyes and didn't think about it anymore. "I accept."

Baby Harik gave me a crooked smile. "Murderer, you're an idiot." Then he flung me hard back into my body. I tripped and slammed into the ground, knocking the wind out of me before I hit a sharp rock with my face. I'm sure I would have screamed if I had any breath.

Margale gave a sinister chuckle. "Visiting gods, eh? I can see they don't like you any more than I do. Get on your horse." He stalked away.

When I got my breath and stood up, I heard Pocklin shouting, "Get over here, sit down, and stay there!"

"Sit on what? The dirt? That bug?" asked his daughter in a pretty loud voice herself.

"Yes! Sit on that bug! I'm your father! If I say to sit on a bug, you squish it with your butt parts and don't argue."

"I'm going where he's going, Daddy. Sorry."

By the time I reached my horse and mounted, Grik stood near my horse, examining me the way she might appraise a gemstone.

Kenzie stood behind her. "Bib, are you leaving? Already and without us? Without Pil?"

"Pil's done with me. Stay and help her, will you?"

"What do you mean, done with you?" Kenzie shouted.

Vargo trotted over. "What's the matter? Do you feel all right?"

Kenzie stuck out her jaw. "Pil has tossed Bib's shoes."

Vargo grinned. "Finally. He never deserved her."

I twitched. "Hell, that's true."

Vargo ignored me and gripped his wife's arm. "Don't run around and bellow like this! All right?"

She patted his face.

Vargo had been trying hard to control every damn thing when in reality he couldn't control anything. That said to me that Kenzie was either dying or pregnant, and she looked healthy. Well, I couldn't control anything about their situation either.

I glanced at Margale, wondering why he hadn't dragged me off my saddle to make me follow him. Talli set her horse next to him, talking quietly but intently and with big gestures. I would probably be occupied with that for a minute or two more. I walked my horse over to Pil and Chexis. Everybody except Margale and Talli joined us.

I said, "Pil, I know you didn't want to ride with some of our taller acquaintances, but I have to ask now. I'm riding to King Hale's capital with Margale to take care of something. Are we going there together, or am I riding alone?"

Nobody said anything for a moment. Then Pil, with her white face and red eyes, said, "I don't know."

"That's an answer," I said. "If you don't mind, I'll come find you when I'm done."

She nodded. At least she didn't tell me to keep walking and not look behind me.

Grik spoke up. "I'll come with you."

"You will not!" Pocklin yelled. "You'll have to put me in the ground before you leave!"

"Stop bellowing like a bull. I'm not putting you anyplace." Grik turned to Kenzie, who was leaning on Vargo. "Do you mind if I go?"

Kenzie smiled. "You're not a slave. You can learn a great amount from Bib. Some of it's useful, and some of it's even moral."

Pocklin spun Grik by the shoulder. "Gretta, I forbid it, and your mother would too if she was here. Look at him. You'll get killed for certain."

She grabbed her father's collar with both hands. "You were knocked silly, so you didn't see him fight. I want to fight like that, and I'm sorry, but you can't teach me how." She pushed the man away. "Bib, I'm ready."

I said, "Young woman, he's right. I doubt I can keep you alive."

"All I want is a chance, that's all. Everybody deserves a chance."

I glanced at Spot, who had fallen asleep in his bag. "Grik, are you a good hunter?"

"What kind of animal do you like to eat? Do you want the males or the females?"

"Get your horse."

"Bib!" Margale shouted.

Everybody was unhappy with just about everybody else, so we had no goodbyes. A few minutes later, in the warm early afternoon, Grik and I followed Margale and Talli at a trot southwest.

By midday, we entered the hills and reached the road about where we'd left it. It curved west, and we followed it all afternoon and through the night, stopping for a bit of rest now and then.

Margale pushed us harder as we neared Hale's capital city,

Scrip. Conversation was impossible at that speed. Nobody had been trying to converse anyway. I decided that Margale was too mean, Talli was too preoccupied, Grik was too focused, and I didn't give a shit what any of them thought.

Late morning on the following day, we drew within sight of the twin hills of Scrip. The shorter hill, Lowscrip, stood about a hundred and fifty feet tall. It housed the city's craftsmen, shopkeepers, laborers, and servants. The other hill, Highscrip, stood fifty feet taller.

King Hale's castle covered a good part of Highscrip but left room for barracks, homes for the wealthy, important warehouses, and two temples—one to Casserak, Goddess of Health and Vitality, and one to Weldt, God of Wealth. Weldt was a very popular god with people who loved money, so he was a very popular god everywhere.

"What's my part in the plan, Margale?" I shouted.

The man opened his mouth and then shut it so hard I thought he might snap a tooth.

"Stay within fifty feet of me!" he yelled.

I cursed the man to the steamiest parts of Lutigan's groin. Telling me what my part in the plan was would certainly be the same as giving me a command. I was still looking for a way to avoid murdering King Hale, but making Margale waste even one command was a worthy undertaking.

As we neared the capital, Margale scowled at Grik. "You stay outside the city."

I said, "Grik has to come with us. She's my chronicler. She's writing the story of my life."

"I thought that was already written."

"That was just the first volume. The great moral teachings will be in this one."

"Plus, I like to fight," Grik added.

Talli beamed. "We can always use more of that!"

Margale said, "All right. Bring her. Bib, stay within thirty feet of me now."

Then Margale led us right through the patrols and sentries as if he were the most beloved man in the city. It astounded me, since I wouldn't have traded him for the smallest rat turd in creation.

The city's market stood on the saddle between the two hills. We dismounted and led our horses weaving through the market. Past the market, we remounted and rode partway up Highscrip until we reached a two-story stone gatehouse into the castle yard.

Margale dismounted, stared at me, and hesitated.

"Just tell me what you want me to do," I said, trying not to smile.

He showed his teeth and called me a particularly nasty name. "The audience will start soon. Stay within ten feet of me for now."

Grik must have looked confused. Talli leaned over and said, "We're talking about the audience King Hale is giving the servants of Queen Apsel. We'll end the war! I've never ended a war. Don't you feel good being part of it?"

Grik smiled. "Yeah, I kind of do. Will we be part of the audience?"

"I don't know."

"Of course, you will," Margale said. "We all will. But look, I need to locate the envoy first. Bring the horses." He nodded at a guard and stomped through the gate without slowing down. I followed him, and the others followed me toward a spreading keep built of brown stone.

I was drawing closer to King Hale and the moment I'd be forced to murder him. But in my experience, situations grow more chaotic as action approaches. Often useful opportunities appear if you stay calm and look for them.

A boy took our horses to the stable, and we walked inside the cool dimness of the keep. Another boy led us up one staircase and past three wooden doors to a poorly lit room of moderate size. Four finely dressed men sat at a table, and they stood when we entered.

"Who are these people, Margale?" asked the oldest one.

"Our bodyguards, Lord Envoy." Margale might have tried to smile, but it came across as a grimace.

One of the men handed Margale a greatcoat, which he put on to cover his worn and dirty traveling clothes. The men of the delegation sat and chatted quietly, but the room stank of tension and doubt.

I turned to Grik and handed her Spot, in his sack. "Please take care of this." Then I turned to the table and spoke up. "So are we going to end the war today? What are the odds?"

The delegates stared at me with huge rabbity eyes.

Margale stood up and said, "Bib, you be—" He cut himself off and may have bitten his tongue to keep from giving me a command.

I said, "Peace would really be something to go home and tell our mistresses about, eh? I admit I may have a little wager on it. I'd like to know—am I on the right side of this thing if I say we'll fail?"

Margale jumped to grab my arm, but I slipped away.

I said to the older men, "Damn, is it that uncertain? Now you have me worried."

Margale couldn't command me to shut up. And he needed me to kill the king, so he couldn't hurt me too badly. I supposed he could break my jaw.

I glanced at Talli to make sure she wasn't about to tackle me. She looked as confused as hell. Maybe she wasn't part of Margale's king-killing plot.

I grabbed the old envoy by the collar. "Come on, grandfather. I know you're not that stupid. Otherwise, you wouldn't be wearing such a nice coat."

Margale grabbed at me, but I threw myself backward out of his grasp.

The envoy shouted, "Margale, do something about this! You'll wreck the audience!"

That was a thought. If I kept raising hell, maybe they'd just cancel the audience. I grabbed the door latch to yell some insane crap down the hallway, but my hand slipped off. I tried again, but my fingers went slack.

Before I tried a third time, Margale seized me from behind by one arm and one leg. He picked me up and slammed me on the table, knocking the wind out of me. Wielding both knives, Grik charged Margale, but he threw a heavy chair at her. She dodged it, but Margale stepped in and punched her in the face.

Grik fell backward and slid down the wall, her face bloody.

By the time I gathered some breath, Margale had set me back on my feet, holding my sword arm with both hands. A soldier had opened the door from the hallway and was ushering everybody out.

Talli hesitated, looking at Grik, who lay in a heap against the wall, with Spot wiggling out of the sack.

Margale barked at her, "Come on!"

Talli scowled at him. "This didn't have to happen. What's wrong with you, lately?"

Margale turned and pushed me through the doorway. We followed the old men down the hall. Talli and Grik stayed behind.

Two minutes later, the soldier led us into a larger much-better lit room. The seven of us fit neatly against one wall. King Hale of Silvershanks sat in a tall chair across the room. Although elderly with deep wrinkles, his hard eyes and trim carriage screamed that he was a monarch who would not hesitate to behead a man if he needed it, or even a hundred men.

Twenty armored guards with bared swords stood in two rows, almost shoulder to shoulder, between King Hale and me.

I whispered to Margale, "Holy crap."

Margale snorted, still gripping my arm. "This will be the most efficient way to do it."

TWENTY-THREE

My first thought was to kill the envoy, which would end
this audience in a hurry. I would rather kill Margale,
but of course, that was impossible. I lurched right to
draw my sword and thrust it into the envoy's heart, but my arm
didn't move a bit. Margale held my arm still as if it were tied to a
tree.

King Hale raised an eyebrow at me.

The envoy glanced over and said, "I apologize, Your Majesty.
He has never been in the presence of royalty before."

I've talked to ten kings and the Father of the Gods too. I thought it, but
my mouth wouldn't say it. I tried to say, "I carried Krak's hand
around in my mouth like a dog," but I couldn't open my jaw to get
that out either.

King Hale said, "Welcome, my lords. I wish for peace, just as
you do. Let us not play at niceties. Here are my terms: Queen Apsel
will withdraw all her armies from my kingdom. She will also pay me
five hundred gold wheels to compensate my kingdom for its suffering. In exchange, I offer her one twentieth of our mines' proceeds
for the next thirty years."

I tried to fall on the floor. My legs wouldn't collapse. I tried to scream at King Hale how attractive he was and invite him to an intimate supper. Maybe the binding would consider that a superior way to kill him. I strangled quietly on the words. I bore down, trying for the loudest fart I could manage. I couldn't produce even a whisper of flatulence.

The envoy said, "You Majesty's wisdom is well known. Queen Apsel offers the following terms: You will pay her five hundred gold wheels for her kingdom's pain and suffering. Her armies will remain in place until she receives said payment. Her ownership of the mines will be negotiated afterward."

The king looked as if he'd bitten down on a poisoned mouse. "That is a . . . fanciful suggestion, my lord. The queen's armies will leave my lands, and she will pay me two hundred gold coins. She will receive one fifteenth of whatever our mines produce for the next forty years."

The envoy sighed. I tried to sigh too but failed. The envoy said, "I'm encouraged, Your Majesty, that our positions are moving closer. May I beg a minute to confer with my colleagues?"

The king nodded.

As the envoy and his cronies gathered in the corner to whisper, I remembered that in a rush, Margale had commanded me not to kill myself. He hadn't commanded me not to harm myself. If I gave myself a spectacularly bloody but not so serious wound, that should make everybody flee the room.

I reached for my knife with my left hand. My heart quickened when I eased it out of the sheath. I prepared to cut myself across the scalp, which should bleed like a waterfall. However, I couldn't move my hand another inch. I tried to shout some extremely bad words in frustration but failed at that too. I couldn't even open my hand to let the knife clatter to the stone floor.

The envoy and his friends returned, and he said, "We have conferred, Your Majesty."

"Excellent," Hale said. "I was tired of waiting."

The envoy smiled as if Hale had told a joke.

Margale squeezed my arm.

"Her Majesty will accept one hundred gold coins in reparations," the envoy said. "Also, her armies shall remain in place until she receives the payment."

Hale frowned.

I saw Margale make three quick movements with his left hand.

Every one of Hale's guards cried out or screamed, then collapsed. A wisp of smoke rose from each head. The king and the envoy's party stared in silence.

Margale said to me, "This is as efficient and practical as it gets." He let go of my arm.

All my efforts to avoid this had failed. I drew my sword and ran across the room toward Hale. It felt like I was being pulled there. The king stood up with a sword in his hand. I thrust at him, thinking that maybe I could just wound him. He parried my thrust.

With my left hand, I jammed my knife into King Hale's chest. He jerked and gasped. I stabbed him twice more, and he collapsed limp back onto his chair with blood running down his chest and belly.

When I glanced back at Margale, he was applauding me.

"You crusty, grunting filth!" I shouted. "You could have killed him yourself!"

"Didn't want to," he said.

Shouts came from the hallway. A guard holding a sword flung open the door. He glanced at all the bodies, then swung at the closest living person, who was one of the envoy's buddies. The guard half-beheaded the old man.

Margale flicked a hand toward the guard. Everything the man was wearing and carrying flared white-hot. After a short scream, the guard dropped, but the heat had set the envoy and one of his men afire. They both ran toward the hallway, shrieking.

"Shit!" Margale snapped.

More shouts and screams sounded from out in the hallway. Margale had blocked our only escape and filled the room with the sweetish stink of burning flesh.

Margale grabbed the surviving old man and reached toward the wall behind the king's chair. A rough man-size hole opened in the stone wall as Margale ran past me shouting, "Stay within twenty feet!" Then he jumped through the hole.

"Crap!" I muttered. He was allowed to tell me how far I could stray without it counting as a command. I had to follow, and I was no closer to killing the man.

TWENTY-FOUR

Margale led me through the audience chamber's wall into the next room, which was a tiny pantry. Nobody was in it, but two big hams hung from the ceiling. Margale dodged them but knocked over a basket of eggs, which smashed against his legs and boots. He snarled a curse as the old man he was dragging flailed into a sack of meal on a shelf. Finely ground wheat dumped onto the floor, and the dust billowed up around us.

It was fifteen seconds into our escape, and we were already marked by pale powder from our hair down. Anybody with eyes would know there was something wrong with us.

Margale turned right, opened a hole in that wall, hefted his club, and ran through it. The next space was a fancy sitting room of some kind. We ran straight across it through the door into the next room, which was a bedchamber. All the polished wood, silk, and ermine told me this might be where King Hale had slept, but I had no time to appreciate it. Margale created a hole in the far wall and jumped through.

He jumped right back out, followed by a guard shouting for help. Margale knocked the man's sword aside and shoved him back through the hole. A moment later, a blast of heat and light rushed at us through the hole, and at least three men in the other room screamed.

Margale had let go of the old man to defend himself. The man scrambled behind a bed and hid. Spinning left, Margale made a hole in that wall. This time he peeked through, and I peered around him. I was looking down a hallway empty of everything but the sound of infuriated shouting from around the corner. Margale grabbed at the old man, who threw himself backward and then crawled under the bed.

I peered under the bed. "You have to come with us. If they find you, they'll kill you for sure."

The man shook his head. Margale flung the bed aside with one hand and picked the man up by the collar of his nice coat. He dragged the man into the hallway before shoving him at me. Then he reached toward the angry voices around the corner. The walls, ceiling, and floor seemed to melt. Then they came together, making a rough stone wall that blocked the hallway in that direction.

Margale sprinted down the empty hallway. I followed and pulled the old man along with me. Three people appeared at the other end of the passage. Margale opened the wall to our right, led us into a darkened room, and reformed the wall behind us. I heard Margale trip over some small piece of furniture, fall, and curse.

I tried to think of a way to get free of Margale but not get killed by Hale's angry subjects. However, as long as I was bound to stay within twenty feet of Margale, I couldn't escape too damn far.

Furniture, metal objects, and wooden things flew and clattered as Margale stood and crossed the near-lightless room. He opened the wall to our left so that we'd be fleeing parallel to the long hallway. Light revealed that we'd been standing in an armory. Margale had been flailing about, randomly throwing around all sorts of sharp and pointy weapons. I could hardly see how at least one of us hadn't been killed or at least maimed.

The next room stood empty except for two lit candles on a bare wooden table. By this point, I was too bemused to wonder what that was about. We crossed the room, ignored the door to our left, and ran through a hole that Margale created in the far wall.

A brown-haired young woman, really just a girl, screamed and then hauled three crying children with her to a bed in the corner. She threw the blanket over them and lay atop it on her back. She trembled, snarled at Margale, and clenched her fists at the same time. He froze as tears started running down the girl's reddening cheeks. Then he backed out, turned, and opened a hole in the right-hand wall.

The next area looked like a big dressing room with fine clothing on shelves and hanging on human forms carved from wood. Margale halted, looked left, right, and up. Then he opened the wall in front of him, obliterating a small fortune in velvet and silk. Another hallway lay through the wall. He turned left and ran down the hall, ignoring five closed doors. When the passageway turned left, he opened a hole in front of him rather than turn. Daylight streamed in, almost blinding me.

Once Margale leaped outside, he glanced around before waving at a tall thin woman wearing a bright red robe. She waved back, and we ran to her. She was young, dark-haired, and pretty in an exotic, high-cheeked way. She was also trying to hold the reins of seven horses. That was about four horses too many to keep quiet.

She gave Margale a stern, questioning look.

"The other three are dead," Margale said.

The woman shrugged.

Several dogs began baying someplace around the corner of the keep. Whoever was in charge must have decided to chase the assassins with hounds. Two of the horses neighed, struggled, and reared at the sound. That set off the other horses. They dragged the thin woman off her feet, and then all seven bolted.

The dogs had chased us for less than twenty seconds and had already ruined our escape.

I said, "I've been underestimating the value of dogs all these years."

Margale grabbed my arm. "If you don't bring those horses back, we'll all die!"

"Maybe. Is there something you want me to do?" I asked.

"You'll be tortured to death like the rest of us!"

"I've been tortured before. But if you want me to do something, go ahead and tell me."

The barking and howling had come closer.

"Bastard! Pacify those horses and bring them back so we can flee! That's my fourth command!"

"I'd love to, you grim thug!" I spun seven yellow bands and tossed one to each horse, convincing them that we were the riders they enjoyed most, and that we were all heading out for a nice ride. The horses trotted back to us, with their heads up and eyes bright.

The four of us mounted. Margale and I each led a horse. The woman let the seventh horse run free.

Margale stared into my eyes. "You may be two hundred feet away from me." Then he kicked his horse and rode toward the wall of the castle yard.

Since I didn't want to be dragged across the yard of King Hale's castle, I rode after him. Margale led the woman, the old man, and me at a gallop east, straight toward the castle's stone wall. A big gap opened in the wall, collapsing a small tower. After we passed through, I looked back to see the fallen stone reform into a rough wall.

Looking at it one way, Margale had bumbled his way through the escape, making quite a few mistakes. However, I had never seen a Bender use his skill with such efficiency. And most importantly, the bastard had escaped, at least for now.

Margale led us down the slope of Highscrip and then angled toward the road that headed southeast. I had never traveled that road, but I soon saw why it existed. The hills grew rugged just east of Highscrip. They would be a bitch to cross, either on foot or on horseback. But a fine, smooth twenty-foot-wide road ran right through the hills in a narrow defile. In places, it was as deep as sixty feet. The road wasn't level but rose up and down gently as it cut through the hills and valleys.

I had never heard of this road, and I'd never seen anything natural like it. A fair number of sorcerers must have struggled and even died creating it. Somebody or something powerful would have commanded them. Feet, hooves, and wheels had worn most of the roughness off, so the roadway was old, or maybe ancient. If the builders were mortal, they were long dead.

If we hadn't been galloping, I would have shouted at Margale to find another route. This one was convenient, but it could be blocked by one fallen tree and a few soldiers who weren't too drunk. When he slowed his horse to a canter, I rode up and tried to give him that advice, but he waved me away.

At last, Margale drew rein. I guessed we had ridden five miles from Scrip. It was only midafternoon, and I shook my head at that. So much seemed to have happened since this morning.

"Bib, you may take advantage of the fact that you're now allowed to be a quarter mile away from me."

I held still and considered that. Obviously, he was keeping me alive to give his last command. Did he want me to ride ahead and get killed by some ambush he suspected? Did he want me to ride far in the rear to defend him against pursuers? Did he want me to find a path out of the defile and lay a false trail for King Hale's outraged subjects?

So far, riding with Margale had helped me escape the people who believed, correctly, I had stabbed their king in the heart. I might well be able to escape on my own now if I could get so far away that Margale couldn't give me a command. Even if he did give me a command, it would be his fifth. After I fulfilled it, I'd be free to kill him.

So, I couldn't hurt the man yet, but I could try to slow him down. Maybe I could help his pursuers overtake us. He might have to use his last command to stop them.

I rode past Margale and the others. "Thanks for the distance, Margale. I guess I'll go ahead and clear the road for us."

Then I spun a yellow band for every horse except mine and convinced them that lions were leaping at them and chasing them. Within thirty seconds, all the riders were on the ground and all their horses were running. I watched the spectacle just long enough to be sure it was actually working. Considering Margale's power and competence, I had hoped that this couldn't be considered seriously attacking him, just seriously attacking his horse. I must have been correct.

I turned to gallop away from both Scrip and Margale.

"Bib, this is my fifth command to you!" Margale shouted after me. The last band tightened around my neck, and against my will I pulled on the reins.

Margale went on, "You will stand behind where I now stand, and you will stop everyone who comes chasing us."

I rode back to him, scrambling for a way to avoid the worst of this. "Margale, I don't believe you can just give me an open-ended task like this. You have to give me a specific end to the task, like sunset."

"An end? You're right. You will stop every one of them until no more people try to pass you. That's a specific end." He jerked his head at me.

I rode past him. "Once I finish this task, I'll be along to kill you."

Margale snorted. His lady friend and the old man were already walking up the defile to find their horses.

I dismounted and walked back toward Scrip to examine the ground on which I'd be fighting. "Hell, Margale, at least give me a hill to die on."

A six-foot-deep depression appeared in the road ahead of me. It spanned the defile.

"Die on that," Margale said. Then a ten-foot-high stone wall rose behind me all the way across the defile, cutting me off from Margale and my horse.

I wanted to curse Margale but didn't have time. I had to prepare.

TWENTY-FIVE

I'd spent many years in the Dark Lands killing anybody who tried to enter. After an embarrassing length of time, I came to understand that the best way to atone for killing a bunch of people might not be killing a bunch more people, even if it's for a good cause.

Also, the cause might not have been as good as I first believed.

Hell, maybe there was no way to atone for the things I had done. Likely those things were why Pil couldn't love me.

However, one thing I'd learned in the Dark Lands was how to kill a god-awful number of people in a short time, especially in a confined space. That wasn't a nice thing to have learned, but it was sure going to come in handy today.

When I left the Dark Lands and returned to the world of man, I lost several advantages that I had enjoyed there. I no longer had enormous vigor or resistance to pain. I no longer had a divine weapon that would slay an enemy at a touch and then terrify all his friends. I wasn't fighting in a land I knew down to the last wrinkle in its chilly black grass.

But I had carried away everything I learned, and I probably knew more about fighting and killing than any man alive.

Also, I had sorcerous power now, which I'd been without for most of my years away. After my deal with Gorlana and Baby Harik, I had over seven squares left. I could put up a ripping great fight with that much power.

The warm afternoon was ripe for thunderstorms. I spent power lavishly to pull together the biggest storm I could manage as fast as possible.

The defile was twenty feet deep here. I spun green bands and pulled bundles of roots out from deep in the ravine wall. They were a bit flimsy, but they'd hold my weight if I was careful.

The rain was falling hard when I saw the first group of horsemen coming at a gallop. I spun ten yellow bands for the first ten horses and convinced them, for the sake of variety, that both lions and wolves were chasing them from my direction. The horses reared and spun. Men fell. Horses galloped back the way they came, crashing into the horses behind them. Those horses panicked and turned to flee too.

I'm not sure how many horses ended up stampeding away. Probably all of them, since no horses wandered back to me. I'm also not sure how many men were thrown or trampled, but the whole force was sufficiently spooked to withdraw.

Using the bundles of roots, I climbed partway up the ravine wall. I only got eight feet high before my arms and legs wouldn't pull me higher. Although Hale's men had paused, it wasn't enough for my task to be considered complete.

I climbed back down and began squeezing as much rain as I could from the storm. I whipped up the wind and pulled in moisture from miles away. This might end up being the most violent storm seen here in a long time.

Before sunset, a rank of four soldiers appeared through the thick rain. I stood just behind the depression, which now had four feet of water in the bottom. I silently thanked Margale for being such an arrogant twat. When I'd asked him for a hill to die on, I was hoping he couldn't resist acting like an ass and giving me the opposite.

Two of the four soldiers slogged through the water toward me with their swords high. I thrust into one man's shoulder and then did the same to the other. They shouted and fell back, struggling out of the water with their swords left behind.

Their two friends charged into the water, and I disabled them in exactly the same way. Their shouts sounded surprised, although I didn't know why they would expect any different treatment.

Another rank of four pushed their way past the retreating wounded. All four rushed into the water together, even though that gave each just a small area of fighting space. The water made things awkward for them, but I still had to rush. I hamstrung one, sliced off another man's hand, and knocked a third silly with the flat of my sword. I thrust into the fourth man's chest harder than I meant to. He fell back and sank under the water. His wounded friends dragged his body away when they retreated, leaving four more swords in and around my defensive ditch.

I had turned back the first eight attackers. Over the next few minutes, twenty-four more men pushed through the hard rain and got the same treatment from me. I guess they then realized the feebleness of their strategy because attackers stopped coming. By then I had disabled twenty-seven and killed five.

I tried to climb out of the defile again but couldn't. More of King Hale's subjects were coming. Flinging three more white bands into the sky, I squeezed out all the rain I could manage.

I heard the rumble before I saw anything. I leaped for the bundles of roots again and climbed as high as I was allowed. I rushed to spin green bands and pull more roots out of the wall. I grabbed onto them, hoping that would be enough.

The road was fairly smooth but rose slightly for a hundred paces back toward Scrip. My storm had spread out to drop rain in the direction of the city. The ground was finally soaked, and the water had no place to go but across the surface.

Now the runoff hit the road in a great rush.

The flood crashed like a furious boar down the defile. Men had to be screaming as they were swept away to die, but I couldn't hear it. The water slammed into me thigh-high on the ravine wall and pulled my legs free. I clung to the roots and hoped they would hold, cursing myself for not expecting such a ferocious flood.

The flood soon wore itself out, and the water began to settle. It left a fifty-foot-long lake pressed up against the stone wall Margale had created. My little defensive ditch was swallowed by the water. A good number of corpses populated the lake. I didn't try to count them, although I knew each one would benefit Baby Harik in our contest.

Everything stayed quiet for more than an hour, but I still couldn't climb out of the ravine. Hale's men hadn't yet given up, then.

I had gotten tired of hanging from roots, especially since my unhealed knee was telling me about it. I swam and waded out of the lake of dead men. Swimming among the corpses was a bit creepy, but I told myself not to be fastidious. After all, I was the one who had killed them.

If I had been one of Hale's men, my next move would be killing me without getting close. I knelt down and pressed my body against one of the ravine walls. Nothing happened for a while. I imagined Hale's nobles and generals shouting over who was in charge and who would give orders. Maybe there'd be knifings.

I let the rain and wind slack off, but I spent the power necessary to keep the thunderstorm handy. Although my power was beginning to run low, I might need the storm again in a hurry.

The night had grown quiet, but my hearing wasn't good enough to notice the twang of bowstrings being released. The arrows surprised me. Hale's bowmen had to be firing blind down the defile, but if they fired enough arrows, one would eventually hit me. A shaft plunged into the wet ground three feet from my shoulder. I couldn't dismantle arrows I couldn't locate, so I needed an offensive move.

Bows had to be fired from within a certain range, and I assumed that the archers were standing on the road. Since the rain had stopped, their commander must have thought they were safe there. I picked the closest likely distance, spun a white band, and coaxed a bolt of lightning from the storm right onto that spot. I created the next band without pausing and threw a bolt fifty feet farther up the road. I kept this going, moving fifty feet at a time, for four more strikes. On the fourth strike, something exploded in a billow of fire.

Screams and curses came down the defile toward me, but no more arrows. When I tried to climb out of the defile, I was still prevented from reaching the top. Well, I heard nothing to make me think that Hale's forces had given up.

In the hours before dawn, I heard the clinking of people in armor trying to be quiet. I unsheathed my sword and stood in front of the lake of dead men. A few torches fluttered to life a hundred paces up the road, then more were lit until about forty were burning. All of them moved down the road toward me.

Within a minute, I could see two armored soldiers trotting toward me with a torch bearer behind them, then two more soldiers with a torch bearer behind, and so on. The first two spearmen charged to overwhelm me. I closed with the first one and thrust into his knee. He crumpled.

These men were armored with heavy chainmail, and their spears gave them reach. I would do better to rush in and attack on the low line. I feinted one direction, shifted the other, slammed the second man with my shoulder, and decided not to kill him either. I sliced him across both butt cheeks. He howled and staggered, backing right into the path of the next two attackers.

I defeated four more men without killing any or being wounded myself, apart from small cuts and bruises I'd been collecting since yesterday afternoon. Then fatigue hit me like a mallet. My unhealed knee started wobbling. I'd had no excess of sleep since leaving Arborswit and not much food either. I might not be as decrepit as one-hundred and thirteen, but I wasn't twenty-three or even forty-three anymore. I could fight more intelligently than these poor, badly trained soldiers, but intelligence wouldn't help my arm lift a sword.

I sliced the next soldier's throat and felt a tingle of vitality zip through me as he died. I cut the next one deep on the leg, a blow that would kill him in a minute. Another bit of vigor chased through me.

Foolishly I had chosen to defend with my back to the lake,

leaving me no options that involved retreat. It was a serious over-sight, so I decided to gain fighting room. I rushed the next two soldiers and killed them both with two slashes. The energy I gained pushed me to kill the two after that, even though I could have easily just wounded them.

I had moved thirty feet away from the lake, which seemed like a decent distance. I mangled the next fellow's sword wrist but didn't kill him, and a bit of energy seeped away from me. I kicked the next man in the groin and then stabbed his knee. When he went down, a little more vitality drained away.

I realized that unless I killed some of my foes, I'd soon be back to my exhausted state. At the very least, I needed to kill one man for each one I disabled.

So that's what I did until the first glow of sunrise.

The soldiers kept coming forward to fight and then dragging back their dead and wounded during all that time. Then they stopped charging at me. Soldiers scrambled to save their wounded brothers, and they threatened to tear out my guts if I moved to stop them. I was happy to let them go.

After the sun had risen high enough for me to see up the road, I spotted a single figure walking toward me. Nobody else stood close to me, nor did any horses. As the figure neared, it showed itself to be a man carrying no obvious weapons.

I held up a hand when the robed man was thirty feet away, and he stopped. He was young, maybe not yet twenty, with short-cropped hair and a freckled face. When he scratched his belly, I real-ized that he was wearing a woolen dressing gown and slippers, as if he'd just gotten out of bed.

"I like mornings like this, especially in the summer," he said in a soft voice.

"Mornings like what?"

"Still. Quiet. Full of the sound of people not being killed anymore. I'm Ratt, the dead king's sorcerer." He waited, but when I didn't say anything, he gestured around. "This was sorcery. Defi-nitely. That's what everybody says, at least."

"Sorcery? That's crap. I'm Krephommer the Lute Player. I don't know what happened here. I just fell into the ravine. Can you tell me the closest place to get a drink?"

"Where's your lute?"

"I had to burn it for firewood," I said.

"But it's summertime."

"To cook with. I can't hold a dead rabbit up against the sun and cook it, can I?"

"Hm. I have heard—and it's just gossip, you know—but I've heard that you are the Murderer." He gestured around us again and raised his eyebrows at me. "If that's true, you must be very old."

"I don't know who that is, and he sounds like somebody I don't want to meet. I don't guess anybody would want to meet a fellow named that."

Ratt pressed his lips together and stared at the ground. "The gods aren't above lying to us."

"That's probably true," I said.

"Every person I know thinks you killed the king. That includes my grandma. And every god I talk to says you killed the king, but that you were forced to do it."

"You talk to gods? Well, look at you!" I whistled.

Ratt stared at me for the first time, and the depth of his eyes surprised me. For a young fellow, he had seen some things. "Murderer, who made you kill my king?"

I thought about lying some more, but the boy looked too unhappy and determined all at the same time. I didn't want to fight him, but that's where this was headed. "Ratt, I was bound by a sorcerer called the Avalanche. He commanded me do it."

"Avalanche? That sounds . . . extreme."

"Wait until you hear this. He's both a Burner and a Bender."

Ratt paused. "I wish I could say you were lying to me."

I immediately decided that Ratt was a Binder and had enchanted some doodad to tell when people were lying to him. I had seen such things before. "I've been given my fifth command. When I finish this task, I'm going to make the Avalanche drink lava, if I can find some. But I have to keep killing or turning back your men until they stop coming."

"I see. A hundred soldiers are walking through the hills right now to attack you from above the road on both sides. They're not riding. They learned better than to ride horses around you. They are bringing plenty of arrows."

"I'd rather not kill them," I said, "but I will."

"The next hundred are bringing lead and a big cauldron to melt it in."

I didn't comment on that. It frightened me a bit. "Who's in charge, now that Hale's gone?"

"Duchess Eldine. A girl. The three heirs ahead of her were mysteriously burned to death in the castle after the assassination. Do you swear that you will kill the Avalanche?"

"I will if I can finish this damn task. As long as your men keep coming, I'm stuck."

Ratt nodded. "I think I can stop the pursuit for now. I can't stop it forever."

"Either the Avalanche or I will be dead long before forever gets here."

"You should check on your task, however you do that, a little while before midday," Ratt said. "You'll know by then whether I've had any success." He turned and trotted back up the road toward Scrip.

"Wait! Do you have any food or water?"

Ratt reached into his sleeve and pulled out a half-eaten loaf of bread. "It's a bit woolly," he said, handing it to me. "Here's an apple."

I grabbed the apple. "Thanks."

He was already trotting away again.

After I ate, I sat against the ravine wall and napped. Maybe somebody would come along and whack off my head while I was resting, but I needed sleep.

As midday neared, I waded across what remained of the lake of dead men. By now I could have counted the corpses with ease, but I didn't want to. I climbed the roots but couldn't escape. I tried again every ten minutes or so. On my seventh try, I climbed right out of the defile and looked around.

I had almost three squares of power left. The land was rough and hilly in all directions, but I'd be damned if I'd climb back down to that road, even on Margale's side of the wall. He had probably taken my horse with him. I jogged east, right alongside the road, looking for a horse, a house, or anything that could provide an advantage.

TWENTY-SIX

hroughout the early afternoon, I jogged beside the road. Soon the defile grew shallower as the hills flattened. At last, the road began gently running up and down with no ravine walls on either side.

I wondered why I hadn't met anybody on the road. I could understand that traders and pilgrims might avoid this road during wartime, but Queen Apsel's soldiers should be carrying messages and bringing supplies. I moved off the road far enough to keep it in sight yet look like no more than a dot to any travelers.

The rugged hills behind me had been covered in short sharp greenish-brown grass all the way from Scrip. Then, within a space of two miles, the grass reached above my knees, and I saw scrawny trees now and then.

A small needle of pain drove into my knee with each step. It didn't slow me much, but at this pace I would never catch Margale, unless he decided to build a house and settle along the road.

Before midafternoon, I spotted the low buildings of a small town. Fields of tall healthy-looking crops grew around it, with flocks of sheep and goats scattered in areas between the fields. The buildings appeared to be built of brick. The town certainly hadn't been attacked and ravaged—at least, not yet.

Maybe I was already in Havenswit, and these were Queen Apsel's subjects.

I would need two horses with saddles to ride hard enough to catch Margale without killing the beasts. I still had a few coins, but only enough to buy a saddle or two. I'd have to steal the horses. That meant being sneaky in the daylight amid a lot of people who probably distrusted strangers on principle. They'd be right to mistrust me, since I was here to rob them.

I had overcome greater challenges, so I jogged toward the town, limping as little as possible. When the people in the fields saw me, they waved. That seemed promising, so I waved back.

Maybe my manner of waving wasn't the right signal to show I was a friend. Everybody sprinted out of the fields toward town.

Walking through the closest field, I kept my hands empty and out at my sides, like the friendliest and least threatening horse thief in all the world. The first arrow flew at me when I was fifty paces from the nearest building. The archer had inferior skills, because the arrow hit the ground thirty feet in front of me. It discouraged me anyway. Since these people were already trying to kill me, convincing them to accept me as a visitor would be a great deal of work.

I found that I couldn't make myself attack them, no matter how logical that might be. They were just scared people in a kingdom at war. They might have survived by killing or chasing away any strangers, and that had proven to be a successful strategy so far.

Maybe when I was young, I might have charged in and slain enough people to get what I wanted. Maybe I wouldn't have; I couldn't say for sure. That had been a long time ago, and it almost seemed like somebody besides me had lived through those days.

Two more arrows flew toward me, no more accurate than the first. I backed away forty paces in case the next arrow was fired with more care. Then I turned to walk parallel to the road but a good distance away from it. I hoped that Margale was following it rather than veering off across the grassy hills. Why would he worry about me following him? I should either be dead or still fighting right now.

Before long, a troop of twenty mounted soldiers on the road approached and passed by without even looking at me. The war was still happening, then. I hadn't ended it when I murdered Hale.

A half mile down the road, Chexis dove down to me, popped his wings once, and settled onto the grassy ground as lightly as a quail.

"Why didn't you kill them?" he asked.

"It's a complicated business," I said, assuming he meant the townspeople. I walked up to face him. "How is Pil?"

"I comforted her for you, since she might have stabbed you a lot if you tried."

"Oh? Well, thank you."

Chexis lowered his head to my level. "Why didn't you kill those people? They tried to destroy you. Back in that ditch, when people tried to hurt you, you killed a lot of them."

"You were watching?"

"Of course. You seem unable to answer simple questions. You're proving it now. A pile of sheep droppings can explain itself better than you can explain what you do. I have to watch you if I want to learn anything. But this business about choosing to kill some people and not others is so inexplicable, I'm forced to ask you what it means. By the way, no dragon would ever kill any other dragon. Did you know that? The fact that you kill any humans at all mystifies me so much I pee fire."

I couldn't help glancing in the direction of his private parts.

"That's a metaphor," Chexis said. "Pil told me that humans understand those. Maybe you're a bit dull, even for a person."

"You called her Pil. Why didn't you give her some other name, like Teal or Lavender? Or a dragon name?"

"I didn't want to. Don't change the subject. Why didn't you kill those people?"

"I didn't want to."

Chexis turned his head to stare at me with one eye. "Are you mocking me? You really didn't want to?"

"No . . . part of me wanted to. But I didn't have to."

Chexis asked, "Have you killed other people you didn't have to kill?"

"Yes, I have."

"Then you're lying to me. Or to yourself. Or to both of us, so stop it!" He whacked his tail against the ground.

"Those folks today weren't a real threat, so I let them live."

"If one of those arrows had flown into your brain, that would certainly have been threatening! Why didn't you kill them?"

"They've suffered enough without getting killed by me!"

Chexis wrinkled his nose, and black smoke wafted out in rings. "That sounds wrong! You know what I'm going to say next, don't you?"

I sighed. "Yes. You're going to ask whether I've killed people even though they were already suffering. The answer is yes."

Chexis sat back on his haunches, almost like a dog. "Did you want something from these suffering people? Maybe something you didn't want from the suffering people you killed?"

I had certainly wanted horses from the townspeople, but I didn't spare them because of that. If I had killed them, I could have just ridden away with their horses. "No, that's not the reason." I shook my head. "It felt wrong to kill them."

"Felt wrong?" Chexis shouted, standing up.

I staggered back, holding my ears.

"You kill some humans and don't kill others because of how you feel?" Chexis yelled. "Are you a bug? A spider? Do you mean that a lizard in the desert has more sophisticated reasons for killing than you do? At least he's hungry." Chexis whacked his tail against the ground again and spun away from me. He yelled at the horizon, "He kills because of how he feels! Is this what mannish means? Sphynthor can't mean I'm like that."

I said, "I promise you there's more to it than that."

Chexis whirled back around to face me. "I came to you because I wanted you to help me understand human things. I have finally learned something from you, Syrtax. I have learned that you don't know what it means to be human!"

TWENTY-SEVEN

Chexis turned away from me and half-walked, half-slithered across the tall grass. He extended his transparent, iridescent wings to fly away.

Some god grabbed my spirit and yanked it with wrenching speed out of my body. Nausea hit me so hard I was gagging when I arrived at the trading place.

I first noticed that the brown dirt patch I stood on was bordered by happy red flowers. Tiny blue and yellow flowers shaped like saucers floated through the air on a cool, sweet breeze. I smelled damp earth, pollen, and cinnamon.

The wind was wafting the flowers from the forest to my left. The forest's leaves were now the palest of greens and covered by the little yellow and blue flowers, which were blowing away in waves. To my right, the bigger flowers in the long field showed magenta petals as far as I could see.

As I watched, every flower's face turned with clockwork precision and then halted facing toward me.

"Hi there, Murderer," Baby Harik said from the highest level of the marble gazebo. "Great job! Just magnificent. You've killed thirty-two more than you've spared so far. Unless you go crazy with mercy now, you'll be serving as my lieutenant sometime soon. Within a month, anyway."

"I'd rather drink poison."

"Come on, is that nice?"

"I'd rather drink poison than serve a grasping, bumbling, semi-diabolical toad like you. I'd rather cut off my fingers. I'd rather kick my mother in the crotch."

"It's sure to be more fun than that!"

"This is less fun than any of those things. Goodbye." I dropped away toward my body, but Baby Harik snatched me back.

"I didn't give you permission to leave," he said.

"Oh. What else do you want to say?"

Baby Harik looked blank for a moment. "I guess just that you're doing a good job. Keep it up. Kill, kill, kill!"

"Marvelous. I feel encouraged." I dropped out of the trading place.

A few moments later, I was watching Chexis prepare to flap his wings and fly off. "Wait!"

Chexis looked back over his shoulder.

I said, "I was bound by that sorcerer, Margale, remember?"

"So?"

"I was commanded to defend that ravine," I said. "If I hadn't been commanded, I wouldn't have killed any of those people. Not even one."

"Really? That's interesting." Chexis walked back to me and lifted his head high. "Are you lying to me now? Are you saying that if you had been commanded to kill those people in the town, you would have been forced to do it?"

"Right, I would have had no choice."

"That stinks."

He sounded so much like a little boy that I almost laughed.

Chexis said, "So you're saying that what a human does has no bearing on who he is."

I frowned. "I don't think I said that. Or maybe it's only true when you've been magically bound."

"Or maybe it's always true. That's something to think about."

"Yes, let's think about it really hard," I said. "Let's take our time. Meanwhile, I'm not bound anymore, and the sorcerer who bound me needs to be stopped."

"Are you going to kill him?"

"Probably. He killed a lot more people than me, you know. He burned down a whole city."

"Oh, I don't want to hear about that!" Chexis said. "You're trying to confuse me. I'm already thinking hard about whether you are what you do. Or not."

"Chexis, can I ride you while you fly?"

"What?" the dragon shouted. "No, you can't ride me!"

"Are you sure? Have you tried?"

Chexis growled. "It would be undignified."

"I don't mean to offend you, but this sorcerer has a big lead on me. I don't see many ways to catch him."

"Well . . . he does sound awful. Maybe I could carry you like you were a dead goat."

I didn't feel like smiling, but I did anyway. "That'll be fine!"

The dragon lowered his head and gazed at the ground. "Although I haven't carried anything bigger than a dead goat." The black patch on his forehead lay forward. "I refuse to carry you to this sorcerer just so you can kill him. I think that's immoral."

"I won't kill him," I lied.

"I'll eat him instead."

I swallowed. "Wonderful."

"Try not to wiggle too much while we're flying. Pretend you're a dead goat. They don't wiggle." The dragon flapped his wings and shot into the air. Then he circled back around and grabbed me under the arms with both his rear claws. He lifted me into the air, leaving my stomach on the ground.

"Go down that road!" I yelled.

Chexis veered to follow the road.

I figured that Margale may or may not have met up with allies, but he'd almost certainly be accompanied by the thin woman and the old man. Chexis and I could fly over them and terrify everybody. When we landed, I'd dispatch the woman, then hold Margale down to be helpful while Chexis ate him. The old man could continue on to his destination, bringing the good news that Margale was dead. It seemed like good news to me.

I started to shout my plan to Chexis, but instead I hurried to lift my feet as we flew low over a big mound of dirt beside the road.

"Watch out!" I yelled.

"You're wiggling! Don't wiggle!" Chexis shouted back. He flew a little higher.

"Be careful!"

"Hush! Let me concentrate!" the dragon called back.

I shouted my plan about terrifying Margale and the others to Chexis. It took only five seconds.

Chexis yelled, "That's more of an idea, or a wish, and not so much a plan, isn't it?"

Before I could admit that he was right, Chexis yelped in an undragonlike way and dropped toward the ground without slowing. I screamed, calling out to Krak, his eyes, his thumbs, and his thundering nipples before Chexis slipped over the road and rose ten feet above the surface.

"We can stop for a minute!" I yelled.

Chexis yelled, "It's fine! Just don't distract me!" He flapped hard but dropped a few feet. Then he jerked right before veering back to the left. I spotted the little tree just before Chexis pulled up, but he still whipped me through a nest of skinny branches.

My body stung in a dozen places. One ran from my right temple to my left jaw.

"Fly over the road! And higher!" I yelled.

The dragon sprang up and then dropped lower before veering off the road. He popped his wings, but he didn't fully halt before he dropped me. I tumbled like a severed head about twenty feet through the grass.

Chexis landed behind me.

I clambered to my feet with bloody little cuts everyplace not covered by clothes. "You said you could carry me!" I shouted, my face just three feet from the dragon's.

"You wiggled!" Chexis yelled back.

"I wasn't wiggling! I was bouncing across the face of the world while you dragged me!"

"What do you expect from me? I'm only one year old!" Chexis shouted.

I staggered back a couple of steps and blinked at that. Chexis looked like a half-grown dragon, but he was still awfully young. Maybe the way he thought and felt about things was less than half grown. If he was human, he'd be a damn toddler.

"I'm sorry, Chexis, that was rude of me. Do you have any ideas?"

"Your unstable weight is altering my center of gravity," he said.

That sounded like it made sense, although I had never heard it put that way. I blinked at him.

"I'm sorry, I forgot that you only have a human brain. Imagine you were carrying a heavy sack of unhappy snakes but had to hold it between your knees. I think I can fix this, though."

A minute later I was lying on my back with grass blades tickling my neck and ears. Chexis stood over me, gripping my shoulders with his back claws and holding my knees with his front claws.

"No," I said.

"Does it hurt?" Chexis asked.

"I'm staring up at your crotch."

"Oh, I see. Turn over, then."

"My back doesn't bend that way. If we go very far, I'll hurt it."

"You have a stupid spine. Your whole body is stupid. I could create a better body out of old bones and mucus."

"I have thumbs, unlike some people."

Chexis sniffed, producing a curl of smoke. "This question may be too hard for you, but I'll ask it. If I carry you headfirst and you slam into something, what part of you will hit first?"

I didn't answer.

"Isn't looking at my groin better than getting a smashed skull?"

"Shit! Damn it to Lutigan's knees and toenails! I guess I can close my eyes."

Chexis flapped his wings and took off with a boom.

TWENTY-EIGHT

(CHEXIS)

Holding Syrtax with all four feet spread his weight much better. I bet I could carry something far heavier than a stringy human sorcerer using that method. I might try a donkey or a small cow. I'd kill it first so it wouldn't wiggle.

This was something really useful that I learned by following Syrtax around. Learning something was a nice surprise. There had been no reason to follow him. Until then, he hadn't taught me any more than that dead donkey could have.

That's not wholly true, I guess. I followed him because he is the most inexplicable human I've met. I knew that wasn't a sound reason to observe him, but if I watched him for insights long enough, something might pop out, as if he were a chrysalis or a dead pig in the sun.

Syrtax said he believes that I belong to him. I heard him say it, although I'm sure he didn't think I could hear him from so far away. It's almost cute, or it would be if it weren't so preposterous. It would be like a frog owning an alligator. Although he is a sorcerer, I guess, so it would be like a big frog owning an alligator.

Following Syrtax had also raised a fascinating thought. Could it be that what somebody does has no relationship to who he is? I think this could be true, or partly true. I ate that nasty human with the metal hat, and it didn't change me at all. Eating a human is a near meaningless act, that's true, so that may be a bad example. I'll need to eat some more.

Once we had Syrtax stretched out properly, I flew quite fast. When I saw ten men on horses ahead, we still had hours before sunset. I tried to listen to the men, but I only heard breathing and a little cursing. I could have learned more listening to their horses blow.

I shouted, "I see them, Syrtax. I'll fly over and burn a few."

"Don't do that!"

"It's all right. I'll terrify the horses too."

I dove on the riders while Syrtax shouted nonsense disguised as advice. Since I could breathe flame about five feet, I aimed to skim six feet off the ground. As the horses began rearing, I realized I was about to slam Syrtax into some riders or even horses. I pulled up to about twenty feet to rethink things.

"Put me down!" Syrtax yelled. "Over there, off the road!"

"I can't see which way your hand is pointing. When you say 'there,' be more specific."

At that moment I felt my entire body tingle. "Something's happening!" My voice sounded high, and I realized I might be a little frightened. Well, concerned.

"I feel it!" Syrtax said. "Margale's trying to set us on fire!"

"He can't do that to me!" I shouted, relieved. I turned to get a better look at the tall sorcerer. He was staring at us with both hands at his sides. "Syrtax, why aren't you burning up?"

"He's trying to burn my clothes, but they can't catch fire! Fly ahead and put me down!"

The sorcerer swept both hands in a little arc.

"Run! Fly!" Syrtax yelled.

"Run? Fly? Which one?"

The sorcerer threw down his hands just as his horse turned and reared.

Four distressing things happened all at once.

First, I was engulfed in a thirty-foot-wide ball of fire for less than a heartbeat.

Second, I couldn't breathe anymore.

Third, all the fire inside my body went out because the air had burned as much as it could.

Fourth, all the air was whisked away from the space around me, leaving emptiness. A fantastic boom sounded as my wings flapped against nothing. I smacked down onto the ground twenty feet below me, twisting so I wouldn't smash Syrtax.

I rolled away from Syrtax and came up on my feet fast while glancing around. All the horses seemed to be attacking the men who had just been riding them. The tall sorcerer's left arm hung limp, and his horse had disappeared into a big hole in the ground.

I only thought I had been fast. Syrtax had already drawn his sword and was sprinting toward the big sorcerer. He was attacking much faster than me. This was so unlikely that I thought he must be using magic to do it.

The big sorcerer twitched his hand. Stone from the road shot up and covered Syrtax's legs to the knees. He fell forward from the waist.

I chuffed but had no fire yet, so I ran toward the sorcerer. He pulled a big club off his back and dodged to the right. When I turned to claw him to death, he swung his club.

Dragons are invulnerable to magic and magical weapons, so I didn't worry as I reached out to claw him, knock him down, stand on him, and then bite him until my jaws were tired. But before I could do any of that, he hit me with his club. As he was swinging, I realized that I was the slowest creature in this fight. I needed to figure out how to be faster!

When the club hit me, I felt my left shoulder crack and break into pieces. It was the worst pain I had ever felt, although I really hadn't ever felt much pain. I snapped at the sorcerer, but he jumped away.

Syrtax threw a knife at the sorcerer, but the evil man hid behind his club. The knife bounced off the club, and I started wondering where in the world that piece of wood had come from. At the same time, I dragged myself over behind Syrtax, who was still locked in stone boots.

The sorcerer ran up and swung his club straight down at Syrtax's head. Syrtax leaned really far and knocked the club aside with his sword. The club scraped down Syrtax's leg, and he bellowed like a dying yak. Then Syrtax thrust his sword so fast I could hardly follow it. He poked the sorcerer in the upper part of the arm that he used for club-swinging. The sorcerer shouted a bad word and backed away while he flicked his hand a couple of times. The stone boots holding Syrtax grew into an entire stone suit, covering his whole body, including his head.

The big sorcerer didn't say anything, but he did smile as he stomped toward Syrtax. He was struggling to lift his club, and before he managed it, I felt a bit of fire inside me. Sticking my head around the side of the Syrtax's stone suit, I chuffed and breathed fire at the sorcerer.

I was only able to shoot fire about three feet, but that was far enough to burn off the sorcerer's beard, eyebrows, and some of his hair. He screamed and stumbled backward as his clothing smoldered but didn't fully catch fire.

The sorcerer said a few more bad words. Then he glanced at his horse trapped in the hole.

I dragged myself a few feet closer to the sorcerer and breathed fire again, this time with a longer flame.

The sorcerer turned and ran down the road away from us.

Syrtax shouted something through his mask of stone.

"Yes, I am injured." I wasn't about to admit to him that I was in agony. "Even injured, I chased away that sorcerer!"

Syrtax said something that wasn't very loud at all.

"Oh! You're dying because you can't breathe."

I scooted around, lying on my good side, and kicked the stone suit with a rear leg. The stone wasn't all that thick. After three agonizing kicks, a lot of the stone had been cracked. Syrtax wrenched his arms free and began yanking at the stone over his face.

"I could kick the stone off your head, but I don't think that would be smart," I said.

Syrtax pulled the stone off his face and sagged. I sagged too and laid my head on the road. I had imagined pain before, but my imagination had been wretchedly bad. I took a deep breath to keep from moaning. That moved my broken shoulder, so I moaned, but only a little.

"The soldiers are either down or running away from their horses," Syrtax said. "I don't see the woman in the red robe or the old man."

I said, "The tall sorcerer ran down the road that way."

"All right."

"Is it?" I asked. "It doesn't seem all right."

"We're alive. That's pretty damn good," Syrtax said. "Margale's a vile son of a bitch, but he's tough. And smart."

"And fast," I said.

Syrtax looked at me. "I guess he is, for a human. How can I help you, son?"

"I don't know," I said. "I've never been hurt like this. I've never heard of a dragon being hurt like this."

"Well, don't give up. I'm not."

"Syrtax . . . Bib, I think I'm feeling something that's sort of like fear, but it certainly isn't fear. Dragons don't feel fear. But I'm feeling . . . a thing."

After a moment, Bib said, "Of course dragons don't feel fear! Whatever you're feeling is appropriate for a dragon, no doubt about that. Rest for a bit. I'm going to take stock of whatever these horses are carrying."

Bib walked away, I guess to sharpen his sword and call Margale names. He left me alone here to feel things and wonder whether I'll fly again.

TWENTY-NINE

The dragon's shoulder looked like hell. It was twisted, and it was bumpy in the wrong places. When he'd rolled up from kicking the stone trap off me, I heard his shoulder pop three times. Chexis wouldn't admit that it hurt, just like he wouldn't admit that he was afraid. I wasn't an expert on dragon health, but he trembled all over.

It was my fault Chexis had been injured. I had browbeaten him into carrying me down the road to catch Margale without a single thought about the young dragon's safety. Hell, they were invulnerable. You could stab them in the eyeball with a magic sword, and they'd just smirk while they were killing you for your temerity. I imagine they would, if dragon faces could smirk.

But dragons weren't safe from weapons forged with divine magic. I had proven that a year ago when I killed two of them using the God of Death's sword. Margale's club must have been forged in the Gods' Realm. I wondered why the gods would give it to Margale, that leaky sack of dead toads.

I gathered up all the food and water in the soldiers' saddlebags. Three of those men had survived and soon woke up. I told them to run and chased them toward Queen Apsel's capital, whacking their butts with the flat of my sword.

When I trudged back to Chexis, I asked if he knew how I could help him or heal him. Then I panicked because he didn't answer, didn't move, and didn't open his eyes. The dragon was just in some kind of heavy sleep. Maybe that's how dragons reacted to being crushed with a god-club.

The sun was dropping, and the moon wouldn't rise until a while after sunset. I wanted to go find some kind of help, because I sure as hell was useless when it came to healing anything, especially dragons. But I didn't want to leave Chexis alone and helpless. I could actually be useful if I stayed to protect him.

As it got dark, I sat on the ground beside the dragon and patted his neck. I sang a few of the songs I'd taught him when he was a baby. I couldn't imagine that would help in any way, but it probably wouldn't make a lousy situation any worse.

Sometime before the moonlit midnight, I saw a pinprick of light on the road back toward Scrip. I stood, drew my sword, and watched it grow larger. When it began moving up and down a little, I decided that somebody was riding toward us with a lantern or a torch. A couple of minutes later, I heard two sets of hoofbeats.

When the riders drew rein, I saw they were Grik and Talli.

I nodded at them. "It's good to see you here looking so well."

Grik said, "Sure, I feel like I've been to a party." I saw that both her eyes were black. Margale might have broken her nose, too. She sounded stuffy.

Talli pointed at me and growled, "You! I heard you murdered King Hale."

"I thought you said he was a greedy son of a bitch."

"That was before you stabbed him in the damn heart with no warning!"

I held up one hand. "I couldn't help it. Margale used magic to command me to kill Hale."

She gasped and then yelled, "That dog-knocker! Mud-sucking bastard! Sometimes you have to know somebody for a whole year before you find out you don't know them at all! I could have poisoned his beer a hundred times, but I was an idiot and just kept sleeping with him like he was the god of sex and alehouses. I'm the world's most awful idiot." She slapped her leg twice, startling her horse.

Grik stared at Talli. "You aren't a little skeptical of this man?" She nodded toward me. "You think he's telling the truth about Margale commanding him? I believe him, but why do you?"

Talli looked down and shook her head. "Oh, I knew Margale was no good. But he was so much fun! Yet I don't think this man here would lie to me. He seems truthful." She squinted at me. "What's your name again?"

I gave her a crooked smile. "Magilyard. Sailmaker."

Grik sighed so deeply her horse flicked its ears around to listen. "Where's Margale?"

"Someplace down the road," I said. "How did you get past the stone wall he left on that end?"

"There's a side path that joins the road farther down," Talli said.

Grik peered past me. "Are there some rocks over there on the road?"

"No, that's a sleeping dragon."

Grik said, "Is that Chexis? Why's he sleeping?"

"He's hurt. I don't know what do to about it," I said. "I wish Kenzie was here. Maybe she could help him."

Grik stared around into the darkness. "I'm not doing anything much, and you're not exactly entertaining me, *Magilyard*. I'll bring Kenzie. Here, take your dog." She reached down to hand me Spot, who was yipping and poking his head out of his sack. "Sorry, he peed in it."

I asked, "Do you know where Kenzie is? Is Pil with her?"

"I don't know where either of them is. Probably someplace safer than this. Give me that lantern, Talli. Bib, I'll find them. I'm taking one of these loose horses too."

Grik trotted her horse over to one of the mounts that had earlier battered their riders. She grabbed the reins and galloped back toward Scrip.

I could see Talli outlined by starlight. "I'm going after Margale as soon as I can."

"Why did she call you Bib? That's an insult."

"She was joking," I said. "It's a pun."

Shaking her head, Talli said, "Whatever you say. Did Margale really kill this dragon?"

"No, but Margale smashed him pretty hard."

"You should leave Margale alone," she said. "He can't be beaten. He can't be hurt. He just rolls over everybody and everything."

"I know it seems that way. But when he ran away from us, he had one arm not working. The other was damaged, and the front of him was singed awfully hard. He's not unbeatable. Talli, are you a sorcerer?"

"No! Why would you think that?"

"Because of your shirt. It's a color you only get using magic," I said.

"Oh, Margale gave me that. He must have made it."

I felt pretty certain that Margale had never enchanted anything. Maybe he was both a Bender and a Burner. I was not ready to accept that he could also bind magic into objects.

I pushed down my anger at Margale and decided to wait with Chexis, at least until morning. I couldn't wait too long, though. We might already be in Queen Apsel's kingdom. If Margale reached her protection, killing him would be a stone bitch. At least he was afoot and wounded.

Talli offered to stand first watch while I slept, and I wasn't too proud to argue.

After a few hours of sleep, I felt ten years younger. I went through the food and picked out anything a dog might eat.

"Talli, what's this war really all about? It can't just be about Hale being an asshole."

She was quiet for a bit before she answered. "Neither Hale nor Apsel is a king or a queen, not really. King Bester is the real king up in Farfall. But he's a thousand years old and they just ignore him.

Years ago, they were Lord Something Face and Lady Twisted Pants. Those are my names for them. Don't tell Margale I said . . ."

"So Margale kills and destroys at Queen Apsel's behest?" I asked.

"He wishes Apsel had married him, I think, although he won't say it. Damn it! My ma said I have the worst judgment in the world about men, and I guess she was right. Shit!"

"Why all the fighting? Is it just for land? Is it really for gold? Do they want to poke each other's eyes out?"

"Oh! Margale talks about that all the time. I think it really is about treasure. That gamy rat Hale mined gold and silver out of his hills, and he hoarded it. The queen could have shipped that ore on the river that runs through her land and traded it for food, and lumber, and cloth, and everything that would make everybody's life better. But Hale just planted his butt on top of that gold and sat there, making everybody suffer. Some people even died because he was a stubborn dog." She kissed at Spot and petted him as he slept.

I considered that. "Talli, I'm sorry for saying this, but you may have the worst judgment about women too. Do you really think Apsel would share with Hale any riches that sailed back up the river?

"Oh . . ." After a few seconds, she made a choking sound. "I guess she wouldn't. I'm an idiot! But I do know that Hale attacked first! I saw it."

"Maybe he wanted to kill Apsel and take her river for himself," I said. "Then he could use it to ship gold and silver."

Talli said, "Maybe they both need to be held down and kicked until they cry. If you hadn't murdered Hale, that is. Do you murder people a lot?"

"I try not to do it for no reason."

"That's good. Really good. Magilyard . . . Bib, I guess, how old are you? I'm twenty-seven."

I tried not to laugh. "Don't make a mistake in judgment about me, Talli. I'm one-hundred and thirteen years old."

She leaned away from me. "I wouldn't have guessed that.

Making sails must be a healthy life. I'm going to sleep now." She lay on the ground next to Chexis and pressed her back against him.

"Aren't you afraid of the dragon?" I asked.

"I guess I should be, but . . . he just seems like he needs somebody to be nice to him. And if he doesn't die, I want to introduce him to a couple of fellows I owe money to."

I glanced at the waning moon, which was headed back toward the horizon. Talli went to sleep while I walked back and forth across the road, watching and listening.

Sunrise came, and Talli woke with no prompting from me.

"I'm going after Margale now," I said. "He may be too far ahead already."

"Leave him alone," Talli said. "You seem nice. Take your friends and go to some other kingdom. Hell, take me with you. Don't let Margale kill you."

"I'm not nice, and I'm going to kill him." I jogged down the road after Margale.

Before I was out of earshot, Talli shouted, "He's awake!"

I ran back to the dragon.

Chexis was muttering to Talli, "Oh, good job, human. Well done. You can see that my eyes are open, so you can deduce that I'm awake. You don't need to announce it to all the fish in the ocean, though."

"Chexis, did your sleep help you? How's your injury?" I asked.

He snorted, and a few inches of flame shot out of his nose. "It doesn't hurt." His body seemed relaxed, but his eyes were dull.

"I've sent for help, and now I'm going to kill Margale. Talli and Spot will stay with you."

"That tall sorcerer . . . Margale will probably kill you. But you should go ahead and try," Chexis said. "You might catch him sleeping or looking at something very interesting."

I smiled and decided against patting his head.

Before I could set out again, I heard a far-off whistle.

Six horses with five riders were approaching fast on the road from the direction of Scrip. I walked toward them and drew my sword. Margale was getting farther away, but I couldn't leave Chexis and Talli alone now.

I glanced over to ask Talli what she thought about these newcomers. She had drawn a big knife and pulled a small metal shield off her back. Now she was stalking toward the horsemen, making it clear what she thought.

One of the riders raised an arm and gave me a big nasty hand gesture.

I nodded and muttered, "That would be Vargo."

THIRTY

Grik returned not just with Kenzie. She also brought Pil, Vargo, Pocklin, and a spare horse for me. Once she'd dismounted, she led Kenzie to where Chexis lay.

Grik nodded at me, but nobody smiled or greeted me, not even Pil. They were all coming from Scrip, where everyone must know I had murdered the king for no reason at all. My companions didn't know that I had been compelled to do it. Even if they had known, they also knew my history. It might not have changed how they felt.

I said, "Pil—"

"You don't need to explain yourself to me anymore." She looked away and knelt beside Chexis.

"Just ten words." I said. "Margale bound me and commanded me to kill King Hale,"

Pil faced me with round eyes. "Are you still bound?"

"No."

"Before, did he command you to not let us know you were bound?" she asked.

"Yes."

Kenzie asked, "How do we know you're not still bound but commanded to make us think you're not?"

"I guess you don't. I would have hoped that sorcerers who were with me for days while I was bound would have figured it out." I tried not to sound critical, but I probably failed.

"I guess I believe you," Pil said. "I know you well, but I believe you anyway. Do you think anybody else knows how to bind you?"

That stopped me. "Margale might have shared my name with the sorcerer working for him, the woman in the red robe. Shit!"

"Then don't get close enough to hear what she says." Pil raised her voice. "Everybody! If you see a sorcerer in a red robe, kill her before she gets close enough to talk to Bib. Don't fail unless you want to see him commanded to kill us all."

Kenzie nodded and knelt beside the dragon's shoulder. She probed it with her open hands while we all watched.

Vargo walked up behind her and laid his hands on her shoulders. "You haven't done this kind of thing, ever. He's not human, not meaning any offense, but you're a human! We have to think about us humans!"

Kenzie reached up to her shoulder and patted one of his hands. "I hear you, and I cherish you. Go away now, or I'll hustle you off and put a spear through your foot to keep you there."

Vargo backed away, muttering under his breath.

"Bib," Kenzie said, "the stories say that you once healed a horrible, bloodthirsty magical creature. How did you do that?"

Vargo spoke up. "You mean the creature that the next week tore apart a village, killed everybody, and made shoes of the babies' skins?"

Kenzie stared at me. "Yes, that one."

"I don't remember any of that happening," I said. "I did keep the spirit Limnad alive until she healed herself once. I healed a couple of other magical creatures when I was young, but I was never very good at it."

"Which would be fine and interesting if had I asked you about that, but I asked you how you did it! Whatever you did, how did you do it?"

"Limnad healed herself—Harik's ass!" I shouted. Chexis had

twisted his neck around and poked his head over my shoulder to look at Kenzie. "You scared me, son."

"You're scared of my head? You must be scared of the whole world. If I break your shoulder too, will you get even more scared?" The dragon's black slit irises had just about taken over his amber eyes. A constant stream of black smoke drifted from his nostrils.

I smiled at him and hoped I looked encouraging. "I was about to say that Limnad had healed herself, so that may not apply here. For the most successful healings, we gathered up magic trinkets, and some magical things that were bigger than trinkets. I healed with one hand and clutched trinkets with the other. Every time one melted, Halla stuck another one in my hand. I went through five or six, I think."

Kenzie said, "All right, then. Who has magic to pitch in for the cause? I would think it's going to take a lot. Things from people close to Chexis should work better."

I drew my sword and held it out to her.

"No!" Pil said. "You'll need that. Here, use these." She opened a pouch and dumped out an assortment of things: two tiny rods made of gold, an acorn, a painted wooden carving of a pig, a little bear cast in silver, a chicken's beak, a wad of cotton, a ruby the size of my thumb, and several other whimsical items. Pil said, "I saw Chexis when he was a baby, so I'm sort of close to him."

Talli had walked away. Now she came back to hand her yellow shirt to Kenzie. Adjusting her jerkin, which was now against her bare skin, she said, "This will feel a little sticky for a while, but he looks so sad lying there."

Vargo held out his sword, which was enchanted so that it yearned to protect his life.

"No," Kenzie said. "I won't use that."

Vargo opened his mouth, but Kenzie cut him off, saying. "I refuse to touch it."

Vargo sheathed the sword and didn't argue.

I pulled off my jerkin and shirt. Then I turned away to take off my trousers and underclothes.

Talli said, "Don't go fight Margale naked. He doesn't really have a sense of humor."

"I won't. I'm just giving my shirt and my smallclothes up for the cause," I said. "It's the least I can do. I hate to leave right now, but I shouldn't dawdle any more over chasing Margale."

"Wait!" Kenzie said. "Keep your dang shirt. If you fight Margale you'll need it. And I may not need your shirt or your sword, but I need you. You should be part of the healing."

It made sense. Proximity and personal connection would make a difference. "All right, I guess. Margale's on foot. But he might leave the road anytime." I wavered.

"I'll go," Vargo said.

Kenzie sputtered.

"Not to fight him!" Vargo said. "I haven't lost every part of my mind! I'll scout after him, so if he leaves the road I'll know. Bib, you can follow me when you're done here."

"That sounds like a really stupid idea." Pocklin winked. "I'll go with you." He turned to his daughter. "Grik, you stay here!"

"Did you hear me volunteer for something?" Grik shrugged.

A couple of minutes later, Pil, Kenzie, and Vargo had tossed in whatever magic bits they felt they could spare. Then Pocklin and Vargo rode east.

"I'll lay all these things out in the order I'll be using them," Kenzie said.

I shook my sword at her.

She ignored Pil's scowl and took the sword. "Bib, I'll put it at the end. I hope I won't have to use it. Come around here and press your hand near his shoulder. Chexis, are you ready?"

"Yes." The dragon gazed around at us. "Is this always the way you treat broken shoulders?"

"It is," Pil said, before anybody else could answer.

"It seems like a complicated and wasteful way to handle things. You should think of a better way to do it."

"Next time," I said.

The healing went faster than I expected. Kenzie moved aggressively and with more certainty than I would have felt. She started with Talli's yellow shirt in her free hand. It gradually melted to the consistency of quicksilver before it soaked into her hand. Pil dropped the silver bear charm into Kenzie's hand next.

Kenzie absorbed all of Pil's enchanted doodads over the next ten minutes, and I could tell she wasn't close to done. Pil pulled off her fireproof jerkin, hat, and gloves, ignoring my objections and profanity. Kenzie absorbed them. My sword lay on the ground, next in the line.

"Here!" Pil reached into a different pouch, hurried to sort through whatever was in it, and pulled out five more trinkets.

Kenzie used those items one by one. She muttered, "I'm not finished," and held out her hand.

Before Pil could hand my sword to Kenzie, Talli screamed, "Dammit!" as she darted in, gripping something hard in her fist. She slapped a pendant into Kenzie's hand. The thing was made of gold, set with diamonds and sapphires, and was bigger around than my eyeball.

I don't know what power Talli's pendant contained, but it gave Kenzie enough to finish before getting to my sword.

Kenzie's face was gray from pain, and she was dripping sweat. She croaked, "How do you feel, Chexis?"

The dragon stretched and shrugged. "Very good. You did a nice job."

Kenzie smiled for a moment, then sagged against Pil, who had stood behind her.

Chexis said, "I thought you might explode and kill both of us. Maybe carrying that baby made you extra careful."

Everybody froze. After a few seconds, Kenzie cleared her throat. "Everybody who already knew, raise your hand."

All of us except Talli raised our hands.

Talli grinned and ran to Chexis, petting him like he was her favorite horse.

Chexis ignored Talli and stretched his neck to sniff Kenzie. She was lying on her side in the dirt, taking shallow breaths. He said, "That helped."

Kenzie muttered, "You'll help me someday."

"Probably not. I'm glad you did it, but I don't understand why."

She lifted her head. "I could help you. What kind of person would I be if I didn't?"

Chexis jerked back as if something had bitten him, and he looked at me. The black patch on his forehead was tousled.

I walked over to stand in front of the young dragon. "She's right, son. People are generous and helpful, like Kenzie. Except for the others who are right assholes, like Margale. We're complicated, maybe more than is good for us. I wouldn't spend much time thinking about it."

Chexis spread his wings and took off right over my head with a bang that hurt my ears.

Pil picked up my sword and handed it to me. "A weapon that Margale can't set afire, and even though the Bole changed this sword, I'm glad you have it, because without a magical weapon, you have no chance." She hesitated. "Did you kill King Hale with it?"

"No, I used my knife."

"Good. I didn't enchant this sword for things like that." She sounded sad, but I could tell she wasn't sad for me. I knew then that I'd been fooling myself. She wasn't going to change her mind about me. Not without magical intervention.

Pil opened her mouth to say something else, but I cut her off. "Fifty years!" I yelled. "Tell me what changed after fifty years! Did I do something wrong? Or not do something I should have? After fifty years, I deserve to know!"

She yelled back at me, "Something wrong? Well, no, unless you count killing enough people to fill up a few towns. That might be a little bit wrong!"

"I'm not the only one here who's killed a town full of people."

Pil's face went red, and my rage dampened a bit. She had been forced to kill hundreds, although they were cursed to live half-dead and had wanted to die to end their suffering. Pil breathed, "I didn't choose that."

"Well, I was trapped in the Krak-damn-it-all Dark Lands and forced to kill there!"

"Hah!" She sneered. "You weren't sent there! You volunteered! You chose to kill all those people! So . . . hah!"

"I was protecting the people of every realm, and you know it!" I shouted.

"Do you know what it was like, living there with you? The first years were fine, because I still thought you could do nothing wrong, but after a while, it was like living with Death. Like I was in love with the God of Death. You had Harik's sword, and you were just like him!"

I felt all the blood run out of my face, and I stared at her with my mouth open.

Pil glared at me, breathing hard, and she didn't apologize or waver.

I stalked toward my horse, picking up Spot on the way. Grik and Talli pretended to rearrange things in Grik's saddlebags, and they didn't look at us.

Just before I mounted, Pil yelled, "Do you know what I wish? I wish that Harik had killed both of us in the Dark Lands when he killed Desh!"

I didn't look back at her.

Pil shouted, "I'll stay here with Kenzie! And I'll try to talk sense to the people of Scrip when they come chasing you. I'll start by not stabbing their new king to death!"

Talli said, "Duchess. They don't have a king now. Duchess Eldine is in charge. I think it's a nice—"

"Shut up!" Pil shouted, and her knife appeared in her hand, out of nowhere.

Grik lowered her voice to Talli and me. "Trutch and her mighty rod! Let's ride away before throats start getting cut!" She kicked her horse into a gallop.

Talli and I followed her east, and Spot rode in his sack. I tried to put Pil out of my mind but failed. Thinking about her made my teeth clench.

I breathed deep and focused. I needed to keep clear and ready for danger. We were traveling to intercept Margale, if my unsupported guess about his location was right.

THIRTY-ONE

alli, Grik, and I rode hard eastward toward Queen Apsel's capital, Brindine. It stood two days away, and I planned to catch Margale before dawn the second day. I also hoped to meet Vargo and Pocklin along the way so they could tell us whether Margale had turned off the path someplace.

We wore the horses down to an uncomfortable state, but it was a damn good thing we hurried. Pocklin would have died otherwise.

As the sun dropped the first day, my butt was tired, my joints hurt, and I felt every bit one-hundred and thirteen years old. But I still spotted the horse before the young women did, standing by itself far off the road, relaxed and eating summer grass as if he had never been touched by a bridle.

Talli shaded her eyes. "It's nothing but a stray horse. Next, you'll want to go poke a tree because it's standing by itself."

I said, "You two go ahead and hold Margale down if you want. I'll be along to kill him." I urged my mount into an easy canter toward the abandoned horse, which I soon saw was saddled. As I neared, Pocklin rose to his knees in the hip-high green grass and waved one hand before falling down again.

Grik galloped her horse past me. Before I had dismounted, she was kneeling over her father. He had taken an arrow in the upper leg.

"I'm happy to see even your grimy faces," he breathed, lying back on the ground. "The ass-flapping bastards ambushed us at sunset. Damn soldiers! I can't walk. I don't think I could crawl if wolves were chewing my feet."

"What about Vargo?" I asked.

"He led them off the other way, calling them everything but whores. They must have figured I was dead or about to be, because every one of them rode after him."

I nodded. "He's a gloomy fellow, but he'll never leave you in danger." Pocklin grunted as I tore his trousers around the wound. His leg was warm.

"It's bad, isn't it? Tell me if it's bad," Pocklin said.

"All right, I'll tell you. Pocklin, without magical healing, you won't live to see the sun set tomorrow." I rubbed my face, feeling wearier than I expected. "We're a day away from Kenzie, who's the only one who can help you. But I don't believe you can last a day."

"I know, you're right." He turned his face away. "Leave me alone here to die here, then," he said in a strained voice. I had seen actors less dramatic.

"Shut up!" Grik yelled, grabbing Pocklin's sleeve and shaking him.

He sucked in a breath. "Stop that! Gretta, you go on and kill some of those galloping turds that killed me." Then he gasped.

I looked around. Chexis was staring at Pocklin from over my shoulder.

Talli murmured, "You do move silently, Mr. Dragon. I didn't hear anything but the wind."

Chexis stretched his neck toward Pocklin. "Are you about to die?"

"The gods are calling me to them," he said.

Chexis stared.

After a few seconds, Pocklin said, "Yes, I'm dying."

The dragon sniffed. "You don't smell very good to eat."

Pocklin tried to scoot away on his butt. He screamed when his foot banged against the ground.

I said, "It's the leg, Chexis. You don't want to eat a rotten leg." I held my breath, wondering whether Chexis would eat the man. Maybe he figured nobody would miss Pocklin since he was about to die anyway.

Chexis swung his gaze toward me. "If I understand things correctly, the one with big hair . . . Kenzie . . . can save him the way she did me?"

I nodded. "She can probably save him. If she were here now, there'd be no doubt."

"Lie on your back, human," Chexis said, raising his head high and stepping to stand over Pocklin. "I'll carry you to her. You can close your eyes if you don't want to look into my groin."

"What?" Pocklin breathed, looking from Chexis to me. "What?"

I said, "Chexis, I fear the pain of flying may be too great for this man. The agony itself might kill him."

"Well . . ." Chexis showed his teeth. "Well, Ceslik burn it all." He sat on the ground almost like a dog. Spot, who had been sniffing around in the grass, sat up and looked at him.

"Wait!" Chexis shouted. The noise made my heart race. "I'll fly back and bring this woman Kenzie here. You won't have to stare into my groin at all!"

"That's . . . that's something to be grateful for," Pocklin stammered.

Chexis slammed his wings against the air with particular gusto, rose, and disappeared in less than a minute.

Without looking up from her father, Grik said, "Bib, go on. I'll stay with Daddy."

I nodded. "We need to ride fast, so that's best. Listen, if Chexis finds—"

Talli yanked at my arm. "Let's go. She doesn't want to hear your explanations. Tell them to your horse."

That felt a little abrupt, but I mounted. Then I said, "Wait!"

"There's a tree over there if you have to squat." Talli pointed at a tree about a mile away.

"I can't take a puppy along to kill a nasty stump like Margale," I said. "Grik, will you watch him for me?"

"Fine." Grik didn't look away from her father.

Talli and I rode east. She knew the city of Brindine well, having lived there for nearly two years. She had already devised a plan of attack for us.

The city stood on this side of a river and was walled on the other three sides. She would get us past the gate guards, who were all her friends, and then joke with them about how anxious she was to surprise Margale and give him his "welcome home" gift. They would snicker and tell her where he was. Then Talli would lead me sneaking down obscure back streets to Margale's location.

She'd distract the man. Then I'd kill him. According to Talli, all I had to handle was the murder. I could leave everything else to her.

I smiled but didn't comment or commit. A suspicion had been creeping around in my mind. Maybe Talli was the source of all these evil events and covered it by acting like a cheerful hell-raiser. She had been awfully helpful for no reason. Could Margale and everybody else really be working for her?

Just before sunset, I whistled, drew rein, and dismounted. Talli halted, and I loosened my sword as she trotted back to me.

"What's wrong?" Talli asked, sliding down from the saddle.

"Talli, does Margale work for you?"

"What?" she yelped.

"Are you the real villain here, giving Margale and everybody else orders?" I watched every detail of her reaction.

Her eyes widened. "No! That's insane! Who told you that?"

"Never mind. I just want to know if it's true."

"It is not!" She laughed. "Nobody works for me, and I don't work for anybody, and I like it that way. How could I give Margale orders, anyway? He doesn't listen to anyone except his beautiful, perfect queen." She glanced down. "That sounded a little snotty, I guess. Well . . . the bitch has a palace, so I bet she can stand an insult or two."

I waited to see what else she'd say.

"Did that answer your question?" she asked.

"One more. Are all these guards really your friends?"

"There aren't many I haven't gambled with and bought drinks for." She smiled. "Maybe not every single one of them's a friend, but at least there are no enemies."

I leaned forward. "When I go someplace where people might want to kill me—"

"Is there anyplace not like that?" she interrupted.

I stared at her for a moment. "I prefer not to go where big bunches of those people gather. Like these gates, no matter how many of the guards are your friends."

"All right, do you want to hop over the wall?"

"Does it have climbing handles?"

"No, I was being sarcastic, you asshole. That leaves the riverside. The current's too fast to swim." She sighed, staring at the ground. "We could ride our horses upriver, steal a boat, float down, and tie up someplace along the shore."

I stared out across the grass to think about it.

"You remind me of my father," Talli said.

"I'm sorry, what was that?" I didn't look back at her, because I didn't want her to see how surprised I probably looked.

"My father. You're like him."

"He was a cruel sorcerer too, then."

"No, he was a priest. The head priest."

This time I looked back with my eyebrows raised. "I can't think of a single thing I've ever done that would make me priestly."

"That's not really it." Talli frowned. After a pause, she said, "When you asked if the guards are really my friends, that's something my father would have said."

I didn't comment. Talli was telling me a lot about herself, maybe to draw information out of me.

"He always thought my friends were bad." She snorted. "I haven't seen the holy old boulder in years. If he saw my friends now, it would strike him dead from shame!" She waited, maybe expecting me to declare that I was her friend.

"Let's get back to this plan," I said.

"I'm his only daughter," Talli pushed on. "Do you have any daughters?"

Both my girls were dead, but I didn't want to say much to this woman about that. "I have two. Let's—"

"I thought so!" She slapped her leg. "I'll bet you don't make them call you 'Father,' do you?"

"Nope. Are we settled on the plan?"

"Wait, I'm imagining you as a daddy! What are their names? Are they grown?"

"We need to go." I walked toward my horse.

"Come on, Bib. I won't move a foot until you tell me that much!"

I turned to face her and couldn't help but imagine four different ways to kill her. I guess it showed, because she leaned away from me.

"Since you're asking," I said, "I killed hundreds of people for Harik so I could save my first girl's life, but she died anyway. It was simpler with the second. I murdered her myself." I waited, but Talli didn't say anything. "Maybe you ought to appreciate the father you've got."

I mounted and rode on, angling to strike the river just south of Brindine. I didn't look for Talli but counted on her to follow. She seemed like a youngster with bad judgment and a desire to raise hell. People probably described me that way, once. It didn't feel as if she was the evil behind all these terrible events.

That just made me more suspicious.

THIRTY-TWO

Talli and I rested the horses once in a while throughout the night. It delayed us enough that we reached the river past sunset, but with light still in the sky. The wind had swung from the south, making the air even cooler than last night's. The damp, muddy smell of water weeds drifted over us, and enough trees grew that we might have lost our way had it been full dark.

Talli spotted a rough wooden hut with a rowboat on the bank, and I found a fisherman out front weaving a basket in the dim light. He was a young fellow named Hune with eyes that screamed suspicion. That changed when I offered to trade him our horses for his shabby boat. If he traded cleverly, he could sell those beasts for enough to buy six new boats like his.

For the next few minutes, I became Hune's best friend. He brought us into his hut and offered us bread. His wife lit a stubby candle using a stick from the firepit in the middle of the dirt floor. The smoke escaped through a hole in the roof, but not before it wandered around inside for a while.

Hune offered to give me nets, hooks, and a heavy club for especially stubborn fish. He tried to put them in my hands because my new boat would be useless to me without those things. His wife suggested that Talli might like some clean clothes, since hers were filthy from the road. We declined everything, but they kept offering. His wife even began taking off her dress for Talli, since it was the nicest one she owned. Two little girls stared at all this from under a table.

We accepted one basket to hold our fish.

The sky had gone black and moonless but full of stars by the time we rowed out onto the wide river. Talli hadn't lied; the water was swift.

"Stay left!" Talli called out, even though we were sitting side by side. "We want to go aground between the two ferries, but we have to move fast!"

A few minutes later, Talli yelled, "Now!" She backed her oar, and I rowed like a demon. Then we ground onto the riverbank. I jumped out and pulled the boat higher onto the sticky clay and dirt.

The riverbank was a dozen feet lower than Brindine itself. A sheer drop separated the two. I saw where floods had washed against the raw wall. However, just a few feet downriver, we found a well-made wooden stairway set into the wall, leading from water up to the city.

Talli pushed ahead of me up the stairs, then jerked to a stop. "Rob? Rob, I'm back in town! Where's the game tonight?"

"The Lamb," came a man's deep, relaxed voice. "You're coming up from the water, and that's odd for you, Miss Tal. Why is that?"

"Hell, you know how unpredictable I am," she said.

I was still behind Talli, partway down the stairs, and couldn't see past her.

"Boys, Talli's here!" Rob yelled.

At least a half dozen voices answered, and they sounded happy about her arrival.

Talli stepped up onto the ground. "If you just have to know, I met a secret sweetheart at the riverbank this evening."

"Who is he?" a man asked.

"Where is he?" asked another.

"Oh, I suppose he's still down there crying," she said.

Men laughed. I poked my head up just enough to see that Talli faced a semicircle of eight armed men, three carrying torches. Two more torches threw a bit of light from a building thirty feet away. I eased my sword out of the scabbard.

"We missed you—and your money!" Some man laughed hard at his own joke.

Talli laughed too. "I'll meet you boys at the Lamb tonight, then. You can buy me a drink!"

"Wait," Rob said. "Margale gave instructions saying that when you come home, we're to bring you straight to him."

"That's sweet!" Talli said. "But I'm headed to see him right now. You fellows don't need to wear out boot leather for me."

"Well . . . he was specific in his orders. And he's been in a bad mood lately. I don't like to piss him off," Rob said.

"But I wanted to surprise him!" Talli said. "I brought him a gift!" Placing her left hand behind her back, Talli held out her palm toward me, a sign for me to stop.

Three more guards arrived, one with a torch.

"I'm sorry, Talli," Rob said. "You've got to come with us. But nobody said we can't joke and talk shit on the way."

I thought hard for a couple of seconds. Maybe I should let them take Talli. At least some of these guards would probably go with her and Rob. I could fight my way through the rest, disappear into the darkened city, and start hunting for Margale.

Or maybe I should follow Rob and his gang as they dragged Talli off to Margale. I'd have to kill any they left behind to keep them from calling out, but Rob and his friends would lead me straight to my enemy.

Talli showed me her palm signal again, this time so hard I thought she'd sprain her wrist.

"All right, Rob, I'll come along," Talli said. "But I want to surprise Margale with my gift! Don't give me away, all right? I mean, he didn't command you to announce me, did he?"

"No. I guess we can do that," Rob said. "Come on, walk beside me. I'll tell you about the riot at the Grapes three nights ago."

Rob led Talli into what looked like a wide paved square. Seven guards walked along behind them, leaving three men guarding the stairs. I wished I could leave these three men alive, but witnesses might be fatal to our endeavor.

I gave Talli and her escorts half a minute to walk away, then I ran up the last three steps. Bounding to the closest man, who was facing away from me, I slashed through the back of his neck. Before he had fallen, I turned and slashed through the front of his friend's neck. Both were dead or dying before they could yell.

I saw the third guard's eyes, huge in the light from the torch he held. He threw the torch at me and lunged to cut my wrist. I leaned aside to avoid him and thrust my sword hard into his throat. Like his friends, he went down before he could raise any alarm.

I stripped off the least bloody shirt and grabbed a guard's helmet, then threw the torch over the little cliff first. The three bodies followed the torch over. I spotted the three torches of Talli's honor guard far across the square and ran after them, shrugging into the guard's shirt and plonking the helmet on my head as I went.

If anybody had noticed all the killing and clothes-changing, they hadn't stopped to speak up. I hustled across the square after Talli and the men, trying to match the pace of a guard who had eaten something bad and was hurrying to the privy.

Talli's drinking buddies with torches gave me a fine trail to follow. Then they turned right onto a street and disappeared while I was still trailing them by sixty or seventy paces. Suddenly I needed that hypothetical privy twice as bad and twice as soon, so I ran like hell.

Rushing around the corner, I chased Talli's escort but skidded to a stop when I saw them just standing sixty feet away. I backed out so I could watch from the corner.

The laughing guards had gathered in a loose circle around Talli, and she was laughing too. By torchlight I saw that her feet were spread as if she were riding a horse.

"And then I told him to pull on the right ear to make the horse go right." She yanked at her imaginary horse's invisible right ear, spun on her right foot, and fell onto the street.

"What happened to him?" a man asked between chuckles.

"Do you mean after the horse stepped on his dick?" Talli asked.

Everybody laughed.

"He jumped up and ran away bent over, holding his crotch, and I never saw him again," Talli said. "If I ever see Goat Boy again, he'd better have my seven bits."

The soldiers ushered Talli down the street again as the laughs turned into friendly insults. She called out, "Goodbye, Goat Boy!" while waving her hand high over her head. Men chuckled. Then she glanced back down the road toward me, still waving, before smiling at one of the guards behind her.

I whispered, "Shit, if she's evil, I need to work with more evil people."

I had no trouble following the herd of happy guards for several more minutes and even caught up to within thirty feet of them. What passerby would challenge me, one guard among a group of nine, even if I walked a little slow?

At last, we reached a granite building about forty feet tall, if the torches on the roof could be trusted. One side of the building disappeared into darkness as we passed it. We walked along the building's front for fifty paces or so. I assumed it was the front, since I saw guarded doors ahead on the left.

Hale had lived in a working castle, prepared to defend itself and its people. Queen Apsel lived in a palace, prepared to sit there, look impressive, and house a lot of servants. Apsel obviously relied on her city's walls and the river to deal with attackers. The guards at the palace gate might be forgiven for not guarding with much urgency.

Rob and Talli greeted the guards, who waved them through. Then they waved the other guards through. I trotted inside fifteen feet behind them, and the gate guards waved me through without looking too hard. They saw a uniform shirt and a guard's helmet, and that was good enough for them.

"This is too easy," I whispered to myself. "She's leading me into a trap."

Talli chattered along a hallway, up two staircases, and down another hallway. As she neared a closed wooden door on the right, Talli shushed all the guards and thanked them in whispers, even kissing two of them. I edged forward with my head down, partly turned to the wall to hide my face from the guards who had already begun drifting back down the corridor.

Talli reached for the door latch with Rob standing beside her. I had edged up across the hall so that I'd be able to see some of the room when Talli opened the door. I drew my sword as silently as possible, hesitated, and drew my knife too.

Talli stood in the doorway and said, "Hello, sweetheart," in a voice that sounded like she meant it.

The room wasn't well lit, but I could make out the edge of Margale's form standing fifteen feet from the door. I couldn't see his face, though. He turned toward Talli and said in a flat voice, "Well. I was worried about you."

"I missed you too," Talli said. "Come on, embrace me!" She held out both arms. She had a knife tucked into her belt at the small of her back, and I swore it wasn't there earlier.

Talli strolled into the room. Looking back, I can't imagine anything more logical for her to do, but her second step led to a lot of pain. She walked at an angle, I guess to make sure Margale couldn't see her back and the knife hidden there. But that step unblocked the doorway.

Margale looked out into the hall and gaped at me.

I felt sure Talli would kill Margale if she could. But she was really the diversion. She had said, more than once, that Margale would be my responsibility. I charged through the door just as Talli ran toward him. She pointed at me with her left hand and screamed, "Margale, help me!"

Margale took one great step and knocked Talli aside with his left arm. At the same time, he reached up to grab the dragon-crushing club off his back. I flung my knife on the run and stuck it in his right forearm. He stopped doing much with that hand, at least for the moment.

I rushed farther into the smoky wood-paneled room. Talli had staggered hard against a cabinet on the wall, and I saw it fall over. A few paces to my left stood the thin dark-haired red-robed woman. She was leaning over Vargo, who was bound to a wooden chair by ropes. Vargo's face was bloody and bruised. He'd been beaten in a professional manner.

I took all this in during two steps.

Vargo slurred, "Bib! Run!"

I swung to lop off Margale's head. It was a simple stroke, but he was shockingly fast for a big man. He saved himself by shifting aside and ducking. I thrust at his chest, but he caught my blade with his gloved hands and held the sword's point away from him. Blood began oozing from his gloves.

Maybe Margale expected me to yank my sword away and slice his hands some more, but I wanted to take his life more than I desired anything else. I dropped my weight and used the leverage to shove my sword's point up, almost touching Margale's throat. His strength stopped me there, but his arms were shaking, and his hands began trickling blood.

Talli had scrambled around the fallen cabinet.

The thin woman with Vargo shouted, "Stop, sorcerer, or I'll kill him!" She stood behind Vargo, gripping the man's hair with one hand and pressing a curved knife to his throat.

Margale grunted, "Surrender and I'll let him go."

Vargo shouted, "Don't give up!"

The woman yanked his head back and ran the knife around his throat, drawing a thin line of blood.

I intended to kill Margale. Hell, I yearned to do it, more than I had needed to take any life in a long time. I gathered myself for an irresistible thrust. Margale might be four times stronger than me, but my leverage was vastly greater than his.

I kept up the pressure against Margale's hands, but I hesitated. This woman was about to take Vargo away from his children and his wife. I imagined telling Kenzie how he'd died. Hell, could I surrender right this moment and find another moment later to kill Margale? Maybe, and maybe I should. I snarled but couldn't make myself drop my sword.

I shouted at the thin woman, "What did you say?"

The woman yelled, "I said, surrender or he dies!"

Sometime in between the words *surrender* and *dies*, Margale's shoulders shifted a bit—he was about to shove my sword aside. I pushed first and thrust my sword an inch deep into the underside of Margale's jaw. I wanted to jam the steel all the way to his spine but stopped myself. He bellowed like a calf as blood began running down the front of his neck.

After a moment, I yanked my sword out of Margale's jaw, but I stayed close enough to thrust into him without taking a step. His palms were leaking blood.

I held up my free hand and smiled without looking at the woman. "I accept your terms! Sorry, I'm old. I didn't understand you right away."

I stepped back but kept my sword trained on Margale, and I pointed at Vargo with my other hand. "When he's free and gone, I'll surrender."

Talli stepped forward, her brow creased and her mouth tight. She looked like she might cry and was actually wringing her hands as she said, "Margale, what can I do to help?"

"Nothing. Just stand there and brighten the room," he grunted, holding his dripping chin with his dripping hand. "Cut the man loose, Parbett." Margale yelled, "Rob!"

The soldier was standing in the doorway with his mouth dangling open, but he stiffened to attention.

Margale said, "Take a couple of men and escort this prisoner outside the city. I mean it. No tricks."

Once Vargo had been cut free, Rob and two men hustled him out of the room.

Margale glared at me. If anything, his brow seemed to overhang more than I remembered. "Surrender, Bib, and do it right now. Back away and drop your sword."

I retreated a step and laid my sword down in front of me. "Well, you have me, you dickless imitation of a hippo. Do you know what to do with me, you mountain of bad cheese?" I was already thinking of more ways to kill him.

Margale shook his right hand, flinging blood, before twitching a few fingers. The floor seemed to melt, crawl up to my knees, and set into stone again. It held my feet tight. Before I could reach for my sword, more stone stretched up from the floor to hold my hands in place with a layer as thick as my finger. It would be a damn fine trap for most sorcerers, but I had other methods of employing magic.

Talli smiled at Margale but had tears on her cheeks. "Darling, I'm sorry. This bastard Bib must have followed me here. Ask Rob, he'll vouch for that. Your poor hands! And your jaw! Thank you for defeating him." She held out her arms, and Margale turned to embrace her, laying his cheek on top of her head.

"Oh, I missed this," Talli said, snuggling into his chest. She twisted a little, then Margale pushed her away from him, holding her by the throat with one huge bloody hand. She was gripping a knife in her right hand, but he held her so far away she couldn't reach his body.

Talli slashed the arm Margale was using to hold her, and he growled. He grabbed the wrist of her knife hand and wrenched it. I heard the bones crack, and her hand went limp, but not before he plucked the knife out of it.

Talli shouted, "You bastard!"

Margale stabbed Talli in the stomach.

She sucked air and stiffened. "You—"

He stabbed Talli three more times and dropped her on the floor. She fell on her side, staring straight ahead.

She murmured, "No, no, no . . ." It sounded like a bird cry.

"Well, that's done with," Margale said, as if he'd just finished throwing out what was left of his supper. He turned back to me with Talli's bloodstained knife still in his hand. He didn't see Talli stop breathing with her eyes open and her right wrist bent sideways.

I strained against the stone holding me but couldn't shift it. I didn't bother yelling at Margale. Talli had died as much because of me as because of him. Maybe more. If I had killed the ponderous son of a bitch when I had my sword inside him, she probably would have lived, although Vargo would have been murdered.

I had more than enough power to call several yellow bands into being and fling them out to find every dog in the palace. As I pulled bands, I sneered at Margale. "Since you murdered Talli, I'll keep calling you a bastard on her behalf."

"You won't do that for long," Parbett said from beside my head. Then she licked my neck. "I'll be killing you in a minute."

"Can't do it," Margale said. "He has to be alive when I start cutting him into pieces." Both Parbett and I looked at him. He shrugged. "Don't ask. We'll take him to the kitchen. Guards! Haul this body away and send someone to clean up in here."

Two guards picked up Talli like she was a dirty rug. Before I could pull bands to call all the dogs near the palace, if there were any, somebody hit me on the back of the head and the world went away.

THIRTY-THREE

Margale did not wake me up by sawing through my leg or my arm. It wouldn't have been my first dismemberment, but I was happy to avoid it this time.

When I opened my eyes, my face was wet, and Parbett was smirking at me with her skinny lips. Then she nibbled my ear.

"He killed Hale?" some woman behind me asked. "Truly?"

I spoke up. "Yep, I put six inches of steel in his heart." I blinked some water away. "Would you like to see how I did it?"

The woman, who I figured was the queen, walked around to face me, her green silk skirt swishing at her feet. She was tall and lithe, with ash-blond hair and slanting green eyes. She examined me. Even with one eye squinting and her lips pursed, she was an exceptionally beautiful woman.

"He doesn't sound as if he's afraid," she said.

Margale walked up beside her, watching me. He had a tight jaw and a huge crease between his eyebrows. I expected more hatred for me in his eyes, especially since I had cut him up quite a bit, but he frowned like I was no more than a fox eating his chickens.

That was fine with me. He'd be even more surprised when I destroyed him with the magic that he thought I couldn't use.

Margale said, "Please stand away, Your Majesty. For your safety." He turned to the queen, and his face settled into adoration that was almost doglike.

Talli had made Margale's love for the queen sound distasteful, but watching his profound obeisance made my stomach shaky.

I focused on Apsel. "He's right, Your Majesty, beware the danger. I spit acid, and I can spit a good forty feet." My feet and hands were still bound by stone. I strained and thought I could feel the stone around my hands shift.

Margale said, "Parbett, go prepare things in the kitchen."

The sorceress sauntered past me toward the door, slapping my ass as she went.

My dogs had gone wandering while I was asleep, but I pulled several bands to gather them back. It brought my reserve of power low, close to two squares, but I still had enough for a few feats.

Apsel took one step back from me. "Margale, it pleases me that you didn't kill Hale yourself. He was awful, but he was my cousin. If you had murdered him, I don't think I could bear to look at you." She smiled at Margale. He closed his eyes and let out a breath.

Now that I had time to examine the room, I saw two doors. One closed door led into the hallway. The other door stood open, and I could see a chamber beyond it. I counted five guards in my room. I also counted a teenage boy and two younger girls in fine clothes.

"You must be the prince," I said to the boy. "If you watch closely, you'll get a lesson on dealing with dangerous men."

The queen laughed and beckoned to the boy. "He is an excellent student! We often enjoy lessons like this. Margale, this man could be useful. What do you think, Your Highness?"

The prince examined Margale but didn't even glance at me. "I think he could be. Look at Margale. This man sliced him up like a goose on the table."

Margale blushed and looked at the floor. "Please don't let him live, Your Majesty."

Apsel looked to be about ten years older than Margale. I tried to imagine him as a giant fumbling teenager around her. Hell, at twenty-five, her beauty had probably been astounding. Young Margale never had a chance.

I didn't give a shit. He had to die. "Your Majesty, I would admire being useful to you. I have skills that allow me to perform services that your other servants might find too challenging."

"Hm. Margale, who else needs to be assassinated?" Apsel asked.

"No, Your Majesty!"

The queen's eyebrows lifted. "No?"

"I mean, please no. You can't imagine how dangerous this man is. You wouldn't believe the way he lies."

"That's not true!" I said. "The lying part's not. The rest . . ." I shrugged.

Everybody in the room looked at the hallway door at the same time. I heard barking.

The queen walked toward the door. "What is that?"

Margale shouted, "It's him!" He grabbed Apsel by the arm and hauled her away from the door. The barking had grown louder.

One of the guards reached to open the door. Margale shouted, but the man's curiosity lifted the latch.

Six dogs rushed into the room before I took a breath. Three were the huge lazy dogs that kings and queens loved. They weren't lazy now. All of the dogs believed that this room was full of other fun dogs to frolic with and plenty of butts to sniff. Sniffing human butts and crotches was just as good.

Every person but me and one little girl was shouting useless observations or commands. The little girl was laughing and chasing the dogs.

While everybody else was distracted, I yanked my stone-bound hands toward my ribs as fast and hard as I could. The stone cracked. After two more yanks, I could see my wrists through the cracks. I hauled my hands toward me, and they slipped out of my soft gloves, which stayed behind in the stone.

Margale was shoving Apsel, the prince, and a girl through the door into the next room, The younger girl was trying to ride a dog nearly as tall as she was.

Margale must have seen me breaking free. More stone rushed up from the floor and created a box that covered all of me except for my head, which stuck up through a hole.

"Cut his head off!" Margale yelled to the guards. The men all looked at me, but none jumped right over to kill me just yet.

I didn't have time to sigh, but I felt like it. I created six more yellow bands for the dogs in the room, shifting the promised fun to the chamber Margale had used to retreat. The dogs bounded that way. One of the hounds needed to take along her new friend, the little girl. Margale had been peeking out through the crack. When five dogs slammed into the door, it burst open.

One of the guards swung at my head, so I ducked into the box. The hole was so tight I scraped my ears and nose raw. I popped my head back up just far enough to see the last dog pull the girl through the door. I ducked my head back down to evade another sword, but the swing knocked Pil's fire-shedding hat off my head. I heard the door slam.

A guard yelled, "Stab him! Stab him down through that hole!"

I hated to hear that because it meant I was about to burn most of my remaining power. I pushed myself against one side of the stone box in case the guards started jamming swords down at me. Then I summoned four red bands and flung one toward each wood-paneled wall.

The bands created astounding pressure in the paneling in almost an instant. All the room's wooden walls exploded, hurling big splinters, small splinters, and wood chunks in every direction across the whole space. The noise was horrendous, which made me happy since I had spent almost all my power. The clatter of falling wood died away.

I waited. The door to the next room opened. I heard the queen say, "Krak. Trutch and Harik. I can't—" The door slammed shut.

I poked my head up. All five guards were dead, and rarely had I seen such butchery. I doubted that any of them could be recognized.

From the next room, Queen Apsel screamed, "Send him away! Give him gold and a horse!"

Margale said something I couldn't make out.

"No! You said he was dangerous! He could have killed my children, but he didn't! He can be reasoned with! But if he can do that from inside a stone box, what else can he do? Reward him and just hope we never see him again!"

"You won't be safe!" Margale shouted. "You're vulnerable, Your Majesty!"

"You will obey my commands! Protecting my children is more important than anything!"

"People use them against you. You can always have more! You're young!"

I began thinking about how to get a horse in here to kick apart this stone box.

Both rooms were silent for several seconds. Then the queen screamed. She kept screaming.

Margale said something and opened the door. Apsel was still screaming, and I thought she might ruin her voice. I saw the youngest girl unmoving on the floor with smoke wisping from one ear.

Margale said, "Goodbye, Bib. I know that Harik will torture you forever." He twitched three fingers toward me.

Nothing happened.

He examined my face and then scanned the room. "Ah, your shirt's enchanted. That won't save you." He stepped back into the other room and closed the door.

Margale wouldn't leave the room if he planned to hurt me by bending something. That meant he planned to burn me. Rock was the only thing around me that wasn't enchanted. It was hard to burn, but anything would burn if it got hot enough.

I rushed to pull my right hand up into my sleeve, and I held the cuff closed from the inside. Then I pulled my shirt up over my head and held the collar closed with my left hand.

The stone might not have burned white-hot. That would have taken a horrible amount of energy. But it burned hot enough for me to see light through my shirt. My exposed left hand must have been shredded by the couple of seconds the heat pounded it. Calling it agony didn't do it justice. The pain was so great I couldn't see, which might have been all right since I didn't think I could stand to look at my hand.

After a couple of breaths, I forced myself to stand and look around. The stone box was entirely destroyed, and my feet weren't held to the ground anymore. I stumbled toward the middle of the room and almost tripped over my sword. It had survived the great burning, since it too was enchanted. I picked the thing up and held it as if I might do something with it, a laughable thought.

Margale opened the door and stared at me, shaking his head and working his jaw from side to side. He glared at me and said, "You're crying, you stubborn lump, so I must have hurt you a little. I'll hurt you a lot now." He pulled the god-club off his back.

I should have run, I guess, but I didn't think I could get far before I fell over. I couldn't fight him. I couldn't fight an angry piglet just then. I considered dropping to my knees and promising to serve him forever, but of course he'd see through that lie.

Before Margale could take two steps and smash out my brains, he stiffened and yelled, "Dammit! You bastard!"

When he turned, I saw Apsel holding the bloody knife that she had jammed into him below the right shoulder blade. Her face was a cry of contempt and grief.

Margale's face held just as much pain and sorrow. "Why?"

The queen's eyes stretched wide, and she shook her head slowly. "Guards!" she shouted. "Seize Margale! He's right here!"

Margale's head dropped. I felt him leave his body to trade with the gods, but I wasn't quick enough to grab on.

Margale straightened and trained a ponderous, iron-hard glare on Apsel. "You'll regret what you've lost here."

"I already do!" she shrieked.

Margale crashed into a guard coming in the doorway and flung him across the hall. The man hit the wall and sagged. Margale slammed the end of his club into the guard's stomach and ran, leaving the man to die.

I didn't know what to say to Apsel, but she wandered back to her dead children as if nothing else existed. Looking around, I found one chair in the room—the one Vargo had been beaten in. I slumped into it and let my head hang backward.

THIRTY-FOUR

As I sat back in Margale's former torture chair, I felt my body warning me that it was time to stop talking, seeing, and doing things for a while. But before I oozed into a sorcerer-shaped puddle, I needed to answer two questions for myself.

First, was I going to kill Margale?

My gut said of course I was. How could I even ask that question? Well, Margale had almost killed me more than once, so stopping to ask myself that question was a damn fine thing to do.

Margale was a hairy ape's ass of a criminal, no doubt about that. He was also insane. Maybe he hadn't been when I met him, but now if he thought Apsel would pat him on the head for killing her children and then skip off with him to make some more, he had lost his mind.

A lot of things can make a person crazy, but bad deals with the gods may be the quickest. The gods are happy to deceive, threaten, and bleed sorcerers who are desperate or greedy for power.

An artistic god won't take away the thing that a sorcerer loves most. He will gradually take other things to distract him or harm his judgment. Once the sorcerer is too damaged to bargain well, the god will force deals that leave the sorcerer unfeeling, desperate, or deranged. An artistic god will turn the sorcerer into the opposite of what he was when all this trading started.

What had Margale been like before he ever met a god? Kind? Loyal? Good company? In the end, an artistic god will let the sorcerer keep the thing he loves but take away everything that would allow him to appreciate it, or even be near it.

It would be nice if the gods would get a different hobby.

So, Margale had access to an extraordinary amount of power, he was crazy as hell, and he didn't like me at all. A smart man would get on his horse and ride to a kingdom with nice beaches.

But Margale had commanded me to commit murder. Only gods were allowed to do that. He had also slain a good number of Arborswit's people. Most of them were guilty of no more than petty wickedness, and they sure as hell didn't deserve to burn alive.

So yes, I would chase down Margale and kill the shit out of him.

That led to my second question. How would I kill him? It would be nice to have a plan other than ride fast, catch up, and stab him until he falls down.

And that led me to the task I had been dreading. I would need power to kill that mad sorcerer, and I had practically none left. I lifted myself upward toward the trading place and called, "Mighty Gorlana, I come to trade!"

I arrived at my normal spot. Mud and dark water squished around my feet. Dank greenish clouds hung above me, and mist hid everything much past the gazebo. The air was so wet it felt like being hit in the face with a hot soaked towel.

I found myself staring into Baby Harik's eyes. He leaned toward me from the lowest level of the gazebo with his hands on his hips.

"I still own you, Murderer." The God of Death snorted and then laughed. "You don't belong to the she-pig of mercy yet, and it looks like you never will! Thirty-two! You've killed thirty-two more people than you've spared!"

"Did you say 'She-pig of mercy,' Baby Harik? I admire your grit! You stand there looking powerful and wise, ignoring the fact that you just uttered one of the saddest and most pathetic insults I have ever heard."

Baby Harik shook his head. "You came calling on me, so you must want something."

"You could have said 'Dour and prissy she-pig,' or 'Drooling she-pig of the damned.'"

"Do you want something or not?"

"Or 'Mumbling she-pig of spite and pointlessness.'"

"Stop."

"Witless mercy-whore who couldn't tell a diamond from a rat's asshole."

Baby Harik jumped to the ground, leaned in, and shouted into my face from inches away, "Shut! Up!"

I managed not to grin. "Baby Harik, in exchange for nine squares of power, I'll provide you one hundred unique insults, each one tailored to a specific recipient."

Baby Harik stood back and rolled his eyes before he returned to the gazebo, jumping four feet to the lowest level with such ease he seemed to float. "I don't need your brain for insults."

"Then . . . I yield to you the honor of making the first offer. The first offer for a second time, since I made the first, first just offer a minute ago."

Baby Harik frowned at me, a crease between his brows. Then a wide grin took over his face. "Say, fighting the Avalanche is pretty challenging, eh?"

I swallowed my irritation. Losing my temper would lead to bad trades. "I expect I'll kill him soon," I said.

"Maybe I could make it easier. I can tell you the Avalanche's true name. Imagine the look on his face when you bind him." Baby Harik smiled.

I knew I should rush to turn down that offer. Despite Margale's craziness, I'd bet that he was a good sight smarter than me. However, I did not tell Baby Harik no. "What do you want in trade for that knowledge?"

"You should be comfortable with this. You will kill people for me."

"A number that only you know?"

"Exactly."

I sneered and told him to take his offer and do something with three apes and a rowboat with it.

Baby Harik shrugged. "If you don't like that, how about this? For the next two days, you'll kill whoever—"

"No!"

"For one day?"

"I won't kill who you say to kill, nor kill how many you tell me to kill."

"Murderer, that excludes ninety-five percent of the possible trades. You're taking the fun out of it." Baby Harik smiled like he was having fun, no matter what he said.

"Forget Margale's true name, I'd just get myself killed with it," I said.

"Maybe not. You might only get some of your friends killed."

I tried not to clench my fists, since it would show him how angry I was. "Pretend I said that thing with the apes and the rowboat again. I want to trade for power. Whose turn is it to make an offer? I lost track."

"Yours. Even if it's not your turn, it's your turn now."

I nodded. "I want eight squares. In exchange, I won't ride a horse for a month."

Baby Harik shook his head, grinning.

"Six squares and no horse riding for a month?"

"Nope," he said.

"Eight squares and no horse riding for a year?"

Baby Harik squinted at me with one eye for a few seconds before saying, "No. What's this business about a horse? Who cares about horses?"

"Riding is important," I said. "We don't have magic chariots like you gods do."

Baby Harik closed his eyes and stretched, reminding me of a cat. "You should see my chariot. No, you shouldn't. It's too exquisite for human eyes to behold."

Anger grabbed at my throat. "All right, I'll stop thinking about it if you'll stop being an oily barrel full of twisted rat members." This wasn't going anywhere. Maybe Harik was just screwing with me.

Baby Harik said, "When this dumb contest with Gorlana ends and she has lost, you'll still get the charm to make the Knife love you again."

"And?" I muttered.

"You can have nine squares if you do not ever use it. You'll have to carry it with you until you die, but never use it." His eyes grew bright, and one eyelid twitched as if he might wink.

I worked my jaw but didn't say anything as all my anger dried like a dead lizard in the sun. I realized I had still been counting on Pil to change her mind.

The charm had to be some god-conjured bullshit to confuse me. But what if Gorlana wasn't lying? She was known not to lie more than half the time. If I traded wisely, I could count on the charm to make things good again. That was what magic was for. Making things happen that wouldn't normally happen.

"Well?" Baby Harik asked. "Don't think too long, the offer might expire!"

I knew I should turn my back on Baby Harik's deal, but without power I might well fail and die. Hell, Pil might die too. I started to tell Baby Harik to climb up his own butt. Instead, I said, "I want to sell you an option."

"What?" Baby Harik yelled, but his eyes widened like I was something good to eat.

"At the end of the contest, if Gorlana has lost, you may, if you choose, compel me to always carry the charm and never use it. In exchange, you'll give me eight squares now."

"That's ridiculous enough to . . . well, why would I do that?" Baby Harik asked. "Instead, I could ignore this option business and compel you if I win the contest. That would cost me no squares at all, thank you very much."

"Think of it like this. When you win, your option means you're not locked into the deal we make now. If something better has come along, you don't have to be excluded. You'll be free to negotiate that deal. Or not. The choice will be yours."

I held my breath and hoped that Baby Harik was too distracted by the fear of not missing out on something to realize I wasn't offering him much of a deal. Everybody was prey to greed for something. They especially feared missing the chance to get the thing they craved. Gods were no different.

The far southwestern kingdoms used options in horse trading, and that's where I'd learned about the practice. For a small fee, a trader might buy an option on a foal, giving him the right to purchase the horse for two gold coins when it turned one year old. If the horse was worth three gold coins by then, the trader would do well. If it wasn't, the trader didn't have to buy the dang horse and could keep his gold coins—it was his option.

"Option? No, that's ridiculous," Baby Harik said. "If I win, I want to win. I don't want to negotiate something new."

"Do you think you're that likely to lose?" I asked.

"No." He grinned at me. "If you really want to sell me this option, then if Gorlana loses, which she will, you'll never use the charm . . . and you'll also kill an unspecified number of people for me."

"No. Pardon me, I now realize that you can't understand simple words like *no* because you speak by farting and peasant dancing."

"Nice," Baby Harik said. "How many will you kill for me, then? I warn you now, you won't take any power home with you today unless you agree to some killings."

I managed not to hang my head. What would Pil think of the thing I was about to say? "I'll kill ten, but not until the contest is over."

"You whiner! You're not as smart as you think," Baby Harik said. "All right, a thousand killings in exchange for three squares."

"Fifty killings for twelve squares."

Baby Harik's eyes bugged as if he'd swallowed something sharp. "No, five hundred for five squares. You see the logic there, right? One square for each hundred murders."

"So a hundred killings for ten squares."

"No, that would be a thousand for ten squares." Baby Harik shook his head.

I shrugged. "I'm bad at math. Ten squares, a hundred killings."

Baby Harik scowled and muttered, "Bad at math? You mule's ass!"

"All right, a hundred and one, a number that's strong as hell, for seven squares, which is equally strong. And if you can't accept this, we can't do business. I've killed plenty of nasty types with no magic at all."

Baby Harik stared at the ceiling of the gazebo. "What does that come to? I just want to know whether you know."

"If Gorlana wins, you get nothing, and I become hers. If she loses, I'll come work for you for four hundred and ninety-nine days, and I'll kill a hundred and one people for you, starting when the contest ends. Also, if she loses, I'll carry the charm the rest of my life but never use it. Of course, it will be your option on me killing the hundred and one people and carrying the charm. Maybe you'll want something else by then."

Baby Harik showed his crooked-tooth grin. "I'll offer you seven squares for this option of yours."

"Nine."

"You said seven!"

"All right, eight," I said.

"Done." Baby Harik sat on a marble bench and applauded. "Go on, Murderer, go win this contest for me! You're so far ahead, I don't think I can lose. I'm sure I won't!"

Before he could throw me back into my body, I shouted, "Wait! Tell me about the Avalanche!"

"Oh!" Baby Harik snorted. "You want me to help you kill the Avalanche. He's a torrent of destruction, so I don't have much reason to help you kill him, do I?"

"I can trade. I'll give you one killing for every question you answer, no matter who wins the contest." I silently apologized to Pil, then wondered why.

Baby Harik stood again. "One death? No, it'll be twenty for each question."

"Five deaths!"

Baby Harik hesitated. "Five deaths for each of the first three questions. For each question after that, you'll kill someone I name."

It looked as if I'd be asking only three questions. If I let Baby Harik choose a victim, it was sure to be someone I would hate to kill.

"All right, I agree. Where is the Avalanche right now?"

"He is in another realm, which he owns."

I blinked. I'm sure I looked like a guppy.

"Isn't that enticing?" Baby Harik asked. "Don't you want to know what it's like, how he got it, all that kind of thing?"

I took a breath. I could find out all that for myself when I got there. "How can I get to his realm?"

"Ooh, I'm not sure that I should say. It feels like cheating."

"Answer the question!" I snapped. I closed my eyes to control my anger. "Your Magnificence."

"Fine, if you're going to be rude about it. There's a river just east of you. Ride downstream a few miles. You'd better do it in the afternoon. Look for a tall tree split by lightning. While the sun is touching the horizon but before it disappears, ride into the river."

I raised an eyebrow. "Really?"

"Don't blame me, I didn't set it up that way."

I waited for more, but he just grinned at me. I said, "All right, I ride into the river."

"You could walk, or ride in a wagon. Or you could flop down the riverbank on your belly. Somebody could throw you. I think any of those would be fine."

"That's all you have to say about it." I was careful not to phrase it as a question.

"You asked me, and I answered you. What else should I say?"

I bit my tongue as I weighed all the things I still wanted to know about Margale. "Please tell me, in detail, how the Avalanche came to have two sorcery skills, burning and bending."

Baby Harik's lips pouted, but his eyes were hard. "That's more of a command than a question."

"I said please."

Baby Harik shrugged. "You have already asked two questions

and condemned ten people to die. Tell me, do you think those ten people are less important than anyone I could tell you to kill?"

"I guess not objectively, but they might be less important to me. It doesn't matter, because we agreed you wouldn't tell me who to kill until the fourth question." I crossed my arms until I realized what I was doing and uncrossed them.

Baby Harik said, "I don't remember it that way. No, we agreed that starting with the third question I would tell you who to kill. Do you have any witnesses to back up your story?"

My face was hot, and I could hear my heart thumping. "Pile of festering black turds!" I shouted. "Pathetic, cheating excuse for the divine. You're the cheapest, most ass-wagging creature in all the Gods' Realm!"

Baby Harik put a hand on his chest. "I like you too. I like you so much that I'll only answer your question if you ask me again. If you stay quiet, you won't be obliged to kill who I say, and I won't tell you what happened to the Avalanche. That's nice of me, right? But think about this. If you stick to our deal like a good sorcerer and kill who I want, you'll be saving the lives of four people. And you've already agreed that the people you choose to kill are no more important than anybody I might choose."

I pushed myself back toward my body, but Baby Harik snatched me again.

The god said, "Murderer, think hard about this. Can you defeat the Avalanche without knowing his secret? I don't think you can. If you fight him and lose, all your allies will die with you."

An image of Talli dying on the floor flashed in my mind. "I have conditions."

"Spit them out." Baby Harik sat again and stretched out his legs, crossing them at the ankles.

I was breathing fast, so I took a few slower breaths to calm myself. It made me feel as calm as a rabid badger. "You can't tell me to kill any children."

Baby Harik nodded, his eyes calm and his lips pressed together.

"You can't tell me to kill anybody I'm riding with these days. In fact, you can't tell me to kill anyone I've ever ridden with," I said.

"I never realized you were so sentimental." He waved a hand. "Fine. There's a place of power in the Avalanche's realm. He entered it and sacrificed whatever it is that places of power tell a man to sacrifice. I can't imagine what it was. He came out with two skills instead of one."

"All right," I breathed. "I'll find out more when I get there."

"Now, let me tell you who to kill." Baby Harik leaned forward and slapped both his knees. "You may not laugh about it now, but you will later. Kill that dragon that's been hanging around you like a creepy dog."

I slogged up to where the brown dirt's edge must be. "No! You can't choose somebody I've traveled with!"

The god rolled his head as well as his eyes. "No and no. I can't choose somebody you've ridden with. The dragon rode once, but not with you."

"But you promised no children! Chexis is only one year old!"

Baby Harik chuckled.

I swallowed and then made myself breathe. "No, that makes no sense! He's a baby, or at most a teenager."

Baby Harik said, "A dragon isn't a child, because a child is human. A young dragon is a wyrmling."

"You're kidding."

He straightened and in fact might have grown a couple of inches taller. "I am a god, and I say that it's so."

I shouted, "I can't kill him! Hell, I don't even have a way to hurt him!"

"I don't think you've looked very hard. Maybe you'll find something lying around that will do the job." He grinned. "And you know that the Avalanche's weapon would do it."

Baby Harik waved and tossed me back into my body with just enough force to knock me and the chair over backward. I felt myself hit the floor. My vision faded to yellow before I passed out again.

THIRTY-FIVE

(CHEXIS)

I need Bib. It makes me sad and a little angry to admit that. More than a little. It pisses me off, as Bib might say.

But I realize that I need to understand some things about humans after all. If I was standing on a crappy island, and I wanted to fly to a bigger, infinitely better island, I'd have to know where the crappy island was. Being a dragon was the better, near-perfect island. Being mannish was the crappy island.

Analogies are always suspect, but this one feels good and explains the situation exactly. It has to be right.

People are too confusing, though. I need Bib to explain them to me, even if his explanations are sometimes weak or foolish or sound like lies. I can learn a lot from lies.

I was flying east to find him and squeeze him until something helpful came out. Bib said that people help each other, except that people like Margale don't. Pil told me, "A thing may seem like help but actually be a kick in the nuts from a lying son of a bitch."

When I asked her what that meant, she said to go ask Bib.

I don't remember anything in the Poems of Dragonkind that says any dragon has helped another dragon, not ever. I suppose

Sphynthor may have deliberately avoided reciting the parts about helpful dragons.

She said that dragons never kill each other, but they do things to hurt each other all the time. What if they're actually helping everybody and never saying anything about it? It sounds like it would be embarrassing if someone found out.

My effort to behave more like a dragon had been wretched so far. I needed to understand about helping and not helping, hurting and not hurting, killing and not killing, and eating and not eating.

I thought I would learn something when I offered to bring Kenzie to help the loud old man with no hair and an arrow in his leg. I expected him to be a lot more grateful when I offered, but he merely looked stupid and babbled. The rest weren't much nicer about it. I could have eaten him and saved everybody some trouble.

Despite their being horrible ingrates, I flew back to Kenzie and explained this opportunity to help a person. She wasn't lying in the dirt whining like a dying goat anymore. When I explained how she did not have to look into my groin while I carried her, she laughed for what seemed like a long time. I began to get annoyed, but at last she lay down so I could carry her.

Pil wanted to stay and talk to somebody who wasn't there yet, which seemed idiotic to me. But once in a while, she seemed almost intelligent. I argued and questioned her until she turned red. I've found that I'm good at making people do that. I got tired of it this time though and left without even saying I'd come back for her.

I flew with Kenzie to the old man with the bad-smelling leg. I would definitely have bitten that leg off and spit it out before eating him. Kenzie helped him, even though he shouted at her when she pulled out the arrow. He was shouting curses, and I recognized them. Bib had shouted them a lot.

The old man and his daughter thanked Kenzie. They helped her lie down and brought her water. They didn't bring me any water, and they didn't thank me either. I would have liked some water. They didn't make any sense. I'd helped just as much as Kenzie had, but it seemed as if help didn't count unless you mash your hands against the person who's hurt.

I asked Kenzie, "Are people only happy with you when you mash on them?"

"No. They're never happy whether they're being mashed or not." Then she signaled me by closing one eye, and I saw how winking was supposed to be done. I looked around to see what she was signaling about, but all I saw was the old man yelling about something called whiskey.

Kenzie flopped onto the ground and didn't keep talking.

I said, "If you would stop lying on the grass, holding your leg, and groaning, you could pay better attention to me. That would be considerate."

She ignored me and went on groaning.

I sat down and applied my intellect to the problem. Bib had been chasing the tall sorcerer, Margale, the one with the dragon-smashing club. I decided to eat that man and drop the club into the ocean. Then Bib could pay better attention to me and answer all my questions.

I flew east in the darkness, about a hundred feet above the ground, smelling the wind and listening for the voices of Bib and Margale. I didn't count on finding them by smell alone, but I might pick one voice out of many conversations happening on the ground.

Unfortunately, I couldn't listen for their voices if they didn't talk.

A spread-out firelit city lay to the east. Other towns and cities I had seen were puny compared to it. Margale was not puny, so by human logic, he probably would live someplace not puny. There would be plenty of people and animals he could hit with his club. If Margale was here, then Bib would show up soon.

Where would a tall sorcerer who crushes things live? Probably in the biggest place in the city. I picked out the biggest building, a sizable rectangle, and landed on the pitched roof as lightly as one hundred hawks landing at the same time. That's awfully light for a dragon, when you think about it.

Bib might be fighting the sorcerer and get distracted if I leaped right into the room. So, I decided to be quiet. I wasn't able to speak from experience, but I couldn't think of many things more disruptive than a dragon running down the passages calling out, "Bib! Bib!"

I decided that I needed to change form. I slithered down an unobserved part of the building, crept up behind a woman who was alone in a shadowy spot, and whacked her with my tail. She fell down. I assumed her form and took her clothes.

This woman's shape was tiny, unlike the one I had used as the guest of Bib and his friends. In fact, it was short and kind of squishy, not strong or intimidating at all. She was a wonderful choice, because I could not turn back into a dragon immediately once I changed.

If I assumed the form of something weak and small, I could change back quickly. If I changed into a rabbit, I bet I could switch back into a dragon within one breath. If I changed into something big and powerful, I could not change back as quickly. The night I'd visited Bib at his campfire, I had first wandered around the boring forest as a big man for a long time. That way I could change back in an instant.

When I found Margale, I planned to stand in front of him as this tiny woman. Then I would pretend to slip, stop my fall by putting my hands on his chest, change into a dragon, and tear out his heart and lungs with my claws. He would be surprised.

But I'd need some time before I could become a dragon again. Bib might be fighting now, or even dying, but I couldn't prevent that as a short pale woman with thin gray hair. I walked around the city for most of an hour until I knew I could change back with no delay.

At the rectangular building, four men stood at a big lantern-lit door, all holding spears. I walked up to one of them, who said, "What want you in here, gran? 'Tis a night too ill to walk the palace."

I wondered what the heck he was saying, then decided to ignore that. "I want to talk to the tall sorcerer. Is he here?"

He grinned. "Margale? You're lagging, old mam. Margale's fled, but he slew Her Majesty's whole family first. Go on home."

I hissed. I should have said Margale instead of "tall sorcerer" now that I could recognize the shit pile of a man by his name.

Human names were hard to remember. Also, I wondered why I had thought "shit pile." It didn't sound like something a dragon would say.

But none of that mattered. I still didn't know what this man was talking about, so I asked, "Has anybody killed him yet?"

"No, but may it be soon, by Weldt's mighty boots and mightier knobs."

I listened but couldn't hear Bib or Margale either. "If you show me where he was and anybody who touched him tonight, I can find him." That was not a lie. He smelled like the underside of an ox on a muddy day.

The man lowered his voice. "Are you the seeing woman?"

I didn't know what that was, but he didn't say it like he wanted to kill it. "Yes."

He snapped his fingers. "Pip, come with me!" Without waiting for Pip, he pulled me inside and down a passage. My little legs had to rush to keep up. Once inside, I heard people arguing, crying, and just talking. I didn't hear Bib. A few minutes later, the man led me through an open door into a room that reeked of blood, smoke, and sawdust.

"Through there, that's where he killed them," the man said, pulling me by the arm into another room that was empty except for some chairs.

I stood in the middle of the empty room that was useless to me. I said, "This room is useless to me. Was a man trying to kill Margale?"

"Uh-huh, Margale had a falling out with his crony there at the end. They carved each other up a bit."

"I want to see that man."

My escort raised his eyebrows. "Why?"

I didn't know what to say, so I looked at him and thought mean things. After a little bit of that, the man said, "All right, come on. They probably haven't tortured him to death yet."

The man led me out the door and down passages for two and a quarter minutes. He stopped at a wooden door and banged on it with his hand.

A voice from inside yelled, "Screw you, we're busy!"

"C'mon, Alan, it's me. I got the seeing woman the queen asked for."

The door cracked open, and a tall man with a lot of hair on his face peered out. He whispered, "Really? Good. Her Majesty's in here fit to eat nails and shit finished cabinets." He opened the door and stood aside.

I walked into a long, narrow room with tools on two walls, a few chairs, a scaffold, two men, one woman, and Bib. He was tied to the scaffold with his head dangling forward.

Being a dragon, I am an expert on many subjects. One of them is burning. Bib's hand had been burned until it wasn't alive anymore. It was just some bones and charred flesh on the end of his arm.

The woman looked around at me. "You're not my seeing woman. Who are you?"

Alan grabbed for me, but I slipped away and ran to Bib. The man standing beside Bib was holding an iron bar. I think he had been hitting Bib with it, and now he raised it to hit me.

This was a wonderful time to stop being this fake seeing woman. I grew into my real form before the bar hit me, ripping apart the clothes I had stolen. I filled a good one-fourth of the room.

The man with the iron bar dropped it, screamed, and ran, but I shot out my neck and bit him in two. Another man had grabbed the seated woman and was dragging her toward the door. He shouted for help as he ran. A third man dropped his sword and staggered back until he hit the wall, then covered his eyes.

I felt like roaring, so I did. Dust fell from the ceiling. The woman screamed. The man against the wall collapsed.

"Bib!" I muttered. "You're still breathing, so don't hang there like an apple. Wake up!"

He did not wake up.

I realized then that I didn't know how to help people who had been hurt. That was why nobody had ever thanked me when hurt people were healed. I hadn't done much to help, really.

Footsteps sounded from the passage, and men began running

into the room. One man stood in the rear and shouted at five men with swords. I slithered forward to put myself between them and Bib. Three of them charged and began slashing at me with their swords. They may as well have been slashing me with sticks of cheese.

I said, "Would any of you like to stab me in the eyeball?"

All the men fell back. I think they were more terrified by me talking than by the fact that they couldn't hurt me.

I roared again. Three men ran out of the room, and one of the men who stayed urinated.

"You!" I shouted, pointing with my tail at the one in the back.

He stiffened and lowered his sword.

"Be nice, or I'll eat all of you, or at least, I'll bite you into pieces. Do you understand? Good. If you have anybody who can help people who have been hurt, send them here. And send some water. And some animal that's been put in a fire. Cooked, I mean. And three goats that haven't been cooked."

He winced and nodded his head a little. I think he tried to smile, but maybe he was trying to make water leak out of his face. I couldn't tell the difference.

I said, "If anybody comes to the city looking for Bib or Chexis, don't hurt them. Bring them to me. And most importantly, if anybody tries to hurt us, or fool us, or do something I don't like, I will burn them all over, bite them in half, and eat at least one of the halves."

All the men ran out of the room. I roared again, just because it felt good.

"Stop doing that," Bib mumbled.

I twisted my neck around and stared into his face. "I came to help you. No, that's not true. I came to ask you to help me. I thought you'd say no to me and then explain why you couldn't help me, and I was going to complain about you and all humans everywhere. Who can understand them?"

Bib looked up at me. "You've been thinking too much about this. What happened to you?"

"Nothing." My shoulders dropped and I sighed. "Bib, I don't

understand anything about humans, and I have tried really hard to learn. It's . . . I think I'm discouraged."

"It's all right." Bib slurred a little. "You know a thousand times more about humans than any one-year-old I've ever met. Can you bite through these ropes or something?"

THIRTY-SIX

With my eyes closed, I heard Chexis say, "You have to answer my questions. I gave you a little dog."

When I looked up, I found that he was curled on the torture chamber floor. I was lying against his side with my head on his foreleg.

My first thought was that I needed to somehow trick Baby Harik so that I wouldn't have to kill Chexis. Well, if Margale killed us both, that would take care of the problem, but I wouldn't call that a good trick. At least Baby Harik hadn't given me a deadline for dragon-killing, so I didn't have to worry about it today.

"You're pretty comfortable to lie on," I said, gritting my teeth. I had been wounded many times but had never been burned this way. It hurt a hell of a lot, so I tried to make light of it. "I thought having my hand burned off would hurt more. It does sting, but I expected agony or something."

"That's good," Chexis said absently, as if I'd been talking about wiping crap off my boot. "Why do people waste time?"

I tried to sit up but fell right back down. I had all the strength of a dandelion. Rarely had I suffered wounds that left me this beaten and drained. I took a couple of deep breaths, preparing to sit up and mean it this time.

"Bib! People live almost no time. Why do they waste that time doing useless things?"

I sat up and leaned against Chexis's rough hide. It felt like a shark's skin. "People don't know when they'll die, so they kind of fool themselves into not believing it will ever happen, unless something whacks them in the face with the reality of death. They don't think about whether they're squandering their time on useless things. By the way, what kind of things do you think are useless?"

"Wearing clothes. And making them."

"But they keep us warm and protect our feet," I said.

"If a place is too cold and the ground is too sharp, you weren't made for that place. Don't go there!"

I chuckled and then winced. "By saying 'don't go there,' you guarantee that every person who ever lived will try to go there."

The dragon's forehead patch stood straight up. "That makes no sense. No sense at all!"

"I didn't say it made sense. If something makes sense, you can be sure that at least half the people will do something different. So, what else is useless?"

"Love. Being in love, or not being in love, and fighting about love. Talking about love, singing about it, and making up love dances, I guess. What a waste!"

"At the moment, I may not be the best person to defend love," I said.

"You're not! You're in love, and it's making you sad. Pil's not in love, and that's making her sad. Why do you spend time on it? Just have babies and go about your business."

I nodded slowly, examining the torture tools on the walls and hoping Chexis would talk about something else.

"Well?" Chexis asked, not letting the subject go. "Why do you spend time on love?"

"Like many things people do, it doesn't make much sense. Every love affair ends unhappily, unless the two folks involved die at the same time. If you asked different people, you'd get different answers about anything to do with love."

"You're the one I want answers from."

"All right. With my first wife, we were trying to build a certain kind of life together. It was hard because neither of us knew what the hell we were doing. Love made us allies better than just spit and a handshake.

"With Ella, we made a crazy and dangerous life together. We always had battles to fight but had fun when we could. I guess love meant we each had somebody who knew us and would care if we got smashed out of existence.

"With Pil, we lived in exile. We took care of each other in that grim place. I helped with her research. She cheered me up when my murders became a burden. We reminded each other of life before the Dark Lands." I shrugged.

"Love sounds stupid. You should stop being in love. Right now."

"I can't just make myself stop." I grinned at him.

Chexis growled, and a bit of smoke drifted from his nostrils. "Why didn't you create a life with Pil? You did with those others."

I felt like he had smacked me with a block of granite. "I . . . well, the Dark Lands could never change. It was a dead place, so I don't guess . . . hell, no wonder she left! I am such an asshole!"

It didn't have to be like that. When the contest between Gorlana and Harik ended, I could use the charm to make Pil love me again. Then we could live someplace that wasn't death all the damn time. May Krak smash it with his little toe, I could fix this!

I felt that if I didn't stand up, I'd be trapped on that floor until I died. With one hand on the dragon's leg, I pulled myself to my feet. I looked toward the door and froze.

The room beyond Chexis was filled with corpses and parts of corpses. I didn't want to count them, but I figured as many as forty men had died there since I passed out. I sniffed, but my nose was full of smoke. That's why I hadn't smelled all that killing.

Chexis said, "They stopped sending men a while ago. It took them a long time to learn they can't hurt me. They're not very smart."

"We have to leave here, Chexis. Something bad will happen if we stay."

"No. This is a perfectly fine lair until you feel stronger," he said.

The dragon's instinct must have been to hole up when things get bad or uncertain.

I asked, "What if they throw something in here that poisons the air? It might not hurt you, but such things can kill me. Let's get out of here. We can find Pil and the others."

Chexis stood up and shrugged. "Your sword is over there. Can you run? Without falling down?"

"Just don't go too fast. We'll go left outside the door, then left again at the intersect—"

"Yes, I know the way." He blinked at me. "Try not to get lost."

Chexis walked and slithered to the door while I picked my way through the bodies. I drew my sword in case some guard fell down in front of me and lay there, waiting for me to execute him. Hell, I'd just bonk him on the head.

When he pushed through the doorway, Chexis caused a great deal of screaming and running around. He hurried down the corridor, leaving me behind. I staggered to catch up. Nobody jumped in from the side or from behind me, so I survived the next hundred feet.

The dragon halted at the intersection and swept his head to breathe fire down all three corridors. I followed him as he turned left. Men on fire jumped and ran in two of the corridors. Ahead of me, a man's scream cut off as Chexis stomped him with a rear foot and moved on. Then the dragon slowed down enough for me to catch up, even though I was gasping and heaving.

A door opened beside me, and a man in plain clothes jumped out with a short sword. He thrust it at my side. Instinct took over as I blocked and whacked his shin hard with the flat of my blade. He fell to his knees, calling me names.

The door to the stairs was closed and apparently barred. The palace's defenders probably hoped to keep the monster away from the other floors. Chexis slammed it with one shoulder and a leg, smashing the door and its bar into wooden chunks and splinters.

Chexis ran over two men and a woman on his way down two flights of stairs. They all seemed shocked and bruised, but not dead. At the bottom, we turned right. Nobody opposed us on the way to the outside door. In fact, if they had been able to get us out of the palace faster, I'm sure they would have.

However, outside we found twenty crossbowmen in a row ahead of us and twenty more lined up on our right. Thirty soldiers stood just behind each group of bowmen.

Using the power I had just bargained from Baby Harik, I spun forty blue bands. I rushed because a crossbow held by a man is a much easier target than a quarrel in flight. Forty crossbows under great tension were rotted, and they destroyed themselves just before I heard somebody shout, "Fire!"

Chexis growled back at me, "Can you fight?"

I answered by swaying and falling on my face.

As I struggled to my knees, I heard the dragon roar. Every soldier and guard in sight grew still. Chexis whipped out his wings and flapped once, creating a thunderous bang as he rose ten feet off the ground. He spouted a five-foot flame, swinging his head in an arc from right to left. Then he slammed to the ground closer to the soldiers and roared again.

Soldiers started running. Once eight or ten had fled, all the rest followed.

"All right, you can lie down now," Chexis said, looking back at me.

"You sound happy," I told him.

"Why shouldn't I be? No human in the world can do what I just did. That was all dragon."

Within a minute, we were four hundred feet off the ground. Chexis had clamped onto my arms and legs, being careful of my burned-up hand. The sun was almost overhead, and I started sweating in the warmth. He turned to fly west.

We traveled west for ten minutes before we saw the army. I estimated a thousand foot soldiers and a hundred horsemen.

Chexis shouted, "Pil is down there! Kenzie too!"

"Are they prisoners?" I yelled.

"I can't tell. But they aren't being beaten, and no one is putting hot things on their skin."

"How do you feel about letting me walk in there alone? I'm not sure how the people of that army will react if they see a dragon."

"I hate that idea! I hate it a lot!"

"Please?"

"All right! Fine! If you want to be on your own, you can just go off by yourself! I'm done with you anyway. I don't think you ever knew that much to start with."

Chexis flew low and landed behind a small rise almost a mile away from the army. He sprang into the air without speaking, leaving me on my back.

"Goodbye!" I shouted. Chexis didn't answer as he skimmed away just above the ground.

I walked toward the army, then I limped toward it, and finally I staggered toward it. I was still a quarter mile away when five horsemen galloped out to meet me. One of them was a big-shouldered sandy-haired man who looked like one of his parents might have come from my homeland.

That man snarled, "You're the pig-humping bastard who murdered the king! Damn you, I'll torture you myself."

I could tell that apologies and explanations would mean nothing to these bastards. "Shit, did any of you really like the king? Really?" I asked. "Of course, I was forced to kill him, so it's not—"

A squatty armored man on an enormous horse yelled, "Shut your damned traitorous face!" He threw his iron helmet at me, and it bounced off my chest. I swayed and almost fell. He shouted, "Get walking, you traitor."

One of the men gave me a sharp poke with his spear. It drew blood and headed me in the direction of the army.

"Fine, I was going over there anyway," I said, gasping and pointing at the mass of soldiers. "You don't have to gouge me. And you, Shorty—I'm not a traitor. Traitors have to serve somebody before betraying them, and I never swore to serve your king. You can call me a nasty son of a bitch if you want to, though."

Shorty bellowed, "Yah!" A second later his horse's gigantic

shoulder bashed me. I went tumbling and sliding across the grass. He shouted, "You'll wish that was all you get! When your hand is deep in your own guts, you'll think happy things about today!"

I lay splayed on the ground, but I raised my head. I saw four more horsemen galloping toward me with at least thirty more some distance behind them.

"Get your ass off the ground!" Shorty yelled.

"That's enough for now," Sandy Hair rumbled. "Leave something for Her Grace to torture."

"Her ass-biting Grace," Shorty muttered. "Hale was the king."

"What did you say?" Sandy Hair yelled, drawing his sword.

I pushed myself up to my knees. The man with the spear knocked me down again, leaving a nice little hole in my shoulder.

I lay on the ground while they argued, and I prepared to drive all their horses mad.

"Stand up, you maggot's ass! March!" Shorty yelled.

Something slammed to the ground behind me. All five horses bolted. I looked around and saw Chexis behind me, his wings out and his teeth showing.

"Thank you, son," I said before letting my head drop to the ground.

Less than a minute later, the four galloping riders halted and dismounted. Grik and Pocklin drew their swords. Pocklin faced the five men whose horses were still running. Grik faced the thirty riders still approaching.

Pil knelt over me and hissed when she saw what was left of my hand. Kenzie went pale. If she healed me, she would take on the pain of that wound.

Pil sat beside me and held my good hand. She leaned in and whispered, "I think this is your dragon now."

I whispered back, "I don't know. Maybe I'm his human. Regardless, if he's within half a mile, you should assume he hears everything you say."

THIRTY-SEVEN

I scanned the enemies at these crossroads and forced myself to take a breath. Everybody should be killing everybody else here, but we had been gathering for three minutes without even one person dying.

Kenzie had healed my burned hand last night. The healing went well but left her devastated.

Just past dawn, I had left Kenzie writhing and calling out for help as she curled up around her hand. Vargo sat holding her other hand, and he glared at me like I was torturing her. I couldn't blame him.

Then I walked ten minutes to the council of war at the crossroads.

Pil and I, flanked by Grik and Pocklin, stood on one side of a rough triangle. To our right stood young Duchess Eldine, King Hale's heir, along with her sandy-haired thug, Drekka, and thirty of their angry-looking soldiers. To our left stood Queen Apsel, some young man in a fancy uniform, and thirty-two of her neck-breakers.

I didn't like any of this. No, that wasn't entirely true. I liked the thunderstorm I had spinning overhead, ready to drop lightning on anybody who said a mean word.

"Thank you all for meeting us," Pil said.

"She brought too many soldiers!" Drekka yelled, pointing at Apsel.

"Are you afraid because we outnumber you by a mere seven percent?" the dapper uniformed man asked in a soft voice. "What a pathetic coward."

Drekka drew his sword. I prepared to cook people.

"Wait!" Pil shouted in a voice that cut through all the noise. "I understand that this might be an important point." She nodded to Eldine. "If it's critical to have equal forces, then you should call for two more soldiers, and I will call for our dragon, who happens to be worth exactly thirty men."

Chexis roared from someplace in the sky above us. I couldn't see him, but Apsel, Eldine, and all their men tried to cower while looking around at the sky.

Apsel pulled herself even straighter and taller, then smiled as if she was imagining how our hearts tasted. She touched the uniformed man on the arm. He murmured to two of her soldiers, and they trotted away toward the city.

"Thank you, Your Majesty," Pil said.

I added, "Yes, that was—"

Pil stomped my foot, and I shut up. It was true, she may not love me anymore, but she sure as hell knew me.

She went on, "We have a common enemy. The sorcerer Margale murdered Queen Apsel's children. He prosecuted the war against Silvershanks with far greater cruelty and destruction than Apsel intended. By magic, he forced Bib to assassinate King Hale, burdening him with the guilt of that murder." She glanced at me, but I kept my mouth closed.

Pil went on, "Margale slaughtered one of our friends in your very own palace, Queen Apsel. He threatens us and everyone we love, so we must come together to destroy him."

Queen Apsel showed her teeth and pointed at me. "Who do we punish for the fifty-three guards and soldiers that man killed while leaving my palace?"

Eldine said, "Excuse me, did you say he killed fifty-three men?"

"That's an exaggeration," I said. "I only killed five and wounded one, and that was to escape torture. The dragon killed the other forty-seven."

I could feel Pil's glare even though she didn't face me. She said, "That is a great tragedy, Your Majesty."

Drekka shouted, "What about our cities burned? That's more of a tragedy than a few guards!"

Apsel's uniformed man shouted an insult at Drekka, who insulted him right back and shook his sword. Eldine was pulling on Drekka's arm, but he didn't seem to notice. Then the soldiers on both sides began shouting. A few men raised weapons. I scanned the area, deciding where I'd call lightning first.

Pil slipped something small into her mouth and swallowed. Then she stepped forward and said, "We have all been hurt!" in a voice so loud I slapped my hands over my ears. People were staggering away from the noise.

Pil pointed at Apsel. "Your Majesty, you know Margale better than anybody, and we're close to his trail. But most of your army is off fighting in Silvershanks."

She pointed at Eldine, who flinched away from the outrageous noise. "Your Grace, you have mustered an army and brought it with you. But you don't know your enemy the way Queen Apsel does. And we"—she pointed to herself and me—"know how to deal with sorcerers. So do we all work together, or do we let the son of a bitch live to murder us all next time?"

After her last word, echoes came back from the Brindine city wall half a mile away.

Nobody said anything.

"Well?" I said in a regular voice. "Did you hear what she said? Murder? Son of a bitch?"

It was as if those words gave them permission to not hate each other for a day or two. Lieutenants were called out. Servants and orderlies brought tables, chairs, maps, cabinets full of war planning supplies, food, and wine.

By late morning, nine people, including Queen Apsel's actual seeing woman, were planning like mad. They decided to strike east, based on the fact that Margale had gone that way. They also planned for at least some of their force to cross the river by ferry. I thought it a sharp decision, since there was no other way across. They were currently working on how to feed the army. All other plans were under development.

As we walked back to Vargo and Kenzie, Pil said, "That should keep them out of our way, because they won't cross the river for two days, or maybe three. Margale has his own realm?" She shook her head and looked away.

"Pil, I need to apologize to you."

She said, "Don't. I don't want to hear it right now. I'm happy you're around, and I don't want to ruin that with apologies and nonsense. If Margale doesn't kill us both, we can talk then. But I think we ought to get drunk first."

I nodded and kept my mouth closed.

Pil and I returned to our little camp, where we found Kenzie kneeling and rubbing Spot's belly. She had recovered from the pain of healing me. Sometimes healing pain faded quickly. Sometimes it lasted a whole day. When she stood, I saw that her face was pale and her eyes sunken, but she smiled. "I'm fine. It doesn't hurt at all anymore."

I had known several sorcerers who healed while they were pregnant, and they had never suffered particularly. But they certainly hadn't experienced healing this arduous.

"She's not well," Vargo said. "You selfish old mule. I told her we should stay home."

"Too late." Kenzie grinned.

Vargo drew his sword, which surprised me. "Bib, are you going to fight that sorcerer? I'll come along. I'll kill anybody you want killed. Oh, and thanks, by the way, for saving my life. Just leave her alone." His face showed no more emotion than a rock.

I said, "Kenzie, stay here. You've done enough. And Vargo, stay with her."

"No," Kenzie said. "You cannot force me. Do you think you'll summon seven pigs to lie upon me, pinning me to the earth, till you're out of sight?"

Pil said, "I agree with Bib, although I can hardly believe I'm saying those words. Kenzie, you should stay behind. Is there nothing we can say to convince you?"

I stared at Kenzie's face and said, "Margale, isn't just cruel. He's dead inside, or at least dying. He can both bury us and burn us. Think about how your hand felt. Oh, I forgot, he lords over a realm of his own. For all I know, it could be as big as the world of man. He could have hundreds of thousands of soldiers fighting for him, and maybe he lives on top of a mountain. What do you say to that? What would your baby say?"

From behind me, Pocklin barked, "Screw all that shit! Gretta, we're going home! Now! Don't even grab something to wipe your butt on!" He snatched his saddle off the ground and walked toward his horse.

Kenzie laughed silently and pointed at Pocklin. "I don't think my baby would say that."

Grik said, "Daddy, I'm staying. This sounds like the battle I don't want to miss." She raised her eyebrows at me.

I said, "Grik, I won't tell you what to do. You may die. But you might live, and I guarantee you'll learn something either way."

The argument took up the next half hour. Vargo and Pocklin found that they were allies, which may have shocked the hell out of them. Pocklin first stated and then shouted demands that Grik and Kenzie go home. Vargo followed that with some sincere though gloomy pleading. Kenzie and Grik stayed calm. Kenzie reminded the men that if she and Grik wanted to go, they couldn't do a damn thing about it. Grik pointed out how ignorant they'd look if they tried.

In the end, all six of us mounted to ride in search of Margale. Some were happier than others about it.

Chexis glided down and eased to the earth in front of us.

Pil said, "We're headed to kill a sorcerer that may have armies, and fortresses, and dogs, and lions, and warships, and volcanoes—"

Chexis interrupted. "I have to kill him. Then I'll take his club and drop it in the ocean, so he doesn't hit any more dragons with it."

I smiled my biggest smile of the past few days. "That was a very dragonlike thing to say, son. I'm proud of you."

THIRTY-EIGHT

e had ridden downstream along the Slatt River since before sunset. An afternoon, an evening, and all the next day had passed since we left the crossroads war council. We pushed hard because the feeling that we'd fallen too far behind Margale had crept up on both Pil and me.

Now the afternoon sun hung low behind us. I sat my horse beside the lightning-blasted tree that Baby Harik had described. If Baby Harik hadn't warned me that the river was our goal, I would have bypassed this tree and never thought about it again.

"This is it?" Pil muttered. I could hardly hear her over the swift water.

"So says the God of Death."

I had told her about the tree and how we'd find Margale. I hadn't said anything about my other discussions and deals with Baby Harik. "He told me to ride into the river here once the sun touches the horizon. You all wait while I scout it. I'll come back then to bring you across."

"I don't want you to go alone," Pil said.

"You'll have to be sad about that, then," I said, "because it's foolish to risk two people instead of one. When did you last hear about two people going to scout together like it was a nice day in the country?"

I went on, "If I don't come back soon, that might be a sign that I got across but can't find a way to return yet. Or I guess it could mean I've drowned. Wait until tomorrow afternoon before you decide whether to follow me. If you give me up for dead, call Baby Harik a bastard for me before you go home."

"We're not giving you up, no matter what," Kenzie said.

"Young woman, how many times in these past two years have you decided I'd be more useful feeding worms than walking around and acting like an asshole?"

She said in a small voice, "A few."

"I'd hesitate before making sweeping statements, then."

After a few seconds of gazing toward the sun, I handed Spot's bag to Pil. He wiggled and yipped inside it. We had rarely stopped, and I'd had to clean out his bag whenever we did. "Here, you take him. He's too little to scout the foreign realm of a crazy man."

I rode down the bank into the river. The current was quick, and the far bank lay two hundred feet away. After the first fifty feet, my horse couldn't touch the riverbed anymore and started swimming.

When we reached the middle of the river, I felt something dragging against my shoulders and head. It seemed as if I was trying to push through a burlap curtain. But the curtain wouldn't give way, and I couldn't get through it no matter how hard my horse swam.

After a minute more, my horse began to struggle, so I slipped off and swam, trying to guide us both back to the riverbank. I got us headed in the right direction, but I lost hold of the horse. I swam toward the bank, trying to keep my head up. The current pulled my floundering horse downriver, away from me.

When I reached the sandy bank, I slogged and pulled a yellow band to search for my horse. I found him on the bank downriver, scared and walking away from me, so I called him back at a gallop. I had expected him to drown, so this was fortunate. Maybe it was a sign of good luck, never mind that so far, I had accomplished nothing and nearly gotten us both killed.

I mounted to gallop back upriver. I wanted to try crossing again before the sun disappeared.

"Baby Harik!" I shouted, lifting my spirit toward the trading place. Almost before I arrived, I yelled, "You're a wheezy chunk of ass crust!"

My breath caught as a hot wind blew in my face out of the nearly pure darkness. I spotted the glow of three volcanoes erupting not far enough away for my liking. Two stood beyond the flower field, and I saw one through the gazebo. The sounds of rumbling and grinding filled my ears. I might need to insult Baby Harik louder than normal.

However, Baby Harik's calm nasal voice said, "Hello, Murderer."

I yelled, "Say hello to my ass! And to the rest of my nasty parts! This gate or door—whatever the hell it is—doesn't work."

"Really? That just perplexes me." He didn't sound confused or surprised at all. "I'm sure it works. Maybe you didn't use it right."

"You said to find the tree and ride in. I found and I rode."

"Oh well! That sounds impossibly simple, right? Don't you think crossing realms should be more complicated than just riding into some water?" I heard the smile in his voice.

"No, I—"

"Answer me. Shouldn't it be more complicated?"

"You have the—"

"Shouldn't it be? Tell me, shouldn't it be?"

I shouted, "Listen, Your Gnat-Dicked Magnificence, I paid—"

"Tell me! Shouldn't it be harder?"

I pretended he hadn't interrupted me. "I paid you a hard price for the secret of reaching Margale, and that's what you agreed to give me."

Baby Harik said, "Yeah, I did. But we didn't talk about how challenging and arcane the process would be. Right?"

I could see that I'd have to at least give him something small to stroke his divine ego. "What do you want?"

"I want the Feather's baby."

"What! No! Forget it." I made hand gestures that I hoped his godlike eyes could see through the darkness.

Baby Harik snorted. "I want that child. On the full moon after the child's first birthday, leave her by a linden tree in the ancient woods of southern Pelleth. Don't bother looking for her the next morning."

"No—"

"You will make this happen," Baby Harik bellowed, "and you won't tell anybody what you're doing or why! You'll never tell anybody! When the child is seventeen years old, she'll appear and kill somebody close to you."

I took a breath and squinted at the darkness where Baby Harik's voice was coming from. "This is awfully . . . mythological," I said. "Like some play about overly proud people at the beginning of time. Do you also want the baby to meet a wise woman and cross a haunted swamp?"

"Maybe." The god snorted and then laughed. "Oh, I just wanted to see which way you'd jump. Why would I want a baby? They're more boring than dogs. Babies can't even fetch."

If Baby Harik's goal had been to fluster me, he'd done a pass-able job. "What do you really want, then? Your Magnificence."

"I want you to kill people, of course. Wait!" he commanded before I could object. "Just one or two. It'll be enough if you kill the Knife."

"No," I said. "Pil belongs to Lutigan. He'll be pissed at us both if I kill her. And I don't want her dead."

"Fine, if that's your decision. Kill any two of the others you're traveling with." He paused. "But if you kill the Feather, she and her baby count as two."

I'm ashamed to admit that I considered killing Grik and Pocklin. However, I said, "I have a counteroffer. If you don't give me the secret of getting to Margale, I'll turn and ride off to the closest city. I'll go to every tavern and alehouse there and tell every tough son of a bitch that I slept with his mother, and that she was less arousing than a sack of sand. When they come at me with a knife or a stool,

I'll cut their wrist, or leg, or maybe their scalp deep enough to stop them but not kill them."

I waited, but Baby Harik didn't say anything.

"Then I'll ride to the next city and do the same. Within a week, I'll have disabled fifty enemies or more, maybe a hundred, and you will lose your contest with Gorlana."

"In that case, the Avalanche will go free," Baby Harik said in a reasonable voice. "He'll return sometime and kill all the people close to you, every one of them. Isn't it better to kill one or two now and save the rest?"

"You can only push a sorcerer so far, Your Magnificence. Give me the secret, or I ride away."

After a few seconds, the god blew out a breath as if he were a whale spouting. "I won't give you the secret for nothing. You have to promise you won't ever call me Baby Harik again. Not to my face and not when referring to me. To you, I will be Harik."

"Hah! I knew the name bothered you! You acted like it didn't, but I knew. I accept your offer, Harik."

Harik grumbled something.

"I'm sorry, I didn't quite hear that, Your Magnificence."

"When you ride into the water, say, 'Hail, Mighty Harik, God of Death and Master of the Dark Beyond.'"

"Oh. You have a new title? Is the Dark Beyond a real place? Or is it just an idea you had one day?"

Harik hurled me back into my body so viciously it knocked me off my horse and to the ground, where I rolled once. I shook myself, remounted, and galloped back up the river.

I found my allies facing my direction. Two of their horses had whinnied, so everybody was watching for me. They stood in a half-circle, except for Pil, who was sitting with her back to a tree, fiddling with something in her lap. Chexis wasn't with them.

"What happened?" Vargo asked, running to help me dismount as if I were a hundred years old. I waved him away.

"We were deciding who to send downriver to find you," Kenzie said.

"Or your body," Pocklin added.

I glanced at the sun. Just a sliver showed above the horizon.

I shouted, "Everybody mount and follow me! Hurry! Now!" I watched for a few seconds to be sure they were in motion.

Kicking my horse, I rode into the river.

"What went wrong the first time?" Grik yelled.

I shrugged. "I didn't know the magic words."

THIRTY-NINE

(CHEXIS)

W e dragons are above the primitive emotion of fear. Lower creatures might be afraid of loud noises or smashing into the ground from very high up in the air, but not dragons. Dragons are fearless. We've written poems about it.

Dragons do feel hatred, though, and I harbored a blazing hatred of water because I felt it was going to kill me. I understood that I wouldn't drown, even if I was underwater for quite a long time. However, "quite a long time" isn't forever. It was possible to get caught for just a minute by an underwater avalanche or by being bitten by the biggest fish imaginable.

Why would that be such a problem? Because that minute might be the one that turned "quite a long time" into "quite a long time plus one minute," and then I'd drown.

Of course, death wasn't certain if I went into the water. A large part of me felt there was at least an eighty percent chance I would die in the dark horrid water, and the rest of me couldn't change the large part's mind.

I had never told Praxis about this, and for the sake of Beymarr's back teeth, I had never told Sphynthor. But whenever they were in the water and I decided to stay out, they criticized me as un-dragonish.

When we got to the river that would take us to Margale's home, I flew down and landed to run beside Bib's horse before he rode into the river again. He and his horse had almost drowned the first time, which I think proved who was right and who was wrong about the dangers of being in the water.

"I'm glad you're coming along to be our ally, Chexis," Bib shouted.

"Of course I'm coming along! I can't kill Margale without coming along."

Bib nodded as his horse's hooves splashed into the water.

"Wait!" I shouted.

He looked back over his shoulder at me but didn't stop.

I reached out and grabbed the horse's tail with one of my claws. The horse made a loud unhappy noise and jumped sideways. I rushed to say, "Something bad may happen. I need to protect you."

"Damn it, Chexis, let go! Stay close to protect me if you want."

I didn't let go. "Close . . . close isn't close enough. You may get lost. I can't protect you unless I'm holding onto you."

"That's kind of you, son, really, too damn kind, but I don't need that much protection. So let go!"

"Yes, you do!" I insisted rather louder than I intended.

Bib stared at me. "How do you intend to do this? Wrap your tail around my waist or something?"

I changed my shape then. I took on the form of a tall awfully loud man I had seen while spying on one of the towns. He'd spent a lot of his time fornicating with different women there, so he must have been likable.

Everybody behind us exclaimed in surprise when I changed, but of course they hadn't seen me do it before. For a moment, I was afraid I might have stretched their limited minds too far, but no one fell on the ground twitching and vomiting.

I jumped and scrambled onto Bib's horse behind him and grabbed him around the body. "All right. Go."

Bib kicked his distressed horse to run into the water and wheezed, "Ease off, Chexis, you're going to break my ribs."

"Go now!" I yelled. I relaxed my grip the tiniest amount and mashed the side of my head against his back.

Kenzie shouted, "Chexis! Do you want clothes? That looks uncomfortable."

"Go! For Beymarr's sake, go!" I yelled.

Bib's horse ran but slowed as the water rushed around its legs. I closed my eyes. "Don't let me slip!" I snapped. I added, "If I slip, I can't protect you."

"You're the one holding onto me. What's the matter with you?"

I didn't answer him. I was too embarrassed and didn't know how to explain how much I despised the water.

When the horse began swimming, I felt something brushing my skin, but nothing was there. Bib said, "Hail, Mighty Harik, God of Death and Master of the Dark Beyond."

Even though my eyes were closed, I could tell that evening turned to bright daylight in an instant. I opened my eyes and saw we were in a different river that wasn't as fast or deep. The horse was walking. Then a massive wall of cold water smashed into my body and drenched me.

I thought I was going to die.

When I wasn't dead, I looked back and saw we had ridden through a waterfall. I craned my neck. This river ran alongside a high greenish stone cliff above us to our left. The eighty-foot-high waterfall spilled from that clifftop.

Far-off horns sounded from several places. Or maybe they sounded far off because of all the loud waterfall noises.

Bib yanked his horse to the right, and soon it climbed up onto the stony riverbank. Everything around us was stone, without a tree or a flower anyplace.

"Down!" Bib yelled as he stopped his horse. When I didn't move, he shouted, "Get down now! Slide off the back!" I looked around but didn't see anything that seemed like it would hurt us. I pushed myself backward and slid off the horse, stumbling a little when my feet hit the ground. I admit I felt a little wobbly. Shaking his head, Bib dismounted.

"Take cover!" Pil shouted.

I glanced around for something to hide behind, but all I saw was a tiny mound of white rocks. They were the only white rocks in sight, so they seemed more like a target than cover, but I followed her there regardless. The horses ran away for a minute and then stopped.

Bib joined us as we lay clumped like mice between the small boulders. He said, "There's the cliff up behind us and a drop-off ahead of us—another cliff, taller than that one. I saw three little stone fortifications. One is on the cliff above us." He jerked his head toward the waterfall we rode through. "Another is right the hell over there on this level."

Stringing her bow, Grik said, "We're in easy range for them—maybe a hundred and fifty feet. They'll have to try hard to miss us."

Bib said, "I saw another fortification at the bottom of the next cliff. Those horns are blowing from all three positions."

Pil was picking through a pouch and maybe organizing things in it. "They were waiting for us, or for somebody like us, and if they'd had their bows in their hands when we came across, we might be dead."

As she said that, some archers fired at us from the closest fort. We all flattened against the ground, and the arrows clattered off the stone.

"That can't go on too long without killing us, especially when the other fort starts firing down at us," Kenzie said. "Bib, you're already clapping together a storm, aren't you?"

"Yeah, but I don't like the feel of it."

"I'll care for the arrows then, as much as I can," she said.

Bib turned to me. "I'd appreciate it if you could turn back into a dragon now, Chexis. We could use a shredding, dismembering, invulnerable dragon ally about now."

I cocked my head at him. My body did it by itself because I was feeling puzzled. A nice bit of human communication became clear to me. "I'm sorry, I can't."

Everybody was silent for a moment.

"Did you say you can't?" Pil asked in a low voice.

"Arrows above!" Vargo shouted. We all threw ourselves flat.

I said, "When I shift, I can't shift back immediately." Pieces of arrows landed all around us.

"Oh," Bib said. "That's a nice thing to know right about now, while we're surrounded and outnumbered. Oh, as far as terrain goes, our disadvantage is spectacular. How long until you can change back?"

"A while."

Bib leaned toward me and dropped his voice. "Less than a day?"

"Oh yes. You seem to be unhappy with me about something!" I was getting angry and thought about hitting him.

Bib was sitting on the ground, and he let his head fall between his knees. "How long?" he muttered.

"Arrows!" Pocklin shouted.

I sat up and looked at Pocklin, then at Vargo, and I realized what they were doing. "Oh, I see! One of you is watching this fort and the other is watching that fort! That's clever."

Grik dragged me down to lie against the ground.

"Chexis!" Bib snapped. "How long?"

I gazed into the sky. "Where's the sun?"

"By Krak and the Unnamed Mother!" Pocklin yelled. "We don't have any damn sun here, do we?" He laughed harshly. "Of course, we don't have a sun! I don't see one. Do you see one? Nobody sees one, 'cause it ain't there, is it?"

I considered how to measure time without the sun. "I don't like to be imprecise, but I'll be surprised if it takes more than three thousand beats of my heart."

Bib paused and then shouted, "Fifty minutes?"

I shrugged. "About that. I don't think humans measure minutes in a uniform manner. It seems like a minute is just whatever somebody says it is."

"You bastard!" Vargo reached over and punched my shoulder.

"That hurt!" I rubbed my shoulder. "But yes——"

"Arrows!" Pocklin shouted.

Grik fired at one of the men who had jumped up to shoot arrows at us. That man fell backward behind the low stone wall.

"Yes, it should be about fifty minutes," I said.

"Wait," Bib said. "Chexis, did it hurt when Vargo hit you?"

"Yes."

"I promise I won't do this, but if I stabbed you now, would you die?"

"Yes. I'm shaped like a human, so I'd die like a human. And I don't know why you're mad at me! I came here to fight alongside you, and I could only get here in human shape. I *came along* to be your ally, even though it's making me really, really easy to kill."

After the next volley of arrows, Bib and the others stared around at each other.

I said, "Well, I think the thing you're supposed to say is thank you."

FORTY

Margale's realm was the driest place I had ever been. I snarled, "I've crossed deserts that looked like pleasant meadows compared to this."

Pil sniffed. "Do you mean besides that river and the enormous waterfall?"

I blinked before pointing away from the river. "I meant over there! But yes, maybe we can do something with all that water, even though I don't sense much of it in the air."

We were being fired on from two directions by two forces, one on much higher ground and both protected by low fortifications. Also, we were hiding in a few rocks and had no damn dragon or lightning. Our situation was bleak.

Although I'd come to this domain with a shade over eight squares, I didn't want to waste them all by calling for storms that didn't exist. I decided to keep trying for a bit longer. We had plenty of heat. All of us were beginning to sweat, and not just from fear of death. I pushed more power into the sky and got nothing back.

I glanced at the river. Pushing that moisture high enough to form clouds would be a shipload of work. I'd come back to it if I couldn't find water that was already where I wanted it.

As I engaged in this futility and also ducked arrows, I appreciated the remarkable new knowledge that I could kill Chexis in his human form. Apparently, I could do it with a knife to the heart or a hard whack on the head. I didn't intend to kill him if I could figure a way out of it, of course. But it was good to know that I could destroy him by waiting for the right time.

Also, I hadn't wanted to admit it, but at times, I got the feeling that Chexis was thinking about killing me. I couldn't point to anything definite. Maybe it was just my natural fear of such a powerful being. But maybe it was the same awareness that sometimes let me know somebody was sneaking up behind me.

Another volley of arrows landed. Kenzie missed one, and it plunged right through Chexis's calf, all the way to the rock beneath him. He stared at it and winced but didn't make a sound.

I scooted over to examine the wound. "Damn, son, I bet that hurts. You must be the toughest boy in dragon land."

"This kind of thing would never hurt a dragon," he said, his voice tight but steady.

"You're not a dragon right now," Pil said.

"You hush!" Chexis snapped. "I am so a dragon. I'm just shaped a little differently for a few minutes."

Vargo muttered, "Yeah, fifty minutes, you boob."

Chexis said, "This wound will be fine when I turn back. The arrow will fall out, so don't worry about me. Go kill those people so they don't shoot me someplace important, like in the neck."

"I'd like to kill them for you," I said. "But I doubt Kenzie can stop all the arrows while we charge over there. And we can't climb that cliff with any speed. At least half of us would die. More likely all of us."

"We'd be a damn sight—arrows!" Pocklin yelled.

Margale's defenders were firing a lot of arrows at us, but they weren't particularly good bowmen. After the next volley landed without harming us, Pocklin went on, "We'd be a damn sight faster on those horses. Maybe we could even gallop back home."

I shook my head, pushing a little more energy into the sky.

Pocklin answered himself before anybody else could. "Yeah, I guess they'd poke three arrows into each horse before they got around to shooting us. Why haven't they shot at the horses already? I guess maybe they need horses. Maybe these bastards just like them."

I wasn't paying much attention to the man's bitching. Instead, I focused on building a storm, and with a jerk, I realized that my attempts had been misplaced. The sky held no clouds and not much water, at least where I expected it. But it contained a reasonable amount far higher up. It was higher than I would have imagined possible. Fortunately, the power I had been shoving into the sky had begun pulling that high water together without me being specific about it.

"Buy me a few minutes," I said.

"How in the rat snot bloody hell do you think we'll do that when we're dodging arrow storms?" Pocklin yelled.

"Like this." Pil pulled something small and round out of a pouch and flung it toward the base of the cliff just below the upper fortress. It flew thirty feet and then rolled to the cliffside, where it bounced off.

Pocklin and the rest watched the object.

Vargo said, "I hope that impresses them more than it does me."

We all dropped when the next volley came, and no one was hit. Grik nocked another arrow. "Pil, it looks like whatever you did has terrified them into firing at us faster."

Pil laughed.

Distant screams came from the high fort. Then fifteen walnut trees shot up behind the stone walls, each carrying a man upward in its branches.

I glanced back at the fort on our level. Nobody there was firing arrows now. They were all looking up at the high fort, where their comrades clung in the treetops.

After fifteen seconds, the trees all seemed to dissolve. Men screamed as they plummeted forty or fifty feet back to the rocky ground. If any of them stood back up, I didn't see it.

"Lutigan damn it with bacon fat," Pocklin mumbled. He scooted away from Pil.

"Should we charge them?" Grik asked, pointing at the fort on our level. "They look stunned."

I could see men over there waving their arms. Maybe they were arguing. None of them were shooting arrows yet. I said, "Wait, don't charge."

I could tell that the high storm was raining a bit now, but the water dried up in the hot air above us before it hit the ground. I aimed in front of the fort's stone wall and brought lightning down close enough to stun everybody but not so close it killed them, I hoped. The enormous thunderclap hurt my teeth.

Harik had lied to me when he said I had killed thirty-two more men than I had left alive. By my count, it had been someplace between thirty-five and thirty-nine. Then I killed five guards in Apsel's palace, which put me at as many as forty-four. I needed to stop killing people if I didn't want to do all the miserable shit Harik had bargained out of me.

Nobody appeared to be moving around behind the stone wall.

Pil shouted, "Now!"

All of us except Chexis charged the little fort. Grik reached it first with Vargo right behind. One man was struggling to his knees. Grik raised her sword to kill him, but Vargo knocked her arm aside.

Grik spun and pointed her sword at Vargo, who raised his own sword.

She snapped, "Why did you do that?"

"Maybe we'll want to question him," Vargo said, stepping between her and the blinking man. "And maybe we don't have to kill men who are on their knees."

Grik charged, knocked Vargo's sword aside, and shouldered him out of the way just before the man stabbed the air where Vargo's back had been. Then Grik swung her sword, killing the man with a cut to the neck.

Vargo frowned at the dead man. "Thank you, Grik. Although my point about not killing men on their knees is still valid."

All the other men from this little fortress were on the ground, some writhing and some lying still.

Pil had knelt beside one. "These aren't men, or they aren't in the way we usually think. Look." She pointed at the man's hands, which each had six clawed fingers, and his head, which had tiny ears and a thick single eyebrow like a ferret lying on his face. His skin was pinkish gray, and his hair was dark brown.

"Tie them up," I said, and I walked around the area. I counted thirteen alive plus the one Grik had killed. Well, I couldn't be blamed for that one. Now that put me conservatively at thirty-one more killed than disabled.

"Krak!" Vargo yelled from the edge of the drop-off. He threw himself backward, tripped, and fell on his butt. Three arrows whipped past him from down below. As he got up, he said, "This whole trip is an awful idea! We should have gone home. We should go home now! That Margale skag will never go as far as Ir hunting for us." He looked at Grik. "I said it yesterday. You heard me say we should go home, didn't you?"

"Did you?" she asked without looking at him. "I wasn't paying attention."

Vargo stomped over to Kenzie, who was trying to question one of the prisoners. We had tied them and sat them on the rocky ground. She was doing a fine job of asking questions, but the soldier stared at her with an expression that was sometimes confused and sometimes disgusted.

Pil squatted nearby, examining the man. "I don't think he understands you."

Grik looked down at the man. "Maybe he doesn't even use words."

Pocklin said, "I bet he whistles, or rubs his legs together like a cricket."

Kenzie reached over without looking and patted Vargo's arm. He grabbed her hand and held it.

I asked, "Pil, do you have a charm that would help us understand this fellow?"

She scowled. "That would be lucky, eh? But no, and before you ask, I'd be happy to cook one for you if you don't mind waiting about seven hours!"

I thought it had been a reasonable question, but it must have struck her wrong. I walked to the edge of the drop-off and peeked over for a couple of seconds. I stepped back just before six arrows flew upward past me from the little fortification below. That didn't matter. I had already memorized the scene.

I pulled a white band, then flung it into the sky. A few seconds later, lightning flared and cracked. The slam of thunder seemed worse here than back home. When I glanced down, I saw sixteen men on the ground not moving, or at least, not moving much. The black lightning mark lay not far outside their fort.

Pil grabbed my arm and nodded. "Bib, look over there."

I hadn't had the leisure to survey much besides our enemies so far. Now I saw that these men a hundred feet below us were on a great expanse of rock. A quarter mile away, it ended in another drop-off, making an immense ledge.

The ledge plunged down into a wide canyon. I could see the other side of it. I gazed straight across but couldn't get a sense of scale. The canyon might have been two hundred feet wide or a mile.

"No, not there." Pil pointed. "Look left."

I shifted my gaze, and the first thing I noticed was that the wide rock ledge below us ran as far as I could see. Someplace between the horizon and me stood a bridge across the canyon. It was probably made of stone, since every other damn thing around here was. The bit of haze in the air washed out any details, but the bridge spanned the canyon in a great arch with no support from beneath.

I snarled. "It was built with magic, for sure. I wouldn't have thought that a stone bridge like that could stand. On this end, it rises at . . ." I shrugged.

"At least thirty-five degrees," Pil said. "That's the kind of bridge I might build if I could twitch a finger and make stone do whatever I wanted."

"Sure," Kenzie said. "I'd likely smack together a stone tower too. Sort of like that one over there." She pointed at a tower of greenish stone near the other end of the bridge. "How tall do you think that edifice is?"

"I couldn't begin to guess from this distance," I said. "Three hundred feet? Knowing Margale's ego, it's probably more."

Vargo walked up behind us. "You must be right, Pil. Those bitty-eared, six-fingered, dob-shite prisoners don't know what I'm saying. Hey, what are you looking at?" He pointed at the tower.

"Well," I said. "Until I am informed otherwise, I'm going to call it Margale's Dick."

FORTY-ONE

After we'd appreciated Margale's architecture for a while, we found some steps carved into the rock, leading down to the lower fortifications. The soldiers manning that post had all recovered, and they had run, stumbled, or been helped away by the time we got there. We were now on the proper level to cross the curved bridge that spanned the canyon. We still hadn't estimated the canyon's width worth a damn.

Vargo and Pocklin helped Chexis limp along in his wounded human form. They both spent most of that time predicting that we'd all die. Vargo moaned about how bad our luck was and insisted that we go home. Pocklin snarled about how we shouldn't have come here in the first place. He also called Vargo a whimpering nugget of scat who wouldn't accept death like a man.

We had to walk, since our mounts couldn't manage the small winding steps. The bridge and the tower didn't seem to get much closer as we traveled toward them. Either they were mighty far away, or they were enchanted up to the gods' drawers.

"Shit!" Pocklin yelled. At the same time, Vargo shouted, "Fingit suck it!"

I turned to see that Chexis was dragon-size again, and the men were on the ground to each side of him. The arrow that had pierced his leg had fallen to the rock, and he was shaking his right rear leg.

I said, "Chexis, I'm glad to see your dragon face again."

"We've been wallowing along as slow as bugs!" he said.

"I know. Stay with us. We don't know anything—"

Chexis snapped out his wings and launched into the air with a fine boom.

"—about Margale's defenses," I said to Chexis's dwindling butt. He sailed toward the bridge, flapping his wings every second or two.

Pil said to me, "It's all right; Margale already knows we're here."

"I just don't want the boy to stumble into some trap."

Pil raised an eyebrow. "Boy?"

"Well, boy dragon. You know what I mean."

"Bib, I could never picture you raising those dragon babies, but now I see it. Come on, everyone!" She tramped along the clifftop, not even glancing to see whether the rest of us were following.

A few minutes later, Chexis came back and landed in front of us. "Humans like big things. I know that for certain now."

"How long is the bridge?" I asked.

"I do dislike your imprecise measures. All your feet are different sizes, and from that springs a staggering degree of inaccuracy."

We stared at him until he shrugged. "The bridge is as long as thirty-six of me."

Kenzie took a second to glance at Chexis from snout to tail-tip. Then, before Pil or I could speak, Kenzie said, "That's over twelve hundred feet. Assuming you're thirty-six feet long, that's about a quarter of a mile."

Pil hissed. "That's thirty-six squared. Hell, it's six to the fourth!"

I said, "Margale's a smart sorcerer. It shouldn't surprise us that he's worked unlucky numbers into all his defenses. Unlucky for us. We'll just have to work harder."

Pil asked, "Chexis, did you measure the tower too?"

The dragon glanced down. "I didn't get as close." He stared around at us. "Not that I was afraid! I didn't like how it smelled. I estimate it's—"

"Don't say it!" Kenzie said. "It'll just dishearten me."

"What are they talking about?" Grik asked Vargo, off to the side.

"I have no clue." Vargo shook his head. "They think some numbers are good and some are bad, and none of it makes sense to me."

Pil said, "It's just the way the universe works, dear. In all the ways we can't see. We've talked about this."

"You talked about it," Vargo said.

"What does that mean?" Grik asked.

Kenzie quirked her mouth and sniffed. "How do you think we do things that seem like they should never happen? Do you know how much math is needed to throw magic, a thing that cannot be touched, and hit twenty arrows in flight?"

"I don't know how much math I'd need to buy a round of beers for the table," Grik said.

I cut in, "An unfortunate number doesn't mean we'll fail. It only means we'll have to work harder." *As if the universe will tie live ducks to our feet before we go into battle.* I didn't say that part, though.

"Look. What is that?" Pil asked, staring at the cliff off to our left.

We all looked, which put the canyon behind us. If Margale had risen out of the canyon then, he could have killed us all with one big swing.

"I don't see a thing. Nothing," Pocklin said.

Pil pointed at a spot seventy feet up and jabbed her finger at it. "There. It's right there!"

Vargo shook his head. "I don't know what you mean, Granda. Nothing's there except rock."

Kenzie said, "It's an opening shaped like a bird, darling. The very likeness of a bird flying exactly beneath you. I think it's a cave. Bib, what do you think about it being a cave?"

"It's a hole, at least," I said, shading my eyes for a moment. Then I reminded myself there was no sun to create glare.

Grik shook her head. "I don't see it. But if you say it's there, I believe you. I'll keep watch while you figure it out." She turned back toward the canyon with her hand on her sword.

I said, "Seems that only sorcerers can see it. Harik told me there was a place of power here."

"Harik told you?" Pil huffed. "Did Harik also tell you there was a place of whiskey and pretty girls who'll listen to you brag all day?" She turned away.

I cleared my throat. "If Harik didn't lie, it's where Margale became a Bender as well as a Burner. I'm going." I walked toward the cliff face.

"You're foolish to talk about climbing to it!" Kenzie called after me. "You still carry that wound in your knee. I'll go."

"The hell you will," Vargo said quietly. "You can't just think about yourself and your sorcery."

Kenzie closed her eyes for a moment before saying, "You're right, I won't go. Bib, you shouldn't either." She trotted to catch me.

Pil ran after me too, her short legs working harder than Kenzie's long ones. "Bib, do you really need to be more powerful? What will it cost? That is, well, will you end up like Margale?"

"No, I'll always be prettier than him. I need to find an advantage. I fear he'll kill us all."

"Not if we work together, and we've defeated worse than him in the past. I can count ten right now, and you can too," she said.

Rather than look at her, I stared up at the cave mouth, still walking. "That was in the past. The past is over."

I could almost hear her eyes narrow and her arms cross. "Go on then, but when you're all sad and broken, be ready for me to point out how stupid you've been. Bastard."

"I'll carry you there," Chexis said. "I'm much better at carrying things now. I could lift you and four goats up there at the same time. I couldn't in the past, but the past is over." He winked at me in an astoundingly human way before grabbing the back of my belt with one of his rear claws.

"Wait! No!" I yelled before Chexis slammed his wings against the air and took off. It felt as if my belt would cut me in half from front to back. I reached up and grabbed the dragon's leg to take off some of the strain.

"I'll swing you inside!" Chexis said. "Yell for me when you want to come down."

"Why are you helping me?" I yelled.

"I want to see what happens!" Then he hovered above the cave opening, flapping his wings slowly. Hovering was not an act he was physically suited to do, but he was a highly magical creature. He swung me with one leg, and I slammed into something invisible that blocked the cave opening. If it had been as hard as stone, I might have been hurt, but it stretched a bit as I struck it.

"Ahh!" I shouted.

Chexis had let go of my belt, but he snatched my left arm and then my right. "That was interesting," he said. "Should I try again? I won't let go this time."

I imagined Chexis smacking me against that opening over and over, like a boy with a rock tied to a string. "No, take me back down!"

When my feet touched the ground, Pil smirked. "Are you softening yourself up for Margale's club? Don't beat yourself senseless before the battle's even joined."

"Chexis was the one who beat me senseless, although I did ask him to do it. Thank you for trying, son."

Pil sighed. "All right, let's go kill that big runny turd and go home."

"Oh, I'm not giving up. I'll climb." I walked toward the cliff face again.

"What if you get there and it's still blocked?" Pil asked, running after me.

"Chexis will bring me down, won't you?"

"I will. This is a peculiar place, and your reactions are fascinating. Why are you climbing?"

"There's no good reason," I said. "I just feel like I should."

Kenzie caught up to walk on the other side of me from Pil. "Chexis, if you're interested in reactions, the first one will be a hideous crash and splatter when he strikes the ground. Bib, have some sense! You're wounded!"

"My knee will always be this way. If I can't climb up there hurt, I sure as hell can't kill Margale."

"If you absolutely have to go," Pil said, "have Chexis fly you almost there, so you only have to climb the last three feet."

I stopped and faced Pil. "I felt this magic when I hit it. When I was flung into it, that is. It's like the bridge in the Dark Lands. It's mean, bitter, and unfair. But it has rules. It's mean to everybody, bitter about everything, and unfair to everyone in the same way. I'm betting one of the rules here is that I have to risk the climb." I turned to Chexis. "That means nobody can hover around to grab me if I slip, right?"

"That would be cheating?" Chexis asked. Everyone stared at him, and he stared back. "I have learned a lot about cheating by watching humans."

I walked to the cliff face, found two handholds, and started climbing. The first twenty feet were easy. The cliff even slanted inward a little. I appreciated that because I wasn't a great climber. In fact, I felt my odds of success were less than fifty percent. But I was convinced that if I didn't succeed here, Margale would kill us all anyway.

At thirty feet, I reached a spot with no good place to grab. I backed down and took a slightly different path with better purchase. By forty-five feet, the cliff went straight up with fewer outcroppings. I was forced to stretch quite a bit—an experienced climber would have handled it fine, but I struggled. I panted and made more noise than a bushel of sticks and rocks thrown against a tin wall.

By sixty feet, my arms and legs were tired, and I reminded myself that this wasn't a good endeavor for people over a century old. I could shout for Chexis to fetch me down, but the cave opened just ten feet above me.

I struggled through those last feet until I reached a spot where my fingers could touch the cliff face less than a foot below the cave. With no other spots close enough to grip, I twisted until I could reach higher with one hand, stretching so far that I thought I'd stand lopsided forever. I was hanging on by the other hand and one foot, reaching as high as I could. I was still an inch from the opening.

Although my knee was screaming, I gathered myself and jumped. I got my fingers over the lip and hung on, then swung to get my other hand inside the cave mouth. I hung there a moment, preparing to pull myself inside.

Two hairy hands reached out of the cave and grabbed my wrists. I thought they were about to shove me out to fall and die, but a scratchy man's voice said, "That's good enough." He pulled me up into the cave, which was about the size of a large hut, with a nice fire in the middle of the floor.

The man who had helped me stood as high as my shoulder and was dressed in a nice tan linen shirt and trousers. He was barefoot, sallow skinned, and hairier than anybody I'd ever met. His straight black beard grew down to the middle of his chest and up almost to his brown eyes. One brutal eyebrow topped his square, blunt face. When he turned toward the fire, I saw that his black hair hung all the way down his back.

"Hello, Bib. Love the stories, by the way. Not as allegorical as everybody says, eh? My name's Simon. Sit by the fire and rest. I won't offer you food or drink. You'd be wary of eating or drinking anything in a magical cave."

We both sat on the floor next to the fire. Two wooden chests and several small bundles lined the cave walls.

"Is this where Margale came to get his power?" I asked.

Simon snorted. "You should have seen his gargantuan ass climbing the cliff. You have to admire his will to get things done, though. What questions does the hero Bib have for me?"

I stared into the fire for a moment, trying to think of a fine question, then I looked upward. To stall, I asked, "Where does the smoke go?"

Simon tilted his head. "It's a magical cave, dumbass." He shook his head and frowned at me.

I heard a distant shout through the cave mouth, then an explosion. Chexis roared, and something made an immense sizzling sound, like the world's biggest piece of bacon. A light flared so bright it lit part of the cave well enough to read.

I jumped up and ran to the cave mouth to look out, but it became a wall of rock.

"Open this!" I snarled.

Simon grinned. "So you can watch your friends be overrun without you? No. You chose to get on this creaky wagon. Now you have to ride it all the way to market. Do you have any more obvious, pointless questions?"

FORTY-TWO

I'd learned in sorcery school that trying to use force on a mystical creature is bad. It almost always fails because sorcerers are weaker, slower, and sometimes less clever than almost any mystical creature you could name. The sorcerer might not die, but somewhere out there would be a mystical creature who hated him. They generally live a long time, with many free hours to think about vengeance.

Therefore, I never attack mystical creatures. Or almost never.

Simon was clearly mystical. I could tell by his odd appearance, his air of superiority, and the buzzing diamond the size of my nose that hung from his necklace. Plus, he sat around in a magic cave. That was strong evidence.

I needed to negotiate. "Simon, I'm willing to forfeit whatever prize I might have earned here if you let me out."

"You haven't earned anything yet. I let you in, so you're in my debt."

"I climbed all the way up here. Doesn't that get me some consideration?" I asked.

"No. Nobody asked you to scale any cliffs. That's your own doing."

"All right. I want to solve this riddle or pass this test, whatever the hell it is, as fast as possible so I can use my new sorcery skill to help my friends. What can I offer you to speed this along?"

"Nothing. Sorry."

I glanced around the cave. "You don't have a bed. I could bring you one. An enchanted bed. What kind of enchantment would you like it to have? Sound sleep? Good dreams? Sex like a champion?" I hoped I could talk Pil into enchanting a bed however Simon wanted.

He grinned. "Beds are for men. And I suppose rabbits. A burrow is like a bed. I don't want a bed."

I held my breath for a moment. "I would never physically threaten you, Simon. But if you don't let me out, I'll make this cave a hell to live in. I'll sing whenever you try to sleep. I'll drag everything out of those chests and bundles, and I'll wallow on it all. I'll walk around behind you asking stupid questions. I'll pee in your fire."

Simon raised one hand. "Stop! There is a way, but it's difficult."

"How difficult?"

"Everybody who's tried it was killed."

"That sounds perfect." I assumed he was exaggerating to dissuade me. "What do I do?"

"Put your hands against the wall blocking the cave mouth. Imagine yourself flying. When you've imagined it strongly enough, the wall will disappear, letting you float to the ground. While you're floating, you'll receive the new sorcery skill."

"Huh. I don't want to insult you, but that sounds implausible. No wonder everybody has died."

"It's a magic cave! Is this crazier than what you do? Making toads dance or calling rain? Have some faith!"

I sighed. If Simon was trying to trick me, maybe I could call Chexis to catch me before I died. That was so farfetched I had to chuckle. I walked to the cave mouth and pressed my palms against the wall.

"Close your eyes and imagine feeling powerful. Invulnerable," Simon whispered.

The stone didn't feel as cool as I expected. The fire crackled. I smelled fresh bread. Simon's diamond buzzed. The back of my neck prickled, and I rolled to my left against the wall. It threw off Simon's aim as he thrust his knife toward my back.

I drew my knife while blocking Simon's weapon hand with my left forearm. He lifted his left arm to block me, so I knelt and drove my knife to the hilt under his left arm. He spasmed, fell on his back, and lay still. Unless mystical Simon carried his heart and arteries in different places than mine, he'd be dead in a few seconds.

"Shit. I killed him."

"You had to," said a high voice. "He's here to protect me from the unworthy, nasty types."

A girl of about fourteen in an embroidered silver dress stood in front of two white-painted wooden chairs. Her hair was brown, and her eyes were steady in her plain, square face. She stood with one leg forward, with a stitched silver shoe poking out from under her skirt.

I glanced back at Simon's body. It was gone. I didn't see any bloodstains.

Facing the girl, I said, "Nice shoes."

She grinned for a moment. "Bib, my name is Benet. I think I know why you're here, but you have to tell me. Those are the rules." She shrugged.

"Show me this challenge. I need to overcome it fast."

She waved a hand. "Are you worried about your friends? Oh, don't do that. Now that you've come so far, time isn't moving for them, at least compared to us. Or maybe we're moving so fast it seems like they're standing still. I'm learning the math for temporal equations, but I'm a little weak."

"I don't mean to slander your honesty, but I'd still like to move this along."

She stepped forward and said, "Please trust me," like a girl asking for a kitten.

"I'll trust you for now," I said. "I want a second sorcery skill. Greater sorcery, like you gave to Margale."

Benet looked to the side and frowned. "Margale. I wish he

wasn't so darn stubborn. Let me tell you all about him. Sit down so we can drink something while I tell you all his secrets."

I blinked and glanced around the room. Except for the hole in a wall leading back to Simon's cave, it looked like the daughter of some wealthy family lived there. Everything was painted white: the bed frame, the dresser with a real glass mirror, and a tall wardrobe. A pink-and-green rug covered most of the stone floor. I smelled a touch of perfume. I leaned toward the hole back to Simon's cave and sniffed. The smell of bread was gone.

Benet came back from the dresser with two engraved pewter mugs. "Here, I got us something a little stronger than beer. Sit down. That chair's a little nicer, so you can have it." She pointed.

The mug smelled like hard liquor, but that wasn't what seemed a little odd about Benet. As I sat, I realized that she wasn't bragging, preening, or threatening, normally three of a mystical creature's favorite things to do.

I bumped my arm on purpose as I sat and spilled a little liquor on the rug. "I'm sorry!" I knelt beside the spill. "Do you have a cloth or towel?" I paused when I saw the pink-and-green colors begin running together as the liquor ate through the rug's woolen threads.

"Definitely stronger than beer," I said.

Benet gave a weak smile and shrugged.

From behind me came a deep, round voice. "Forgive me for deceiving you—twice—with these distractions."

When I looked for Benet, she was gone. The back wall of her room had opened into what looked and smelled like a large barracks, with weapons hanging ready and bunks along the walls. I saw one person, but I hadn't yet stepped through.

He was big, not like Margale, but big in presence. His energy filled the whole space. He looked mature and maybe even middle-aged with some white hair I could spot from thirty feet away. His wide-jawed face was unshaven, with large eyes and slightly upturned lips. His rough leather clothes wouldn't be out of place on a battlefield, and he held a five-foot-long sword with its point against the stone floor.

"Oh hell, you're forgiven," I said. "We spilled a little poison, but that's nothing to men like us."

He smiled, showing two broken teeth. "I'm glad. We can't award the prize to any old miscreant who can climb some rocks. To be deserving, a person must be both devious and clever. You've shown yourself to be both."

I stayed back in Benet's room and didn't walk into this new space yet.

"What about strong and brave?" I asked. "Are you here to test me on that?"

"Of course not! I am Nubbin, the Red Warrior. It would be dishonorable to challenge you unprepared. Come in, and we shall talk about your coming trial."

"You mean listening to you wasn't the trial? That's disappointing."

Nubbin laughed hard and long, I guess to show that he wasn't offended. That meant he was pretty damn offended. Anybody called the Red Warrior would expect me to kiss his ass and beg for advice.

I drew my sword. "It's not that I don't trust and revere you, but my hip's getting tired. I don't know how you haul around that giant hunk of steel."

"I don't carry it to battle much anymore," he said. "Only when I'm fighting giants or demigods. Come on, I'll show you my everyday weapons. They have exceptional utility." He turned and walked toward the back wall, skirting a rough wooden table. Halfway there, he turned and beckoned me.

"This little girl's room is awfully nice. Maybe I'll sit on one of these white chairs for a while." I pulled a chair around to face Nubbin and sat on it.

Nubbin wandered back to me, rubbing his chin. He walked through the opening and sat beside me on the other white chair. He smelled like leather and oil. "Bib, let me explain this situation in its entirety. You want the prize of greater sorcery. I want you to have it. I do. But I am obligated to beings greater than either of us."

"Gods? Void Walkers?" I asked.

"No . . ."

"Demigod? Spirit? Pissed-off imp?"

"No, no, and no."

"How about a bridge guardian, or unicorn? What about a dragon?"

Nubbin shook his head.

"Then how much greater than us could they be? You're the damn Red Warrior! Bring your masters out here and let me talk to them."

"That's not possible."

"What is possible, then?"

Nubbin said, "Come with me to the barracks. We'll discuss the details there. This little girl's chair is hurting my ass."

I sighed. "All right, Nub." I smiled at the memory of my friend, Desh, known to the gods as the Nub. He'd be laughing at me now. "I'll come with you." I stood up but got my sword's scabbard tangled between the chair legs. "Here, hold my sword a minute. Damn scabbard." I handed the weapon over.

The first thing Nubbin did was look closely at my sword. That was natural. Anybody in the world would have done that. The next thing he did was jerk and gurgle as I drove my knife up through the bottom of his chin.

Nubbin clattered to the rug, creating a chorus of worn leather and steel buckles. I resheathed my sword and fetched one of Benet's towels to clean my knife. When I looked back at Nubbin's body, it was gone.

The sound of applause came from a good distance away, past Nubbin's barracks and through part of the room that opened beyond it. Somebody in there with a smooth, powerful voice called out, "Congratulations, Bib!" You are only the second person in an age to make it to the final room."

I drew my sword and strode into the barracks but didn't walk into the next room. "How long is an age? I've always wondered." A bent young man was sitting on what looked like a throne. To me, he resembled a frog on a lily pad.

"Bib, I am Zoffar. I keep the prize safe and share it with the worthy."

"That sounds like a great responsibility," I said, walking into his room, which was cramped but decorated in marble and gold.

"Oh, trust me, it is." He leaned partway back on his throne.

I thrust my sword through his chest.

"Criminal . . ." he gasped.

I walked past him as the back wall of his room opened onto a pool of water surrounded by marsh grass and mud. A pale yellow water spirit, a lot like Limnad, rushed at me. I sliced off an arm and then her head.

If she had been a real spirit, I'd have been dead before I raised my sword.

I shouted to no one in particular, "It would have been more believable if you put her in a river instead of that drip of a pond."

The next room looked like a stone courtyard, and a short grim priest pointed at me from across it. "Stop! You are condemning yourself in the eyes of the gods."

"Yeah, I've done that and gotten over it." I slashed his throat. He grabbed his neck and fell.

In the next room, I paused when I found a massive being with a glowing chest and hands of fire. She was more impressive than any demigod I had ever faced.

"You've reached your goal, Bib. Here is the prize you seek." She held out an intricately worked silver bracer.

"Thanks, but do you want me to burn my hand? Just put it on the table." I pointed toward a heavy oaken table against the wall.

She reached toward the table, and I sliced her arm deeply. I struck her neck with the return stroke, and she eased onto the floor like a bundle of cotton. The fires on her hands died, and her chest stopped glowing.

I glanced around for the wall that opened to the next room, but none of the walls disappeared. I chewed my lip as I stared back at the corpse.

"Crap."

I walked a couple of rooms back the way I'd come, but it was just a bunch of empty space with no bodies on the floors. When I came back to reexamine the unnamed glowing woman, her body was gone. I didn't know whether to be relieved that I hadn't killed the wrong person or pissed off that this wasn't finally over.

"Bib," said a familiar voice from behind me. I turned to see my mother, glowing and a bit transparent, the way most spirits of dead people present themselves. "You've almost gotten whatever this thing is that you want. I don't know what it is, but I guess it's important, since you've gone off to be a mighty sorcerer, and you must have and do all kinds of outlandish things. Why didn't you ever come back to see me one last time? Why didn't you tell me I had a granddaughter, the poor thing?"

I smiled at the ceiling. "Well, that was a mistake. My real mother wouldn't say that many words to me in a whole year." I whipped my sword through the ghost, and it dissolved.

None of the walls disappeared, but a wooden door appeared in one of them. I leaned in close to the door and shouted, "Get ready to be killed if you can't deal with me for what I want!"

I hesitated. The door was plain wood and a little warped. Nothing distinguished it, but I felt like I had stood in front of it before.

I grabbed the latch and pushed. The door opened, silent and smooth. Light sprang through from the room beyond.

A woman's voice said, "Hello, Bib. I baked some ginger cakes. Would you like to have one?"

FORTY-THREE

The voice didn't sound like it should belong to one of the universe's great powers. It sounded like the voice of a well-off tradesman's wife who appreciated good things and was probably smarter than her husband. But I knew that voice, which belonged to the Unnamed Mother of the Universe. It was a name given by her children. She admitted it was pretentious and even a little ridiculous. However, she did not tell people to stop calling her that.

A tall lantern on the table hid the woman's face, and suspicion wound through me. Voices were easy to mimic.

"I don't like ginger cakes anymore," I said, still standing in the doorway and glancing around the room. "If you really were the entity you want me to think you are, you'd know that." The bare walls were built of pale tightly joined stone blocks. A small sideboard stood against the wall on my right, and a large cabinet stood on my left, both made of rich brown waxy wood. Two yellowing wooden pitchers sat on the sideboard, along with a silver tray holding the cakes in question. The smell of ginger mixed with the scent of lamp oil.

"Are you sure you don't want a cake?" she asked. "I put on

chocolate buttons. Bib, your mother would be disappointed." The woman lifted a long bright knife and rested her hand on the back of a bone-colored stuffed chair. Another chair like it stood on the other side of the table. They were angled to face both the door and each other.

The cakes really did smell like my mother might have just brought them from the kitchen. I pointed my sword at the woman. "This isn't the Dark Lands, so you're not the Unnamed Mother. And if you were her, you wouldn't need that little bit of steel to protect yourself from me."

The woman stepped out from behind the lantern and lowered her knife. My sword's point wavered. She sure as hell looked like Mara, the Unnamed Mother. She was a robust dark-haired woman standing so straight she looked taller than she was. Her brown eyes crinkled at the corners, and her pale oval face had a slight double chin. White lace cuffs showed from the sleeves of her long dress, which was striped dark green and pink.

"How can I convince you?" she asked. "I could describe Krak's nastiest habits. Ask you to think of a number between one and ten thousand and then guess it. What's something that only you and I know?" She grimaced. "That would be difficult. I don't think you could know something that's so exclusive nobody else but me knows it."

The woman hurled the knife at my chest. I turned and knocked it aside with my blade.

She grinned. "If that's how you wish to behave, I won't prepare a gift for you next time. Pick it up, dear, we don't have much time."

I smiled and shook my head, taking a deep breath. "Everything outside is frozen while I'm in this cave, so we have as much time as we want."

She settled on a chair, sitting as straight as if the chair back didn't exist. Raising an eyebrow, she said, "Everything's frozen? I'm astounded that you would believe such an obvious lie."

My teeth clenched extra hard because I had been so stupid.

"Fetch your knife and bring a pitcher," she said. "You can pour for me this time. Oh, perhaps that's something only the two of us know. I poured beer for you last time. And mind that you don't catch your foot on the rug!"

I hurried back with the knife in one hand and a pitcher of beer in the other. "Fine, I accept that you're Mara. It's wonderful to see you, and thanks for the knife. May we please get the challenge done quickly now? I'd like to get the new power while there's still time to help my allies."

"If you rush, perhaps you'll die. That wouldn't help anybody." Mara raised a tall, wide pewter flagon, one of two that had been on the table.

I poured for her and then for me. She stared at the empty chair, so I sat. I drained my flagon, and despite myself, I relaxed a bit. "I really do have a battle to fight."

Mara glanced at the knife in my hand. "You're welcome."

"Yes, I am grateful. Sincerely! Is it enchanted? What does it do?"

"It's marvelously shiny."

I grinned at her. "Yes, it's bright, it's pretty, and the beer makes me think of beaches and beautiful girls." I paused. "Are Pil and the others already dead?"

"Not yet. But they will be if you don't begin cooperating."

"All right!" I snapped. "I apologize. What do you need me to do?"

Mara smiled so that her eyes almost disappeared. "I told you many things when we last met, and quite a lot of them were secrets, or almost secrets. Now you will tell me things. I think that Murderer is an appalling name for you. What should your name be?"

"Are you going to change my name?"

"Of course not! You're not a fool, so don't say foolish things. Humor me. What *should* it be?"

"Uh, Not-a-Fool. Knife-on-the-Floor. Hell, I don't know!"

"Take this seriously."

"I don't know how many people I've killed, Unnamed Mother, but it's been a lot. How could my name not be the Murderer?"

"I know precisely how many you have killed," she said. "It is knowledge that would do you no good. Close your eyes. Very well. Within a minute, the answer will come to you. You'll know when it does, and then you will tell me the name. Don't say anything until then."

I silently called Mara a nasty, rim-rolling cow's crusty asshole. It didn't make me any less pissed off at her, and then I felt guilty for thinking mean thoughts about her. I didn't know what name she was looking for. I tried not to picture Pil and the others assaulted by hundreds of Margale's pinch-faced soldiers, but I failed. Hopefully, Pil still had a pouch full of magical crap that was awful enough to scare away a few hundred men. Vargo and the others would have to protect her. If Kenzie called a wind, she could fill the enemies' eyes with—"

Mara slapped my face hard enough to make my ears ring. "What was the next word you were thinking?"

With one eye closed, I rubbed my cheek. "Chicken beak."

"It was not!"

"Was so. From now on, I'm Chicken Beak." I didn't know why, but I hesitated to even hint at having a name so ambiguous as Dust. "Chicken Beak the Magnificent."

Mara sighed. "No one will ever call you that."

"You underestimate how persistent and annoying I can be."

"It doesn't matter. Fine. Chicken Beak. If Gorlana had named you Chicken Beak all those years ago—"

"My life would have been totally different, right?"

"No, it would have been almost exactly the same. It might have looked different to you, though."

"Humph. Am I done? Is . . . is this name going to give me the extra power?"

"No. Is power really what you came here for?" Mara asked.

That stopped me. "I'm pretty sure it is. Unless there's something more useful."

"Margale demanded extra power."

"He sure as hell got what he asked for. Are you the one who gave it to him?"

"No, someone else did it."

"But you can give me powers like that?"

"No." She shrugged. "But I can convince somebody else to do it."

I started to tell Mara I wanted the power of a Breaker. That way if Margale bent something into a shape I didn't like, I could make it not exist. But the way she was smiling at me made me pause.

"Unnamed Mother, I ask that you give me whatever you think will serve me best."

"Flatterer. Well, there are alternatives to receiving a new power. I'm speaking of your lost ability to heal."

I stared at her for a couple of seconds. "Good, I'll take that."

"Don't you—"

"I'll take that," I said again. "Please."

The Unnamed Mother of the Universe stood and nodded. "Goodbye, Bib the Chicken Beak." She looked down, but I saw a grin. "You may leave through that door." She pointed to a wooden door that hadn't existed a few seconds earlier.

"Thank you." I stood, hesitated, and jumped over to cram a dozen cakes into a pouch. Then I ran out the door and slid to a stop just before hurtling out of the cave mouth and down the cliff.

FORTY-FOUR

(CHEXIS)

Bib has nothing else to teach me. He hates Margale, but he climbs all the way up to a magic cave so he can be like Margale and do whatever Margale does.

He wants Pil to love him, but he won't just ask her what she doesn't like and stop doing whatever that is. He keeps doing more of what he's been doing as if suddenly she'll feel differently about it. Even I, a being who doesn't believe in love, know that's an ignorant way to go about things.

Bib told me he killed lots of people and then tried to atone for it by killing lots of people. I had to ask him to repeat that twice.

So, this is the thing Bib taught me, although he didn't know it: being human means totally believing two opposite things at the same time without going crazy or realizing how foolish it is.

It's so outlandish, I forgive myself for not seeing it sooner.

I am a dragon. Sphynthor taught me. Bib taught me things too, and they were not dragon things but seemed useful. I had believed dragon things and human things at the same time, but they're opposite.

Thinking like that is what it means to be human. It's *mannish*.

Now that I know this, I can certainly avoid thinking that way in the future, so I am done here.

I flew toward the river that led back to the world of man, and I ignored the shouting and clanking behind me. Margale's soldiers had rushed over the bridge before Pil and the others could get there. As I flew away, they faced eighty-seven soldiers charging to hack them apart. More soldiers were coming across the bridge.

Oh well. If Bib's friends didn't die now, something else would kill them soon. Humans hardly lived any time at all.

I was glad to be leaving before Bib came back out of the magic cave, since I had decided to eat him before I left. I should eat him to obliterate the human bits he put inside me. I hated to go back on something once I've decided it. It's like breaking a promise to myself, and I am very important to me.

But Bib kills dragons, so he might not be so easy to eat. Leaving was for the best.

I heard Bib shout, "Chexis!" from behind me, probably from the magic cave. The sound didn't make me happy, since now I'd have to kill him. I turned, flew back to the cave, and found Bib standing in the cave mouth. He was staring at the sky, and I could feel he was doing something magical to it.

He yelled, "Carry me down there to help them!"

I should probably have just started biting him, but he had given me an idea. If he let me carry him away from the cave, I could drop him. Then he wouldn't have a chance to kill me. I would fly down to where he landed and eat him there.

It was a clever plan. Even Sphynthor might say it was good. I reached out with my rear claws and grabbed Bib at the shoulders, then I flapped and flew away from the cave.

I didn't drop Bib right away. If I flew over to where everybody was fighting, I could drop him on one of Margale's soldiers, or even two. I was still mad at Margale for smashing my shoulder, so killing his soldiers would be fun.

Bib had done a bad thing to me by teaching me to be human when I was a baby, so I should want to kill him.

I flew over Margale's men.

"Put me down over there, by Pil!" Bib yelled.

I ignored him, but I did drop lower so I could aim better. Maybe I could drop Bib on three soldiers.

"No, back over there!"

"I'm sorry." I didn't mean to say that and can't imagine why I did. It just burst out of me like a jet of flame. I flew past the mass of soldiers and circled back.

Bib was quiet then. When I reached the soldiers again, he said, "That's all right, son. I trust you."

I flew past the soldiers again without dropping him, although I intended to every second. They fired a few arrows at us. Most of them fell short, but one flew twice as fast as the others, hurtling to pierce my left wing. Nothing had ever made a hole in my wing before. I didn't know how hard that would make flying.

I slid sideways, wobbled, and almost flipped all the way over. I plunged toward the ground, struggled up a few feet, and twisted toward Pil and the others. I let go of Bib about ten feet off the ground, and I am sure he mowed down at least three soldiers. I hit the ground and slid, knocking down a few more soldiers.

By the time I stood, Bib had already killed two men and was limping toward a third. I battered a man to death with my tail, clawed another, and scorched two so badly they probably wouldn't live. Then Bib poked a soldier with the shiny knife in his left hand. Light flashed so brightly it hurt my eyes, and the soldier stumbled before wandering away.

Within a minute, the soldiers pulled back. A few of them ran away. Bib limped to join Pil and the others, and I followed him. I didn't know what else to do.

Kenzie and her mate both lay on the ground with their eyes closed, both wounded in their left shoulders. When I looked at them, my shoulder tingled where Margale had smashed it. Pil had gathered up a few small rocks and was doing something magical with them. The man with no hair was guarding them all, and his daughter trotted over to us.

"Really sweet of you to come back, you two," the daughter said, staring at Bib and then at me. "Are you all right?"

Bib flexed his knee but nodded. "I see that Kenzie started conjuring a storm. I'll keep working on it. Are you wounded?"

"Not so much." Blood had trickled down the side of her face. "Kenzie and Vargo were both hurt bad."

Bib walked over to the wounded people, examined them, and said, "I'll heal Kenzie first, then she can heal Vargo. That way I might still be able to use my left arm a bit. Chexis, I understand if you leave. This isn't your fight."

"You're right, it's not!" I growled. "If I weren't so reckless as to let them put a hole in my wing, I could fly away, and by Ceslik I would! But since I'm stuck, I'll help you. I won't stand far away and watch you all be killed. I'll stand next to you while you're killed!"

I thought Bib might comment on my generosity and courage, but all he said was, "When I signal you, rush over there to this end of the bridge and prevent any more soldiers from coming across it."

"Oh." I paused. "They had an arrow that put a hole in me. I don't see any reason they couldn't have more. And Margale has that awful club. I may be killed."

Bib nodded. "You're right, I can't ask you to do that. We all have to decide for ourselves. Think hard. There's a damn good chance we'll all die."

"Why don't you turn around and go back?" I gazed at the river that led out of this realm. Without looking back at Bib, I said, "Is it revenge?"

"Margale is a dire and wicked sack of piss. One of the worst I've ever seen. If we kill him here, we'll save all those he would have hurt and killed in the future."

I considered that. A dragon would never kill another dragon. But that meant a dragon would never kill a dragon today to save other dragons in the future. To do that would presuppose the ability to know the future, which was a silly idea. We could end up with a lot of killing now to prevent bad things that might not happen anyway.

I told myself that this was another human thing that made no sense. Then I pictured Margale smashing my brother with his god-club.

Walking closer to the canyon rim, I eyed the bridge and decided I could rush to it fast if Bib signaled me. I didn't know what the signal would be, but Bib looked busy healing Kenzie and talking to Pil at the same time. I'd wait a few minutes to ask him what the signal for a reckless and doomed attack was.

FORTY-FIVE

When Chexis carried me down from the cave, he gripped my arms so hard I imagined they might pop off. I wondered if he was afraid that he'd drop me, but that didn't make much sense. A couple of days earlier, he had flown along dragging me through trees and against the dirt, and he'd shown no concern that he might hurt me.

Then Chexis ignored me when I asked him to put me down. Well, maybe I didn't ask so much as demand, and that could have ruffled the boy. He flew me over the mass of soldiers and then turned for another pass, and that revised my thinking. Maybe I had offended him somehow, and he intended to show me who was in charge. I guess if he was really mad, he might drop me to my death. If that was his plan, he had outmaneuvered me handily.

But he might be clamping me so tight because he hadn't convinced himself to kill me, not deep down.

There wasn't a damn thing I could do to stop him, so I decided to use guilt. It had worked for my mother, intimidating my sisters and me more than if she'd carried a battleax in each hand. I told Chexis I trusted him and then scanned the ground in case he dropped me anyway. I could hope to land on some of the softer rocks, if there were any.

When arrows flew at us, I prepared to pull some bands and dismantle them. That proved unnecessary for most of the arrows, since they flew nowhere near us. But while I was looking damn hard for archers, I saw Margale's red-robed sorcerer Parbett fire her arrow. It hurtled with fierce speed. I was able to hit it with a blue band, but my magic didn't destroy it or even slow it down. I felt sad but not shocked. Only an enchanted arrow would fly that fast.

Chexis jerked hard and slipped sideways when the arrow tore a hole in his wing. The arrow wasn't just magic, it had to be enchanted with divine magic. I imagined one of Fingit's demigod toadies banging away on the thing, but I didn't imagine that for long. Chexis plunged, lifted a little, and dropped me at twice my height above the ground. I slammed into two soldiers, wrenched my knee, and scraped half my face on the rock before I came to a stop and started killing on all sides. I didn't have the leisure to be nice to my enemies, and I needed the vitality my sword would give me with each kill.

Chexis landed in a heap but bounced up and ran toward me. He clawed, whacked, and bit a path through Margale's soldiers. They endured only a small amount of our fury before they withdrew toward the bridge. I estimated there were seventy of them, with more coming across every minute.

After a word with Chexis, I needed to do several things that were equally important. It looked as if Kenzie had been pulling together a storm before she was wounded. It had drifted apart a bit, so I spun several white bands to draw it together. At the same time, I knelt over Kenzie and examined her wound.

Pil put a hand on my shoulder from behind. She panted as she said, "Did you get what you went after?"

"No, but I got something I wanted." I began pulling green bands that would help Kenzie's shoulder wound close and heal.

Pil gasped. "Fingit and Krak and their little white bear! You can heal!" She hugged me around the neck.

"Stop it. I might make her grow a third arm." Pain was sinking into my left shoulder as Kenzie's mended. Without looking around, I said, "Pil, what are your orders?"

I heard her snort. "This is a mess, so I'm making you leader, and I'll walk around clearing the field of busted weapons. Never mind. If we want to get Margale, we'll have to cross the bridge, but he can collapse the bridge and drop us a mile into the canyon whenever he wants."

"A mile?"

"It looks like a mile to me," she said. "Maybe it's the perspective, you know. Staring down at your probable death might make it seem deeper. A mile, a thousand feet, a hundred feet—it doesn't make a howling bit of difference when you hit the ground."

Kenzie opened her eyes.

I said, "You're going to be fine, young woman, and I'll be finished in a minute. Then you can heal your husband."

She tried to sit up, but I pushed her back down. She asked, "How bad is he?"

"Bad, but not so bad that you can't save him."

"Bib, you're healing me!"

"Sure. I think I'll put a sign on my chest that says, 'Yes, I heal now. Buy me a beer.' You're done."

Kenzie shifted and knelt over Vargo. Pil was talking to Pocklin, nodding as he pointed at something about Margale's men. Grik was questioning a wounded soldier. He did nothing except glower until he pulled a hand free of his bonds and jumped at Grik, scratching her face with his claws. As he struggled to his feet, she thrust her sword into his chest.

"Damn it!" Grik shouted. "Damn every one of them to be limp forever!" She used her hand to dab at the scratches on her face. "Bib, we've captured three since you climbed up that wall, and none of them will talk. One of them broke his arm trying to pull free. It's like they think we're monsters or demons."

I scanned the sky. "Maybe Margale has convinced them we're vile, baby-eating, granny-stomping, hell animals. We're beautiful, but that's only so we can lure them to a horrible death."

"I'm glad you think this is funny," Grik said. "We'll probably die here."

"Hell, Grik, that's no way to think! We're outnumbered, with no viable options, and we're facing one of the most dangerous sorcerers I've ever met. This is the time for confidence. If you ride around all morose, you're just waiting to die. But all kinds of opportunities show up during a battle, when nobody really knows what the hell's going on. If you're confident and alert, you may grab one."

"What if there's no opportunity to grab?" she asked.

"Then you die. But at least you spent your last hours fierce, with your foot on the world's throat, not whining because of bad fortune."

Grik smiled and sheathed her sword. "I'm going to search these bodies for arrows. I've run low."

I turned away and pulled a couple of white bands to work on the storm. Then I froze. Something about the second band felt wrong. I tried again.

Bands of different colors don't have an innate sequence. There was no such thing as bands of one color being arranged next to another color. But ever since I was a boy sorcerer, I had thought of them in order because that made it easier to grab the right color. For me, from left to right, they were red, yellow, green, blue, and white.

Now I sensed some color beyond white, and I had never felt that before. I gently pulled from that new place, using a tiny amount of power. That created a dull gray band.

I hadn't been the finest student in my sorcery school, Gallinn on the Mere. But I had managed to stay awake on the day we studied bands and colors. This was a gray Breaker band, ready to make something not exist anymore.

I glanced at the ground and spotted a pebble. I sent the band to wrap itself around the pebble, then I imagined twisting it. The band disappeared, taking the pebble to oblivion with it. It also took a pit out of rocky ground the size of a bucket.

Right away, I redefined "tiny amount of power."

One law of sorcery is that simple feats take less power than complicated ones. For example, creating fire was simple, while convincing rats to swarm underneath a man's clothes was more involved. I learned that when I was eleven.

But I had thought that simple feats might take half as much power as complicated ones, or maybe a fourth as much. Now that I had actually disintegrated something, I realized it cost a tenth as much power as a more challenging feat, such as creating fog. Maybe it cost even less.

Closing my eyes, I whispered, "Shit! I mean, thank you, Unnamed Mother. I'll use this to . . . well, you wouldn't believe any of my promises, but I'll do my best."

I scanned the field. It looked as if Margale's men were massing to attack again. I guessed about ninety would charge in a minute or so.

I shouted, "Kenzie! Can you call lightning yet?"

"Almost!" she answered, staring at the sky.

"Well, hurry, and stay behind me! Pil, when they charge, you and Vargo run seventy feet to my right. Grik, you and Pocklin run seventy feet to my left."

"What?" Pocklin shouted. "You've lost your mind!" He turned to his daughter. "He's lost his mind." Pointing at me, he shouted, "I don't mind fighting, or even dying, but I won't be cut apart like a lamb for roasting!"

"Grik, you go. He'll follow you," I said.

Grik nodded. "Sure. It looks like you have plans."

Pocklin sputtered.

Pil asked, "Bib, what are these plans?"

"No time to explain. If you ever loved me, trust me now. Everybody, hold your ears! This will be loud! And Chexis, you stand here beside me!"

"Here they come!" Vargo shouted.

Vargo and Pil ran right. Grik and Pocklin ran left, with him cursing all the way.

Margale's men didn't approach in good order, or in much of any order. They came in a great mass, and only the ones in front could see us. A few of them angled to meet our left and right flanks as our people raced into position.

I pulled four gray bands, considered the situation, and pulled one more. I flung them, and they spread like warm butter to cover eighty by sixty feet of the stony ground. I twisted, and a thundering boom sounded as air rushed in where rock had disappeared to a depth of ten feet. At least fifty men fell as I destroyed the ground under them.

Every one of the soldiers, and not just the ones in the pit, slowed down, stunned by the noise.

"Attack!" I shouted. "Kenzie, work on the lightning. Chexis, stay with me."

I ran to the edge of the pit and counted the men in a few moments. Fifty-four of them were struggling to their feet. Every man was naked from his toes to his waist.

"Did you mean to do that? To have their genitals hanging out like that?" Chexis asked. "Is it to demoralize them?"

"I wish I could say yes, but this disintegration business is new and my control lacks precision."

"They'll just crawl up on each other's shoulders and climb out, won't they?"

I nodded and spun more gray bands. Another explosion sounded as I disintegrated the pit down to twenty feet deep. Some of the soldiers were cowering, others were stumbling, and some were shouting at me, probably curses and threats. A few began stringing bows.

I pointed left. "Go help Grik and Pocklin. Stay away from the bridge for now."

"Why?"

"That's where that dragon-maiming arrow came from."

I half-limped, half-ran to Pil and Vargo.

Many years before, Pil had created an enchanted knife that was surpassingly sharp. She preferred to fight with it, and I had trained her in combat for decades in the Dark Lands. She hated killing, but she didn't hold back now. Vargo guarded her flank as she marched through the soldiers, cutting them down. Soon they were running from her.

"Don't chase them!" I shouted.

"Don't chase them?" Pil smirked. "What do you think I am, a milkmaid with a stick? Don't chase them, indeed."

"Sorry, I got carried away by the glories of command." I gazed over at Chexis and the others. Soldiers on that side were retreating too. I imagine the retreat had begun when a dragon showed up to fight them.

Margale's men had fallen back to gather around the bridge entrance. I nodded at Kenzie. During the next fifteen seconds, three strokes of lightning landed on the mass of soldiers. After that, the few not lying motionless on the ground crawled or staggered back toward the bridge.

"Chexis, go to the bridge now!" I bellowed.

The dragon half-ran, half-slithered to the bridge entrance, burning and stomping survivors along the way. Once at the entrance, he breathed fire at anybody who came near.

The bridge arched high above us, and anybody on it could look down as if they stood on a hillside. I spotted Parbett in her red robe among the soldiers as she raised her bow.

I spun a gray band fast, hoping that only the arrow was enchanted, not the bow. I hurled the band to envelop the bow and twisted. The bow disappeared. The arrow slipped away from Parbett, bounced on the rock, and skidded over the edge into the canyon.

Even from so far away, I could tell that the sorcerer was spouting profanity like a kettle.

Chexis held most of the soldiers bottled up on the bridge. Two came forward to face him. He burned one man alive. He played with the other one a bit, tossing him in the air before batting him into the canyon. Kenzie set herself to dismantling any arrows that might come our way.

"Well, we made it to the bridge," I said to Pil, wiping sweat off my face. "What now? If we cross, Margale can just bend it enough to make it fall down with us on it. Or he can bend the spots under our feet to create holes. We'll fall through and die. Then he can repair the holes and still have a nice bridge."

Pil sighed. "He certainly used magic to make this thing, but once he was done, the bridge wasn't magic anymore, was it? Now it's just plain old rock that he's finished with."

"I don't like this, but keep going."

"If I enchant the bridge itself, then his magic won't affect it."

"Uh-huh. Why don't you enchant the whole canyon too? And when we go home, there's an ocean right there waiting to be enchanted," I said.

"Asshole. The bridge is big, but it's a discrete object, and I could perform the tiniest enchantment possible, one that wouldn't cost much power, relatively. And I could take some negative consequences to bring the cost down."

"How much do you think it will take?"

"Fourteen squares, or maybe fifteen."

"Krak's mistress riding on a pony! Is that all?" I rolled my eyes.

"I think it's possible. I have three squares now, and well, I have two of these." She reached into a big pouch to pull out a leather bottle with a wax stopper, then she showed me just the top before she tucked it away. Each of those bottles held one square of power. She said, "Those are the last two of the ones Desh made."

"You carried them around all these years?"

"Well, no." She paused. "You probably don't want to hear this."

I pointed around us. "Is it going to make all this worse?"

"Limnad brought them to me the night after we left the Bole."

I paused. "I don't know what to say to that."

"She came to congratulate me on breaking your heart. She offered to bring me what was left of your heart, but I thanked her and said maybe later."

I nodded slowly. "I appreciate that, although you were right, I didn't want to hear it. So, you need ten more squares. Ten is the most I've ever gotten in one trade."

"I intend to bargain better than you." She grinned.

"I'm coming with you to trade."

"No, I don't want you there!"

"Hell, I'm definitely coming now."

I felt Pil lift herself toward the trading place, so I grabbed on to come along.

FORTY-SIX

I arrived in the trading place and found something I had never seen before. The brown dirt I stood on was so dry that when I moved my foot, dust rose like smoke. The forest was gone, replaced by a great field of bare gray earth. I saw a distant green valley on the other side and maybe a mountain beyond that.

The field of flowers to my right had been obliterated too. Where they had been, empty gray dirt stretched as far as I could see.

I felt as if it should be hot, but the air was still, not hot and not cold. It was awfully damn dry. My lips felt chapped within ten seconds.

"Be careful," I murmured to Pil. "Something's wrong." I didn't know whether she heard me. She didn't have sight in the trading place like I did, and she could only hear what the gods wanted her to hear.

Pil belonged to Lutigan, the God of War, so I wasn't surprised when he swaggered out of the dimness deep in the gazebo. Most of the gods created perfectly beautiful forms for themselves, although the new Harik hadn't followed that tradition.

Lutigan openly despised beauty. When he clenched his fists, fierce ropes of muscle sprang out on his scarred, pitted arms. His great chest was protected by scraped red armor made from the skins of the fourteen most terrible monsters he had killed. Maybe that was bluster on his part, but I never challenged him on it. His red hair hung wild, and his scowling face was so sharp I could imagine him beating enemies to death with it.

The God of War pulled one of his fourteen divinely enchanted swords off his back and pointed it at me.

"Hello, Mighty Lutigan," I said.

Pil added, "Yes, you—"

"Be quiet, Knife." Lutigan bit each word and spit it at her. He stepped toward me and showed his teeth.

I swallowed. "How've you been, Your Magnificence? I haven't seen you since the family dinner. Has it really been seventy years?"

Centuries ago, one of Lutigan's randy demigod sons showed my umpteenth great-grandmother how they do things in the Gods' Realm. That put a whisker of divinity through Lutigan's line into my blood, which I didn't care much about. Lutigan had made it clear that he didn't give a shit about it at all. He regularly killed his sons if they pissed him off.

The God of War, my incredibly distant great-grandfather, took another step toward me. I managed not to shuffle backward, but I did shiver.

He said, "How dare you come here . . . Chicken Beak?" He locked eyes with me. I didn't know what the hell to do.

Lutigan snorted. Then he blinked twice, turned his back to me, and laid his sword over his shaking shoulder while he laughed. "Dammit! Krak curse it with piles! And those little lizards with poisoned spines too!" He laughed some more. I didn't say anything. As long as Lutigan wasn't laying a curse on me or planning my death out loud, I considered myself to be ahead.

At last, he turned to face me, wiping his eyes with his free hand. "Gorlana told me I'd laugh. I owe her three of those chubby flying horses. Chicken Beak. Only you would be so ridiculous. Nobody will ever call you that again, but you certainly brightened my day."

Pil said, "May I speak, Mighty Lutigan?"

"Go ahead."

Pil probably intended to face me, but having no sight, she turned toward the corner of the gazebo instead. "Chicken Beak? What the hell?"

I waved a hand, even though she couldn't see it. "Just a little fun Mara and I were having over beer and cake."

She raised her voice. "The Unnamed Mother? That's who gave you this new power? And the old power? Again?"

"That's right, and she was sweet about it too. You should have come along," I said. "It's probably too late for you now."

Lutigan set down a foot, not quite hard enough to count as a stomp, but it was an attention-getter. "That's enough of this silliness. Knife, I see that you have a bridge problem, and I can guess what you want to do about it. You'll need a lot of power, maybe more than you want to pay for. You've always been hesitant about making the hard deals."

"It's kept me alive. And sane," Pil said.

"Maybe alive. But sane? You married the Murderer. Looking back, does that seem like sanity?"

I heard Pil's teeth clack together, and I closed my eyes. If she wanted to make a decent deal with Lutigan, she couldn't afford such emotional reactions.

"I want ten squares," Pil said. "I extend to you the pleasure of making the first offer."

"Hah!" Lutigan barked. "For ten squares . . . you'll make sure the Avalanche survives and goes free."

"If I plan to do that, why would I cross the bridge? I wouldn't need any power."

"That is a point," Lutigan said. "All right, blind him first."

Pil said, "Somebody will heal him, and then one night he'll smash us in our sleep with his giant club."

I added, "How did he get that club, anyway? Who made it?"

"Bib," Pil grated, "that's not the main point right now!"

"Sorry, I thought the knowledge might be useful. But . . . go ahead."

She said, "I can't let Margale live. He's too dangerous. Mighty

Lutigan, you're the God of War. I'll join the first war I find as I travel, and I'll win it for the side I choose."

"That's vague. You might join a little skirmish and call it a war. I will select the war, and I'll choose which side you join."

I wanted to tell her not to take that deal, that she'd be entirely in Lutigan's control, but I stayed quiet.

Pil said, "For ten squares of power, you choose the war, but I choose the side I help."

"I don't like the choosing aspect of this deal," Lutigan said. "It seems weak. Uncertain. I feel disgruntled by it." He swung his sword, and I felt the air swish from fifteen feet away. "Knife, in exchange for ten squares, war will follow you the rest of your life. You will fight in war after war until you die."

I choked but managed not to speak.

Pil said slowly, "Mighty Lutigan, I understand your position. My offer for ten squares is that I will be involved in wars for the next year."

"Ten years."

"Two," Pil said.

"Five," Lutigan said. "And five is as far as I'll go."

Pil was breathing hard, but she couldn't be aware of her body in the trading place. "If I accept that, I want twenty squares instead of ten."

Lutigan almost smiled. When gods smile, it's never good for people.

"You've bargained well, Knife. You can have twelve squares in exchange for five years of warfare, and once you defeat Margale, you will take his club to the Bole and destroy it. I believe you know where that is, right?"

Pil held her face still. "I do. I accept the bargain."

"That's good, damn good. Farewell, Chicken Beak."

I would never claim that the God of War giggled, but as he tossed us toward our bodies, he did sound a little blithe.

Back in my body, I said, "I'm sorry you had to make that deal, Pil. I wish I could have helped."

She looked at me, and I flinched. She wasn't angry, but her face had a hardness I had never seen.

I whispered, "That deal changed you, Pil."

She squinted at me. "Really? I don't think so. I feel the same as always. Now, let's enchant this bridge so we can kill every son of a bitch over there."

FORTY-SEVEN

P il knelt at the very edge of the bridge to examine its stone surface. Chexis breathed fire at Margale's soldiers to keep them back. The dragon set an incautious man ablaze, who ran screaming straight off the side of the bridge. He fell like a flaming meteor all the way down. Chexis roared at the sky and then laughed when the soldiers scurried back, bunching themselves on the narrow bridge and knocking two more of their cronies over the side.

Pil patted and rubbed the bare rock. She pressed her ear to it. I didn't see her taste it, but maybe I missed that while I watched for arrows.

I had taken over arrow duty while Kenzie healed my knee, or healed it as much as possible. She would come away from the effort with a sore knee and a limp of her own. She had said, "Bib, this battle will hang on your skill of arms, not mine, and if you can't spring about, then you can't fight worth crap. Nobody cares if I'm gimping along behind."

From far away, the bridge had looked like a string arched across the canyon. From closer, it had still looked narrow. When I reached the span, I saw that it was eight feet wide and about twenty feet thick where it joined the canyon wall. Eight head-spinning feet with no railings would let people pass each other, but there was no practical room to fight side by side. The battle would take place between two individuals at a time, facing each other, until one was killed and somebody moved up to take his place.

So when I killed a man, I would need to rush up and take his spot, then face the next man. Doing that would get us across the bridge.

The bridge looked about a quarter mile long. How many steps might that be? Lackadaisical walking-around-town steps would be about two and a half feet long. But we'd be in combat and pushing hard, so I figured each step to be three feet long. I called the total four hundred and fifty steps.

When you walked onto the bridge, it angled up sharply, at least thirty-five degrees. Then it curved all the way to the top of the arch, which was level for a space. It curved back down toward the side where Margale's Dick stood. I assumed the bridge was about as steep on the far side as it was on this side.

The journey would be two hundred and twenty-five climbing steps to the middle, fighting one-on-one all the way, then two hundred and twenty-five steps down to the other side. I assumed we'd be fighting the whole time. I couldn't think of a reason why the soldiers would suddenly run away or do something whimsical like fling themselves off the bridge unasked.

I also assumed that I would go first. Everybody else seemed to assume it too.

"Chexis, I want you to do me a favor," I said. "Don't go onto the bridge."

"But that's where the people are. The ones that are fun to kill."

"I don't want you to risk getting shot with another of those horrible arrows. And if you fall off the bridge and can't fly, you might hurt yourself."

"I don't think it's possible for the ground to hurt me, no matter how hard I hit it."

"Maybe not. But you're a heavy creature. Your weight might be too much for the bridge, and if it collapses, we'll all die. Well, except for you, I guess. Just please, don't go onto the bridge."

Chexis grumbled, sounding like a little boy who's been told he can't play with the chickens, but he promised.

Kenzie finished with my leg, and I thanked her as she took over arrow watch.

I squatted beside Pil. "What do you think? Can you enchant it? Or do we go home? I suppose I could try to destroy the foundation of his tower, but it's a long way off. I'd need more power, and ten thousand pounds of collapsing stone probably wouldn't kill that bastard anyway."

"I can do it," Pil muttered. "I'm going to enchant this bridge so that any bugs crossing it will walk slightly slower than they would normally."

"I haven't seen any bugs."

She winked at me. "I know. The fact that no bugs will ever be affected makes this enchantment a bit less costly." She hesitated. "But it's a huge enchantment. I had to accept something bad to create it."

I raised my eyebrows at her. Then I realized I was holding my breath.

"I'll tell you when it's time," she said.

I didn't insist that she tell me now. It would only piss her off, and I didn't have the right to ask anyway. I did dare to ask, "With all the magic baubles you used up healing Chexis, have you spent them all? Do you need to create more?"

"I have a few," she said, concentrating on the surface of the bridge, her nose a few inches away from the stone. "There's not enough time to make more."

Pil's enchantment required only a few more minutes, but it left her sweating and shaky. She breathed, "Damn, it's big, but the charm is simple. Fairly simple."

I helped her up. Pain had been pulsing through my left shoulder since I healed Kenzie's wound, but mine wasn't a wound and couldn't be healed. Nothing could be done about it. I simply wouldn't be able to fight with my off hand.

I pulled the bright knife out of my belt and handed it to Pil. "I can't use this, but maybe you can. Mara gave it to me. When it strikes somebody, they fall into a kind of daze."

Pil raised one eyebrow at me. Then the world's most accomplished sorcerer became six years old by saying, "Ooh, it's shiny!" She took the bright knife in her left hand, then summoned her surpassingly sharp knife from the tiny realm where she kept it. Pointing behind me at Grik, she said, "Should we put her third in line so she can shoot at people above us? Or below us when we get to the other side?"

I turned and beckoned Grik over.

Halfway to me, Grik yelled, "Hey, are we already starting?"

I whipped around to see Pil pass Chexis and charge up the steep bridge to the closest enemy.

"Dammit, come back!" I shouted, running after her.

She ignored me and startled the soldier by lunging and stabbing him in the chest.

"Don't go first! You'll have to beat them all!" I shouted this obvious fact as if that would change her mind. "Let me do it! I have this sword . . ." I trailed off, realizing that this was the bad thing she must accept. She had to go first.

Pil was a small woman. Although strong for her size, she didn't have the leverage needed to wield a long weapon in an extended fight. She used speed to close with her enemies and finish them with the knife.

By the time I reached her, she had killed another man, pushed the body out of the way, and climbed a second step up the bridge. That left four hundred and forty-four to go.

She parried the next man, stepped in, and scratched his arm with the bright knife. Light flared and I looked away. He shook his head and wandered over to plunge off the bridge. He never screamed, but Pil gained another step.

Pil gave the next man's arm a brutal cut but didn't kill him. As she pushed past, I whacked the back of his head with my sword's pommel, then followed Pil, leaving the limp fellow for Grik to deal with. I began treating each wounded man that way. I didn't know for sure what Grik did with them, although in a minute I glanced back and saw no soldiers flopped on the bridge or running away.

Pil fell into a rhythm, defeated another dozen men and climbed one or even two steps each time. With four hundred and twenty-five steps to go, a wide-chested man with a smug smile and a cleft chin stopped her dead. He didn't move like a sword master, but he seemed born to be Pil's deadliest opponent. He shaved some skin from her right thigh with his curved sword and ten seconds later gave her a shallow cut from collarbone to breastbone.

I bounded to help, but that risked pushing her over the side. Then Pil shoved the bright knife away in her belt and grabbed something out of a pouch. A great flash blinded me.

Within a couple of breaths, I could see again, at least enough not to stumble off the bridge. Pil must have knocked the Chin and the five men behind him over the edge and was about to stab the next man in the chest. I rushed to catch her.

Blood had begun soaking her shirt, and Pil was moving slower. Her shoulders moved up and down as she breathed, but she stabbed the next man with the bright knife. It flashed, and she shoved him off the bridge as he stumbled.

"Pil!" I yelled. "Take my sword!" I didn't say that it would invigorate her. She damn well knew it would.

"Bite a pig!" she shouted without looking at me.

"What?"

Some seconds passed before she slipped inside the next man's guard and cut him in the groin. He howled and fell to his knees.

"Bite a fat hog's ass!" Pil yelled as she stalked uphill to the next man with four hundred and ten steps to go. Once she had killed him, she tossed her head three times and sprang up the slope as if she had just gotten out of bed.

She defeated the next eighteen men without pausing. Then she stumbled, panting, and was almost killed. A soldier knocked her sharp knife out of her hand, and it flew, spinning, off the bridge. The man raised his sword to split her head, but she stood, lunged against his body, and cut his throat with the knife that had just plummeted off the bridge. He didn't live long enough to understand that Pil could pull that knife into its tiny realm from anywhere and then bring it back to her hand in a moment.

The bridge had become less steep as we neared the top of the arch, and Pil drove herself forward two steps. Some order must have come from the enemy's rear, because the soldiers had begun crowding toward Pil. She wounded the next man and yelled some profanities at the soldiers, even though they couldn't understand the words. She put away the bright knife and grabbed what looked like a small tomato from a cloth pouch. She hurled it thirty feet ahead, where it exploded, flinging glop onto everybody under it.

The men shouted nasty-sounding words at her but stopped when two of them fell on their asses. Everybody stood with ginger stiffness, and I realized that the part of the bridge ahead of Pil was as slippery as butter.

Pil leaned forward as the closest man slid toward her. Her footing seemed solid. The slope wasn't as great here as at the bottom, but it was just steep enough. As each soldier slid screaming down toward her, she shoved him off the bridge, one way or the other.

Soon every soldier within twenty feet of Pil had slid or been pushed off the bridge. No more soldiers walked out onto that part of the bridge.

"Move over, I'll go past you!" I yelled.

"Don't! You'll slip and fall off," Pil said, panting.

"Back up, then!"

Instead of moving, she looked me in the eye. "I can't blame this on that dog's knob Margale, can I? It's me deciding to kill these people."

"That's right, darling. I'm sorry."

"I knew that. I just wanted to hear somebody else say it."

"Come on," I said, reaching for her arm.

Pil slashed and just missed my arm. She left a neat cut in my sleeve. I jumped back. Pil snapped her fingers and ran up the bridge toward her enemies.

Pil had caught her breath and sprinted up the slope that wasn't slippery anymore. She plowed into the next soldier, who hesitated to step out and attack her. Once she crippled him, she had almost three hundred and eighty steps to go.

An arrow flew past me up toward the enemy. I glanced back at Grik, who smiled. Since the bridge arched up away from us, she could see the soldiers fifth or sixth in line past Pil.

The soldiers became a lot less anxious to press forward into Grik's line of fire. Without that pressure from behind, Pil could gain two steps and sometimes three when she defeated a man. Grik fired until she had spent all her arrows.

Pil gained some strength, but it didn't last long. She was far more skilled than any of these men could be. Also, sorcerers possessed greater toughness and vigor than regular people. But physically, Pil was over forty. Muscles that old just don't endure as long as muscles half that age. She was still defeating each man, but she was taking small wounds as well as a deep puncture in her hip. Sometimes she didn't gain a step at all when she beat a soldier.

"Take this damned-to-Krak's-left-nut sword!" I yelled.

She was panting too hard to speak but shook her head.

When Pil had three hundred and thirty steps to go, I sheathed by sword, drew my knife, and hurled it into the next soldier's chest. She stepped up and killed the following man, whose eyes had gone wide. By the time she defeated that soldier, Grik was passing me her knife. Pil gained another twelve steps before we ran out of knives.

Pil dropped to her knees before she reached the next man. He ran forward, but not too fast, probably realizing that if he killed her, he'd still have to fight the rest of us. Before the soldier reached her, something blinded me again.

"Dammit, Granda!" Vargo shouted. "Stop doing that! We might fall off!"

When my vision cleared, I saw that the next dozen soldiers only existed from the waist down. I had seen both Pil and Desh do this before. The trinket didn't disintegrate the men from the waist up, not precisely. It was impossible to disintegrate a living creature. Instead, it burned them with such fury that they were vaporized.

Pil was lumbering forward to meet the next soldiers.

I ran to catch her. "Pil, stop! Let me pass! Let me go first!"

"No!" she yelled in a strangled voice.

I ignored her. Just before I ran past her, she swung her knife back toward me in a ferocious cut. She could have disemboweled me. Hell, she could have cut me in two.

I raised myself toward the trading place. "Mighty Gorlana! I come to trade!"

Mighty Gorlana must not have wanted to bargain with me. The trading place didn't appear. I gritted my teeth and called for Harik, but he didn't answer either.

I tried Fingit, the God's Smith; Lutigan, the God of War; and Trutch, the Goddess of Life. Fingit probably liked me enough to avoid running me down in his magic chariot. I felt the other two would at least swerve a bit. I didn't know what the rest of the gods thought about me at this point. They technically owed me a debt, but immortal beings had short memories.

It didn't matter, since nobody I called answered. I didn't try the Father of the Gods. Calling Krak was like trying to open a locked door by burning down every house in town.

Pil's next enemy raised his arm for a swing that might crush her skull. Without thinking, I spun a gray band and disintegrated his sword. He fell off balance, and Pil stabbed him in the throat. She shook her head and moved to the next soldier, with three hundred and seven steps to go.

I disintegrated the next soldier's sword too. After Pil crippled him, she yelled, "Stop doing that! You'll need that power!"

I answered by disintegrating the next man's sword.

She killed that man. "Stop!"

"I'll stop if you use my sword!" I shouted, holding it out to her by the blade.

She fought the next man for half a dozen strikes each before nicking him with the bright knife. "Bib!" she panted as the light flared. "I don't want your sword! Either of them!" She choked out a laugh.

I might have laughed too if the next man hadn't missed her forehead by a finger's width.

She stabbed the man below the ribs with the bright knife, which flashed. He sighed and ambled forward, tangling himself in her arms. The man behind him raised his sword with both hands and rammed it through the soldier's body and into Pil.

It didn't look like the wound in her stomach was too deep, and it might not be fatal. But the man who had stabbed them used his sword's hilt as a handle to heave both Pil and his comrade off the bridge.

FORTY-EIGHT

There was no way Pil could be dead. She was alive when I'd last seen her, and I hadn't touched her body, so as far as I was concerned, she still lived. The soldier who had stabbed her was backing away, waving his hands for somebody to give him another sword, so I could probably have taken a second to look over the side.

I didn't look. I knew she was alive, and I didn't want anything to make me think differently.

I took advantage of my sword's love of cutting. I sliced a leg from the man who had stabbed Pil. He fell over, bleeding to death.

Pil had dropped the bright knife before she fell, but I couldn't do anything with it. My left arm was still weak from healing Kenzie. I stepped over the knife, hoping somebody behind me would pick it up.

The next six men lost an arm above the shoulder, a head, and another leg, plus two slashed throats and a thrust through the midsection for variety. I felt a wash of energy with each kill until my body hummed with vigor. But that must have been the limit. No more energy flooded into me when I killed the next man.

Earlier when had I dropped fifty men into a big pit, I figured that counted as defeating them without killing them. It put Gorlana eleven vanquishings ahead of Harik in their contest. If I kept killing all the way across the bridge, Harik would catch up and then get too far ahead for me ever to recover.

But if I didn't kill enough enemies, my extra vitality would drain away. I resolved to wound a man for each one I killed. It would keep my energy high and prevent me from killing more than I simply defeated.

That plan worked well, at first. I used my unnatural energy to rush my enemies as if they were drowsy cattle. I shoved the dying aside or off the bridge. I bounded past the injured, and I shocked the ones behind them with how fast my sword arrived to wound them or end their lives. I treated forty-one of them this way.

I cursed a little at Pil. She could have come through this unharmed if she had just stayed behind me. As I thought that, a bent and tanged clump of sharpened stakes flew from behind my immediate foe and almost bashed out my brains. I knocked it aside with my sword, but it was heavier than it looked. It scraped a gash along my left shoulder before it sailed past me and bounced. By the way Grik shouted, it may have hit her.

The soldiers farther back hurled two more of these missiles. Kenzie rotted the wooden stakes, which left the cores—big rocks covered in wax. I charged the closest man, figuring the throwers wouldn't risk bashing their friends. I sliced that man's neck and moved on without pausing.

As five more stake-clumps sailed over my head, I tore through the soldiers as quickly and brutally as I could on that narrow span. I cut and killed nine men before I reached the little wagon half-full of these twisty-pointy bashing clumps. The man behind the wagon flung one hard at my chest. His eyes went wide when I disintegrated it, and he backed away into the man behind him. That man shoved him toward me again. Lunging across the wagon, I stabbed him in the throat.

By that point, the bridge was almost flat, with two hundred and thirty-five steps to go—only ten from the midpoint.

I raised my sword and watched its point shake. I felt powerful, more dynamic than ever, but my whole body was trembling. I mumbled, "Pil, how much of this charmed power is too much?"

My arms began shaking so hard I figured I could only wield this magic sword as skillfully as a plow hand swinging a fence post. I drew a breath, raised my sword high, and roared as I raced toward the next soldier. I swung the sword as hard as I could manage, aiming for his arm but hoping to hit him someplace between the head and the waist. He lifted his sword to block but shrank back, and I cut off his free arm below the elbow.

It defeated him, but I'd have felt more encouraged if I hadn't been aiming for the other arm.

I pretended it was the greatest victory since Lutigan slew the Crushing Void Toads. I roared at the next man, swung, and hoped for the best. After killing five men and wounding eleven, my body stopped shaking.

Not knowing what other capricious behavior my sword might display, I pushed on fast but was careful not to kill any more men than necessary. I did not fall into a rhythm. That was the last thing I wanted these sons of bitches to see from me. I always pressed them, but on occasion I might sprint hard, defeating two or three in as many cuts, just to keep their friends wondering.

That lasted until I had a hundred and ninety steps to go. I raced down to the next soldier but jerked to a halt when three spear heads thrust out at me from around him. I saw that the spears were of different lengths so that three men could stand back a bit, almost side by side, and threaten to puncture me.

I lowered my sword and waited while the soldiers thrust their spears a few times, daring me to come closer. Then I spun gray bands to destroy the bit of shaft behind the spear heads, which fell and hit the bridge with a clank.

The battle didn't fall silent, but it did quiet down a bit as every-body around stared at the spearheads lying on the stone. I could just make out Kenzie snickering behind me.

I swept the shafts aside, ducked, and bashed the closest man with my shoulder. That knocked him into the three scrambling spearmen, and all four went down in a pile. I killed two as I passed them and wounded the other two before leaping toward the next soldier. I slowed and wounded the next three to prevent my body from getting overwhelmed by power again.

I had reached a hundred and eighty steps from the end, and the bridge had gained a definite downward curve. As I fought my way along, I still felt full of vitality, but my arms and legs didn't respond with as much snap. Maybe the spell on Pil's sword could only push flesh so far.

As the soldiers became less eager, I began gaining two or even three steps when I defeated a man.

Then chanting rose from someplace ahead and grew louder. I wounded a man, stepped past, and faced a line of six tall warriors in chain armor under white-painted and lacquered cuirasses. They were led by a young man of average size wearing no armor that I could see. He was bald, with an aggressive mustache, and he watched me like he was already drinking my life.

"Why aren't you chanting too?" I yelled at him. "Don't know the words?"

The man smiled at me but answered only by relaxing as he pointed his slim sword at my face. The relaxation bothered me. It reflected both training and experience. The sword concerned me more. It glowed with a watery blue light.

I reminded myself I should be most concerned by the fact that he was younger and probably stronger than me. He might be faster too, even if I was crammed to the eyeballs with my sword's vitality. My best bet was to draw him out and delay until he tired himself out. However, he might be ready for that, since I had fought my way across the bridge and wasn't even breathing hard.

I made a conservative thrust with the option of retreating, just to make him chase me. He answered with a near-perfect lunge, aiming for my heart. I held my ground with an obscure parry I had never seen anywhere outside the Dark Lands, and I riposted into his throat. His body snapped tight, but he stayed up, dying on his feet. With my sword arm, I shoved him back toward his chanting buddies, the better to destroy their morale.

"Grab his sword!" I called back to Grik. As I advanced on the tallest chanter, I silently thanked that pain in my butt, Bixell, who had trained me in the Dark Lands and had saved my life again.

Only the first chanting soldier showed any appetite for fighting me. I hamstrung him and passed by as he fell. By then, the others were trying to run, but the advancing soldiers behind them blocked their way. A few of the shorter men got knocked or tossed off the bridge. That finally routed everybody. I followed to make sure they didn't change their minds.

I trailed along a few paces behind the soldiers, making mean faces and waving my sword. That decision to trail behind instead of pushing them may be what saved me. With about seventy-five steps left to the end, the rearmost chanter combusted in white-hot flame. Heat hammered me for a moment before I pulled a gray band to destroy everything around the charred corpse, including the air. The light and heat disappeared with a great popping sound.

Margale had turned his loyal, though retreating, soldier into a weapon by setting everything he wore and carried on fire in the most intense fashion.

The fire-shedding clothes Pil gave me protected nearly all my body. But fresh burns created piercing pain in every spot where my clothes had been cut or torn. The hat protected my head, but nothing had shielded my face. I fell to my hands and knees and then rolled onto my side.

I heard Grik shouting, "Krak! Krak, is he alive? Damn it!"

"Bib!" Vargo shouted. "Can you hear me?"

"Of course he can't hear you, you boob!" Pocklin said. "He's got those black bits where his ears ought to be."

FORTY-NINE

I felt hornets crawl across my face, stinging me in waves as I lay on the ground. I slapped my cheek and shouted, "Agh! Krak ream it with fire!"

Somebody grabbed my hands. "Stop that! It won't get better if you pick at it, so leave it alone!" Pocklin said.

My thoughts wandered through the pain until I eventually realized it didn't hurt as much.

Pocklin pulled to help me sit. The stinging on my face faded even more.

I glanced around and saw that I was still on the bridge, maybe a hundred steps from the end nearest Margale's Dick. Grik stood facing the tower, holding her bow. While Kenzie was healing me, Vargo had scavenged arrows from soldiers' bodies back across the bridge. As I watched, Grik shot a soldier who was climbing up the bridge toward us. "You're not burning *my* face off, you dog turd!" she yelled.

Soldiers fired a few arrows toward us from the foot of the bridge. They all fell short or went wide. Margale's men were brave, but they couldn't fire arrows any better than they could chew gravel.

I asked, "Why are we so far up the bridge?"

"An archer might have a lucky draw," Grik said. "No evidence that's ever happened to these fellows before though, except for magic arrows." She shrugged.

"I guess you could have pulled back farther to be sure," I said.

Pocklin said, "This is the farthest young Kenzie figured we could drag your ass without killing you. Stand up."

I swayed for a few seconds but steadied on my feet. Feeling the hilt of my sword at my belt, I took a deep breath. I truly didn't feel much pain. "I don't know why I was ever afraid of getting burned up. This isn't so bad."

"Funny. I'll laugh out of my ass," Grik said. "Come talk to Kenzie while she can still speak."

Kenzie lay with her head in Vargo's lap, writhing and panting.

I knelt beside her. "I'm here. Thank you," I said.

"Go to hell." I realized she was staring at nothing and wondered how badly my eyes had been burned. She said, "Listen, first I healed you no more than to keep you alive. You were a whimpering mess."

"Um, thank you for keeping me alive."

"Then I healed you enough for fighting, but that bit won't endure."

"So part of it's temporary. Once that healing fails, what will I be able to do?"

"Scream. If you're lucky, pass out. You may have two hours. No, not that much, not that at all. Close, though." She sighed and went limp.

I stood. "Two hours to fight our way to the tower, break in, find Margale, and kill him." I glanced at Grik and Pocklin. "You can't come. You'll be set afire and kill us all."

Grik held up her left hand. She was wearing Kenzie's soft gloves, and the lengthy sleeve of her shirt was rolled up. "I changed into Kenzie's fire-shedding clothes. Daddy changed into Vargo's."

"Huh. What will you fight with?" I asked. "Margale will burn your weapons hot enough to melt off your arms."

Pocklin said, "Vargo there gave me his magic sword!"

"Loaned!" Vargo shouted.

"Sure, loaned, and it's a noble gesture from such a down-mouthed, dribbling little squid like him."

Grik drew the watery blue sword we had taken from Margale's champion. "We're coming. That nasty cobb killed Lemlin. I know, his men did the killing, but it equals the same."

Her father raised Vargo's sword. "We'll run this Margale criminal to ground, and I'll shove this sword up his bottom before I tickle his throat with it."

I gazed at the gray-green tower and the empty expanse of rock in front of it. I figured the tower was two hundred and forty feet tall and forty feet across. It stood a hundred and fifty steps from the end of the bridge. A road ran from the bridge past the tower and off into some rocky hills.

I examined the space in front of the tower and felt daunted. It was an open half-circle. The flat side ran three hundred paces along the cliff's edge with the bridge in the center. The tower stood straight across from the bridge in the middle of the curve.

The space was so regular it had to have been fashioned by magic. Margale himself had probably done it, using whatever vast amount of power he had acquired. It was filled with rows of stone breastworks facing the bridge. Each row stood higher than the one before it so that the end of the bridge was under fire from every spot where an archer could stand.

I began pulling the storm together. I might need three or four storms to cross that space.

"Gonna make some joke about how you handled worse before?" Pocklin asked me.

"I have. But there was nothing funny about it. We need staging areas—places along the way where we can pause in cover. Once we get among their positions, most of them won't be able to fire at us."

"Ah. Instead of a thousand arrows, only a hundred will be fired upon us," Grik said.

"Right. If we can't deal with a hundred arrows, we have no business trying to kill Margale."

Both Pocklin and Grik were silent.

I smiled. "I'll create trenches to hide us as we run—and I'll take care of the arrows. You'll fight anybody who's in our way. When we reach the tower, we'll open the door. Once we're inside, I'll collapse the wall above the door to block it. Then we'll find Margale, kill him, and cut off his head to terrify everybody into leaving us alone while we retreat. Easy."

They watched me but didn't say anything. I didn't blame them. I couldn't begin to list all the things that could go wrong with this plan.

A faint rumbling rose from the bridge. The bridge had suffered a great pounding today, and it shouldn't have shocked anybody if it failed. I glanced back at Kenzie, who was still passed out. We could carry her and run, but the shortest path off the bridge was toward Margale's tower.

The rumbling grew, and a crunching sound came along with it.

"Grab Kenzie!" I yelled, but Vargo and Pocklin were already seizing her legs and arms. I needed to hide her someplace if we ran toward the tower. I might create a deep trench where arrows couldn't reach her.

We started running. As I scanned the area, I saw a thirty-foot-tall stone crenellated tower in the middle of it. I couldn't believe I'd failed to notice it before. Maybe Margale had just created it.

Somebody wearing bright red stood on top. It would be a fantastic spot for Parbett, where she could attack the whole field with arrows and magic. So far, I had seen no one but her wearing red.

Red was a poor choice for the battlefield, since it made her a target. It was probably enchanted, but she could have enchanted a brown robe just as well. It was vanity.

Hell, before I criticized too much, I had to admit that I possessed a sizable dose of vanity myself.

The rumbling and grinding grew louder, but the bridge wasn't shaking at all. Then I jerked to a stop as Chexis climbed up from the side of the bridge, his claws digging deep gouges in the stone. The rumbling ended once he had writhed onto the surface of the bridge.

He blinked at me and said, "I'm going home now. I have a lot to share with my brother."

"Um, thank you for telling me. Chexis, remember when I asked you not to walk out onto the bridge?"

"You were mistaken, Bib. This bridge would hold twenty dragons. What's wrong with your face?"

"Margale burned me up, but Kenzie made it better. Chexis, is there anything you want to do before you leave? Do you know enough about how not to be human?"

"Oh, that." The black patch on his forehead swept back. "I'm not interested in that anymore," he declared as he flipped his tail. "Human things are as meaningless as bugs farting. Only babies would care about it!"

"We're not very interesting compared to dragons. The complexity of dragons is vast."

Chexis laughed. "Don't try to 'butter me up.' That's a human thing to say. There's no way to say that in my language, but I don't care what other dragons think. Being a dragon is what I say it is."

I nodded. "You define the reality of it."

"Yes!" Chexis's tail whacked against the bridge. "It's almost as if you're capable of having that thought on your own."

Behind me, Pocklin whispered, "Could you ask him not to do that thing with his tail?"

Chexis slapped his tail against the bridge again as he stared at me.

I smiled. "We're about to take vengeance on Margale. As a dragon, are you interested in vengeance?"

The dragon laughed again. "If I say yes, you'll agree with me that vengeance is satisfying. If I say no, you'll tell me how unsatisfied I am and that I need vengeance." He waited, but I didn't speak. At last, he said, "I have no opinion on vengeance. You dick."

I stepped back and smiled.

"I like that phrase. You dick. It's useful in almost any situation."

"Sure, I use it myself sometimes. Chexis, I am able to heal again. Do you want me to heal your wing so you can fly?"

The dragon was silent for several seconds. "Obviously I do. But

I don't want to owe you one of these 'favors' you talked about. No matter what you said, they are not free."

"You won't owe me a single thing."

"I know that you think that will be true, but it won't. Goat Drag was a long time ago, Bib."

"Yes. Please reconsider. I need your help with Margale—you can see that, son. But I won't let you suffer just because you don't fight him."

The dragon was silent for a few seconds. "If I help you, then you would owe me one of those favors. That could be interesting." Chexis pushed his face close to mine. "Go ahead."

"Go ahead what?"

"Pet my nose. You've been wanting to for days."

I patted his nose three times. It was rough, like a shark's skin, dry, and warm. "Thank you for allowing me this familiarity. I feel honored."

"Of course you do. But now . . . I have to hurt you."

I backed away fast, almost knocking down Pocklin, but I didn't draw my sword. A more futile act couldn't be imagined.

Chexis eased back away from me. "I climbed down the cliff on that side of the canyon and back up on this side. I found Pil at the bottom. She was alive."

"I knew it!" I jumped and jabbed my fist in the air.

"She used some kind of floaty magic, but it didn't floaty all that well. She'll die soon, if she's not already dead."

My new plan to save Pil took five heartbeats to create, and I explained it with my very next breath. "If I heal your wing, will you fly me down to Pil?"

"Yes."

I drew my sword. "I'll use this up to heal you. Turn this way."

"All right." He shifted around on the narrow bridge.

"Bib!" Vargo shouted. "Do you want us to carry Kenzie all the way back over the bridge? Should we wait for you there?"

"To hell with that!" Pocklin shouted. "What about your first plan with all the trenches and collapsing doors and shit? Are we tearing up that plan and throwing it in the ocean?"

I paused. I had to abandon the first plan, that was true. The chance that Kenzie and Vargo and the others would survive was no better than spit puddling on a hot stove. Margale's men would catch them, maybe before they crossed the bridge.

But what were they to me, really? I'd known Pocklin and Grik for a few days. I had ridden with Kenzie and Vargo through some tough spots, but they weren't people I adored, like Pil.

If I let Margale live . . . well, how many people would a brutal, insane, vastly powerful sorcerer kill? Dozens or probably hundreds. But I didn't know any of those people either, not at all. I had loved Pil for most of a human lifetime.

If I didn't help her now, it would be like dashing her body against the stones myself. I knew I couldn't really hear her calling for me, but I damn well heard her anyway. She had to be suffering. I pictured her face. She looked scared and alone.

Somebody might ask me what Pil would do in my place. I didn't know what she'd do. To be honest, I hoped that she'd come save me. That's what I was going to do for her.

A god pulled my spirit up from my body. That usually didn't make me happy, but this time I grinned like a hound. When I arrived in the trading place, the sunlight was smooth and rich, while the air was cool, but I hardly noticed anything around me except the marble gazebo.

I had expected the Goddess of Mercy. I got the God of Death instead. Harik sat on the edge of the gazebo's lowest level, letting his feet swing. "Greetings, Chicken Beak."

"Hello, Mighty Harik."

He chuckled. "I don't know what you were actually thinking when the Unnamed Mother asked for your name, but you're going to regret acting like a smartass with this Chicken Beak business."

"Better than being a chicken gizzard. I leave that for you, Mighty Harik. You are the gamy, withered, slippery gizzard of woe."

Harik rubbed his chin. "Gizzard of Woe. I like it. Maybe I'll make it one of my official titles. You have a problem. You need to save the Knife, and you need to slaughter the Avalanche, and you can't do both at the same time. Are you prepared to deal?"

"I am prepared to listen to your offer, Your Magnificence. Do you still like being insulted, by the way? Oh crass, ignorant, flimsy, crumbling pit of emptiness where divinity ought to be?"

Harik threw out his hands and smiled. "Wonderful! I am prepared to keep the Knife alive for an extra ten minutes, giving you more time to save her before she's kicked by the mule of mortality. Do you like that? Mule of mortality?"

"I love it. If I have a son, that's what I'll name him." Ten minutes was a sadly short amount of time, but usually Harik's first offer was ridiculous. "Mighty Harik, what do you think about keeping her alive for ten extra hours, and for the sake of symmetry, providing me ten squares of power?"

"All right."

I stopped breathing and waited for him to correct himself.

He smirked. "Did you hear me, Chicken Beak of Murder? I would agree."

"I see, Mighty Harik. What do you propose that I offer in trade?"

"Oh, something uncomplicated that you might even enjoy. You will perform a certain number of killings for me. And only I will know what that number is."

"No!"

"Are you sure?"

This was the same deal I once made with Old Harik, trying to save my daughter's life. It didn't save her, but I killed a lot of people because of the bargain. Some of them had done nothing to deserve death.

I said, "I have another offer—"

Harik said, "There is no other offer. Take this deal or let her die."

I drew a deep breath. "You dangling clump of filth. Scummy, crusted puddle of . . ." My cursing failed.

"Before you suggest something else, let me explain your situation," Harik said. "I'm giving you everything you want, right? So, you'll have to give me everything that I want. We won't have any chirping back and forth like little birds. Take it or don't."

I opened my mouth to say no, but nothing came out. I tried to say no four more times. I knew how Harik's deal would really work. I would spend the rest of my life hunting and killing people who I thought deserved to die. A lot of them might really deserve death, but some wouldn't. My judgment in these matters could be shaky.

That would be my life. But Pil would survive.

I started to say yes but coughed instead.

My daughter had died anyway, regardless of the deal. Maybe some random damn thing would slay Pil too. But maybe she'd live. Maybe she'd live and fall in love with me again.

I clenched my teeth. I wasn't making a decision. I was silently whining about the fact that I had to make a decision.

It came to this. If I saved Pil, I would kill a lot of people, and Margale would go free to kill a lot too.

If I let Pil die and stopped Margale, he wouldn't slaughter people, and I wouldn't have to either.

Before I thought about it much more, I said, "No," and let Pil die. I felt empty, but that was all right. I was about to fill that space up with rage.

I let myself drift back toward my body. Harik stopped me while I was still in darkness. "If you change your mind, Murderer, call out. The deal is still open for now. Oh, you should start killing more people regardless. Gorlana is ahead by eight victims."

"Really?" I asked, not paying much attention. "That seems off."

"I guarantee you it's not! You could at least kill a few extra to make it close."

I returned to my body and saw that everyone was watching me. I spotted the bright knife in Grik's belt, grabbed it, and screamed as I hurled it as far as I could into the canyon.

Grik opened her mouth and closed it once before saying, "That is the most wasteful thing I've ever seen a person do! That was magic! One of us——"

Pocklin interrupted, "Look the other way, Gretta. He had to let her go."

I stared past the dragon's neck at Margale's tower. "We're back to the plan with the trenches and the collapsed door."

"Oh, Bib . . ." Chexis said. "let me give you that favor. We can come up with a better plan than that."

FIFTY

"That shorter tower is the problem," I said to Chexis. "See the woman up there wearing red? I think that's the sorcerer Parbett, who fired that divine arrow that put a hole in you. She may have more like it."

"Can you destroy her from here? I'd like to see her hit with lightning," Chexis said.

"I need to get a bit closer. Let's heal your wing first."

Chexis whipped his head around to stare into my face. "If you heal it now, I'll owe you a favor. I don't want to get behind on the owing of favors. After I help you, then we can talk about what favor I want."

"You wouldn't owe me anything, Chexis. I'll just help you."

"Do you know how silly you sound when you say things like that? You sound like one of those seals that barks in the ocean. Onk! Onk! Onk!" He stared at Parbett's tower again. "Are we really going to let Pil die?"

"I can't talk about that and plan an assault at the same time."

Chexis stared at Parbett's tower again. "No, don't heal my wing yet. If the sorcerer shoots me again, maybe she'll shoot me in the same wing."

"That would be mighty unlucky," I said.

Chexis stared at me. "If she shoots me twice in that wing and you only have to heal me once, how is that unlucky? No, I'll help you fight until you get to the big tower. Then you'll owe me a favor, and I can decide what I want it to be."

"Aren't you worried I'll get killed before you can get your favor?"

"Onk! Onk! Onk!"

"Very well, I agree!" Right away one of my top ten rules became *When a Dragon Offers to Fight for You, Say Yes.* "Everybody, stay back."

I trotted down the bridge until I could pick out details on Parbett's tower. It was one column of stone, not made of stone blocks. That unsettled me a little, but I concentrated and pulled two gray bands. A soldier charged me, but Grik put an arrow in him.

I flung the bands to cover a big wedge of tower right under the crenellations.

When I twisted, that wedge disintegrated. The tower's top thumped down on one side, slid, and crashed to the ground, taking Parbett and two other people with it. I didn't pause to appreciate the destruction. I flung two more bands over a wedge at the bottom of the tower. When I destroyed it, the whole column teetered and fell to smash everything that had just fallen off the top, including Parbett, I hoped.

I beckoned everybody else. "I can't guarantee I killed them, but I know I got them dirty and made them sad." I squeezed past Chexis, who half-ran, half-slithered down the bridge faster than a horse. A dozen soldiers had been massing at the foot of the bridge to attack us. They saw Chexis and scattered.

I kept pulling together the high storm I had been nursing for the past half hour, even though I wasn't certain I'd need it. Drawing my sword, I jogged down the bridge, followed by Grik and Pocklin.

When I reached the end of the bridge, I stopped with my head cocked. Grik and Pocklin didn't ask me why. Chexis had already rushed out and turned left to run behind one of the closest rows of breastworks. He reminded me of one of those little dogs that hunts gophers. Screaming men jumped or dragged themselves out of the way. Legs, arms, and whole bodies flew into the air ahead of the dragon, and to the sides as well. Archers from all over the area fired arrows, most of which missed. A few bounced off Chexis's scratchy hide.

I shook myself and ran down the road. It didn't seem likely that Chexis would need my help, but he might appreciate it if I cheered.

Chexis reached the end of the first row and rounded onto the second, headed for the ruins of Parbett's tower. He paused to roar before chasing more soldiers. Before Chexis reached the row's end, Parbett stepped out from the tower's wreckage and raised a bow. She had timed her attack well and had the dragon at point blank range. While she drew back the bowstring, I spun a gray band and hurled it to cover her entire person.

I tried to destroy everything on her. Magic things resist being disintegrated, of course. Parbett's arrow was enchanted, so it survived. Just like earlier, the bow she was now holding didn't. She must have thought, *Who needs a hard-to-enchant magic bow when you have easy-to-enchant magic arrows?* The bow disappeared, and her arrow fell to the ground. Her clothes went away too, except for her boots. Her pouches were destroyed, and all the magic trinkets and doodads she carried in them tinkled to the ground around her shiny magic boots.

Parbett froze for a moment when she saw me sprinting toward her. Then she knelt, grabbed a magic bauble without taking her eyes off me, and tossed it at me.

I guess it could have been a charm to make my bones melt. Instead, a happy campfire appeared in front of me.

"Wrong one?" I yelled as I hurdled the fire.

Parbett was in the middle of calling me a terrible name when I sliced off her head. A wave of energy trickled into me.

I pointed at the little piles of magical trinkets. "Grik! Gather those up!"

She muttered, "Throws away a magic knife and wants me to pick up this shit."

Chexis had turned to the last row on the left side. None of the soldiers even pretended to hold their ground. I turned to the closest row on the other side. All the men there were fleeing. At Margale's tower, soldiers shoved each other to get out the main door, where they turned onto the road and ran the hell away toward the hills.

I caught and killed three retreating men. The rest had run too fast and too far to worry about.

"Stay away from bodies!" I yelled, pointing at Pocklin. "Anything that's easy to burn, stay clear!" I trotted to Chexis, who had finished chasing all of Margale's gophers out of their hiding places. "What about your wing, son?" I asked him.

The dragon turned his head to look at me and blinked once. "You're about to ask for another favor, aren't you?"

"I am."

"Bib, you eradicated that nasty sorcerer with the arrows. Do you want to consider that to be a favor I owe you?"

"Only if you want to think of it that way. It doesn't matter to me."

Chexis hissed. "Fine, I think of it that way! Ask! What do you want?"

"If I hang onto you, will you climb to the top of Margale's tower with me?"

The dragon let his tongue dangle out of his mouth and said, "Bleaugh."

"Um, is that no?" I asked.

"It just popped out to express my disgust, but all right, I'll help you. Anything else?"

"No."

"Grab onto my neck."

I held up one hand. "Just a minute." I shouted, "Grik! I'm not going to collapse the door and trap you two in there. Count to two hundred, then go inside and raise hell. Make it really loud but stay on the bottom floor. If Margale shows up, run like mad. I'll be along in a minute."

When they had nodded with adequate expressions of understanding, I ran back to Chexis. I climbed onto his back, using his foreleg as a step.

"You have a bony back," I said.

"Your butt smells like dead pigs. Hold on."

Chexis dug into the stone wall with his foreclaws, then with the rear. He didn't climb as fast as he could run, but he made the two-hundred-and-forty-foot trip before Pocklin and Grik entered the tower.

Hopping down, I said, "Thank you, Chexis. I can't ask you for anything more. Now I owe you two favors. I'll try not to get killed before you want them."

"I could just eat you now. I think that would be like two favors."

I froze.

The dragon laughed. "By Beymarr's fifth claw, you're gullible. Go kill Margale. Don't play any gambling games with him though. He'll cheat. He'll . . . cheat his ass off."

I put a hand on the dragon's shoulder. "Cheat his ass off? Are you all right?"

Black smoke poured from Chexis's nostrils. "Of course I'm all right! Dragons can talk about asses if they want to! I can say any of the interesting things I've heard humans say. All of them, if I care to! There's nothing wrong with a dragon doing that." He took a deep breath before blowing smoke and a lick of flame. "I'm fine. This is just . . . this is fun! Better than Goat Drag. Go kill Margale, and don't die."

Chexis crawled over the side and back toward the ground. A few breaths later, I heard Pocklin bellowing over the sound of weapons clashing.

I counted to fifty and pulled a band to clear a Bib-size hole in the roof. Only silence floated up, so I poked my head down inside. The room was a twenty-foot circle and well lit by deep windows. The ceiling was twelve feet tall. It seemed to be a large art studio. I saw a dozen painted panels, an easel, a small marble statue in progress, and a long table with tools and molds for metal casting.

I muttered, "Margale, I wouldn't have expected it."

The floor was a bit far down, especially with a bad knee, but I didn't see a ladder anyplace. I lowered myself with my arms and dropped. Halfway down, I was grabbed at the waist by a loop of stone that whipped out from the wall.

Margale stood in the doorway with his god-club in one hand,

wearing four cows' worth of heavy leather armor. His brow looked thicker than ever. "Wouldn't have expected what? That you'd have to come this far for me to kill you? That you'd abandon your wife to die? That I'd smash the face of your damned pet dragon after you're dead?"

I didn't answer. Instead, I destroyed the ring of stone holding me so I could drop to the floor. Then, just as I had done to Parbett, I disintegrated everything on Margale that wasn't enchanted.

His left boot disappeared, but nothing else.

"The left boot?" I yelled. "Why just the left? What the hell does the right one do?" While I was babbling, I destroyed part of the ceiling over him. The undestroyed parts fell toward his head.

Margale sneered as he bent a stone shield out of the wall to protect himself. Then he stepped back out of the room. To me, that meant he was going to set something in there on fire to hurt me.

I pulled four bands just that fast and wiped out everything in the room except me, including the door Margale was behind.

Margale shouted, "Damn you with Krak's fist!" as he ran toward me, raising his club. I prepared to cut through two cows of armor and disembowel him, but a big lump of rock popped out of the floor and smacked my side. I was knocked against the wall.

Before Margale could bash my skull, I created a big hole in the floor under him.

He created a stone ramp in the room below to catch himself.

Margale made a hole in the floor under me, but I was already jumping toward him. I hit the lower floor, rolled, and slashed toward his throat. He blocked with his club.

We were in some sort of workshop now, but I didn't look hard. I pulled some bands and disintegrated everything in it.

"Stop doing that!" Margale yelled as he swung at me.

I threw myself backward. "How many rooms do you have here, Margale? Maybe I can empty them all."

I thrust at Margale's heart, but I only pierced three of the four cured cow hides protecting him there. He swung at my legs, and I jumped back. I didn't dare block his god-club straight on. I faked another thrust before slashing at his head. Even at an angle, his block made my arm shiver.

Margale retreated and bent open a hole in the floor under me. As I fell, I grabbed the edge with both elbows. He raised his club and used magic to pull the entire hole across the floor toward him. I felt like I was tied up in a damn wagon, rolling toward my death. Before he swung, I stretched out my sword arm and cut off three of his bare toes.

Margale roared, pulled the hole snug around me, and made the floor throw me at the wall. In the air, as I was disintegrating the wall before I hit it, I wondered whether it was possible to defeat a person who can make the floor throw you at the wall.

The space beyond the wall was a torchlit stairway about eight feet wide. I was still flying but losing speed. I disintegrated just enough of a hole in the far wall that I could stop myself with my arms and legs before I flew through. It was a fine decision, since this was an outside wall, and we were about two hundred feet off the ground.

I ran down the stairs to the next doorway. I saw a room full of weapons, so I kept going down the steps. Halfway to the next landing, I disintegrated one of the stone steps and the two torches closest to it to darken the stairwell. When I reached the closed door, I pressed myself against it, raised my sword, and waited.

"Bib!" Margale shouted as he thumped down the stairs, probably trailing blood from the stumps of his toes. I heard him trip at the missing step, clatter, and come down the steps in a crashing tumble.

Margale slid down to me, but I had forgotten how damn big he was when he's right next to you. I had to jump aside before I could swing, but his mile-long leg flailed out and knocked me over on top of him. His mass dragged both of us down the stairs. I let go of my sword along the way for fear I'd slice my own throat.

I had two thoughts on the trip down. First, maybe this was why he was called the Avalanche. Second, if Margale got a good grip on me, I would never leave this tower alive.

We clinked and thumped to a stop on the next landing. I found one of Margale's wrists and brought up my leg to lock his arm. It was a desperate act. I probably wasn't strong enough to break his arm. The only other thing I could do with the damn arm was let it go, whereupon he'd crush my throat. Even if I could break his arm, he'd probably crush my throat with his other hand. This was not a winning strategy.

I reached with my free hand and gouged Margale's eyes as hard as I could at that angle, which must have hurt like hell but wasn't enough to blind him. I let his arm go and jumped up just ahead of his grasping paw. Then I ran into the nearby room to find some implement of death I could use to destroy the man.

I found myself in a bedchamber. The bed coverings were white and fluffy. Maroon velvet curtains hung open, and large windows let in a fine wash of light. I saw several pieces of pale carved furniture, including a heavy dresser, a matching wardrobe, and some small tables with chairs. Any of the chairs would be crushed by one of Margale's legs. A big ornate *P* was carved into the headboard.

Before I could disintegrate Parbett's frilly shit, four stone loops from the wall grasped my wrists and ankles, then pulled me against the wall. Margale rushed limping into the room. As I was destroying the stone holding me, he grabbed the dresser and shoved it ahead of him with great force.

I disintegrated the dresser. Or I tried to. Parbett must have enchanted the thing for some purpose, because it refused to not exist. Margale slammed it into my legs, and pain shot up my thighs into my back. I screamed as I destroyed the floor under me. I fell two feet and hit a stone platform that Margale must have created under the floor to trap me.

Just as I disintegrated the platform to escape, Margale swung his club overhead at me. I leaned so that he smashed my left shoulder rather than my head. I'm sure the blow's full force would have killed me, even hitting my shoulder, but I had already been falling. As it was, I heard bones snap, and it became hard to breathe.

I dropped to the room below, and pain blinded me. Well, I didn't need eyesight for what I was about to do. As I scrambled into the stairway, I spun a white band and pulled lightning down onto the floor under that dresser, since it handily stood beside one of those nice big windows.

The horrific light and great boom stunned me. My hair stood on end, and I felt myself vibrating. It was awfully damn close. Well, to hell with it. I threw another lightning bolt at the middle of that room above me, then a third bolt across the room for the sake of thoroughness.

After that, I disintegrated everything in the two rooms above me, including the floors. My sword landed, clattering, a mere two feet from my hand.

Margale, charred and smoking, landed on his back in the middle of the room in front of me. He struggled to sit up and failed.

Grabbing my sword, I dragged myself upright and limped to Margale, whose feet were toward me. I stepped up to cut off his legs. He opened a hole in the floor and dropped himself, but I gave him nasty cuts across both thighs.

I wasn't sure I could fall through the floor into the next room, the one Margale had fallen into, smack onto the stone floor, and not pass out. So I stumbled down the stairs, hoping that he'd been stunned when he plummeted to the floor. It would be better if the fall broke his neck. I stepped into the room and saw a hole in this floor too, right in the middle of two rows of stored furniture.

I spun to flee, pulling a gray band to destroy everything in the room. I was a shade slow. Everything erupted in white-hot flame that lasted half a second before it all disintegrated. It threw me across the landing, where I hit the wall and blacked out.

When I woke up, Margale was just dragging himself up the stairs to kill me, grinning in the way great piles of crushed rock would grin, if they could. Before he could raise his club, I destroyed the landing and stairway under his feet. He created a ramp to catch himself, but I had gotten his rhythm on that maneuver. I wiped out that ramp the instant he created it, then did the same with the next ramp he made. He thumped hard onto the landing below and groaned.

While Margale shook his head, I pulled a gray band and flung it at Margale, sending a big sphere of air around his head into oblivion. Air rushed into the emptiness with a bang, which I hoped would stun him. He gulped like a carp on the shore but pushed himself to his feet anyway.

Before I could destroy the floor under him again, Margale hurled his divinely powerful club up at me. I threw myself aside, and the club pulverized part of the stone wall beside me rather than obliterating my head. When the club rebounded off the wall, I reached to grab it but missed. It dropped back down the stairwell. Margale stretched to snatch the damn thing out of the air, and he hauled back to throw again.

I turned to retreat into the room at an energetic hobble, but I hadn't learned Margale's rhythm as well as I thought. He twisted the stone around the door and slammed it shut while I was in it. The door caught my left leg and broke it below the knee. I destroyed the doorway and everything around it.

Falling, I crawled and wriggled across the floor trying to protect my shoulder and hide my location from Margale. A moment later, from the room below me, Margale opened a hole in my floor, where I'd just been lying.

I kept crawling, and the next hole he made was farther from me. Margale must have been guessing about my location. I angled and tried not to groan.

Three blunt lumps of rock grew out of the floor, stretched, and bent over to smash the floor like hammers. One of them struck the floor right in front of my nose.

Margale opened a hole two feet away from my elbow. I peered through it at an angle, and I saw that the room below was stocked with piles and bolts of cloth. It would make a hell of a fire.

The next hole Margale opened was the farthest away from me yet. I needed a distraction, or at least cover. I guessed roughly where Margale was by the pattern of holes he'd created. I crawled and wriggled past the stone lumps whacking the floor and holes opening, and I put myself over a big stack of blankets I had spotted.

I pulled four blue bands and aged all the soft cloth in the room, except for my pile of blankets, until the cloth was so rotten it would fly into tufts floating in the air if something hit it. Then I destroyed enough floor to knock over the wooden racks holding the cloth. They fell in a chorus of bangs, filling the air with bits of floating rotten cloth.

I destroyed the floor under me and landed on the blankets, and I managed not to die immediately from the pain in my shoulder. I pushed up onto one foot and looked for Margale through the crap in the air. If he was still in this room, he wouldn't start a fire here yet. He'd kill himself too.

Margale was swaying a little but about where I expected he'd be, facing away from me and peering through the cluttered air. Wishing I knew how to hop stealthily, I jumped like a crippled rabbit toward the man with my sword ready.

Margale turned, snarled, and swung his god-awful club two-handed at my unbroken leg. Maybe I should have retreated and stayed out of grappling range. His strength was deadly no matter how many toes he lost or how badly his legs were cut. But instead of jumping back, I hopped inside his swing and slashed. His club fell to the floor. So did both his hands.

As I hopped backward, Margale kicked the knee of my hopping leg. The knee produced a grim crack as pain circled around and through it.

Margale fell to his knees, glaring at me for a second before he stared down at his severed hands. I lost my balance and plopped onto my butt. Then I felt his spirit leave to trade with the gods. I grabbed on.

FIFTY-ONE

The first thing I noticed when I arrived in the trading spot was warmth. It didn't feel like a hot day or even a pleasant day. It felt like lying in bed under two good blankets on a cold night. The warmth seemed to have eased its way through me.

I looked up and saw three suns throwing different shades of yellow light between towering clouds.

Normally I looked around at my surroundings first thing—the gazebo, the forest, and the field of flowers. This time I looked for Margale. He stood two arms' length to my left, staring at nothing. In this place I could see as the gods saw, but Margale didn't seem to be allowed sight.

He was allowed to have hands. He appeared entirely unhurt. It was a shame he couldn't feel that, or anything else. It was such a horrible shame that I had a hard time not laughing.

I expected Harik to be in the gazebo, and he was, lying on a bench with his arms crossed as if he might be napping. Gorlana sat one bench over, one braceleted hand in her lap and the other poised gracefully in front of her. Maybe she was ready to blast something out of existence. Maybe she was ready to primp her hair. It was hard to tell.

Just above a whisper, Margale said, "Mighty Harik, I beg you to trade with me."

Without thinking much, I said, "That's no way for a sorcerer to talk to a god, Margale. You have to shout like they're dull and nasty dock workers. Otherwise they run all over you."

"Bib!" Margale said it like I was a disease, and he stared around blindly. "I'll kill you when we return. I'll cut you into parts for frying!"

Without sitting up, Harik said, "That would be interesting. I haven't seen anybody fried in vengeance for several years."

I chuckled. "I don't see how you'll do that with no hands, Margale."

Margale said, "Your Magnificence, I want you to restore my hands."

This stopped being amusing really fast. "You'd have to give up a lot for that kind of godly intervention," I said.

Still lying on his bench, Harik whipped his head around to glare at me. "Murderer, you aren't part of this deal! But you're right. Avalanche, for that you'd have to give me quite a lot."

"I'll let all his allies live if they leave my domain. I will utterly destroy the kingdom of Silvershanks and bring its wealth to Queen Apsel. Oh, I want to be fully healed too."

"I don't think Margale can accomplish it," I said. "Queen Apsel hates the shit out of him."

"She won't hate me forever." The pain in his voice jarred me.

Harik sat up and stomped toward me. "Murderer, hush! Would you like to hold your tongue in your hand until you leave here?"

Gorlana said, "Harik . . ."

Harik smiled at her. "He belongs to me, dear. Go cuddle one of your own sorcerers." He stood. "Avalanche, I know this doesn't sound like me at all, but I'm not interested in destroying any kingdoms."

Margale twitched. "You're not?"

"No. I want this nasty tramp you're infatuated with. I want all your memories of her."

Margale held still for a couple of seconds. "Apsel? No! Hell no!"

Harik shrugged. "Then you'll die. The Murderer will stab you in the eyeball or do something else just as, well, I have to say, just as creative. What you have is obsession, Avalanche. You don't love the woman! You just think you do."

"I can't make that deal." Margale stared at the brown dirt under him. "I'll give you something else. Something big."

I wasn't sure I'd take that deal, if I was Margale. It sounded profoundly painful for him.

"Not interested!" Harik said. "I don't want anything big, and you should be grateful that I'm being so generous. All I want is your memories of that woman."

"But—"

"There's no other deal for you! Give up your memories of her or die."

After a few more seconds, Margale brought up his chin and took a deep breath. He was about to take the deal, go back to the tower, and beat me to death one bone at a time.

I said, "Mighty Harik, may I speak?"

"Oh, why not?"

"I want to trade! I want you to fully heal me too. I want you to save Pil's life too. Oh, and give me six squares of power."

Harik chuckled. "I thought the Avalanche was greedy. Chicken Beak of Murder, you know what I want."

"Why?" I yelled. "Why do you want me to kill until you say to stop?"

"You know why."

And he was right, I did. I said, "Old Harik trapped me in this same deal. Although I was such a pain in the ass, I think he regretted it later. You believe that if you can trap me the same way, it will show the other gods you're every bit the God of Death and not some pathetic, underpowered fraud terrified that everybody will find out how scared he is."

Harik stiffened as his eyes flared at me.

"What, you don't like that insult?"

"You have my offer, Murderer."

Margale spoke up. "Your Magnificence! I beg you to repudiate the Chicken Murderer's offer!"

Harik grinned. "Repudiate? Do you think that impresses me?" He pointed at me. "Do you accept my offer, which will give you a chance to survive? And it will definitely save the Knife."

I admit, I thought about agreeing. But I had turned the deal down once recently, and I realized I was past risking the murder of people for no damn good reason. Besides, even if Margale was healed and I was broken like an old chair under a fat man, I might still beat him. It wasn't impossible.

"No," I said.

Without hesitating, Margale said, "Yes, I accept."

Gorlana bent her head to look at the floor.

Harik took time to say some arrogant and self-indulgent crap. I used that time to think. Margale would expect me to open the floor under him, or maybe drop some ceiling on top of him while he was still kneeling.

Could I reach out to slash him, even with my broken bones? Probably not. His club was closer to me than to him. Could I drop my sword and grab his club? Hell, why would I do that? I could kill him with the sword more easily than with the club.

I decided to do the stupidest thing imaginable and hope to surprise him. When I arrived, I'd throw my sword at him. Then I'd reach for the club while I dropped the ceiling on him. After that, I'd improvise.

Harik said, "This ought to be interesting. And fun!"

He slammed me back into my body. It knocked me over onto my broken shoulder, and my vision faded for a moment. Then I sat up fast to throw my sword.

Before I could fling the weapon, I saw that Margale hadn't moved. While I watched, he sagged until he was slumped, staring at the floor in front of him. He didn't move, although I could see he was breathing.

I scooted forward and poked his chest with my sword. He didn't react. I didn't know what had happened, but like this he couldn't hurt me with weapons. He couldn't use magic. He could try to hurt my feelings if he wanted. That would be fine. As soon as I could stand up, his life would end.

But I didn't understand what had happened to him. I needed to know before I did anything else. I raised my spirit through my head and shouted, "Mighty Harik, I come for answers."

My spirit was yanked with a force I had rarely felt. When I reached the trading place, I was dropped sprawling on the brown patch of dirt. A cloud of dust rose from it, and I sneezed.

I stood and looked around, then looked again. The forest was gone, and so was the field of flowers. Bare rock stretched in all directions, and daylight settled on everything. The day was bright, but the sun was absent. Just a minute had passed since my last visit, but now the trading place looked exactly like Margale's dry realm, although I saw no canyons, bridges, or towers.

Harik stood in the center of the marble gazebo's lowest level. Behind him stood a row of four imps—the gods' nasty servants, thugs, and foot soldiers. They were nine-foot-tall slabs of muscle with floppy ears, flat noses, and eerily human mouths. Their skin ran from pale green to deep blue, and they wore ragged clothes.

Harik laughed and slapped his leg. "That was wonderful, the whole thing was. Now to the killing! Do you need any advice on throat-cutting?" Harik snickered.

I ignored everything he had just said. "The Avalanche belongs to you, doesn't he?"

"No. Maybe. Not technically."

I stared.

"Oh, Krak's sack, yes!"

"You told him about me, right? You gave him my name and had him bind me!" I stepped to the edge of my dirt patch. "If we both belong to you, why?"

Harik pointed at his chest. "God of Death! Pay attention! I like death, and the two of you delivered a fine crop of it."

"When will he come out of the daze he's in?"

"Daze? Never."

I shook my head as I thought about that. "Never. I beat him then."

Harik nodded. "Technically. We might say he defeated himself with his last trade."

"I like to think I helped. Why did he have so much power?"

"I traded it to him, you bucket of spit!" Harik laughed, and the sound made me feel clammy. "He did enough hideous crap with it to make me smile. And that's all he wanted from me—my smile and enough power to make a demigod shrink and scuttle away."

"How much did he pay?"

Harik laughed again. "He paid everything! I emptied him like he was a pitcher of ambrosia. The last thing he held onto was that chintzy twat he lusted for, and he even gave her to me at the end. Now he's empty. Really empty. If you leave him alone in that room, he'll sit there until he dies of thirst. So kill him! It'll be merciful."

I narrowed my eyes. "The word 'merciful' sounds abnormal coming out of your mouth, Your Magnificence."

"Funny. Hurry up, Murderer, and kill faster! Gorlana is ahead by four pathetic maimings, but killing the Avalanche when you return will be a nice, aggressive move. And you deserve to kill him. As enemies go, he was a boulder. A hillside. I encourage you to kill him!"

All four imps turned and walked into the back of the gazebo.

"Go! Kill!" Harik said, flinging me back toward my body. Then I was yanked back to the dirt patch.

A smoky blue imp hurtled from the back of the gazebo, smashed headfirst into a marble column, and hit the floor, limp.

"This is all normal. Happens all the time," Harik babbled. "Goodbye!" He threw me out of the trading place, but I flew right back in as if yanked on a string.

Harik faced the back of the gazebo and stepped aside, clenching his fists. Two imps, one lavender and one sky blue, vaulted out of the gazebo with their heads flopping. They tumbled past on each side of me and came to rest forty feet behind the dirt patch.

Gorlana, Goddess of Mercy, stalked out from the darkened back of the gazebo, pinching an imp's wrist between her thumb and forefinger. The imp whined and shuffled along on its knees, trying to keep up. She sat on a bench, let the imp go, and smoothed her diamond-laced green gown. "Harik dear, what have you boys been talking about?"

I said, "Since you're ahead in the contest, Mighty Gorlana, I can kill the Avalanche without ending up as Harik's slave."

She tilted her head toward Harik. "That's just as misleading as it can be, isn't it? As of this minute, Harik and I are exactly tied."

I stared at the ground, ashamed that I would take Harik's word about anything. "So if I don't fight anybody until the contest ends, it'll be a tie. What happens then?"

"Things stay the way they are," Harik said.

I said slowly, "I'll just—"

"No, you won't," Harik said. "If you sneak off and hide someplace, I'll send waves of men to kill you. And you'll kill them instead." He grinned.

Gorlana sighed. "I think we're finished with this fun."

"No, we're not," Harik said. "The Knife is still alive, but barely. You can't climb down to her in time. You can't fix that snotty dragon in time to fly down, so she'll be dead if you don't take my deal to kill people."

"Shit!" I said. "Wait! Bring her here so I can talk to her."

Harik shook his head. "If you want to chat with her, take the deal."

I glanced at Gorlana, but she shook her head.

"I can't."

"You've just killed her." Harik slammed me into my body just as brutally as he had last time. I fell onto my smashed shoulder again. It drove the air out of me, but I stayed awake.

Grik charged into the room as I struggled back up to sit facing Margale. She stared around, pointed her sword at the sorcerer, and said, "Why isn't that piece of filth dead?"

"I am contemplating his destruction before I decide how he must die. Also, if I stand up, I think I'll puke."

"I'll kill him," she said, as her father walked into the room behind her.

That didn't seem right, since I was the one who had nearly been slaughtered while defeating the man. She didn't move toward

Margale, though. I thought if she did, I might create a hole and drop her into the room below.

I made a decision. "Grik, I'm not going to kill Margale. I won't try to stop you, but he's broken in his mind and his body both. Pocklin, help me outside."

FIFTY-TWO

Pocklin got me down the stairs, although it was an agonizing, harrowing event.

"Thank you," I panted. "Find some long rope."

Pocklin raised his eyebrows but trotted back into the tower.

I was slumped against the tower wall when Chexis ran from the bridge to join me. He said, "Since you're alive, I'd like my first favor."

"I need to ask one more favor, son. I know that makes three."

Chexis lifted his head, hissed, and then chuffed. Actual flame flicked out of his nose. "This is not the act of a civilized creature, but I guess you're no more than a rodent. No more than a bug under a rock. I'm ashamed to know you."

"I want you to help me save Pil."

"Finally. That should have been the first favor you asked for." The dragon lowered his head, and the black patch on his forehead tousled.

"With your injured wing, how well can you fly?"

"I can't fly at all," Chexis said. "I can fall extremely well, though."

I took a breath. "Do you fall like a melon? Or do you sort of flutter like some leaves?"

Chexis blinked at me. "I don't know. Would you like me to test it? If I hit the ground, it will hurt, but I won't be injured. Unless this canyon has been enchanted by a god." He shrugged.

Pocklin returned with a long rope.

"We don't have time for experiments," I said. "I can't hang on, so Pocklin will tie me onto your back. Then you'll run over to the canyon and flutter down to Pil like a beautiful clump of leaves."

Chexis didn't say anything. Pocklin helped me up onto the dragon's back. I shouted a couple of times and cursed him a lot. He tied me on tight.

"How will you untie these big old knots?" he asked. "I tied them damn tight."

I panted. "Won't be a problem."

Chexis ran to the canyon's edge and stopped. I respected that he might need to consider the endeavor for a few seconds. He said, "I believe—I strongly believe—that you're about to die. I wish you wouldn't die."

"Thank you, Chexis. If I do, I bet Kenzie will make good on my favors. She owes me for teaching her how not to blow herself up."

"It sounds insane, but I don't even care about the favors." Chexis launched himself off the three-hundred-foot cliff.

The first few seconds made me optimistic. We glided nicely and didn't turn upside down. The dragon's wing didn't collapse or snap off. I didn't know what else to expect, but things seemed good so far. Then Chexis plummeted tail-first for a couple of seconds. I was too scared to curse the gods, which is about as scared as I ever get.

We spun in a circle and then upside down, which tested Pocklin's knot-tying skills. But Chexis's wings flapped hard, sounding like an old bedsheet in a gale, and he brought us upright. We rose for a second and then nosed over, with Chexis flapping so we'd ease down instead of dropping like a meteor.

One hundred feet from the ground we spun upside down again and kept spinning for a couple of seconds. Then Chexis roared and flapped just his injured wing until we were right-way-up again. We dropped straight down from there until Chexis flapped hard twenty feet off the ground. Then we smacked into the ground.

Later on, Chexis assured me that I lived only because of his supernatural dragon senses. I told him it helped that we landed next to a big pile of rocks instead of on them, and Chexis claimed credit for that too. I couldn't argue, since I passed out when we hit the ground.

By the time I woke up, Chexis had run to Pil, who was lying on her back. A shocking amount of blood had splashed out from where she landed. I disintegrated part of the rope, and Chexis rolled onto his side to put me on the ground next to her.

Pil's breath was so faint I couldn't feel it at first. I placed my hand on her chest and spun a green band so I could find the most dangerous injuries. After thirty seconds, I still didn't know which injuries those might be. I had found so many I needed to pause and create a plan. If Pil hadn't possessed a sorcerer's toughness, I'm sure she would have died long before I reached her.

I ignored all the broken bones and mended every place she was losing blood. Then I healed some of her beaten and bruised insides. Pain crept into me as I was healing her, but compared to how much I already hurt, it was like pouring a bucket of water into a creek. I avoided ticklish things like her broken back. By the time I finished, she was breathing easier and asleep. Chexis lay down and curled up around her.

Pulling another green band, I sent it inside myself to see what my fight with Margale and my trip down the canyon had done. I had hardly learned anything when Kenzie's not-quite-two hours of healing reached its limit and let the burns on my face reappear. She had said it wouldn't kill me, but I wasn't prepared for this pain. It was like pouring a bucket of water into a delicate crystal goblet and then slamming the bucket down on it. It went on for a few seconds. Maybe it was a minute. It might have been days, but I passed out before I could ask anybody.

FIFTY-THREE

(CHEXIS)

The day after we defeated Margale, I watched Spot lick Bib's unconscious face with great energy, just the way I'd seen him licking his own anus. His own butthole. That's the way Bib would say it. I wouldn't propose that there's poetry in the word *butthole*, but I knew I wouldn't forget it. I'd think of it whenever I thought of Bib.

I thought about licking Bib's face too. He had been lying limp for more than a day, which seemed like an unreasonable amount of time. Maybe licking would help.

But of course, licking wouldn't help any more than roaring in his ear or whacking him with my tail would help!

I had already tried those things.

Bib was just a human. The world that Praxis, Sphynthor, and I lived in was filled with humans of all shapes, smells, and flavors. They covered the world like frogs. Or like grass. Insolent grass. Bib was just another blade of grass.

I swept the ground under me with my tail, settled, and watched Bib sleep.

Kenzie glanced back at me as she limped over to Pil, who was still sleeping too. "He'll be well soon, dragon. It's better he sleeps for now." She sat beside Pil. Kenzie had said that Pil needed more healing and needed it faster than Bib.

After the battle, Kenzie's mate had found some stairs carved into the canyon wall, and he brought Kenzie down to heal us. He himself didn't do anything but stand behind her, worry, and complain. I asked her if I could eat him since she was finished with him, but she said there was a small chance she'd use him in the future.

Kenzie healed my wing, so I owed her a favor, but she wanted to use that one to pay off one of Bib's favors. That meant he owed me two.

I asked her, "Do you want to make up a poem about who owes who how many favors? It's an excellent way to remember things."

"Oh, no," she said without much care. "Unless it climbs up to twelve digits or so, I won't forget."

I decided I should terrify her for daring to mock me. But the father and daughter shouted at us about food before I could do that. They arrived, hauling water and food from Margale's home. Based on everybody's response, that was the only thing they lacked to be perfectly happy and live in the canyon forever.

The next day, Kenzie healed Bib until he woke up. Then she lay down on the dirt and moaned while Bib healed Pil. Then he lay on the dirt, moaning. Pil sat up, smiled at me, and asked for water.

During all this healing, nobody asked anybody else for favors. I decided that they didn't understand how human bargaining was supposed to work.

That night, when Bib and Pil at last could both walk, they sneaked away from everybody else. Spot followed them, yipping, and I followed Spot. Pil and Bib sat on the ground facing each other. I sat to their side where I could see them both.

Pil said, "Chexis, I'm sorry, but this is a private conversation."

"I won't tell anybody."

Bib said, "We'll be sharing some very personal information."

"Oh. Don't worry, I won't be embarrassed. Go ahead."

They nodded to each other, and Bib said, "Just to paint the landscape, I still love you."

I spoke up. "I've been meaning to ask. What is love? Really. There has to be something about it I don't understand."

Bib stared at me.

Pil sighed. "You know love when you get it. You know it when you lose it. All the rest of the time . . ." She shrugged. "It's hard to tell."

"That sounds awful! You shouldn't want that. Both of you, stop doing it," I said.

Bib didn't answer me. He said, "Pil, I assume you don't love me."

"No, I'm sorry. I don't anymore."

"I have a strange question," he said. "If you could make yourself feel however you want . . . just decide how you want to feel and make it be that way, would you want to love me again?"

"Probably," she said without waiting. "Well, maybe. It's a complicated question." She grinned. "Do you have a simpler question? About cooking pie, maybe?"

"No, not even about pie. Pil, we were friends a long time before we were in love, and allies before that. I'm still your friend and ally, and I hope you're mine."

Pil stood. "I will be, as long as you don't let me fall off any more damn bridges."

They walked back toward the others, talking about what they'd do when we all left this realm. I was glad they were talking about that. I didn't think they'd like to live in this canyon forever.

I had thought that Bib wasn't teaching me much, but I ended up learning things. I'm not sure how that happened, but it did. I needed to share it all with my brother, Praxis. The best way would be carrying Bib across the sea to our island so he could teach it all to Praxis. Maybe Bib would teach us even more things. It would be a favor he could do for us.

I hadn't realized until tonight that Bib and Pil were still friends. I'd have to take her too, since without each other, they'd be sad.

Bib might say that coming to our island to teach us would be an exceptionally big favor. It was a good thing he owed me two.

FIFTY-FOUR

We made Vargo moan and bitch for three days after we rounded up our horses. We had abandoned them on the plateau by the river, so they had plenty of water. But it seemed that nothing grew in this realm, or at least nothing grew anyplace we could see.

Margale had stocked his tower with vegetables, fruit, and some grain, which would have to do until we got the horses back home. Every day, Vargo, Grik, and Pocklin enjoyed the privilege of climbing three hundred feet of stairs, walking a mile along the canyon, crossing the bridge, loading up food, crossing the bridge again, hiking a mile the other direction, hauling the heavy bags by rope up two shorter cliffs, feeding the horses, and then returning. The entire task required more than half a day, which was a measure of some conjecture, since this realm had no sun.

Ever since Margale was defeated, Pocklin had been in a jovial mood, which meant he cursed only half the things he saw while journeying to feed the horses. Grik carried the heavy sacks as if she had been born to do nothing else, but she muttered quite a bit as she hauled them.

While I was sitting on the ground resting, Grik walked up to me.

"Here." She tossed the bright knife at my feet. "I won't go find it for you next time." She walked away before I could thank her.

When we had all healed enough to travel, I visited the tower. I hadn't decided what to do about Margale. It didn't matter, because he was gone. Nobody ever confessed to killing him, but conspicuously close by I found part of a big clawed footprint in blood. Only one creature in this realm could make a print like that, as far as I knew.

We rode into the river and crossed back into our realm. I hadn't much confidence that it would be so simple, but Pil told me not to worry and even teased me about it. She was the expert on such things, so I shut up.

Riding back to Brindine took a few leisurely days. We arrived in the afternoon, crossed the river by ferry, and then entered the city. Chexis flew above the city, high enough not to be seen in the partly cloudy late-summer sky.

I hoped we could ride through town unnoticed by gawking at everything like raw villagers who happened to be well-armed and leading horses. However, Talli's friend, Rob the Guard, spied me and waved.

"Where have you been?" he asked. "Why did you ride away without us? Did you bring that ten-times-damned dragon with you?"

Pil smiled, and Rob relaxed into a smile too. She said, "Oh, the dragon's far away from here. We left to scout an hour ahead of the time when we thought you'd leave—dawn the second day after Margale ran away."

Mouth open, Rob stared for a few seconds before he started laughing. He kept at it until his face was well-reddened. "They ain't left yet! Last I heard, they were planning the order of march. Nobody wants anybody else to get behind them."

Pil nodded. "That figures, but Margale's dead, so they don't have to worry about that now."

Rob sighed. "Damn good news. I didn't care to fight him. Which one of you killed him? You can be sure the queen will reward you."

I said, "He jumped off a cliff in a fit of regret. It was considerate of him."

Rob waited, his eyes scanning us, but nobody called me a liar. "Hm. I'd better ride to tell Her Majesty."

I said in a solemn voice, "You might tell everybody that Margale killed me."

"I can't lie to the queen!"

"If the duchess and her raw killers think I'm in the city, they'll skip over here with their army and not stop burning shit down until I'm dead. You can tell her the truth once they're out of sight."

"Bib, I don't think lying would be proper." Rob shook his head.

Pil said, "I do understand your position, Rob, since the queen might want to give Bib to the duchess as a peace offering. If that appears to be her plan, then the dragon is in that cloud right there." She pointed. "And he's listening to all that we say."

Rob swallowed. "In that case, lying to her . . . would be an act of loyalty . . . sort of. Come with me to the palace so you can wait for her while I ride out to report." He shouted for some nearby guards. "It wouldn't be fit for you to walk the streets with no escort, like you were a trollop or a pumpkin farmer."

Rob called to every guard we saw on the way to the palace. By the time we got there, we had a twenty-three-man honor guard making sure we didn't run away.

We were fed, and that evening Queen Apsel received us in a small but richly appointed sitting room on an upper floor of the palace. The furniture was dark and probably centuries old. A window looked down on a garden full of bright late-blooming flowers. Apsel was generous with her wine, which was so good that it might have been what she normally drank. After we explained what had happened to Margale, she stared at floor. "So he's dead."

"Extremely," I said.

"Are you sure? It seems impossible that anything could kill him, especially . . ." She cleared her throat as she looked me over.

I reached out to Kenzie, who handed me a big item that I unwrapped. "I'm sure you recognize Margale's weapon, Your Majesty. Does this convince you?"

She nodded with her face tight. "Thank you for bringing it back to me. Lay it on that table."

I waited, hoping it was a joke. "We didn't bring it here so that it could lie on your table, or for your friends to come look at it and say, 'Ooh.'"

Pil nudged me.

"Your Majesty."

Apsel's head had come up like a hawk's. "That weapon has been in my family's armory for fifty years. It is mine!"

Pil said, "You must admit, Queen Apsel, that the weapon has caused great misery. Without its influence, Margale might never have gone mad. I've been commanded by the God of War to take it to a secret place and destroy it."

"What place?" the queen asked.

"A secret place," I said. "A place that is secret and not to be known." I raised one eyebrow.

"No! I won't let you." Apsel glanced at one of the four guards in the room but didn't give an order.

Pil nodded and said, "Your Majesty, please let me apologize for being rude and unclear. We are required by the gods to take the club away, with our thanks for your wisdom and generosity, and destroy it so it will never shatter anybody else the way it did your faithful and loving servant, Margale. And with no intention of ill will or threat, I must tell you that the gods call my friend Bib here the Murderer, and he's proven that he knows how to kill kings." She pressed together her lips and raised her eyebrows in apology.

Queen Apsel leaned forward with her face as hard as a chisel. I thought I could see her trembling all over, and her fists clenched until her knuckles were white. All the guards shifted their feet and gripped their weapons tightly.

"Margale had a room prepared for you in his tower," I lied. "The blanket was white and fluffy. Big windows, but not big enough to crawl out of. It had a mighty impressive lock."

"We have to destroy his weapon," Pil added in a soft voice.

Apsel seemed to shrink a bit as she nodded.

We rode out of the city shortly afterward without buying provisions or even stopping for a drink.

Pocklin and Grik lived northeast along the coast, and this would have been an excellent time for them to leave us and ride home. They argued over it, unsettling the horses with their shouting. At last, they agreed that Grik would come with us, and Pocklin would bark curses about it as he rode along with her.

To reach the Bole, we rode a great arc around Scrip, just in case its people harbored any sore feelings over me murdering their king. Halfway around the city, just after midday, a patrol of eight Scrip horsemen appeared in the distance, rode to cut us off, and then hailed us.

When we reached speaking distance, I stayed in the back with my shoulders hunched. I glanced at the sky, hoping Chexis would stay up there. Pil called out, "A fine afternoon to you, men! I think we're lost. Could you point us toward a town with a blacksmith? And a tavern?"

The heavyset soldier in front took off his helmet and scratched his woolly brown hair like a dog with fleas. Before he said anything, the three men behind him all yelled at the same time, calling me a murderer (obviously true), a traitor (untrue because the old fellow wasn't my king), and a baby-killer (debatable). All eight of them then tried to ride through or around my allies to reach me.

It was a short but bloody fight. I killed a man who was riding up behind Grik, then gave another man's sword arm a long nasty cut. I roared at a third man so ferociously he fell out of the saddle. Unhurt, he ran away toward Scrip. A few of us had small bruises and scrapes, but nothing worse.

Afterward, Pil glanced at me. "Someday I'd like to revisit someplace where the people don't want to kill us."

I thought up a couple of sarcastic comments but didn't say them. Then I realized that she sounded as if she might stay with me! I opened my mouth and then snapped it shut, realizing the high probability that I'd ruin this moment with a foolish remark.

I muttered, "Maybe I am changing, at least a little."

In the early afternoon, some god invited me to the trading place by yanking my spirit like it was cold molasses. When I got there, I found dust blowing. The forest and the flowers had all wilted. The golden sun, burning purer than any earthly sun, made me sweat within seconds.

Gorlana stood on one side of the gazebo's second level. "Murderer, we won!"

On the lowest level, Harik yelled, "You did not! It was a tie!"

"Untrue." Gorlana smiled.

"It's a tie! Everything stays as it is!"

Gorlana gazed at him with eternal calm as he twitched.

Harik shouted, "No! It doesn't count! He didn't even touch the man, and he didn't use magic."

Gorlana said, "Would that warrior have bounced out of the saddle all by himself?"

Harik paused. "Maybe. You don't know."

I blinked some sweat out of my eyes. "You mean the man I just yelled off his horse? That counts as a victory?"

"Lutigan, Trutch, Fingit, Weldt, Effla, and Fressa all said it does." Gorlana giggled with a careless hand over her mouth. "Welcome home, Murderer! We'll have so much fun together!"

I felt a chill even in that terrible heat.

"As a gift of celebration, I shall give you four squares of power. Don't forget to say thank you."

"Thank you," I muttered.

Harik sneered. "You think you've won, and maybe you have. But you may not enjoy your victory." He stalked into the back of the gazebo and disappeared. His exit would have been more dramatic if he'd worn a cloak, or a robe, but he achieved some fine predatory menace.

"You'll find your other prize hiding snug in your pouch when you get home," Gorlana said. "When you break it, the Knife will love you again."

"If she wants to."

"Of course! Goodbye, dear Murderer. We'll talk soon!" Gorlana tossed me back into my body and restrained herself so that I was shaken but didn't fall off my horse.

I reached into my pouch and pulled out a garnet the size of my thumbnail, linked to a golden chain through a tiny hole. I hurried to shove it back into my pouch.

The next time we stopped to rest the horses, I took Pil aside and showed her the charm. "Gorlana gave me this."

She lowered her voice as she leaned toward the charm to examine it. "What does it do?"

"If you want to love me, it will make you do it."

Her eyes popped open, looking twice their normal size, and she stepped back.

"I'm not going to use it," I said, holding it out to her.

"That's a hell of a concession!" she snarled. "You create something to alter my mind and then claim to be a hero because you don't use it!"

"I didn't ask her for it." I paused. "But I didn't turn it down when she offered."

Pil snatched the chain away from me. "I know you don't mean to do foolish things like this. You just do them. You're . . . oh, sometimes you're like one of those whirly things in the desert. You just bounce into stuff."

"It won't work unless you want it to," I said.

"I heard you." She eased the chain over her head to her neck, pushed the stone inside her shirt, and patted it. "I'll think about what to do with it."

Pil hadn't used the necklace right away and then jumped into my arms. That was disappointing. But she hadn't thrown it on the ground, stomped on it, and spit on it either, so I felt a bit of optimism.

The Bole came into sight in the early evening. The tall pine trees all swayed in one direction, held the bend, and all swayed back the other direction. I watched them do this nine times before we halted.

"Nine is the least fortunate number of all," I muttered. Pil must have been listening because she looked back at me and nodded.

Chexis landed to join us as we dismounted. "Set Spot loose so he can run around and pee on things."

I dismounted and set Spot on the ground. "I hate this place," I said to nobody in particular. "Let's go in and finish this before it gets dark."

"Who said you're going with me?" Pil asked.

I paused. "I guess I just assumed you wouldn't want to go alone. I sure as hell wouldn't."

Kenzie gripped my shoulder and pointed at Chexis. "Something's wrong."

The young dragon leaped a few feet into the air, circled, landed, and ran a hundred paces away from the Bole while twisting his long neck around to stare at it. He chuffed three times and breathed fire toward it, then stared at it with his wings spread.

I ran toward Chexis yelling, "What's wrong?" Halfway there, I realized it might not be wise to run into the middle of all that leaping and fire-breathing.

A few seconds later, I wasn't concerned about those things. In fact, I forgot about them until I ran things through my mind later.

Two dragons glided over the Bole, dropped, and hovered over us. I recognized Chexis's mother, Sphynthor, although I knew her by the name Red. Despite the name, she was a medium blue at the head shading to darker blue all the way back to her black tail-tip. She was paler on the bottom than on the top.

Otherwise, she looked about like Chexis, although she was more than twice as big.

The other dragon had to be Chexis's brother, Praxis. His size matched his brother's, and he was dark green across his entire body.

That was the extent of my first observations, because my gelding lost its mind as I stood trying to hold the reins. He reared and pulled free, then galloped back toward Scrip. All the other horses were doing the same, if I could trust the sounds of neighing, cursing, and hoofbeats.

Sphynthor boomed, "Chexis!" in a profound voice loud enough to make me want to run. She then spat out thirty seconds' worth of dragon speech. The longer she talked, the more Chexis seemed to shrink. He broke in to say something in a small voice for a few seconds, but she cut him off and continued the verbal pounding.

By now, all us humans had gathered in a respectful clump fifty paces from the dragons.

"Should we run away?" Vargo asked.

"You go ahead. I'm staying." I leaned toward Red, trembling but trying to notice any details.

"Getting closer won't help!" Pil yelled, holding my arm. "Bib, you don't speak the language. Let's go."

She pulled at my arm, but I held still. "I guess it's crazy, but I don't want to leave him by himself."

About that time, Sphynthor produced a fierce fifteen-foot-long tongue of flame. She fanned it by swinging her head from left to right. While that was happening, Praxis landed beside his brother, and they bashed each other's shoulders. It looked friendly, although it might have broken some of my bones. They bashed once more and leaned against one another.

Sphynthor ignored her boys and boomed, "Chartreuse!"

I stepped forward away from everybody else. "Yes, Red?"

The dragon lowered her voice until it sounded like something ground out of the Trenches of Death. "Come over here!"

FIFTY-FIVE

I strolled over to stand thirty feet in front of the dragon Red. I had sat closer than this to her jaws before, but never when she was raging. We had discussed philosophical ideas, and she had chosen me to care for her babies. I had come to believe that she wanted people to be terrified of her, but she despised people who were.

So, before I spoke, I pressed my knees together to keep them from knocking and tightened my sphincters against unfortunate displays. "Greetings, Red. May I say that you've raised a damn fine son? Well, two sons, I'm sure——"

Red roared at me, showing the flames snapping in her throat. I staggered back two steps but didn't fall.

"Be silent!" she growled.

I stayed silent. I stood still and didn't breathe.

"What horrors have you wrought upon my son?" she growled.

Chexis spoke up. "There weren't any horrors. I didn't see one horror."

"Quiet!" Red shouted at Chexis.

He kept talking. "I learned a lot from Chartreuse about humans and why they do things."

"That's nothing to be proud of," Red rumbled.

"Maybe I shouldn't be. But we are three dragons living in a realm with thousands and thousands of humans. If we kill every human we see, at some point even their tiny minds will decide to send enough men and god-magic to destroy us."

"Hah!" She chuffed for emphasis.

Chexis said, "Dragon One and Dragon A aren't saying, 'Hah!' Humans killed them."

I hoped he didn't glance my way, since I was the one who killed them. Chexis walk-slithered to join me, and his brother came with him. "A human almost killed me, but Chartreuse saved me."

I cut in. "That's not quite accurate. We saved each other."

Chexis leaned his head toward me and murmured, "Do you want to be eaten? If you don't think that would be fun, be quiet and let me talk." He looked back at Red. "Chartreuse can help us avoid humans. Or if we can't avoid some batch of them, he can teach us how to kill them so that no one will ever know."

"Hah!" Red answered with a lot less emphasis.

"Wait," I said. "I didn't agree to any of this."

Chexis whispered to me, "Yes, wait. Wait until you hear the whole plan."

Praxis spoke up in our language for the first time. "What can we learn from Chartreuse? I don't disbelieve you, Chexis, but I am curious."

My breath caught. Hearing Praxis's voice was like walking into a waterfall of comprehension, confidence, and even love. That voice must have been an innate magical ability for him.

If he was anything like his voice, he might end up being the most dangerous creature in the world. I tried to imagine what he'd be like when he grew up. All I could picture him doing was whatever the hell he wanted.

While I was busy being stunned, Chexis was answering his brother. "He knows everything about sorcery and a lot about horses, which are very important to humans. He knows all about every human weapon. He talks to the gods and learns their secrets, especially Harik."

Red roared. Old Harik had waged war on dragons thousands of years ago. The dragons didn't win.

Chexis wasn't just shaving the truth about my capabilities awfully thin, he was slicing it into pieces. I put a hand on his shoulder, but he shrugged me off.

The young dragon went on, "Chartreuse knows the human philosophies, and that would help us kill them. And best of all, he knows how to do illogical, stupid things and live through them."

Red sighed, and smoke wafted out of her mouth and nose. "It sounds a tiny bit interesting. But the logistics would be tiresome."

"I plan to bring him home with us, so he can teach us everything there," Chexis said.

Praxis thumped his tail against the ground. "Smart."

"Chexis, I haven't agreed to this," I said.

The young dragon stared into my face from a foot away. "Bib . . . you owe me two favors. This is what I want. Don't worry, we'll bring Pil." He bounced his shoulder against Praxis again, who shoved him back and laughed. "Mother, we should bring his mate too. People aren't smart, but she's the smartest one I've found, and Chartreuse might be sad without her. He might not work hard." He leaned back toward me and whispered, "See, it's working!"

I muttered, "Chexis, I don't want this."

Chexis pulled back his head. "Really? Why not? Helping dragons is an incalculable honor."

A man behind me screamed. A woman joined in.

I spun but didn't see the problem at first. I ran back toward my people, scanning for danger and whipping out my sword. They were running, staggering, and crawling away from a figure that hadn't been there when I left.

Gods almost never manifested in the world of man in their actual person. I understood it to be a difficult thing to accomplish, even for a god. When they did, it was never good for people. Sometimes it wasn't good for thousands, or tens of thousands, or even hundreds of thousands of people.

"Hi, Murderer!" Harik waved at me with one hand while balancing his five-foot-long war hammer of blue flame in the other.

I slowed down to face Harik from a distance that felt safe but certainly wasn't. I called to him, "It's a beautiful evening, isn't it, Your Magnificence? Now that you've seen it, why don't you go home?"

"You defied me, Murderer. You dared to mock me in front of other gods. I've come to punish you."

I said, "I belong to Gorlana now. Don't you think she'll be pissed off if you kill or maim her property?"

"I didn't say I'd harm you," the god said. "I will punish you. I'm here to kill things you care about." He turned and threw his hammer at Grik. She jumped aside. The hammer's blue flames scorched the side of her head as it passed, taking her ear with it. Grik was knocked sideways, spun in a circle, and fell.

Pocklin ran and knelt beside her.

"Damn it! Fingit did a lousy job with this thing." Harik ran to grab his hammer. He ran at least twice as fast as a human. The god pointed at Grik. "May Krak rip off your other ear, sword-whore! But he's not here, so I'll come back to you!"

"Kenzie!" I shouted, running toward her. "Club!"

Kenzie had been carrying the club ever since we took it from Margale, and she had been complaining about it just as long. Now she ran to me, holding out the weapon. It had been forged in the God's Realm and was our only weapon capable of hurting Harik, at least theoretically. I dropped my sword and grabbed the club.

By the time I turned back to chase Harik, he was sprinting toward Pocklin and Grik. Just before he reached them, he pivoted left, swung his hammer, and broke Vargo's sword as the man tried to block. The hammer went on to crush Vargo's chest, and he flew more than thirty feet. Kenzie screamed and ran toward him.

Harik pointed at Grik. "Fooled you, eh? How did that feel, Murderer?"

I ran as hard as I could to kill him before he hurt anybody else. A cloud of steam appeared around Harik, along with brilliant bits of light popping inside the cloud. I hoped that Harik couldn't see through Pil's magical distraction, but he waved his left hand to make the entire cloud disappear.

The dragons had pulled back but were now roaring and charging Harik. The boys ran on the ground beside each other while Red flew above them.

"Murderer, can't you see how ridiculous it is to have a pet dragon?" Harik laughed, ran to meet the dragons, and hurled his hammer. It smashed Red on the neck as she twisted her head away. She slammed into the ground and threw a cloud of dust and grass as she slid toward Harik and then lay still.

"Which dragon should I kill next? What's your preference, Murderer?" Harik laughed.

I ran up behind the god and slammed the club into the back of his skull.

Harik staggered forward and turned to face me, holding his head. "You dick! That was unfair, and you'd better not do it again." He wrenched the club from my hands and hurled it spinning out onto the dry dimming plain. I couldn't guess how far he'd thrown it.

Harik turned back to the dragons just as Chexis leaped on the god, leading with his claws. Harik smacked into the ground underneath Chexis, who began biting at Harik's head.

I looked for a way to help, but I didn't know what I could do. I probably shouldn't get between a thrashing dragon and a struggling god.

Then Harik kicked Chexis away using one leg. The dragon was hurled backward but caught himself in the air with a pop of his wings. Harik jumped up. His clothes were shredded, but he didn't seem to be bleeding, bruised, or even hindered. He smiled and raised his weapon as he walked to meet Chexis.

I saw Praxis diving like a falcon on Harik from behind. Chexis held still, making himself a target while Harik stalked toward him with his hammer upraised. Just before Praxis crashed into the god, Harik spun, knelt, and delivered a hammer blow to Praxis's chest. He tumbled across the grass like trash in a strong wind.

A few seconds later, Chexis jumped at Harik, who hadn't yet set himself for another swing. The god stood up and punched Chexis on the side of the head. The dragon flipped over sideways and fell on his back.

Neither Chexis nor his brother were moving.

The God of Death stared around, grinning. "That was invigorating! Oh, get a good look at this next one, Murderer!" He trotted toward Pil.

I charged after him. If he heard me, he didn't care enough to look around. All I could see was Harik's back and Pil's strained face as she backed away from him.

I pulled the Unnamed Mother's bright knife, closed my eyes against the flash, and stabbed Harik in his divine kidney. It was like stabbing a plank wall. However, Harik stopped, stared into the distance, and shuffled a few steps.

"He's dazed!" Pil yelled.

"Great!" I yelled back. "I can't keep stabbing him every few seconds until he gives up and goes home!" I squeezed my eyes shut and thrust with the bright knife again.

"Bury him!" Pil yelled.

"Why?"

"He won't like it!" she screamed.

I pulled eight gray bands and destroyed the rock under Harik's feet, making a two-hundred-foot-deep shaft. He plummeted into it. Before he hit bottom, I created another two-hundred-foot-deep shaft under the first one. While he was falling down that shaft, I disintegrated chunks of the walls all the way down so that the shafts would cave in on Harik. When I figured he must have hit bottom, I created a ninety-nine-foot-deep shaft below the first two.

I shouted at the ground, "That's four hundred and ninety-nine! That's the number of days you wanted me to serve, you weasel-tit bastard!"

I kept on collapsing the walls down there, although I was working blind.

"Do you think that will save us?" I asked Pil, feeling lightheaded.

"Yes," she said.

"What? Yes? Just yes? How?" I yelled.

She grabbed my arm and squeezed it hard. "Three reasons. First, Harik is a fairly new god and not yet fully come into his power, so he probably can't dig himself out of all that. He'll do what gods normally do when trapped, which is go back to his own realm from down there."

"Then he'll come back here and smash the rest of us!" Pocklin said from behind me, where he was helping Grik stand.

Pil waved that away. "No. Manifesting is a lot of work. Otherwise gods would do it every time there's a festival in their name. So Harik probably won't have the power to come back soon. And if I know gods, all the others are mocking Harik with divine cruelty right now because he screwed this up so badly." She swallowed. "He claimed he'd kill us all, but he only got one of us. Can you imagine what Trutch will say to him? Or Sakaj? I don't think he'll risk coming back to fail again." She stared at the ground. "But he did kill Vargo."

Vargo had been brutally smashed in the chest and was dead before he landed. Kenzie sat beside his body, holding his hand and humming. Grik's wound was painful but not serious. I glanced toward the dragons, but none were moving yet.

I ran over to Praxis and Chexis. Harik's hammer had left a big depression in Praxis's chest, and he lay limp. If he was breathing, I couldn't tell. Chexis was unconscious but breathing fine.

I checked Praxis again, and he surprised me by not being dead. He was breathing once every couple of minutes and was horribly wounded, at least as far as I could tell. I wasn't an expert on dragon wounds and bodies.

I spun some green bands anyway and tried to heal Praxis of his worst wounds. However, the farther I went into his body, the less I was able to affect it. Dragons were deeply magical, and magic tended to resist other magic. That was why a magical sword couldn't be disintegrated or set on fire. I found that I wasn't able to help Praxis with his most serious wounds.

Sighing, I examined Red. I wasn't able to find any bit of life in her, and I feared that Harik had killed Chexis's mother.

I retrieved Harik's hammer, which was far too heavy and awkward for me to ever use in combat. We found that its fiery blue head made an admirable torch. Pil and Pocklin took it to retrieve Margale's club and found it in the dark after a two-hour search.

"We live bizarre lives because we're sorcerers," Pil said, "but this is the strangest day in a long time. What are we going to do with Harik's hammer?"

"We could send it to Apsel to put in her armory. Or to lay on a table," I said.

Pil smiled a little and shook her head. "Maybe we should find a way to return it to Harik, unless we want to be attacked by dead armies and chased by dead animals."

Harik had never been known to raise creatures from the dead, but of course Pil knew that. We tried to laugh about it, but nothing seemed funny.

Chexis was still asleep, so I checked on Kenzie. Pil sat with her, near Vargo. He had been part of Pil's family and one of her favorites. They were silent, and both seemed calm. Most of the things I could think of to say about grief sounded damn foolish. A couple might be comforting, so I said those. A couple more seemed so stark that saying them would be like sticking a knife into mourners, so I shut up and went to sit with Chexis.

The quarter-moon broke the eastern horizon, and a short while later, Chexis shook his head and flipped around to stand upright. "Did we kill the God of Death?"

"I'm afraid not. He hurt us badly."

Chexis held still, and I saw that he was staring at Praxis.

"Your brother's alive but gravely hurt, and I haven't been able to heal him," I said.

Chexis walk-slithered to his brother and began circling him. "I'm not surprised. We're magical as heck at our core, but just regular magical at the outside parts. But dragons act this way when they're hurt. They seem like they're going to die, but they don't. Soon you'll be able to tell him everything you told me."

When I didn't answer, Chexis laughed. "You don't know about dragons, so he looks dead to you, but he'll be walking before the sun rises. He may be flying by then. Come back at sunrise, you'll see."

"I'm sure I will." I hesitated. "I think your mother's dead."

"She is not!" Chexis hurried over to where Red lay.

"If she's living, I couldn't tell it," I told him.

Chexis circled Red, stared into her face, and laid the side of his head against her neck. Thick smoke streamed from his nose the whole time.

I asked, "Is she alive?"

Chexis turned and walked back toward Praxis. "You should go away, Bib."

I went back to camp, ate a bite, and then I lay down but couldn't sleep. I felt bad about leaving Chexis alone, no matter what he said.

I walked back toward the young dragons. It wasn't sunrise yet, but hell, maybe Praxis was already better.

Praxis wasn't walking around or flying either. Chexis was dragging him away one heave after another, teeth clamped on Praxis's neck. I didn't know what to say, and this seemed like something I shouldn't interrupt, so I walked back to our cold, fireless camp.

I managed to sleep, but when I woke, the night was still dark. The moon told me that morning would arrive before too long. Something touched my cheek.

"Bib. Wake up," Chexis whispered. He poked me again with his dragon lips.

It was still dark. "What is it?"

"Be quiet and come with me."

We moved in near silence out of camp, although Pil, who was on watch, saw us and waved. Chexis led me toward the Bole.

I said, "I'm sorry if your brother's not—"

"Be quiet. Talking is . . . un-magical."

We entered the Bole and felt our way to the lake. I usually knew exactly where I was, but my bump of direction always failed at the Bole. Chexis swished across the lake. Things in the water bit me just like the last time I was there, except these were bigger and crankier.

I saw that Chexis had dragged his brother to the hollow tree that was the Bole itself. He said, "I see now that my brother isn't going to survive. Bib, you're a sorcerer, so save him."

"I'm sorry, I tried. It didn't work."

"But we're next to this awful thing that makes this part of the world shake. It must give you more power. Otherwise, why would you ever come here?"

"The Bole is powerful for certain things," I said slowly. "Mainly for destroying things. I don't think I can use it to help your brother."

"You can. Dragons are more magical than humans. Far, far more."

The idea of using the Bole to heal such a magical being daunted me. If I was successful, I'd accept the pain of the dragon's horrible wounds. I wasn't sure what that would do to me.

Chexis was staring at me, and I realized I couldn't just refuse to help him. I nodded and said, "I'll try."

Then I wondered what I could sacrifice to the Bole. "Chexis, since dragons don't have scales, we can't give one of your brother's loose scales to the Bole. Can you think of anything else of his we can give it?"

"Bib, that's an awful idea. It makes me want to hide in a cave and sleep for a year. We can't put any part of Praxis in that revolting tree."

"We need something," I said. "The Bole doesn't care if we sit here forever."

"I have learned that sometimes you aren't fully truthful, Bib. You saved Praxis's life when he was a baby, so save him now." When I didn't say anything, he went on, "You can poke holes in me if that will help. Not just my wings either."

"I can't see how that would help."

"Are you sure? You can do it. That hairless man's daughter found the arrow that shot me, and she's been carrying it."

That was news, but there was nothing to say about it to Chexis. I shook my head.

"Bib, I didn't want to do this, but . . ." Chexis lifted his head high above mine. "You owe me two favors."

"I'm sorry, son, that won't help."

He blinked twice. "You can have a hundred favors. If you die before you use them all, I'll give the others to whoever you say."

"If I could help him, I'd do it for no favors at all," I said. "It simply won't work."

Chexis lowered his head and murmured, "I'm being foolish about this, right? Praxis has to die, doesn't he?"

"No, you're not being foolish. You're just grieving."

"Has anybody important to you ever died?"

"Yes," I said. "More than one."

Chexis raised his voice. "Well, teach me something then. Tell me what to do. Because I don't know what to do."

FIFTY-SIX

(CHEXIS)

Bib told me to do something pathetically foolish. He said, "Let yourself be sad." Clearly, he didn't know anything useful and didn't want to show his ignorance.

Then I thought about how often he had obviously been wrong and foolish. But he turned out to be right a surprising number of times.

"Bib, telling me to let myself be sad is like telling me to let myself digest food. I don't think I could do anything about it if I wanted to. Is there hidden, helpful wisdom in what you're telling me? Or are you making a simple, food digesting–type statement?"

"I don't know about food, but I'm not sending hidden messages."

Praxis was lying on his side. I flopped down with my shoulder against his and laid my head on his neck.

"My brother is very smart," I said. "Smarter than me. Much smarter than you. One time he made a devastating argument proving that all existence began the moment he and I hatched. It was silly, but I could never refute it. Did you know we hatched at the same time?"

"I know. I was there."

"It would have been better if he lived."

"Even if you died?" Bib asked.

I lifted my head to stare at Bib. "Obviously."

It hit me then. Being human had nothing to do with that "believing two things at once" crap. I could hardly accept that I had ever thought that. Being human was about watching people important to you die, and then having to live some more without them.

In normal dragon places, I could live a thousand years before any dragon I knew died. And I probably wouldn't like that dragon even a little bit, unless it was Praxis. I might never be sorry that any other being died.

"You said I'm grieving?" I asked. "That's what humans do, not me. They have a lot of grieving."

"They grieve."

"Strange wording, but fine, it's a human thing. I don't think any other creature that exists could grieve. It's too inconvenient. And it must feel . . . I can't think of an adjective bad enough for how it feels."

I slapped my tail against the ground. Praxis's skin felt cold. "I don't want him to be dead!"

Bib stared at me for a few seconds. "Remember that this is not your fault."

"It's certainly not his fault. Even I can make that argument."

"Maybe it's nobody's fault except Harik's," Bib said.

I hissed and felt the fire inside me cooling down. "Praxis is going to die." I said it because it didn't seem true. "Half of all existence will be gone."

Without planning to, I jumped up, slammed my wings against the air, and drove myself into the sky. Once I got aloft, I realized that I didn't know where I was going. I just didn't want to watch him die.

FIFTY-SEVEN

I didn't call after Chexis when he flew away. He was in a lot of pain, and maybe he didn't even understand why.

The sky above the pine trees was growing lighter, and the sun would be above the horizon soon. I sat down beside Praxis. His skin felt cool, but still I saw him breathe now and then.

I lifted myself to trade with Gorlana. I didn't know what I might offer, but she must want something. She ignored me. I called other gods, but they stayed silent too. I gritted my teeth and called on Krak, but even he ignored me, even though I had once carried his hand in my mouth.

I tried again to heal Praxis. My green bands moved slower and slower as they sank into the dragon's body until they stopped, stuck like a cart in deep mud.

One more idea had surfaced while I was boiling the problem in my mind. I hated this idea. It was stupid and scared me a little, so it was probably the right one.

I stood up, walked to the hollow tree, and drew my sword, which was enchanted to be exceedingly sharp when cutting. I leaned against the tree with one arm, adjusted my stance, and slashed. My left hand fell to the ground, and the wound hurt like a poke in the eye and a broken heart all in one. I cursed all thirteen gods, their eyes, their tongues, and their hands.

I might never be able to restore that hand, since healing was beginning to not work on me. But I believed this was the best chance to save Praxis. After all, my hands fed Praxis when he was a baby. They comforted him and dragged goats for him. My hands killed to keep him alive.

I pulled a green sheet, just enough to stop my wrist from bleeding. Then I picked my hand up off the ground, hoping it was enough, and tossed it into the Bole.

The hand burned up, sparking bright enough to hurt my eyes.

I was sadly unfamiliar with dragon guts, but I found my way around Praxis's insides well enough after a while. I healed his most damaged parts until he could breathe so frequently that no one would mistake his green body for a big grassy lump on the ground.

It may not have been the worst pain I've ever experienced from healing someone. It might have been the third worst, or even the fourth. I realized then that nobody knew I was at the Bole. Pil might have already destroyed Margale's club, and if so, she wouldn't come back. I couldn't count on Chexis coming back either.

I started crawling, hindered quite a lot by having no hand on my left side. The Bole was a small place, though. I hoped that the biting things in the water would leave me some skin on this trip across.

By midmorning, I reached the lakeside, and I made myself ready for the stinging, if the lake chose to sting me. Glancing to my left, I froze when I saw Pil thirty paces away, standing on the other side of the water. She had propped Margale's club over her shoulder and didn't look toward me.

I thought about calling out but didn't. She had forbidden me from helping her destroy the club. Actually, there weren't too many things she needed my help to accomplish, and this probably wasn't among them. I decided to hide and not bother her so she could cross the water and walk into the trees undisturbed.

If I really needed help, I could call for it when she passed by on her way out of the Bole.

Pil waded into the water until it reached her thighs. She stopped there and used one hand to pull Gorlana's garnet charm off over her head. She weighed it in her hand for a couple of seconds, closed her eyes, and tossed it into the water.

Pil slogged across and trudged into the trees, never showing any sign that she had seen me.

I felt as if maybe that hadn't really happened. Or perhaps Pil threw something else, and I just thought it was the charm. By the time I had crawled halfway to the others, I had conjured up four other explanations for why I hadn't seen what I had just seen.

I saw it though, and I knew it. All I could do was carry it around with me like a big rock and try not to think about it.

Pocklin spotted me and helped me rejoin the others. I put off all their questions and didn't delay restoring my hand. Pocklin watched me work and made observations as if he were at a furious dice game on which he wasn't betting. When I finished, I possessed a hand that was untanned, soft, and whole again.

Pocklin whistled. "Could you have made it bigger than before? So that you can have a great, huge fist for bashing drunks and nasty boys prone to groping?"

"I've never tried." I stretched and wiggled my fingers. "I could put it to the test on you. Hold out your hand."

The man stepped back. "Hell no! I can whack them with both fists if I have need to."

"Maybe you're not looking for a bigger hand. Are you saying you'd like me to slice off something else and make it grow back bigger?" I grinned, pulled my knife with my new hand, and almost dropped it.

I succeeded in not flinging the knife into Pocklin's arm. I suppose I looked natural enough doing it because he showed no concern. He just ground his teeth and stomped away.

I walked off a ways and experimented with my knife. No matter how tightly I tried to hold it, my grip remained weak. The hand looked normal and was as sensitive as before, but it had far less strength.

Spinning a green band, I examined my work and found that the muscles in my hand hadn't been restored to their full glory. I tried twice more to repair it but failed. I had to conclude that my hand would never fully heal, just as my knee wouldn't.

Maybe I ought to have made everybody aware of my lazy hand, but I didn't. I told myself it was none of their concern. I told myself I had been a deadly bastard with only one hand in the past. I didn't want to tell myself that I had grown leery of admitting weakness these days, as if somebody was always waiting, ready to use it against me.

When I acquired the Breaker skill, I didn't expect to use it to dig graves. We buried Vargo at midday. We had no spade, since the horses carrying our gear had fled from the dragons and never returned. I could have used magic to search for them and call them back to us, but I had spent a great amount of power these past few days. We hadn't ridden far into the wilderness, so horses would be a mere convenience, unnecessary for survival. I chose not to spend any of my remaining power to spare our feet. Kenzie didn't volunteer to bring back the horses either, and I didn't ask her.

I used only enough power to destroy one grave's worth of dirt. Kenzie insisted that Vargo's fire-shedding clothes be given to Pocklin. Such magic was too valuable to be left in the ground. Vargo would wear Pocklin's normal clothes when we buried him.

Ever since Vargo died, Pocklin had walked around grim and sometimes sniffling, as if he hadn't called Vargo a son of a bitch a dozen times a day. When Kenzie gave him Vargo's clothes, Pocklin broke down and had to walk out onto the plains to collect himself.

We gathered enough dirt to cover Vargo by digging with pathetic little sticks far into the afternoon. I had thought Chexis might dig with his claws for us, but he didn't come back and hadn't said where he was going.

Spot dug with gusto.

Kenzie held a sorcerer's skepticism about the gods, but Vargo had been devout. Grik spoke over his grave in brief powerful sentiments that almost made me roll my eyes.

The dragon Sphynthor, also known as Red, still lay unmoving nearby. I assumed she was dead. I felt grateful that nobody wanted to dig a hole for her.

I waited until sunset, resting and watching for either Praxis or Chexis. Neither dragon appeared. I slept through the night without dreaming, which I welcomed. My dreams were rarely comforting.

The next day, I suggested that we not dawdle any longer on this dry prairie, since we weren't carrying much food or water. Pocklin and Grik's town lay three days' walk toward the ocean and then five more days along the coast. They knew of some fishing villages on the way. I began making suggestions about the journey. My suggestions might have sounded like orders.

"I won't be walking to that place," Kenzie said. "I'm not meaning to speak insultingly about your town or people." She nodded at Pocklin and Grik. "But I want to go home to have my baby, that she not know foreign lands before her own."

"She?" Grik asked.

"My baby's a girl." Kenzie said it the way she might say "Rocks fall down."

Pil said, "Our home in Ir is the other direction from yours, friends, so goodbye and take care in these dangerous places."

"Maybe we'll meet again someday." Pocklin smiled but wiped his eyes. "It'd be strange, but hell, maybe we'll save your life next time."

I said, "Pil, if I remember rightly, we could find villages and farms north of here, dotted on the countryside like fleas. It's a bit in the wrong direction to reach Ir, but if we trot over there, we can provision ourselves and buy horses. I don't care to wear out these fine boots on the long walk to Ir."

Pil gazed into my eyes, as calm as if she was training an arrow on a deer. "You're not welcome on Ir. Maybe you forgot. You should go somewhere else."

I truly had forgotten that the Goddess of Life had exiled me from my homeland. I coughed around the lump in my throat. "I don't mind waiting someplace on the mainland until you're done."

"I may never be done," she said. "I may stay there forever. I'm too old to fight on bridges and get thrown into canyons."

"You're not too old. I doubt any living person could have fought her way up that bridge the way you did."

"Except you."

"I had a damn magic sword!" I drew the sword and shook it in the air. "That you made, by Krak's crushing eyebrows!"

She grinned a little. "All right, I'm not too old. I could kill a thousand men, chopping them up one arm or leg at a time."

"Damn right you could!"

"The problem is that I'd kind of like to do that now. The problem is that it sounds like fun. You said I had changed, and I guess I did, and I have no business riding from kingdom to kingdom looking for bad people so I can kill them and all their friends and pretend I did something heroic, when in fact, I was nothing except a bloody-handed bitch." She breathed hard and stared at me. "So I'm going home and staying there."

I drummed my fingers on my leg. "What about your deal with Lutigan? Fighting in wars?"

"Wars will have to come to me."

"Well . . . could you sound a little more definite about all this?"

We laughed over that for longer than it deserved. Then she said over her shoulder, "Kenzie, we're leaving. Gather up anything you want to take."

"Pil, take Harik's hammer," I said.

"What?" Her eyebrows came up. "Why? I'm not going to be running around the wilderness stabbing and bashing things. You take it."

"Harik already has plenty of reasons to hate me," I said. "But he doesn't care about you, or not much. And you are the one who suggested sending the hammer back to him somehow. That makes it your task."

Pil shook her head but didn't say anything.

I smiled. "Do it for me. I'll use guilt. You made me sad, so take away this divine weapon so I don't have to screw with it."

"All right! But I have to say it's an awkward note to part on."

We hugged, and I whispered, "I still love you," and Pil whispered, "That's all right, go ahead and do that."

I sat down and watched Pil lead Kenzie away. They gave the Bole a wide berth, appearing smaller as they went. I stretched out my legs and watched them until they weren't much more than hash marks on the horizon.

Grik said, "Come on, Bib. At this rate, we'll be walking in the dark!"

I waved without looking at her.

Pocklin muttered something to Grik, and she shut up but kicked the grass. Spot sniffed my boot, flopped down on it, and fell asleep.

When I couldn't even pretend to see Pil anymore, I rolled to my feet. Spot yelped, and my back popped twice in a disquieting way.

"Finally," Grik muttered. She led us northeast at something close to a trot.

"Slow down, Grik," I said.

"Why? You're not so old. I watched you fight."

"Good. What did you learn by watching me fight?"

She did slow down and ticked off a dozen observations.

"Not bad," I said. "It sounds like you almost understand one or two of them."

We tromped on for a minute before she asked, "Which ones?"

"We can chew over it when you allow us to stop for the night."

We smelled the salty ocean for half a day before we reached the first fishing village. It had no horses for sale. It had no horses of any kind. One fisherman offered to sell me three groupers so we could ride them along the coast through the waves. Then he and all his friends laughed at me until they wept. One of them strangled and coughed himself red.

We bought food and water, then left in the morning.

Grik had become cooperative and thoughtful once we started discussing combat. I realized that she had been such a pain in the ass lately because she thought I would never teach her anything. For the next ten days, we marched along the coast from dawn through midday, then I trained Grik until sunset.

Grik was smart and willing to try anything, and she was a solid fighter already. I taught her things that had cost me years and blood to learn. By the time she reached home, I believed she could defeat a good portion of the people I had fought throughout the years. In these remote lands, she might never meet anyone who could match her prowess.

When we reached Splinterfale, Pocklin's hometown, he invited me to stay as long as I wanted. I told him that was nice, but I'd rather be hit in the throat with a club. I smiled at him as I said it. Then he offered me a horse and provisions for my journey, wherever the hell I was going.

I had lost my taste for riding far and fast. I took the food, left the horse, and walked out of town before dawn without waking anybody.

No one and no place demanded my presence. That made my hair creep, since I couldn't remember the last time that had been true. I found that it was impossible for me not to have some obligation or goal, even if that goal was to get drunk and puke.

I estimated that I could walk to Bindle Township in six or seven weeks, if the place even existed anymore. I hadn't seen it in over seventy years. I had lived there with my first wife and our daughter, who had both died almost eighty years ago. Hell, just about anybody I had known there must be dead too. But in all the world, it was the closest thing I had to a home.

Spot and I strolled along the coast, in and out of the surf. The puppy couldn't run fast, especially stopping to sniff everything, including his own butt. I wasn't in a hurry.

At sunset on the third day out of Splinterfale, I decided what to do about a problem that had been vexing me. I picked up a piece of driftwood, and on the sand, I wrote in letters as tall as myself:

Harik—

You commanded me to kill Chexis, but you didn't say how soon I had to do it. I'll tell you when I get around to it.

That made me chuckle once in a while until I fell asleep.

I dozed long into the morning. The late summer sun was making me sweat by the time I woke up. My body felt heavy, and I wondered whether Harik had infected me with something. I forced myself to trek along the beach, since we would need food and water soon. We were sure to find a fishing village. I'd have to pick the bones out of fish for Spot, but I didn't have any other duties.

Just past midday, a flying dragon whipped right over my head from behind me. It felt as if the creature had brushed against my hat as it passed. I recognized Chexis as he climbed with a couple of powerful flaps and roared. Then he wheeled to land in front of me.

"Bib! We were wrong!"

"That statement can apply to a great deal of our behavior."

"Praxis wasn't dying! He rested for a few days and then flew home. I was moping around the island and thinking up poems to honor him and Sphynthor." Chexis lowered his head. "She really is dead. Praxis found her when he left that horrible shaking place."

"I'm happy for you about Praxis, and I'm sorry about your mother," I said.

Chexis lowered his voice. "I want a favor. If ever I am doing something precipitous, like assuming that my brother is dying and then flying away to . . . ah, not grieve, but something like it, please stop me."

I nodded. "I promise I will. But don't feel bad, son. I thought he was dying too."

"Since you're a sorcerer, maybe you should have known he was going to survive. You could have told me. But I guess that awful Bole might have confused you. Where's Pil?"

I couldn't help glancing west toward Ir. "She went back home."

"Without you? Aren't you sad?"

"I am, but it's what she wants."

After a pause, Chexis burst out, "This is perfect!"

"Oh? I'm trying to be noble about this shit, but I can't go so far as perfect." I grinned but couldn't quite hold it.

Chexis kept going as if I hadn't spoken. "I expected to find you both here, and I wanted to ask for a big favor. You would probably need to owe me two favors for me to even ask, but now you only owe me one."

"What is this favor? Maybe it's a one-favor task. You never know. To be clear, I will not go live with you on your island."

Chexis laughed. "Oh, it's nothing like that. I want you to help me kill Harik."

I counted to ten, watching Chexis, but he didn't twitch. At last, he said, "I mean that I want you to help me avenge Sphynthor by killing the God of Death, in case I wasn't clear."

After a pause, I asked, "Again?"

"Yes, again, like in the stories. Please. You've done it before, so you must know all the tricks."

"I'm sorry, but that's a bad idea, son. I'll tell you all the reasons why, if you stay the night, because that's how long it will take. I'll start with two facts. Harik can only be killed in one place. Also, I don't know how to get a weapon I could use to do the job. Oh, and he can kill a dragon with one blow."

All the tendrils on Chexis's forehead patch slammed forward. "I don't care."

"Chexis, he may be listening to us right now and know that you plan to kill him."

"I don't care! I'm going to kill him!"

"Why don't you write insulting poems about him and spread them around?" I suggested. "I can help with that."

"I'm going to kill him, and I need you to help me!"

I shook my head at him. "I'm sorry, Chexis. This is bigger than a one-favor task. Even with the best weapons and luck imaginable, I doubt that you and I could accomplish it."

Chexis shouted, "That's why it's perfect!" As I winced from the loudness of his voice, he went on, "We'll bring Pil with us! Then we can kill Harik, and you won't be sad!"

"No, that won't work. She's not leaving her home in *Ir*." I winced when the word *Ir* came out of my mouth. "And she wants to stay there!"

"She'll change her mind. And when I bring her, you'll owe me another favor, which will make two. Then killing Harik will be your favor to me!" Chexis launched himself into the sky.

"Stop!" I yelled. "Let's talk! You can't just snatch her off the street in front of her house!"

"That's a good idea!" Chexis yelled back at me as he flew west.

I knelt to pet Spot as I watched Chexis dwindle, and I wondered how I'd explain to Pil that this wasn't my idea. Hell, even if I could convince her of that, I'd still have to prove there was no way I could have stopped Chexis. It wouldn't help that I'd told Chexis where to find her, or that I'd suggested the plan for kidnapping her.

How Did Bib's Adventures Begin?

Find out in *Death's Collector*—Book 1 in the Death's Collector series!

A WIZARD COMPELLED TO KILL. A slaughter he vowed to prevent. A murderer who pissed off the wrong guy . . .

Bib the sorcerer hates how much he loves his job. Cursed by the God of Death to collect lives, he focuses his thirst on snuffing out only lowlife losers and contemptible ass-clowns. But when innocents under his protection are brutally murdered, Bib flips the switch on the ultimate revenge spree.

Bent on obliterating the bum responsible, Bib is more than a little miffed when he discovers the shocking truth about his own degenerate nature. But knowing the type of killer he is inside, the reluctant hero won't be stopped until he mows down every evil dude in his path.

Can Bib fight his way to redemption before he loses his soul to bloodlust?

Death's Collector is the first book in the darkly humorous The Death-Cursed Wizard fantasy series. If you like snarky heroes, top-notch magic systems, and epic sword and sorcery, then you'll love Bill McCurry's addictive tale.

BUY *Death's Collector* to flirt with darkness today! On sale at: tinyurl.com/2kzbnyjt

. . .

READERS ARE SAYING:

"OOZING WITH SARCASM AND HUMOR."
—Quella Reviews

"WE LOVED this book from start to finish."
—OnePageToAnother

"I JUST FINISHED Book 1 of *Death's Collector*. I read constantly and usually start skimming within a chapter. I savored every word of your writing. The carefully correct grammar, the deviously dark psychology, the Nobel Prize–winning curses—I cannot thank you enough for capturing my imagination."
—Jean L. H., direct sale reader

"*DEATH'S COLLECTOR*, the intro to the saga of Bib, the death-cursed wizard, leads you gently by the hand into the life of a good man who became obligated to kill people for the God of Death. And then it trips you and dumps you into the muck and the blood and the guts and laughs at you. This irreverent book is the memoir of a man who kills people and likes it for beings that he neither loves nor respects, a truth he tells to their powerful faces every time he meets them. But underneath the deadly sardonic exterior is a gold-leafed heart that wouldn't mind loving again if the opportunity presented itself."
—Ted S., Amazon reader

ALL OF BILL'S books are on sale at: tinyurl.com/bmccurrystore

ABOUT THE AUTHOR

Bill McCurry blends action, humor, and vivid characters in his dark fantasy novels. They are largely about the ridiculousness of being human, but with swords because swords are cool.

Bill was born in Fort Worth, Texas, where the West begins, the stockyards stink, and the old money families run everything. After college, he moved to Dallas, where Democrats can get elected, Tom Landry is still loved, and the fourth leading cause of death is starvation while sitting on LBJ Freeway.

Although Dallas is a city that smells like credit cards and despair, Bill and his wife still live there with their five cats. He maintains that the maximum number of cats should actually be three, because if you have four then one of them can always get behind you.

CONNECT WITH THE AUTHOR

BMcCurryBooks.com
Facebook.com/Bill.McCurry3
Instagram.com/bfmccurry

Sign Up for Bill's Newsletter!
Keep up to date on new books and on exclusive offers. No spam!
https://www.bmccurrybooks.com/contact-us-2/

PLEASE LEAVE A REVIEW

Please leave a review on the platform of your choice!
https://linktr.ee/reviewdragonsawkw

Milton Keynes UK
Ingram Content Group UK Ltd.
UKHW040655160324
439418UK00015B/142/J